I0561409

Jeannie's Golden Key

Unlocks Time Travel

Jeannie's Golden Key

Unlocks Time Travel

Book 1 of the Kopaz Series

Dale Groutage

Copyright Material

Text and all material, including illustrations, pictures, and songs, © 2022 by Dale Groutage

Copyright Office Certificate of Registration, Registration Number TXu-908-088

Jeannie's Golden Key is the intellectual property of Dale Groutage. All rights reserved by Dale Groutage. Except as permitted under the Copyright Act of 1976, no part of this publication may be reproduced, distributed, or transmitted in any form or by any means, or stored in a database or retrieval system, without the specific written permission of Dale Groutage.

ISBN: 978-0-9984403-8-5
Library of Congress Control Number: 2015909484
The Kopaz Series™ Independent Publishing Platform
Neenah, Wisconsin

Dedicated to the Travelers of Life

To my lovely wife, Nancy, and my three exceptional children, Phil,
DaleAnn, and Lane—thank you for your love and support.
We travel our worldly journeys together.
To my Desert Pirate friend, Robbie—thanks! Our adventures in a coal
camp in the 1950s made us who we are today.
We travel on—our journeys are not yet complete.
Two very special people—who gave me life and sent me on the road to
search for hope—are no longer with us. They sit on their lofty thrones
above and smile—their earthly journeys are complete. My father, Fred,
spent twenty-five years in a coal mine. He taught me to never give up.
My mother, Katharine, made our little abode in the desert and our
lives in the ever-present shadow of a bleak existence just a little piece of
heaven.
For all of us who travel on, our journey not yet complete,
there is an old Navy saying:

Fair winds and following seas!

Table of Contents

	Prologue	ix
Chapter 1	A Coal-Black Tomb	1
Chapter 2	Vulture in a Graveyard	7
Chapter 3	A Sweet Voice and a Lonely Ride	13
Chapter 4	Nightmares	16
Chapter 5	A Missing Pirate Returns	22
Chapter 6	Let's Go Snooping	27
Chapter 7	A Crazy Man Spots Her	33
Chapter 8	Lord Mochcom, Good Servant of Zuron	39
Chapter 9	Monkey in a Palace	46
Chapter 10	Crazy LeRoy's Evil Secret	56
Chapter 11	Pirate Log Day	62
Chapter 12	The White Face of Ziz Reveals the Path	72
Chapter 13	Pirate Legends	83
Chapter 14	Sacred Legends	87
Chapter 15	Zanzee, the Mystical Egyptian Cat	107
Chapter 16	The 1955 Chevy—What a Wild Ride!	116
Chapter 17	Uncovering Secrets—First Clue	128
Chapter 18	Uncovering Secrets—Second Clue	138
Chapter 19	Zanzee Points the Way	143
Chapter 20	Supernatural	153

Chapter 21   Treasure or Hoax? · 160
Chapter 22   The Black Disciple · 170
Chapter 23   The Further We Dig · 177
Chapter 24   Treasure · 190
Chapter 25   Bow and Arrow Lead the Way · · · · · · · · · · · · · · · · · · · 203
Chapter 26   The Golden Key · 216
Chapter 27   First Love, First Kiss · 225
Chapter 28   Rosetta Stone · 236
Chapter 29   Unraveling Mysteries—Jeannie Teases · · · · · · · · · · · · · 247
Chapter 30   Intipraimi—A Combination Code · · · · · · · · · · · · · · · · 256
Chapter 31   The Disciple of Darkness · 270
Chapter 32   The Garage · 274
Chapter 33   Farewell · 277
             Dale Groutage · 287

Prologue

How could the simple, hardworking people of CoalVille—coal miners and their families, living in the Scarlet Desert of Wyoming during the 1950s—know that a war was raging in the heavens? That the war was a high-stakes game of good versus evil, a winner-take-all contest between warring factions of the primeval gods? That the outcome of this game could bring about the end of life as they knew it and would impact their existence for eternity? That Crazy LeRoy, the lovable, mentally challenged man, was not who they thought he was but a disciple of the dark god Zuron—the essence of an ancient evil that preyed on little children, its reign of unthinkable horror stretching back thousands of years?

Life was a challenge for the people of CoalVille, and the desert did not reveal her secrets easily. For eons, dirt, wind, and coal seams had concealed a mystery among the petroglyphs and volcanic formations in the mystical Scarlet Desert—the mystery of death, which has gripped every member of the human race with its secret powers since the dawning of time. But the indigenous people, the Kashome, who had lived in the Scarlet Desert for centuries, had legends of the Chosen One, whose sacred name was Neferzul. According to legend, Neferzul would come forth and use the power of the sun to open the gods' portal into time and space and pass through it onto the celestial battlefield, right into the middle of the war of the gods. Traveling the Highway of Time, Neferzul would receive from the gods that most precious gift, eternal youth.

The beliefs and traditions of the Kashome people date back to the time when Prince Kashom of the royal family of Kopaz arrived in the Scarlet Desert. When he came, he found only a few native inhabitants remaining, from a tribe called the "Ancients." For some unknown reason, most had died off. One, however, the daughter of the chief, was still young and beautiful. Her name was Star-of-Night. Kashom and Star-of-Night fell in love and married. Their offspring eventually became the Kashome, who inhabit the Scarlet Desert to this day. Star-of-Night grew old and died, but Kashom had traveled the Highway of Time, so he never grew old but remained eighteen forever. To this day, it is said, Kashom still lives in the desert. His whereabouts, however, are unknown to all.

The legend of Kashom foretold that Neferzul would be of the direct lineage of Prince Kashom. She would have silky, black hair and sapphire-blue eyes exactly like the supreme goddess, Neferdor, wife of the supreme god of the universe, Viracocha. But legends tend to get lost in the pages of time, and eventually, they come to be viewed as nothing more than the idle talk of past generations.

For the hardworking people of CoalVille, the reality at hand was simple. They had no inkling of this raging battle of the gods. They were immersed in a war of their own, battling poverty and the monster that was their coal mine. It was a shaft leading thousands of feet below the desert floor, and it buried its victims alive.

When the hand of fate intervened in the coal-mine casino, the shrill sound of a whistle would alert everyone in the coal camp. The gambling hall where the high-stakes game of life and death was played was a small black chamber at the end of the mineshaft. Entering the chamber was a perilous game; the miners called it "miner's Russian roulette." But without the game, they would have no income, so they played on.

It was the end of February 1958, and the monster had claimed another victim. On that sad occasion, the grieving communities of CoalVille and Granite Springs met in the old wooden church to celebrate the life of yet another fallen hero. But no one from those communities was aware that a search was even then underway for a special teenage girl—a girl bearing the sacred name of Neferzul. Even more mysteriously, she was destined to inherit a throne of power at the council table of Supreme God Viracocha and his quorum of primeval gods.

These grieving souls, family and friends of the fallen hero, had no idea what was going on around them. They were just hardworking people whose only ambition was to scratch out a meager existence digging for coal in a hellhole, thousands of feet below the earth's surface in the Scarlet Desert.

CHAPTER 1

A Coal-Black Tomb

It was the morning of the day of the funeral. In the wee hours before dawn, howling winds were shaking the old house and rattling its windows, pulling Danny Roberts, shivering on his bed, deeper into his own special hell. At seventeen, he should have been filled with zest for life, but the reality of death was pulling him into a dark nightmare corner, his mind whirling, searching for answers. *Why did you do it? Why did you let my father die? Who are you, anyway?* Demons of depression seemed to be rushing forth from the blackness of his room. The walls seemed to be closing in on him, and his body tensed in response to the idea.

The wind died and in the stillness of that moment, Danny's thoughts turned to conversation with the blackness filling his bedroom. His hand gripped the corner of the old tattered blanket that was covering his legs. He spoke to the nothingness surrounding him: "Are you God, and can you hear me?" Tears welled in his eyes.

Questions of deity had consumed Danny's consciousness. He was battling with the age-old mystery of life and found no serenity in knowing his questions had never been answered. Hatred weighed on his soul as he whispered his words: "Why are we on Earth? No loving god would put us in this hell and make us wallow in misery!"

The coal company–owned house clung desperately to its foundation as the wind kicked up and started hammering it again. Danny's canker sore of hate seemed to grow larger with each blast of wind pounding the old house. He snarled his words against the rhythm of the rattling windowpanes: "Are you just playing a game with us? How can you be so cruel?" But as the wind died down again and his words faded into silence, he knew there would be no answers.

The void closed in on him. The fear of death and what follows hung over Danny as it had for countless millions of humans since the dawning of time.

Five days earlier, on the snowy twenty-fourth of February 1958, a cloud of black coal dust had belched from the mouth of the mineshaft, and the whistle had blown. The monster had claimed another victim—Johnny Roberts had been buried alive. The all-too-familiar aftermath of a horrific mine accident once more settled on the small community of CoalVille like a smothering cloud of hopeless doom.

Like on so many other occasions, family, friends, and neighbors gathered in the century-old wooden community church on Main Street in the town of Granite Springs, located ten miles south of CoalVille, to pay their last respects to a fallen hero. In their own ways, they were dealing with the stark reality of death. Johnny Roberts would spend eternity in the Scarlet Desert, buried thousands of feet beneath the earth's surface in a coal-black tomb.

And so it was that on that bleak, cold Saturday morning, the first day of March 1958, Danny Roberts clutched his mother Darla's hand as they walked sadly behind the empty, flag-draped coffin. Darla Roberts's long, pleated black dress swirled around her slender legs with each step as she and Danny made their way toward the chapel doorway. Danny's load of pain—almost too much for a teenager—grew heavier as they approached. He wished he could crawl into a hole to escape the stark reality, but he could not escape the bitter truth that lay ahead.

My god, I'm doomed. I'm going to end up like my dad—buried alive.

Danny trembled as thoughts flashed through his mind like a horror movie. He seemed to be watching as the monster of the coal mine snuffed out the life of his father.

By ten thirty, the funeral was well under way, but Danny could not escape his thoughts. That monster of a coal mine had always devoured those who dared to enter the shaft leading to the small cavity. That chasm two thousand feet beneath the ground where his dad and his dad's best friend, Hank, had been working, was nothing more than a beckoning tomb, just waiting to usher its next victims into eternity.

Suddenly, Danny's mind seemed to explode with sound. *Kaboom! Kaboom! Crash, kaboom!* He seemed to hear the dank dungeon of the coal mine bellowing with pain as the shaft leading from the chasm to the earth's surface collapsed. He envisioned the wind that gusted from the collapsing ceiling picking up his dad, who was crouching like a baby on his hands and knees, and hurling him against the coalface at the end of the pitch-black void. He could only imagine the savage force of the blast that had slammed his dad against the wall, let alone the torrents of pain that must have shot through his body. A vivid image entered his mind of his beloved father lying helpless under a pile of coal. It was all in his head, but it was as real as real could be. Danny's body twitched uncontrollably as he imagined his father gasping for air, buried under the pile of coal and unable to utter words—but every breath only drew more coal dust into his lungs. The phantasm of his father's final gasp made him tightly squeeze his mother's hand.

He knew exactly what his dad's last mortal thoughts would have been. *I can't bear the pain—it's so dark in here. Darla…Darla…I love you, sweetie! I love you, Darla. I love you, Danny—farewell, my loved ones—my God, take me home!*

Danny seemed to drift into an altered state as he pictured his dad's final moments, but his body continued to tremble, as if in sympathy with his father's convulsions under that pile of coal. Then, he saw, as clear as day, an image of his father's limp body, lying helpless on its back in that coal-black tomb. He trembled no more.

With a face as somber as one of the stone carvings on Mt. Rushmore, Danny stared at the bodiless mahogany casket not more than two feet in front of him. His throat tightened as his mind fixed on a single thought. *My god, how will I ever get out of this hellhole? I'm doomed—I am going to end up like my dad, buried alive. My god, I'm doomed!*

Never having known a life outside his shambles of a coal camp tucked between two small hills in the Scarlet Desert of Wyoming, Danny had no fit words to express the bitter sadness that was piercing the very core of his being and ripping his soul from the foundation of hope that he had always clung to. His dreams of escaping the shackles of CoalVille were fading into the abyss.

Yet his sad countenance did not go unnoticed. Standing next to her mother in the old wooden pews of the chapel, Jeannie LoneTree, a strikingly beautiful teenage girl with silky-black hair and sapphire-blue eyes, was watching a tall, strong, handsome boy walk by. He didn't notice her.

Oh, Danny, what are you going to do? My wonderful Danny, how can I help you? I wish I could hold you in my arms, your body next to mine, and make the pain in your heart go away.

Tears spilled from Jeannie's eyes as a knot gathered in her throat. She leaned forward a few inches from the pew where she was standing and turned her head to get a better look at Danny walking down the aisle. He had shaggy, sun-bleached blond hair and stunning emerald-green eyes, and he had captured her heart long ago. A pang of sadness pierced her soul.

She knew she was in love with him. There had been a time when they had shared that first young-love attraction, but now he kept his distance and held his feelings locked up inside. Just watching Danny as he held his mother's hand was enough to make her heart pound. She struggled not to bolt over the wooden bench in front of her and race into his arms.

Mrs. Hastings nodded her head with each note as her long, thin fingers pushed on the yellowed keys of the old pipe organ, filling the chapel with the sounds of "Amazing Grace." As at so many previous funerals for miners buried alive, she was loudly singing the words:

Shall I be lifted to the skies
On clouds in gentle breeze,
While others reach to grab the prize,
Sailing on bloody seas?
Amazing grace! How sweet the sound

That saved a wretch like me.
I once was lost but now am found,
Was blind but now I see.

Life in the Roberts home would never be the same; Johnny's final farewell was but a formality for family, friends, and neighbors. Crowded into the old wooden church with standing room only, people craned for a final view of the bodiless casket as the funeral service drew to an end. As they listened to Mrs. Hastings's beautiful voice and watched Danny and his mother walk down the aisle, their conversations centered on the tragedy of Johnny's death, the Roberts's loss of a loved one, and the many similar deaths that had preceded this one. Occasional rays of sunlight filtered through drifting clouds, penetrating the stained-glass windows and bringing the congregation brief moments of heavenly warmth.

Moving slowly and tensely toward the double doors, Danny felt chills run down his spine at the horrifying prospect of his future. *I don't want to end up like my dad. I don't want to get caught up in the cycle of life that has dominated CoalVille for generations. It can only end with me buried alive.* Mine accidents had taken the lives of at least ten men during the past year; one was the father of Tony Lopez, his best friend. *I won't do it. I won't live here. Somehow I'll find a way to get out of here.* He shuddered as he thought about how his parents' love had ended in tragedy because they got stuck in a coal camp.

Clasping Danny's hand tightly, Darla stared at the multicolored stained-glass figures on the windows in front of her, directly above the large wooden doors, of the Baby Jesus in Mary's arms. Searching for answers, she looked past the figures to the sky.

"It's a beautiful casket," she mumbled through the tears running down her face and over her lips. "Johnny would like it."

As the procession inched its way closer to the chapel doorway, Darla spotted a filthy black coat, a piece of rope dangling from one of its pockets. The coat was hanging on a hook attached to the back wall of the chapel. Lost in grief, she never gave it a second thought.

Finally walking through the church doors, Danny and Darla were met by fresh wet snow blowing in their faces.

CHAPTER 2

Vulture in a Graveyard

The plains of the Scarlet Desert were far from welcoming to a straggling stranger, and they were certainly not representative of the beauty of most of southwestern Wyoming. Howling winds and blowing snow would set the backdrop for Johnny Roberts's graveside service in a wet, muddy cemetery.

Danny turned to his mother and said sweetly, "Mom, we're not going to ride in an old black hearse. I'm going to drive, and we'll go to the graveyard in Dad's pickup."

The funeral procession—led by the hearse, with a stream of cars following—wound through the streets of Granite Springs, making its way toward the cemetery. Behind the black hearse, which was a 1944 Cadillac, was a shiny red truck with the young, grief-stricken Danny Roberts at the wheel.

Danny's mother had been a high school homecoming queen, and her incredible beauty had captured the wild imagination of the entire football squad. At age thirty-three, she still looked like she was only twenty-three. Her friends in CoalVille said she was gifted with eternal youth. Danny was definitely proud of having such a beauty queen for a mother, and his awareness of her beauty made him rather protective of her, wary of anyone who might want to take undue advantage of her.

As Darla sat beside her son on the front seat of the pickup, her thoughts drifted back and forth between Johnny and Danny. She was trying to comprehend Johnny's death and the aftermath that would surely follow, but her mind played tricks on her, making her imagine that he was still alive. Her senior year in high school flashed through her mind; she thought of the many exciting and steamy times she had had with Johnny, who had been the star football quarterback and led his team to the state championship, and of being his homecoming queen. Those memories brought tears trickling down her cheeks. *I don't know if I can go on without him!* Yet she knew that her lover no longer being in her life would not only leave a hole in her heart, but would also leave her and Danny with no source of money. Her tears of mourning for her husband turned to tears of panicked hopelessness. *What will we do? How will we ever make it?* Lost in her own world of grief, she stared vacantly at the hearse in front of them.

Where are you, Johnny? Can you call my name? I want to talk to you. I want to hold you in my arms.

Driving through the ornate cast-iron gate, Danny saw row upon row of marble tombstones through the windshield. The undertaker's son directed Danny to their designated parking spot.

"We're here, Mom," said Danny as he pulled into the reserved space next to the hole in the ground. He jumped out of the truck and walked to the passenger side. Opening the door, he took his mother's hand and gently helped her out. "I think they want us to stand over there," he said as he watched the funeral parlor's assistant point to the brass railing next to the newly dug grave.

I hope this doesn't take very long. I don't know why we spent the money on a casket. Dad's not in it. She wanted twenty-four red roses in a mahogany coffin. I don't think he would have cared. Oh, well, that's what Mom wanted. I just want to leave. I hate this creepy cemetery.

"Keep holding my hand, Danny. It's awful muddy, and I don't want to fall down. I need you, Danny."

"Sure, Mom, I'd be glad to," said Danny. But it wasn't only his mom who was terrified by the unknowable future. The stark reality lying ahead had hit Danny like a baseball bat upside his head. *Why the hell did we spend a ton of money to bury roses? My god, why did Mom listen to Pastor Duncan and buy a casket? What are we going to do? We don't have any money. Those bastards that run the CPC, our lovely CoalVille Progressive Company, won't waste any time. I hope they don't kick Mom and me out of our house before we get the rent paid—we'll be on the streets!* He shivered in the cold weather.

Umbrellas popped open as friends and neighbors got out of their cars and slopped through the mud, making their way to the gravesite. As the casket was being unloaded from the back of the hearse, Danny's mind meandered on. *Why'd the sun go behind the clouds? Crap, now it's going to rain or snow or both. My dad is gone. This isn't going to bring him back—an empty box in the ground with that bastard rambling on about bullshit that won't do a thing for my dad.*

Shivering as she stood in the snow, Darla stared at the hole in the ground. Her Sunday dress shoes were covered with mud, but she didn't notice. Her long black dress expressed the same mood as the clouds overhead—dark and dreary.

As Reverend Duncan scanned the crowd, his attention was drawn to a beautiful girl standing twenty feet behind Danny and his mother. He could only make out part of the young girl's facial features; his view was blocked by the crowd standing in front of her. *Hmm. I wonder—could it be?*

Danny was trying to pay attention to Pastor Duncan, but fluttering motions off to his left distracted him. When he realized what was making them, he flinched. Then he slowly turned his head to stare at the unusual sight. It was a black vulture, sitting on a giant leafless cottonwood tree not far from Pastor Duncan. Its outstretched wings formed a ghastly silhouette in the dark, eerie branches of the tree.

Oh hell, that's a scary bird, thought Danny.

Aackk! Aackk! The vulture's howling screeches pierced the air, creating an eerie graveside racket as Pastor Duncan started reciting his parting words for the deceased. "For the wages of sin is death, but the gift of God is eternal life through Jesus Christ our Lord," he intoned in a loud voice, competing with the vulture's screams.

Danny's heart jumped as he watched the giant bird leap from its perch high in the tree less than thirty feet behind the preacher, raking the air with its wings to get its flight under way. The black vulture's vocal interlude subsided as he glided through the flurries of snow, over the crowd of people standing in the mud next to a bodiless casket being readied to be lowered into a hole in the ground. An ominous, foreboding thought leaped into Danny's mind. *Holy shit—why was that bird so close to the preacher? That's not normal—is it? Why was that bird even here?*

As the vulture disappeared into the distance, he returned his attention to Pastor Duncan, trying once more to comprehend the significance of the graveside sermon.

"The wages of sin bring condemnation. Be valiant and conduct your life with harmony in Christ—for if you do, your death will be glorious as you meet your maker."

A wave of silence descended on the graveyard as Pastor Duncan ended his sermon and stepped back from the coffin, then approached Darla Roberts. Struggling to walk, he hobbled, his legs twisting with each step—the result of a childhood accident that had left him lame. Finally, he stood two feet in front of Darla. He smiled as he reached to place the American flag in her hand—the flag that had draped the casket moments earlier. Because Johnny had served in the military during World War II, he had received military honors at his funeral.

Darla's long, brilliant auburn hair glimmered in the sunlight as it streamed through a crack in the clouds. Her dark-blue eyes sparkled with tears.

Trying to be inconspicuous, Pastor Duncan stared at Darla's beautiful hair—hair that flowed like silken strands of red gold over her shoulders and down her back—hair that shimmered with dancing rays of sunlight. He let his fingers slide gently over her hand, which clutched the flag. His heart pounded, and there was only a single thought in his head: *Darla is thirty-three years old but doesn't look a day over twenty-three. Oh, my! She's gorgeous!*

Danny was watching every movement Pastor Duncan made, and he had a good idea of what was going through the preacher's mind. *You filthy old bastard!*

Pastor Duncan lifted his arms. With the sleeves of his ornate robe falling down around his elbows, he spread his hands like a waving politician.

Not moving an inch from where he stood, training his eyes on Darla, he recited Psalm 23. Strangely, he condensed the passage.

"Let us pray. The LORD is my shepherd; I shall not want. Thy rod and thy staff they comfort me."

But no one seemed to notice. Watching intently, the onlookers moved their heads in sync with every word and every movement the preacher made, admiring his loving concern for Johnny's widow.

Pastor Duncan dropped his arms, the billowing sleeves falling into position, leaving only his hands uncovered. His prayer completed, he returned to the brass railing surrounding the open grave as the coffin made its final descent into the muddy hole.

Unmoved and irritated by the preacher's words, Danny stiffened. His face was drawn with lines of anger. "What the hell does this guy know about wages? He's never worked a day in his life!" he rasped.

"Danny, shh. Pastor Duncan is telling us about Johnny and eternal life."

The grey-haired gentleman standing next to Darla tilted his umbrella to protect her from the wet snow blowing in her face.

Pastor Duncan took note of the old man next to Darla and gave her a smile. He lifted his arms in the air, his sleeves flapping in the snow-filled wind. He looked directly at her as he made his concluding remarks, which were spoken loudly and clearly.

"May we find peace and comfort in each other's love. Yes, my friends, if we're in need of love at this time in our lives, we can reach out and embrace each other's hearts with our friendship. I'm always here for you, my friends."

Danny was grappling with piercing emotions. A bitter sadness filled his soul as he once again visualized his dad being buried alive. A tear rolled down his cheek. His mind was consumed with one thought: *That coal-black tomb has taken my best friend from me—my wonderful dad!* He stood motionless next to his mother and stared at the snow flurries swirling around the mouth of the grave.

The pastor's final words cut through the crisp March air like a sharp knife. "When you're alone and need comfort, please come to see me. I'll be here to guide you through your sorrow. Amen."

As Danny realized the true message of the preacher's parting words, another emotion took over his feelings. He glared at Pastor Duncan, and the canker sore of hate grew larger in his heart as his mind created a vision of the crippled preacher reaching to touch his mother intimately.

CHAPTER 3

A Sweet Voice and a Lonely Ride

The clouds parted for a few minutes, letting the sun shed some warmth on the bleak scene. Danny heard a voice coming from somewhere in the crowd behind him: "I'm here for you, Danny." It was a sweet voice, one he recognized, and it made him turn quickly.

Searching the crowd, he spotted Jeannie LoneTree standing beside his best friend, Tony Lopez.

Jeannie threw her hand in the air and waved as she watched Danny standing next to his mother. She knew that the pain in his heart was almost more than he could handle. Their eyes met.

I wish it had worked out between Jeannie and me, reflected Danny sadly. As tears spilled from his eyes, he heard her say, "Is there anything I can do? I'll call you. Drive safely. Take care of your mom."

"Thanks, Jeannie!" he replied, bravely mustering a smile. He turned to his mom and noticed she was shivering. "Mom, the graveside service is over. Let's go." He reached with one hand and pointed with the other. "Let me have your arm, Mom. Watch your step. The truck is right over there."

They reached the pickup. Danny opened the passenger door and helped his mom get in. As he walked around the front of his truck, he noticed the preacher still standing in the same position, now gawking at

Jeannie. He stiffened a little.

"Why the hell is that damned fool staring at Jeannie?" grumbled Danny to himself, glaring at the preacher. "What a pervert! If he doesn't stop it, I'm going to kick his ass."

Holding onto the steering wheel, he jumped into the driver's seat. He reached out and grabbed his mom's hand. "It'll be okay, Mom. Let's just go home." *The ride home is going to be a long one*, he thought, as he put the '55 Chevy in gear. The Chevy that had once been one of his dad's favorite possessions now belonged to him.

It was a ten-mile journey to their home in CoalVille on the outskirts of town. Clutching the steering wheel, Danny gazed out over the hood at the western horizon. The sun, drifting in the late-morning sky, was illuminating the long flat top of White Mountain for as far as he could see. Silver-lined scarlet clouds floated along the golden ridge, which seemed to kiss the sky.

As he drove his newly inherited truck with his eyes following every movement of the majestic clouds, Danny drifted into a world of his own, one locked away in his mind. He reflected on the good times he and his parents had shared together. A lump grew in Danny's throat as he daydreamed of times gone by.

We had difficult times, but hard times never lasted—they passed, and everything always turned out okay. I remember the time I went with my parents to Granite Springs to shop—Mom and Dad were concerned they didn't have enough money to buy food for the next week. We were headed to the grocery shop, and my parents didn't want me to know they were broke. To avoid embarrassing them by my awareness that they were penniless, I said, "I'm going to walk down North Main, and you guys can pick me up in a half hour at Paul's Confectionery Store."

I looked in the window at Paul's store and saw a necklace made of beautiful gems sparkling in the sunlight. I stood there thinking about how much my mom would love to have those jewels hanging around her neck. Then I heard the sound of my dad's truck. He hollered out the window as he and Mom cruised by to pick me up: "Danny, time to go. No gems today, son—maybe tomorrow. You're a dreamer, Danny—maybe someday you'll find the treasure you're looking for."

Danny chuckled to himself as he thought of how his dad had always kidded him about dreaming of treasure.

Yeah, we may not have had rich man's food, but we had each other, and Mom always managed to scrape together a dinner for us. Those were good times. And one thing I'll always have? My dreams—dreams of finding treasure in the Scarlet Desert.

Nightmares

Danny's recurring nightmare—cries for help coming from a deep hole, followed by a loud bang—flung him from the security of sleep. *God, I hate this!* Danny winced as he shot straight up into a sitting position.

In the stillness of the black night, a cloud drifted away from the moon, exposing its face and allowing a sliver of light through the bedroom window. For a brief moment, the illuminated cracks in the plaster on his bedroom walls took on ghostly shapes that danced in rhythm with the flickering moonlight that shone through the branches of a tree, waving in the wind outside Danny's window. He stared at the eerie figures, watching them fade into pitch blackness as the moon's light was once again concealed by the ever-moving clouds of the dark night.

The demon of memories hiding in the cobwebs of Danny's mind and the nightly loss of sleep were taking its toll on him, pulling him into the depths of depression.

Drifting in and out of sleep in the blackness of night, he prayed for daylight to come. Finally, the first rays of light stretched across the sage-covered desert, painting it blood red. It was Tuesday morning, the eleventh of March 1958.

Thank god, it's morning. I hate dark nights. God, why can't I just sleep? Through his window, Danny watched the sun peek over the eastern horizon and start its daily climb into the skies over CoalVille.

With those first rays of light, the wind on the Scarlet Desert picked up speed. It rattled the windows of Danny's bedroom. He lay on top of the threadbare covers of his bed, listening to the sounds the wind made. The Crisp March air whipped through the small crack of the opened window and across the nightstand next to his bed. Papers from a school assignment two weeks old fluttered from the stand and skittered like spiders over the floor.

For now, he was free from his nightly routine of nightmares. But it was not over. Two weeks had gone by since the CoalVille mining accident that had killed his dad, but time had not mended the hurt that consumed his being. The thought of his father being buried alive continued to haunt him. Unpredictably, the horrible sound of a yipping coyote would seize his mind, and he would see an image of the creature prancing over the lifeless, colorless body of his dad, as real during the day as it was in the dead of night.

Fighting the cruel taskmaster of depression had left him exhausted and incapable of interaction. He didn't want his friends to see him in this state.

"Danny, I think you ought to go back to school today," Darla called. Standing next to the window over the kitchen sink, she reached for the geranium pot on the sill and put it in the sink.

No response came, so she called again. "Danny, are you up?"

She looked at the sunlight shining through his partly opened bedroom door, then at the clock on the wall. "Danny, it's seven o'clock, and if you're going to school today—well, I think it would do you good to get out of the house and see your friends."

There was no response. She walked from the sink to the large coal-burning stove, still staring at his bedroom door. *I hope we can get a life again. I know what Danny is going through! God, I hope we'll be okay.* She tensed as she thought about their situation, but she knew she had to do everything she could to get her son out of the debilitating depression he was falling into. She called to him again: "Coach Bollas called yesterday and wanted to know how you're doing. He wondered if you'd be in school today to rejoin your Pirate teammates. Your buddies need you—you guys need to prepare for the upcoming Superior High basketball game. You know, Danny, the CoalVille Pirates have lost their last three games, and you're their star player—they need you."

She didn't hear him stirring. "Are you awake?" She started walking in the direction of his door. Before she reached it, he answered.

"Yeah, I'm getting up. I'll be out in a minute."

Danny swung his legs over the edge of his bed and tried to muster the willpower to move on with his life. He thought about his dream of being the star varsity player this year—his third year of high school. CoalVille High was one of the smallest schools in Wyoming, but it had always had great basketball teams. The CoalVille Varsity Pirates had captured the State Championship in Class B basketball three times in the last four years.

The Superior Grizzlies beat us by one point last year and kept us out of the state tournament. That won't happen this year.

The full morning sun was now sitting on the eastern horizon. Darla gazed out her kitchen window at its brilliance. Though she was struggling herself, she knew that a certain special girl might be just who Danny needed to get his life back on track.

If anybody can help him, it will be Jeannie LoneTree.

"Jeannie called last evening after you had gone to bed. We talked for a few minutes. She's concerned about you. I think you need to go back to school. Danny, Jeannie is a sweet girl—she sure thinks the world of you. She told me that she can't get excited about cheerleading when you're not on the basketball court leading the Pirates to victory."

Darla lifted the cast-iron lid on top of the stove. She reached into the coal bucket next to it and grabbed a large piece of coal, then put it on the fire. "It's nice and warm out here, Danny. If you hustle, we can have breakfast together."

Standing next to the stove, rubbing her hands over its heat to warm them, she continued talking about Jeannie. "Danny, Jeannie came to see you three times last week. I know she only stayed a few minutes on each visit. I guess she sensed you were pretty sad. Maybe she didn't know what to say to you. I think you need to talk to her. She would like that."

For obvious reasons, Darla choked up with thoughts of young love as she talked about Danny and Jeannie. Her discussion brought back old memories—memories of her first love, Johnny Roberts. *Our wedding night was a warm summer's night. We made love for the first time that night, lying on a blanket under the pale moonlight at the base of Boar's Tusk in the soft sands of the Scarlet Desert.*

Suddenly she started, thinking about something unusual that had happened on that evening almost nineteen years ago. *Johnny and I never did figure out who put that strange jewelry and that gold note on the blanket we made love on. When we woke in the morning and found it next to us, we were frightened. We thought someone was spying on us. We never did figure out who it was. Although we were poor, we were scared by what the note said and never sold it or the jewelry. We followed the instructions engraved on that gold note. Johnny is gone now, and he'll never know. Maybe someday I will.*

Danny watched his mom through the partly open bedroom door as she walked from the stove to the sink. *She must be thinking about me being sad. Yeah, Mom is right. I need to get my life back on track.*

He jumped off his bed and walked through the kitchen past his mother on his way to the bathroom, wearing only his white boxers with red polka dots.

"Mom, I'll hurry in the bathroom. We'll have breakfast together before I leave for school."

Then, just like that, it was there—his image staring at him. The silent oval mirror displayed his movements and gave him a clear view of himself. "How did my 'stiff upper lip' end up so limp?" he muttered. He slapped his face. "Get with it, guy! Either start living or just stay in the damned hole you've crawled into!" he mumbled, grinning for the first time in two weeks. His image stared intently at him as he muttered, "I wonder why she called. She's Tony's girl."

"What did you say, Danny? You know, Jeannie will be glad to see you. I really like her—she's a neat girl."

"Mom, what did she say about me?" Danny asked as he finished brushing his teeth. "What did you guys talk about?"

"Oh, we just talked! You know, girl talk! I think you and Jeannie have a lot in common."

Danny thought about Jeannie as he finished his grooming in the bathroom. He knew Jeannie was an open person and had probably told his mom a lot more than his mother was revealing.

Hmm, what did Jeannie tell my mom? I don't think Mom is giving me the whole story! Yeah, at one time, Jeannie and I had something going, but that ended when she got involved with Tony. This is just strange. Oh well, maybe she just wants to be nice to Mom because she knows what we're going through.

"Tony also called to see how you're doing. All your friends will be glad to see you back in school." There was a pause. "Danny…"

Then, for a few minutes, there was silence. *I wonder why Mom stopped talking.* He cracked the bathroom door open a little wider so he could see what was going on.

The wind had picked up speed and was whistling through cracks and holes in the walls of the fifty-year-old house, making strange noises—like sounds that emanated from a flute.

Suddenly, for whatever reason, Darla was lost in sorrow. Perhaps it was the wind and its strange, sad noises that really brought home the desperate situation that she and her son were in. Perhaps it was the thought of the unknown future—her future or Danny's future. Who knew?

Coming out of the bathroom, Danny noticed his mom sitting at the table, tears in her eyes, staring out the window. He walked to the table, put his arms around her, and gave her a strong hug.

"Mom, we're going to be okay. I just know it. We'll find a way to have a good life. Mom, I just love you! You're the greatest mom a guy could ever have. I'm going to be here for you, no matter what! We're a team! We'll make it!"

Darla's tears of sorrow turned to tears of joy. She reached out and grabbed his hand. "Thanks, son! Hurry and get dressed—we have a few minutes to have breakfast. It will give us a little time together before you go to school."

Danny came out of his bedroom wearing blue jeans and a white T-shirt. He sat next to his mother. For a few minutes, they quietly ate their cereal together. It was Danny who broke the silence. "Mom, can you remember what Jeannie said?"

She smiled, clearly cheered up. "Yes, Danny. She thinks the world of you and wants you back in school!"

When they had finished eating, Danny got up and went to his room. He grabbed his school bag and started walking to the back door. "See ya later, Mom."

"Danny, don't forget to pick up the mail on your way home from school." There was a short pause, and then she added, "Say hi to Jeannie for me. Tell her to call me more often."

He laughed and said, "Yeah, Mom, I will." Then he walked out the back door.

CHAPTER 5

A Missing Pirate Returns

"Finally! Danny will be back in school today. I can't wait to see him," Jeannie whispered to herself. *I'm so glad Darla called a few minutes ago to let me know!* She was beaming; she could not stop the excitement building in her mind. Jeannie was absolutely sure he was the one. The very first moment she had laid eyes on Danny, her heart had throbbed.

She was looking in the mirror as she got ready to go to school. The image in the mirror smiled back at her, seeming to say, "He's the one!"

Brushing her long black hair with one hand, she reached to pick up two rhinestone barrettes. She pulled her hair back on each side and put them perfectly in place, making her look like a teen model ready for her debut under the bright lights of the fashion-show runway.

There would be no slow walking on her way to school. She left her house without finishing her breakfast, her heart pounding at the simple thought of seeing him again. She tried to imagine a first kiss with him and trembled at the thought. She thought spending her life with Danny would be more than she could ever hope for or dream.

For twenty years, the CoalVille high school had been located in a two-story brick building between Middle Camp and Lower Camp. Eighty-five students attended. Behind the main school building was another brick building—the gymnasium. To the west, just a short walk away, was a new, smaller brick building—the grade school. The entire school complex sat on ten acres, which included a dirt football field and a track facility one hundred yards to the west of the gymnasium.

As he walked into the school building, Danny ran into Tony. "Danny, you look great. I like the James Dean look—blue jeans and white T-shirt. Sure good to have you back, guy."

Despite his grief, Danny broke into a smile. "Good seeing you too, Tony," he replied, trying to be upbeat for his best friend.

Tony gave a nervous laugh. His choice of words was guarded; he knew the pain that still existed in Danny's heart. "We have a lot to catch up on. How's your mom? I know what you're dealing with, Danny. It's the shits! If I can help in any way, you know where to find me."

"Thanks for your support, Tony. You know, if it were anyone else, I'd know they were bullshitting me. Coming from you, it means a lot! Thanks! Mom is having a rough time. You know what I mean."

Gratitude sparkled in Tony's eyes. "You were there for me, Danny, when I lost my dad. We'll get through this together," Tony said. Then he noticed it was almost time for classes to start. "See ya later. I've got to run!"

For any young man who had just lost his father, the first day back at school would be difficult. Danny would need all the friends he had to help him cope with life without his dad.

Danny's morning classes seemed to last forever. Finally, the noon hour arrived, and Miss Anderson dismissed her typing class for lunch. It was customary for most of the students to eat in the cafeteria, located in the building next to the high school. Three of Danny's teammates, DeWayne, Robbie and Clint, gathered in the hallway outside of Miss Anderson's room. They talked about Danny on their way to lunch. They weren't sure what to say to him, but they knew he was the best player on the basketball team. Without his skills, they would not win the state championship.

But they were too late to catch him. Danny had taken off by himself and was sitting alone at a lunch table, surrounded by the hubbub of kids carrying on conversations about the upcoming Grizzlies-Pirates game. The only thing Danny could focus his attention on was a bug making its way across the floor. It got to the wall and started to climb but was unable to hang onto the slick surface, so it fell to the floor and made another futile attempt with the same result.

Jeannie raced to the cafeteria, looking for him. Her heart was pounding. She had not seen him go through the lunch line or walk to his table. She went through the lunch-service line. Holding her tray of food, she scanned the room for him, but the kids surrounding her blocked her view. *Oh no! Where's Danny?* Her heart sank. She sat down.

Then, she spotted him. Her heart picked up speed. *What's he doing by himself at that table clear across the cafeteria? He's staring at a bug. Okay! We'll fix that.* A spark of joy swept through her as she jumped to her feet. *I'm not going to eat this macaroni and cheese. This stuff stinks. I've got to catch him before he decides the same thing and leaves.*

As she walked swiftly toward him, almost running, her mind filled with thoughts. *Danny, we'll get through this rough time in your life. You captured my heart the first time you spoke to me.*

She thought of their first adventure. *It was a year ago when he and his parents moved from the Winton coal camp to CoalVille. I immediately planned an adventure to get him alone. I asked him if he wanted to go horseback riding in the desert. God, did he get my attention! His answer still rings in my mind. "With you, anywhere!"*

She was now running across the cafeteria floor as she recalled what he had said when they were out riding Alex's horses. *We had stopped our horses to get a drink of water. We were throwing rocks into the pond at the base of White Face Cliff. Out of the blue, he said, "You're beautiful. You have such soft white skin. You have beautiful black, silky hair. And those sapphire-blue eyes—they must be a gift from the gods." We hit it off instantly. Who wouldn't after a start like that?*

But then, they had started drifting apart. She slowed to a walk again. It had been almost a year since Tony's dad had been killed in the mines. *I spent time with Tony, just being his friend and helping him get through that tough time in his life. Danny thought I cared more about Tony than him. Things went south at that point.* She stopped and paused for a moment, thinking about the many days she'd spent with Tony after school. *We just talked, but Danny didn't know that. Yeah, I can understand why Danny thought I cared more for Tony than him.*

As she started walking again in his direction, one thought pushed all the rest out of her mind. *Oh, my strong, handsome Danny, you have no idea how I feel about you! Maybe soon you will. I'm going to be here for you. We'll get through this together. Danny—it's you—not Tony. Soon, my love, you'll know!* She smiled to herself as she gazed at the young man she was falling in love with. As she took her final steps to his side, she shivered with joy. *Oh, Danny—that silly boy thinks there's buried Incan treasure somewhere in the CoalVille hills.* She chuckled to herself.

I remember our first conversation when we were horseback riding through the desert—he told me there was a reason why CoalVille High School adopted a pirate as their mascot. I asked him why. He was quick with his answer: "You know, there's a legend of buried treasure in the hills around CoalVille."

He's a dreamer—a tall, handsome dreamer! Wow! I wonder how he feels about me? We have a lot of fun together, and holy cow, he's one good-looking guy! Does he realize that girls are more fun than dreams of buried treasure?

Finally, she had her chance to talk to him alone. The words that popped out of her mouth were not planned. She was so excited that just the chance to say anything was all that she wanted at the moment.

"Danny, quit staring at that goofy bug. You know, Danny, if I had to live my last seventeen years over again, I wouldn't blink."

"What are you talking about—you wouldn't blink?" replied a surprised Danny, looking at her with a puzzled expression.

"Well, Danny, that phrase means life is so short that if you blink, you might miss something. In fact, it's too short to spend looking at a bug climb a wall!"

"Ah. You've got a point!" He smiled and gave her a brief wink.

That's my Danny. Did he just wink at me? And, then, before he could say another word, she asked, "What are you doing after school on Thursday and Friday?"

He hesitated momentarily. "I don't know—what do you have in mind?"

Jeannie's eyes widened. "Adventure," she shot back.

He hesitated again. Then he asked, "Is Tony included?"

She knew she had to get serious and make her point clear. "Danny Boy, Tony will be there, but he's just a friend—no more than that!" She smiled.

He gazed at her for a moment. *Tony's just a friend! Hmm.*

Her eyes didn't move from his. Her intent was to drive her point home with no ambiguity. Now she spoke very softly. "Danny, there was never anything between Tony and me. I just wanted to help him get through a sad time in his life."

Danny's face broke into a huge smile. His mind was finally at peace about Tony. *Damn, I'm glad that's cleared up. He's my best friend, but my best buddy and Jeannie being together would leave me the odd man out.*

Jeannie looked at him with a long searching gaze, then reached out and touched his arm. *That's more like it, Danny. I knew I could get you to come out of your shell. Danny Boy, you and I are going to have lots of fun!*

"See ya Thursday after Miss Carter's class," she said. She paused briefly, then added, "Danny Boy? We'll go snooping!"

"Okay," said Danny. "Sounds like old times again."

Jeannie winked her sapphire-blue eyes at him, brushed her hand along his arm, turned, and headed for the door just as the lunch bell rang and signaled everyone to return to class.

Wow! She's gorgeous! Yeah, Jeannie, you're the only one that can call me Danny Boy, and I think you know it! I just love that little bounce-skip in your walk. He watched her walk away. *Snooping? I wonder what she has in mind!*

Suddenly he jumped to his feet, flipping back his shaggy blond hair, and hollered, "Oh, Jeannie!" She stopped and turned around. "Mom says hi. She wants you to call more often!"

Her hand went to her mouth, and she blew a quick kiss his way, hoping she wasn't overstepping. "Tell her hi from me. I'll call real soon."

Instantly, Danny threw his hands in the air and pretended to catch the kiss. Then he slowly drew his fingers across his mouth and saw Jeannie smile with sweet surprise. His mind was no longer filled with the visions of his dad being buried alive. Now it was consumed with the image of a beautiful girl.

Jeannie's heart jumped with a surge of joy as Cupid's arrow pierced it. She left the cafeteria thinking of nothing but what was to come next. *Oh Danny, soon you'll catch a real kiss. I can't wait until you're wrapped in my arms and our lips meet for the very first time.*

CHAPTER 6
Let's Go Snooping

"Let's go snooping, guys!" said Jeannie. It wasn't hard for Jeannie to convince Danny and Tony to go snooping. Why would it be? Snooping in a crazy man's house for hidden treasure would intrigue anybody with a sense of adventure. Curiosity was a powerful driving force, especially if you were living in poverty and there was a possibility of discovering a stash of old Spanish gold coins. Breaking the law by entering a filthy old house seemed trivial. They had no idea of the risk they were running or the door of horrors they were about to open.

Danny, Jeannie, and Tony met under the lone cottonwood tree in the only patch of grass on the west side of CoalVille High School. The afternoon sun was warming its branches, which were just starting to bud with new leaves. With all the metaphorical fences mended between Danny, Jeannie, and Tony, this was their new rendezvous spot where they would gather after the last class of the day. Most of the students had already left the school building and were on their way home, but Danny, Jeannie, and Tony were making plans.

"What do you think, Danny?" asked Jeannie as she reached out and took his hand.

He smiled. She didn't have to persuade him. *God! Jeannie, I just want to be with you. I don't care what we do!*

But there was something else on Danny's mind. "Jeannie," he asked as he gazed fondly at her face, "I know you have an ulterior motive for going up to Crazy LeRoy's place, but answer me this. Don't you think that Crazy LeRoy is a strange bird? Maybe there's more there than meets the eye."

Jeannie turned and faced him. She was about to answer his question, but as she looked past him for a moment, two kids wandering out of the brick building caught her eye. Eddie Calhoun and Terry Zumford were arguing about something as they walked down the concrete steps. Their voices were louder than normal, but Jeannie couldn't hear what they were saying.

There was a long pause as she followed their unusual hand movements and shouts. It appeared to Jeannie that Eddie wanted Terry to do something, but Terry was reluctant and was waving his hands in disagreement.

I hope those rascals don't follow us. They are always snooping into other people's business, thought Jeannie as she watched them leave the schoolyard. *They sure are sneaky buggers.*

Danny noticed Jeannie's lack of attention and gave her hand a slight squeeze.

She turned away from Eddie and Terry and said sweetly, "Danny, why do you think we're going to his house? Just to snoop? I don't think so! You know how, when Mr. KeeLord went missing, they found a stash of Spanish gold coins in his house? Where did that old man get all that gold?" Her face lit up with a smile. "The rumor is that KeeLord and LeRoy hung out together. Maybe they found a treasure. I just want to snoop around and check it out. Who knows what we'll find?"

Jeannie squeezed his hands and gave them a tug, then turned her head to swirl her long, shiny black hair. It caught the afternoon sun with a flash. "Follow me, boys. We'll make our plans!"

She wanted to turn and go, but she couldn't. Danny's hand didn't release hers but pulled on it gently. Touching Jeannie's soft hand was like holding a silk pillow—an electric one that sent a tingling sensation through his body. "We have a few minutes," he said.

Jeannie was thinking, *We need to get going.* Her curiosity was pushing her to get their plan of snooping in motion. "Danny, what time is it?" she asked. She turned her head and looked at Tony to get his reaction, but his face was blank.

Tony watched as Danny reached for something in his pocket. Danny pulled on a gold chain connected to his belt loop. The thing attached to the chain had always mystified him, but that didn't matter; he owned it. He smiled as he thought about his prize. *A watch I never have to wind! I can set this down for months on end, and it just ticks away. How cool is that? Shit, nobody would ever believe me if I told them it never stops!*

It was unknown to any of them at the time, but a slight diversion was in the making that would have dire consequences—a diversion caused by Danny's mystical watch that would eat up precious seconds of time.

Danny glanced sideways as he looked at this watch. Tony caught it. His eyes didn't move. He was watching what Danny was doing.

"Danny, where did you get that neat watch?" asked Tony.

Danny had rehearsed his answer in his mind a dozen times. Knowing his response to questions would have to be a little white lie, he had it down pat. "Oh, this was my dad's. He gave it to me two days before the mine accident. Look at the fob and intaglio!" as he unhooked it from his belt loop. "My dad's grandmother gave it to him on his sixteenth birthday. The watch and fob are solid gold."

"Wow! That's neat," said Tony.

Danny looked at Tony. Tony looked at the watch.

"Yeah, I want to keep it special. It means a lot to me," said Danny in a quiet voice. His strong, massive fingers tightened around his golden treasure.

Jeannie was now caught up in the intrigue. Going snooping could wait for a few minutes longer. After all, this was her first adventure with Danny since the death of his father, and she had no intention of letting their plans spoil a special moment.

Still holding Danny by one hand, Jeannie could sense he was tense about something. She had no idea of the secret he was concealing about his golden watch. She took his words at face value and accepted that it was a gift from his father. *He must be thinking of his dad. It has to be hard for him.* She tried to imagine the anguish in his heart at his father having been buried alive not more than two weeks ago. Watching the way he gripped his prized possession—a gift she thought was from his father—got her thinking, *Yes, Danny, you have a treasure—a golden watch your father left you. What if you had the real treasure—your father?*

Then, a flash of joy crossed Jeannie's mind. She thought of the legends of her people, the Kashome, especially the legend of Kashom. For centuries, her people had waited for the legend to be fulfilled. Perhaps they were waiting for just such a glorious gift? The heart of the legend of the Pearl of Time was eternal youth—a gift from the gods.

Maybe someday, Danny, the gods will grace you with the gift of your father. Wow! Wouldn't that be wonderful if Supreme God Viracocha stepped in and gave you a gift more precious than a golden watch—the return of your father, forever eighteen years old? She couldn't take her eyes off him.

Still looking at his watch, Danny asked, "What do you think of my watch, Jeannie?"

She didn't answer him immediately. Standing under the tree, she looked at him with a sparkle in her eyes, and her mind started drifting again.

I stood next to my parents in the back of the chapel on that horrible dreary day. I was at a loss about what to do. Oh, how I wanted to jump over the pew and race to your arms! She remembered the tears that had filled her eyes and the lump that had gathered in her throat as she watched Danny and his mother walk behind the flag-draped, bodiless wooden coffin.

As the procession inched its way closer to the chapel doorway, I saw Darla turn her head and look momentarily at a filthy black coat with a piece of rope dangling from one of its pockets. It seemed out of place on that hook on the back wall of the chapel. She then took Danny's hand and looked at him sadly. My heart ached when I saw the pain in Darla's countenance. I remember how they walked through the church doors and were met by blasts of fresh wet snow in their faces.

But now things were going to change. Still holding Danny's hand, Jeannie looked fondly into his eyes, thinking, *Oh, Danny, you have no idea how I feel about you! Maybe soon you will. I'm going to be here for you. The last weeks have been pure hell. We'll get through this together.*

As the silence dragged on, Danny asked, "Jeannie, why are you staring at me?"

She winced slightly. Although not moving an inch, she slid her tongue across her lower lip as she continued to look at him.

"Danny, can I see your watch?" Jeannie asked. "You can leave it on the chain. That's okay."

He gently pulled on her arm. "Well, you have to come a little closer." She did.

"Here ya go," Danny said, holding his watch in front of Jeannie. Then he dropped it, letting it dangle on its chain between them. The other end of the chain he had hooked to the pocket of his T-shirt.

He grabbed Jeannie and pulled her next to him. No longer dangling, his watch was pressed tightly between them.

She wasn't interested in his watch anymore. True, the thought of reaching between them to see if she could locate it was a little intriguing, but she didn't. Instead, she slid her arms around him. She pressed her small breasts against the tightly stretched white T-shirt covering his bulging chest muscles and squeezed him as firmly as she could. She could feel him breathe heavily against her. "How much time do we have to change our clothes?" Jeannie whispered as she made eyes at him.

Danny and Jeannie were the same age and had the same birthday, which was coming up on the twenty-fourth of March 1958. At sixteen, only two weeks from his seventeenth birthday, this was new to Danny. He'd never had a girl in this position. But that didn't stop his mind from taking off. *My god, Jeannie—you sure know how to get a guy worked up!*

He put his arms around her. His massive forearm muscles and biceps tightened as he squeezed her gently. He put his lips next to her ear. "Jeannie, do you know what?"

Sweetly, she answered, "No! What?"

He whispered into her ear so Tony couldn't hear what he said.

Tony rolled his eyes, letting Jeannie know he was getting a bit annoyed at being left out. Jeannie caught Tony's reaction, so she waved to him as Danny was whispering in her ear. But she didn't have much attention to spare for him. Her eyes were beginning to shine at Danny's words, but she didn't say a thing. She was plotting.

She slid her hand up Danny's side, tickling him with every move. Leaning back a bit, she moved a finger to her lips and licked it. She extended her hand to his face and touched his lips with her wet finger. Joy swept through her as she pressed her face to his. Her soft white skin slid along his cheek, and her mouth found his ear. She whispered ever so quietly, "Danny, you and I are going on a treasure hunt. Who knows what we'll find?"

His two hands moved to either side of her face. He gently moved her head so he could look into her eyes. His face broke into a huge smile. His mind had found peace, thinking about the girl of his dreams. *Jeannie, I found my treasure. It's you!*

She looked into his eyes with a long, searching gaze, reached to touch his arm, and smiled. *Yeah, Danny, you think "whoa." I'm just starting to get you worked up! You just wait and see! I have a lot in store for my Danny Boy!*

Tony had had enough. "Okay, guys, enough monkey business," he snapped. "What's the plan?" He looked at his wristwatch.

Danny grinned as he looked at Jeannie. "I guess Tony wants to get going."

She slid her fingers down his back and said, "Yeah, we'll have to continue later."

Danny released her. "Let's see, how about if we meet back here in fifteen?" he said to Tony. His eyes returned to Jeannie as he said, "It's three fifteen, so let's meet here at three thirty."

"Sounds like a plan," Jeannie replied. "The school is about the same distance for everyone, so that should work. We'll watch from the hill behind Crazy LeRoy's house to make sure he has left for his walk. When we know he's gone, we'll have fun snooping for treasure in a crazy man's house. Who knows? We may just find a pot of old gold coins. That's what Danny wants, right?" Jeannie threw him a quick, smiling glance and skipped off toward her house.

Danny watched Jeannie for a few moments. His heart was pounding, and his mind was blank except for one thought.

That Jeannie—damn, she's got a great body!

CHAPTER 7

A Crazy Man Spots Her

It was a strange twist of fate. In a romantic interlude not more than half an hour earlier, Danny and Jeannie had been standing locked in each other's arms. As their bodies had been pressed against each other, the golden watch on a chain had dangled between them, ticking away precious seconds—precious seconds that gave Crazy LeRoy the time to leave his house and spot them on the streets of CoalVille.

Had the romantic interlude never occurred, their plan to watch from the hill behind LeRoy's house to make sure he had left for his walk would have happened. Under that scenario, there would have been no opportunity for a chance meeting on the streets.

Jeannie had already returned to their rendezvous spot next to the high school steps and was waiting. She laughed happily as she saw Danny racing toward her. "Right on time," she said, unable to take her eyes off him. She giggled and blurted out, "I wish we were still standing together with your watch dangling between us. That was fun!"

Danny, Jeannie, and Tony took off from their schoolyard rendezvous and headed to Middle Camp on their way to LeRoy's house. He lived at the end of CoalVille in the section of town called Upper Camp. There had been three houses in Upper Camp: LeRoy's, KeeLord's, and the Danielses'. When KeeLord had gone missing three months ago, his house had been torn down. In the walls of his old shanty, the wrecking crew had found a stash of gold coins. For some unknown reason, the Danielses' house had burned to the ground within a month of KeeLord going missing. The Daniels family had moved away, leaving LeRoy the only resident of Upper Camp.

The trio hadn't walked long before they noticed someone approaching them. LeRoy had rounded the corner, leaving Upper Camp, and was now walking on the sidewalk through Middle Camp on the north side of the street.

"Hey, look! There's the crazy one!" shouted a surprised Jeannie as her eagle eyes spotted that familiar severe limp. She had not anticipated running into him.

Nobody in camp really knew much about LeRoy. He kept to himself. In fact, he was rarely seen by the people of CoalVille, except when he walked to Granite Springs. Most people had never talked to him, and he knew very few of the locals. He was just there. Nobody knew where he came from or who his relatives were. People in CoalVille just accepted him as the crazy old man who lived in Upper Camp.

LeRoy stared at the kids walking toward him.

"Hi, LeRoy. How are you doing today?" Jeannie asked as the three greeted him.

"Hi, I is Crazy LeRoy. How do you do today?"

Everyone knew that LeRoy always introduced himself by saying, "Hi, I is Crazy LeRoy," no matter whom he was greeting.

"LeRoy, where're you going? Granite Springs or the desert?" Jeannie asked.

"I go desert. Where you go?"

Jeannie giggled. "Oh, we're just out horsing around in the hills."

LeRoy gripped the handle of the shovel that he always carried. He dug his long fingernails into it. A gold ring on his left hand, with a large black stone set in it, flashed in the afternoon sun as his fingers wrapped around the wooden handle. "Okay," LeRoy said. He didn't stop to address Jeannie; he mumbled his answer, staring at her momentarily, and kept on walking.

Jeannie and Tony waved goodbye to LeRoy and walked ahead, but Danny stood motionless for a split second. *Why did that old bastard look at*

Jeannie like he did? he wondered, thinking over the conversation between Jeannie and the crazy man. But even more puzzling to him was the unusual ring on LeRoy's finger.

Another thought entered his mind. *Did I imagine it? I don't think I did. My god, there was a strange-looking beam of purple light coming from the black stone of his ring. Hmm, where on earth would a crazy man get a ring like that?*

Pausing briefly, Danny reached and touched the large ring, set with an emerald, that hung from a gold chain around his neck. A strange emotion filled his soul. *LeRoy's ring behaves like mine. What is going on?*

Noticing that Jeannie and Tony were walking on, he turned and ran to catch up with them, but couldn't help turning his head to look at the crazy man one more time. *Who is he? He's one odd duck!* As he caught up with Jeannie, he remarked, "He's a lunatic! He's in the middle of a lake, and that crazy nut doesn't have his oars in the water. Hell, he doesn't even have his boat in the water!"

Part of LeRoy's weekly routine was to walk to Granite Springs, come rain or shine, seven miles over the hills and desert lands as the crow flies. He made this trek Mondays to get groceries and Sundays to people-watch. Nobody had ever seen him drive a car or truck, although he did have a green 1948 Ford truck that he kept parked in a dilapidated shed next to his house. As far as anybody knew, he hadn't driven it for the seven years he'd lived in CoalVille. Another mystery that people wondered about was his trek each Thursday afternoon at three thirty in another direction—toward the Boar's Tusk in the Scarlet Desert. That was the extent of what people in CoalVille knew about him.

Danny reached for Jeannie's right hand. She nearly said something, but before she could, he jumped in and asked, "Do you think that crazy old coot is for real?" He looked directly at Jeannie's shining face.

She dropped his hand and skipped a few steps in front of him. "Who knows? He's an odd duck, just like you said! Come on! You know it! That guy hasn't had all his wheels turning in the same direction for who knows how long! I do have to admit it's strange that nobody knows much about him. He's a crazy mystery if there ever was one."

Danny lengthened his stride to catch up to Jeannie. He stepped in front of her and turned around to listen to what she was saying. Walking backward, he reached out and took both of her hands. He smiled and looked into her sparkling blue eyes as they caught the light of the sun, which was getting low in the sky.

Suddenly, something out of the ordinary caught his attention as he looked over her right shoulder. The sun was shedding its late afternoon rays not only on Jeannie but also on someone down the street from them. It was LeRoy, not more than fifty yards away. The strange behavior of the supposedly crazy man sent a chill up Danny's spine.

LeRoy's limp was unmistakable. Danny stared. His mind whirled as he looked at LeRoy's grungy old coat. It was black and filthy and flapped against his legs. *Why the hell does he have a piece of rope dangling from one of the pockets?* As Danny watched him hobble for a minute, he noticed that LeRoy stopped briefly at the edge of the sidewalk and planted the blade of his shovel in the gutter, resting his foot on it. He leaned on its wooden handle and rolled his hat back to get a better look.

Just as Danny was watching him, LeRoy was staring at Jeannie. *It's Neferzul! It's the one I've had to wait for! Now the game begins.*

LeRoy seemed to be preparing to take a step, but he changed his mind and remained still. He let the sunlight hit his ring finger, and once again, Danny observed the purple beam of light emanate from the crazy man's ring. But Danny had no idea what evil thoughts were filling LeRoy's mind.

Mochcom, masquerading as LeRoy, was taking pleasure in a memory of bygone days. The remembrance was crystal clear. It was as if it had happened yesterday, but that was not so. His murder of Princess Aerapondes of the royal family of Kopaz centuries ago was sending a wave of pleasure through his black soul.

His long bony fingers stroked his goatee while the other hand gripped the wooden handle. He smiled as he thought, *I sneaked up behind her. As my breath fell on her shoulders and the back of her head, I covered her mouth with my hand and squeezed her with my powerful arms. She tried to scream, but no sound came out. I tore the chain with the golden key from her neck. As she squirmed, I knew terror had overcome her. I dragged her to the river's bank.*

LeRoy's thoughts raced on with pleasure, savoring his heinous deed, that cold-blooded murder in the faraway land of Kopaz a long time ago. *She held her breath. My hands tightened on her mouth, holding her head under the water. It seemed to last forever. But then, she went limp. She floated away over Yellshome Falls.*

As he gazed at Jeannie, his heart pounded as he anticipated the murder of a young girl who was the spitting image of Princess Aerapondes.

"Yes!" Mochcom mumbled. "I had the golden key of the supreme goddess Neferdor once. The gods' gift to Neferzul will soon be mine again!"

He turned his head—just slightly—as he left the sidewalk and started walking toward the Scarlet Desert, his long, filthy black coat swaying back and forth in the breeze with each gimpy step.

"What's with that crazy old man?" Danny said, cringing. He was still holding Jeannie's hands and walking backward, but he couldn't take his eyes from LeRoy.

Jeannie detected the sudden tenseness of Danny's body. She tried to follow his weird facial expressions, knowing he was deep in thought.

Danny's thoughts were no longer on the large ring set with a black stone, but something more serious—a crazy old man most definitely eyeing a seventeen-year-old girl. His mind exploded with questions. *Why is LeRoy staring at Jeannie? I caught him. What does he want with her?* He watched LeRoy head off to the barren hills. "That weird old bastard—who is he? Why was he staring at us?"

As Danny watched LeRoy limping along, a large, black vulture swooped out of the sky and landed on the ground ten feet in front of the crazy man. The remembrance of a similar bird at his father's graveside service sent a chill up Danny's spine. As his muscles tensed, Jeannie's grip tightened a bit, which made Danny refocus his attention. In an effort to keep from alarming Jeannie about the crazy old man staring a hole through her, he turned his questions to another subject—the shovel.

"Why does he always carry that shovel with him? Is he digging something up or burying something?" asked Danny, still not taking his eyes off LeRoy.

Jeannie wasn't paying a lot of attention to Danny's words. She was looking at him. She wanted him to look at her and not at the crazy old man.

But Danny wasn't distracted by her smile. "He's hiding something! You know it!" Danny voiced his concern. "How come nobody knows much about him? I'm concerned that he may be hiding who he really is! That filthy old man—what's with that goofy answer he always gives? 'Hi, I is Crazy LeRoy.' Don't you think he may be acting or pretending to be someone he isn't?"

This time, Jeannie did pay attention to what he was saying, but she wasn't affected by his concern. "Danny, you're being too analytical. He's just a crazy old fool who lost his marbles someplace along the line. He lives in a stinky hole at the end of Upper Camp. Nobody in his right mind would live like he does. Come on, Danny—sane people don't act or live like he does. Forget about him—we're going snooping! Let's have fun today."

Tony went forward, walking more swiftly now. He wasn't interested in getting involved in a conversation about a crazy man.

Danny wasn't going to give up. His intuition was hard at work. Something strange about LeRoy was gnawing away at him. He turned to face Jeannie.

"Don't give me that Miss Know-It-All answer, Miss Jeannie. You know what I mean. He's an odd duck! And I think he's hiding something, and I'm not the analytical one. Tony is!"

Spinning around, Tony jumped into the conversation in an effort to change the subject. "Keep me out of this looney-tunes discussion about a crazy man," Tony snapped at Danny. "We all know the guy is nuts!"

"Yeah, he is more than nuts. He's a total weirdo!"

CHAPTER 8

Lord Mochcom, Good Servant of Zuron

Lord Mochcom's long bony fingers slithered around the wooden handle of his shovel, clutching it, as the image of a beautiful young girl with long black hair, eyes of sapphire blue, and soft, white skin consumed the dark citadel of his mind. He screamed, "*Yes!* I've found her!" and stopped walking momentarily. His perfectly manicured fingernails dug deep into the handle as he raked them down the shaft. Gazing at the sky, he smiled with pleasure as he imagined ripping the girl's heart from her chest as she squealed with fright and pain.

The sweet sounds of creatures singing for a mate to bring new life into the Scarlet Desert halted briefly as Mochcom gently laid his shovel in the white desert sands, which glistened in the warm afternoon sun. He lifted his arms and began a howling, cackling chant, startling an unsuspecting meadowlark, which took flight from a cedar tree fifty feet away. His eyes roved back and forth as he searched for his disciple, Black Vulture. "Where are you?" he roared. "You must follow her and report her pattern of movements to me!"

Mochcom resumed his walk in the Scarlet Desert. *That filthy outside of my house is a good disguise. No one would ever suspect a crazy man was once the high priest of the royal court of Kopaz. If these people in this town ever realized the lavish palace that I live in, they would be shocked. Safe in my hiding place, I still have my long black ceremonial robe with inlaid jewels and the golden rope that ties it securely to my waist when I perform the sacred ritual of Capacocha!*

CoalVille was home to coal miners and their families, but it was also home to Lord Mochcom—Prince Dark Soul. While three CoalVille teenagers were seeking adventure to lift their lives to a higher plane of happiness, Lord Mochcom of the Dark Side had a different quest—to find the gifts from the gods and become the supreme holder of eternal youth. His quest for power had taken him on a journey through time, stained with the blood of innocent victims.

The Black Disciple of Death, Black Vulture, circled the outcropping of a sandstone formation not more than two hundred feet in front of Mochcom. He screeched loudly as he glided through the air, tilted his wings to slow his flight, stretched out his talons, and perched on the highest point of rock, now only one hundred feet in front of Lord Mochcom.

"You must not disappoint me, Black Vulture. Your mission is essential for me to gain my ultimate glory. The reign of death we will leave behind us will be our badge of honor. We must please Zuron, the great god of the underworld. He's counting on me, and I'm counting on you." He raised an arm and motioned Black Vulture to follow.

Mochcom walked on toward the Boar's Tusk—two lava rock pillars, towering four hundred feet above the Scarlet Desert. He struggled with each painful limp he took. His ranting and raving to the god of the underworld went unnoticed by any onlooker.

"Eminent God of the Dark Side, you have given me precious gifts—my ring, which was once worn on your finger, is my shield, and Black Vulture, your disciple, leads me to my victims. My ring will shield me from the powers of TRPOV, the Royal Prince of Viracocha, and Black Vulture is my faithful servant, helping me carry out my acts of horror as I trap TRPON, the Royal Princess of Neferdor. Black Vulture leads me to the young girls with the sacred name of Neferzul. He showed me where Princess Aerapondes was—I drowned her. Vulture showed me where Moon-of-Day was—I pushed her into the crevasse, and she is gone forever! Now I'll use your gift and will trap the third Neferzul, whom I believe is TRPON. Oh, yes! Vulture will lead me to her—soon she'll be mine."

Lord Mochcom lifted his eyes to the sky. "God of Darkness—host of the Black Temple—Negra Pantheon—I'll be patient. This time I will not act in haste. I'll wait until Neferzul shows me where the gifts of Viracocha are hidden—the five worox stones and the emerald star. This time they'll be mine forever. *Yes!* When I have the gifts from Viracocha, Neferzul's blood will drip from her heart in my hand. Her heart will beat its last beat in my hands—her blood will be my gift to you! Oh, Great God of Darkness, I'm your servant. With your help, Mighty Zuron, I will fulfill my mission and control the power of eternal youth!"

His constant agony suddenly erupted violently, and Mochcom stumbled and fell. His legs flared with excruciating pain, as if pierced with a red-hot dagger, caused by twisted bones from compound fractures that had happened centuries ago.

Sitting in the warm sands of the desert, he rasped, "I've waited patiently for centuries to get the gifts of Viracocha." He raised his outstretched hands to the sky and roared, "Mighty Zuron, Great One of the Dark Side, I, Lord Mochcom, have been your faithful prince for eons. You know my works of horror—I was Gorom Mochcom, the high priest for the royal court of Kopaz. I carried out your wishes."

Slowly, with the aid of his shovel, he rose to his feet. Resting the shovel handle against his chest, he raised his arms to the sky again and continued addressing his master. "It was I who followed your desire to thwart the will of Viracocha. It was I who sought his gifts. It was I who took possession of those gifts so I could honor you. It was I who killed Aerapondes, the first Neferzul—the special 'living doll' of Neferdor—Viracocha's wife."

He struggled to steady his feet, using his shovel as a crutch.

"When I possess all the gifts from the gods—the golden watch, the golden key, the five worox stones, and the emerald star—I'll have supreme power over eternal youth. Viracocha will no longer have control through his human emissary, the Royal Prince of Viracocha."

Mochcom was certain of the changing of time and the coming of the royal prince. *We do not know yet whom Viracocha has designated as his royal prince, but we know he is now on the Earth or soon will be. We know the time is at hand when the gift of eternal youth will be entrusted to more than just the royal family of Kopaz—we know that gift will be bestowed upon the Royal Prince of Viracocha, to give to whomever he will.*

He gazed at the Boar's Tusk on the horizon. "I must find the one to whom Viracocha has given the golden watch. I must kill him before he knows who he is and get the watch. Viracocha wants his royal prince to be the one who determines who is entitled to the gift of eternal youth. Little does he know that it will be me, Lord Mochcom, and not the Royal Prince of Viracocha."

Black Vulture listened intently as Mochcom rambled on. He swooped to a scrub cedar tree not more than ten feet from Lord Mochcom and found a dead branch for his perch. His wings fluttered in rhythm with the ranting and raving of his master.

"Working together, you and I, Mighty Zuron, will defeat the cause of Viracocha. We will take away the power he will give to his prince. Viracocha will not have an emissary—I will destroy his emissary," Mochcom bellowed. He leaned on his shovel and stared into the sky. "I'm your emissary—and yours alone. I'll carry out your will. You'll have the glory and honor of defeating Viracocha through me. You will have supreme control of eternal youth! Yes, Great One, soon you'll be the supreme god—you will take that honor and title from Viracocha!"

Black Vulture bobbed his head, swishing his beak through the air in a motion that signified concurrence with his master's rant to the god of darkness.

"Mighty Zuron, Great God of the Underworld, help me! Help me! You know where Kashom has hidden the gifts. Help me find them! I'm your loyal servant!"

Mochcom's pointed goatee and mustache twitched as he ground his teeth in irritation. He stood not more than a quarter mile from the Boar's Tusk. His hand dropped to his leg. He tried to massage it to relieve the pain, but to no avail. The ache in his legs left him no choice but to rest on a large, flat sandstone rock.

Clutching the handle of his shovel, he gazed at the western horizon. Long, silver-lined crimson clouds glided across the top of White Mountain, which gently kissed the skyline. The ever-changing kaleidoscope of colors cast by the setting sun illuminated an expansive vista of the purple-sage-covered hills of the Scarlet Desert. It was Mother Nature's way of saying good night to her vast creation—a landscape that she would greet in similar fashion the next day with the first rays of the rising sun.

Suddenly, Mochcom heard something. He squinted to focus on any movements that might be going on around him. At first, he thought it might be the wind, but his innate ability to detect the unusual, honed over centuries, made him suspect otherwise.

He cocked his head in the direction of the sound. "What's that? Damn, it must be! Oh, yes," he rasped as he listened to the familiar tinkle. "Where is he? Kashom's black cat is around here!"

A black tail twitched above the sagebrush. *"Oh yes! Vulture, get him! Find him! Kill him!"* Mochcom howled in rage.

Black Vulture leaped from his perch and beat the air with his wings to propel his body into flight. He swooped over Mochcom and glided in the direction of the black tail.

"Get him! Bring his dead body to me!" Mochcom's excitement flared as he watched his bird of death dive for its prey.

Zanzee the cat raced for cover, hearing the flapping sounds of Vulture's wings as the bird closed in on him. He yowled in fright as he searched for a refuge. He spotted one—a crack in a large rock not more than fifteen feet in front of him. His long, slender legs thrust him toward this safe haven. Without a moment to spare, he leaped through the air and vanished into a hole. Vulture diverted his flight so as not to crash against the face of the sandstone formation.

A surprised, innocent black-tailed hare scurried from the hole and emerged from the rock. Vulture spotted him. He swooped down again, plunging his deadly talons into the flesh of his unsuspecting prey, and released a howling scream signifying his kill.

From his dark, confined hole, Zanzee peered through the crack into the sunlit stage of the afternoon desert, where the drama of death was unfolding.

Black Vulture was standing on the twitching body of the dying animal.

Before the hare could make a movement in its quest to escape death, Vulture dug his talons deep into the warm flesh. The hare went limp. Crimson blood oozed from the gaping wound.

Vulture lowered his head. Holding his prey secure with his legs, he sank his beak into the exposed flesh. He yanked his head in upward motion, ripping a large piece of meat from the dead animal.

Not making a sound, Zanzee lay motionless in the secure haven of the rock as he watched Vulture quietly devour the rabbit.

Vulture's silence told his master that a feast was underway. His glee at visualizing the death of Leg Breaker's cat diverted Mochcom's attention from his rant to thoughts of the god of darkness—lord of the Black Temple—and filled his soul with joy. He began chanting the words "Negra Pantheon" over and over. Then he screeched, "To me, Vulture!"

Vulture returned.

"Where's your prey?" roared Mochcom. He was unable to see behind the rock, which blocked his view of the kill and aftermath. "I see the blood dripping from your claws and beak! Did you kill him? I want the body of Kashom's cat!"

Vulture hopped in front of his master. He regurgitated a bloody black paw and blinked.

"Good boy, Black Vulture. We've stifled the magic of Leg Breaker's cat forever!"

Vulture screamed as he lifted in flight and headed toward the Boar's Tusk.

Mochcom watched his faithful friend circling the Tusk and imagined the dead body of a black cat rotting in the desert, with the maggots crawling through the decaying flesh. His gaze took in the massive towers of rock projecting their majestic silhouettes against the deep blue Wyoming sky.

"Yes! Great and mighty Zuron, if you help me to find the five worox stones and the emerald star, I'll honor you with acts of horror. I'll be the sole controller of eternal youth throughout eternity! It will be you, Zuron, working through me as your emissary, who will bask in the glory of the world's horror and misery." Lord Mochcom smiled as he looked to the skies.

CHAPTER 9

Monkey in a Palace

The two-rut dirt road was covered with weeds, old tin cans, and broken bottles. The trio walked gingerly. "Watch where you step," warned Tony. "This is a garbage dump!" They turned off the main street onto LeRoy's driveway.

LeRoy's house was 150 feet off the road, nestled in a carved-out area at the base of a small hill. A rock wall behind the house kept dirt from sloughing off the hill, offering protection from some of the elements. The roof of the dilapidated shack had had most of its asphalt shingles blown off. In their place, LeRoy had nailed down strips of tar paper, but the wind had managed to rip most of it apart, leaving unsightly black flags waving from his roof at passersby.

When they reached the end of the driveway, Tony said, "Anyway, you guys, we're here. This is one creepy place! Do we get on to what Jeannie planned and start our snooping?"

Before Jeannie could answer, sounds came from the house. *Meroww, meroww.*

"Hey, there's a cat in there! Let's go! I'll bet it's cute," yelled Jeannie.

Danny cringed as he looked at the old wooden shanty. "I don't know, Jeannie," he said in a sullen voice. "That cat may be some old scrawny devil that will claw the crap out of us. I don't want to look for it!"

She grabbed his hand and pulled on it. "You're no fun. Come on. We came to snoop, so let's snoop!"

Walking toward the house, Danny pointed and said, "Let's check to see if he left the back door unlocked." He stopped and looked at Jeannie. "Are you sure you want to do this?" He was still not comfortable with her decision.

Jeannie had no doubts about her adventure plan. She didn't hesitate. "*Yes!*" she yelled. "See if the door is open!"

Not sure he wanted to go through with breaking into a house, Danny hesitated, but there was no hesitation from Jeannie. She pointed at the door. Danny took her silent order. Gingerly, he checked it. "Hey, we're in luck."

Tony laughed, looking at Danny out the corner of his eye. "Well, best buddy, looks like you take orders from the same lady general that I do."

Jeannie waited patiently until Tony had finished. "Get going, Tony," she replied, giggling. "We came to snoop, so let's snoop! And that's an order from the lady general!"

They all laughed and stepped just inside the doorway together.

"Holy jumping catfish," yelled Tony. "Get a load of this!"

Never in his entire life would Danny have expected the sight he was looking at. "You have to be kidding me! What the hell is this place?" he shouted as he dropped his hand from the door, spun around, and looked at the surprised Jeannie.

There could be no denying how unusual it was, especially for three poor teenagers who seemed to be stepping right into their fantastic dream of finding something of value just by snooping. The house they were peering into was a palace, at least on the inside—a treasure trove disguised by a filthy old exterior. It was a combination that was not commonplace in a coal camp.

His eyes darting around the glistening room, decorated with what appeared to be golden objects, Danny said, "My god, Jeannie, look at this place. Holy shit, this kitchen looks like a king's palace."

And that it did. Even though the outside of the house provided a perfect illusion—a rattletrap old house—the inside was completely different. There were golden vases on marble tables and eye-catching medieval tapestries adorning the walls.

Crowded together just a few feet inside the doorway, they gaped at the brilliance of the white marble walls reflecting the streaming light around them. What they saw was a kitchen, but a kitchen fit for a palace. Staring at the most unusual sight, Jeannie said, "Whoa! Get a load of the sink! Are those faucets gold? It sure looks like they are. Let's get inside and check this out!"

She grabbed Danny's hand and started the procession through the doorway. "Holy shit, this place is immaculate! There isn't an ounce of dirt anywhere," Danny said as he stepped inside. "Holy shit again! Look at the table and chairs!"

That was it for Jeannie. She had had it with his cussing. She yanked on his arm. He spun around to look at her, and she made a motion of washing out his mouth with soap. Danny rolled his eyes and pretended not to understand.

"Danny! Stop your cussing! You don't have to make your point with swear words!"

Of course, that was just the signal for him to have more fun. He pretended to zip his mouth with two fingers and spoke through them. "Okay, Miss Princess Jeannie. Your wish is my command," came the muffled words through his cupped hand. Looking squarely into her eyes, he dropped an eyebrow and gave her a wink. *Come on, Jeannie, let a guy be a guy! We have our own language.*

Her glare was a bit more persuasive. He knew he had better clean up his language, so he said, "Sorry! I just got carried away." He paused, but she said nothing. He knew her look meant business. In a softer and more sincere voice, he asked, "Are we still friends?" She smiled, and he too smiled, with relief. Then he turned his attention back to the house.

"Check out this table and chairs," he gasped. "Holy Mother of Saint Andrew and Horse Pucky," said Danny and then paused. Their eyes locked. She said nothing, and he continued. "You didn't hear me cuss. Just a few holy words."

She smiled at his comment, so he charged on. "As I was saying, Holy Mother of Jesus, these chairs are made of silver." Unable to resist the temptation, he grabbed the back of the chair and tried to slide it along the floor with one hand. It didn't move, so he used both hands. "Holy S! They have to be solid silver! They weigh a ton!"

Jeannie quickly pointed her finger at him. He laughed and said, "All I said was 'S.' What's wrong with that?"

Saying nothing, she wagged her finger at him.

His fingers slid over something unusual on the chair back. As they glided over the lettering, he noticed the same words on top of the silver table, shimmering in the sunlight. "Check out the gold inlay on the backs of the chairs and the table. What do you think it means?"

He paused and waited for an answer. No one said a thing, so he charged on. "I have an idea," he said, pointing to the inlaid gold. "'HHP GM' means 'Help, help, please—get me!'"

HHP

GM

Laughing, Jeannie answered, "No, I don't think so, Danny."

Suddenly, the sun vanished behind the clouds, and its illuminating rays, which had moments earlier turned the reflective marble walls into mirrors, were gone. Now the cavernous room was only dimly lit. A heavy feeling of oppression shot a cold chill up Tony's spine, and all traces of his humor also vanished. "This place gives me the creeps! In fact, it scares the hell out of me. I don't want to dilly-dally!" he remarked, peering into the blackness of the now lightless house.

The two windows in the room were both secured by thick shades—heavy, ornate tapestry coverings that did not allow an ounce of light to enter. Tony's mind went into high gear. *My god, zero light comes through these shades. They completely conceal the inside from the curious glances of stray onlookers who might be passing by and want a glimpse of what's inside. As Danny says, holy shit! They'd never notice this palace hidden behind the disguise of a crazy man's old house.*

As he looked at the weird expression on Tony's face, Danny too felt the ambience shift. As he stood in the dark palace, what he had seen earlier flashed through his mind. *That crazy old bastard has a ring like mine.* Although they had made it no farther than the middle of the kitchen floor, Danny's intuition was now telling him not to venture into the adjoining rooms. Motioning with his hand, pointing to the doorway, Danny said, "Let's get out of here. Come on, you guys. Something is not right. This place gives me the creeps, and I think that crazy old bastard is hiding who he is.

Jeannie disagreed with Danny. "I don't think he's hiding anything. He's a crazy man. Come on. Why do you say he is hiding something?" She laughed as she looked at Danny's uneasy expression; it did nothing to stop her curiosity. "Well, you may be right. He may be hiding something. Who knows? You gotta admit, this is way creepy! What's with all the marble and medieval tapestries? Is this camouflage for something?" With a strange little smile on her face, she continued, "We haven't gone in the other rooms. Don't you think we need to check them out?"

"*No!*" snapped Danny as the image of LeRoy's black ring flashed in his mind. "This place gives me the creeps! Let's get out of here!"

She snickered. "Come on, guys. If I can do it, so can you." Jeannie pointed at the door. "We may find something really neat through here!"

Danny rolled his eyes and wrinkled up his face even more. Jeannie stuck her tongue out at him. In response to her gesture, he reached to tickle her in the side, puckering up his lips and replying, "Yeah, like what?"

Jeannie jumped sideways, avoiding Danny's hand. She started laughing again as she noted that the uneasy look on Danny's face was still there.

A little swifter this time, Danny grabbed Jeannie's arm. "Come on, Jeannie. I don't care about snooping in a palace. You know, Jeannie, don't you think it is pretty strange that a crazy old man lives in a palace disguised as a shanty? This place is way too spooky for me!"

In a sweet voice, Jeannie replied, "Danny, it is strange and unusual. But that old man is weird. Who knows why he built his palace? He's nuts! What other explanation is there?" She poked him in the side and added, "Anyway, that's what we came to do—to snoop around and find out what's up here. Come on, Danny. If I can do it, you can."

Danny looked at her and grinned uneasily. "Okay," he said, "but I don't like this place."

Tony had already walked ahead of Danny and Jeannie. "Boy, this is one scary place," he said, standing by the door leading from the kitchen to the living room. Each step of Tony's shoes on the polished green marble floor sent sounds echoing off the walls.

Danny listened to the eerie floor music and didn't move. "What would we see if there were more light in here?" He stared around the dark living room. *Do we really want to mess around up here? I don't think so!* He was not persuaded they should stay and snoop. "Jeannie, something tells me we need to get out of here! Something is not right. Let's skip the snooping and get the hell out of here!"

"Danny, I told you to quit cussing! Do I have to wash your mouth out with soap?" snapped Jeannie, pointing her finger at him.

"Begging your pardon! What cuss word? What are you talking about?" He flashed her a bewildered look. She didn't buy his innocent facial expression.

Staring him down, she said, "You know exactly what I'm talking about. Okay, guys, enough bantering. We're here to go snooping. Let's go!"

Tony's keen eye observed the dynamics between Danny and Jeannie, but he chose to say nothing.

Danny didn't let it go. He looked to see where Tony was. "What did I say? Tony, did you hear me cuss?"

Now Tony had no choice, except to respond while trying to remain neutral. "Don't drag me into this!" he said from across the room.

A little smirk crept across Jeannie's face. "Oh, never mind. You know when you cuss, Danny! Don't give me that 'What did I say?' business," she said in a motherly tone. Then she gave him a stern look and said, "Well, here's what I say. Keep your tongue under control!"

Danny stuck his tongue out and grabbed it with two fingers. "Okay, Jeannie, I've got me tongue under control." He winked at her.

"Good! Oh, by the way, you have a cute little wink, Mr. Me!"

Gingerly, they walked across the kitchen's green marble floor, Jeannie leading the way. She held Danny's hand, tugging slightly to make sure he followed her.

The sun came out from behind the clouds, and enough light filtered through the doorway from the kitchen to let them see some of their surroundings. Indeed, no sooner had they walked into what looked like a living room than a burst of light penetrated their dark surroundings, causing the white marble walls to momentarily flash their magnificence. And not only the walls lit up. Something more intriguing caught Danny's eye—a yellow sheen. "Holy smokes! Get a load of this!" he said, pointing at it. "It looks like that candle is sitting on a little gold table!"

Holding Jeannie's hand, he gave a gentle nudge to move her toward it. He stroked the gold. "Oh my god! This is worth a fortune! We struck pay dirt!"

Then there was a soft chuckle from the darkness near the covered window in the living room.

Spinning around on one foot, Danny dropped Jeannie's hand and darted past Tony. He stopped briefly and stared into the blackness of the room, rolling his eyes in the direction of the window. The heavy tapestry was swinging back and forth. Slowly it swung back into position, once again stifling any light that tried to get in.

Danny's mind churned with thoughts of possibilities. *Who just stuck their head through that window and cackled at us?*

Jeannie bolted to his side and grabbed his arm. "What is it, Danny?" she whispered, holding onto him tightly.

Suddenly, all three kids heard loud voices. "*Hey!* What are you *jerks* doing in there?" Someone was shouting in the yard behind the house.

Jeannie felt her heart drop. "*My god!*" she screamed. The loud voices coming from outside had startled her. She jumped sideways, still holding onto Danny, and almost pulled him over.

"Who's out there?" Tony yelled. The unnerving sounds had caught the three of them off guard.

Danny charged to the window with lightning speed, lifting the tapestry to get a peek at who was outside. "It's those idiots, Eddie and Terry," he shouted. "They're in the backyard."

None of them had expected that. "What? Why are they here? Those jerks! Why don't you and Jeannie go out and see what's going on? I'll take a look around in the bedroom and see what's in there," said Tony.

Danny raced outside and sprinted toward Eddie. He grabbed him. Jeannie stood back and just watched.

"Why do you guys always have to follow us and be such jackasses?" Danny snapped at Eddie, gripping him by the arms and staring him in the face. "You guys are always asshole bullies, but do you know what?" He didn't wait for an answer. "You guys are nothing but wimps. Why don't you get a life?" He pointed his finger at Eddie and wagged it a little. "You know, Eddie, I could wipe the ground with your ugly mug. You're such a nerd."

Eddie pulled away and said to Terry, "Let's leave these fizzle-jerks to their misery." He knew he was no match for Danny, who was bigger and a lot huskier than he was. His mind was racing as he and Danny faced each other. "You're a donkey jackass! I—I—I'll hit you with a big rock!"

Danny grunted angrily. He gave Eddie a sharp pull on the ear. Eddie squealed, *"Ouch!"* He reeled and backed away from Danny to stand two feet from the bedroom window above his head.

Inside the house, Tony suddenly heard a noise: *clang, bang, kersmash!* He froze. His mind raced. *What the Sam Hill? Is someone in there?* His hand started shaking as he reached for the bedroom doorknob, and he hesitated as he turned it. Now with his Cub Scout flashlight out, he peeked through the partly open door. On the bed was a monkey jumping up and down. It started squealing and then darted for the window. Startled, Tony just stood there, but a smile crossed his face as he saw its hind end disappear through the window.

Danny, standing in front of Eddie, saw the monkey before Eddie did. His face lit up. Eddie was puzzled. *What's Danny staring at, and why does he have that grin on his face?* He was still holding his ear, which was in excruciating pain where Danny had pulled it.

Yelling and screaming, the monkey flew through the air and landed squarely on Eddie's shoulders, knocking him face down into a hog wallow.

"Oh no! Who hit me?" yelled Eddie.

Grins crept across Jeannie and Danny's faces. Their cheeks lifted and their eyes sparkled as they watched the episode unfold. Their laughter was building, just waiting to explode. Finally, Jeannie looked at Danny, who nodded enthusiastically. Their laughter filled the air as the monkey did its thing.

With his nose in a stink pile, Eddie had only one thought. *Oh no! They're laughing at me with my face in hog crap.*

Jeannie had enjoyed watching Danny handle Eddie and Terry like a pro. The monkey was just the icing on the cake.

Danny chuckled, thinking, *I didn't have to rub your face in it. The gods of fate just wiped your ugly mug in the washbowl of hog heaven!*

The strange idea of a monkey living in a palace in CoalVille hadn't yet registered with Danny and Jeannie. They were caught up in enjoyment of the school bully getting his just reward.

Terry watched his friend pick his face out of the stink pile. He turned and sprinted for safer ground. Still, in the midst of his flight, he couldn't help but snicker to himself. *That was the funniest thing I've seen in my life—a monkey getting the best of Eddie!*

"Wait for me," shouted Eddie, in hot pursuit of his friend. *I'll bet Terry is laughing at me. If he tells anyone what happened up here, I'm going to beat the snot out of him.* As they ran away, he wiped hog mud from his face with the sleeve of his shirt. He turned his head, sandy-brown hair waving in the wind, and hollered cuss words at Danny and Jeannie. "You jackasses! I'll get even with all of you, come hell or high water!"

Then the strangeness of the situation hit Danny. A zillion questions shot through his mind. He blurted out, "Where the hell did that monkey come from, and where did it go?"

Shaking her head, Jeannie said, "This is bizarre. A crazy man, a palace, and a monkey!"

"Jeannie, it is bizarre," said Danny, "but even more bizarre, who unlocked the back door to this palace? I don't think Crazy LeRoy would leave the door open, do you?" Hiding his expression from Jeannie, Danny froze momentarily; no matter how strange the monkey and the palace were, his mind kept going back to one thought. *That crazy man has a ring with special powers. What does his ring do? Is it equivalent to mine? My god—if it is, we've got problems. He has supernatural powers.*

Yet try as he might, Danny could not hide his body language from

Jeannie. She watched him and knew he was uneasy, but she never suspected that his thoughts were on a ring set with a black stone that emanated purple light. The palace and monkey were foremost in Jeannie's mind as she answered Danny's last question. "I don't know, Danny. Maybe it was the monkey!"

CHAPTER 10
Crazy LeRoy's Evil Secret

In the interim, back in Crazy LeRoy's bedroom, the hind end of the monkey had vanished from Tony's sight, leaving the tapestry to swing back into place. Now there was once again only a small sliver of light filtering around the edges. Tony's eyes were not yet accustomed to the dimly lit room, and he was consumed by an oppressive feeling of darkness. *This is one freaky, scary place!*

His eyes followed a ribbon of sunlight that stabbed through a the thin slit in the window curtains. His mind was racing. *Is that something on the wall? There's a painting that looks—oh my God! It looks just like Jeannie!*

Tony swayed where he stood. The strangeness of what he was looking at seemed to enfold him. He reluctantly approached the wall. His small Cub Scout flashlight wobbled as he walked toward the painting, which was at least four feet by six feet. The flashlight didn't put out much light, but it was all he had. "Holy shit. This is a painting of Jeannie. What the hell is going on?" he mumbled in the darkness.

Although he noticed the caption across the top of the painting, "DEATH TO NEFERZUL BY CAPACOCHA," he had no idea what it meant.

At that instant, the wind fluttered the tapestry on the window. The sliver of light danced around on the squares of white marble used to construct the walls. Oddly, it landed on a piece of marble that was a different shape from the other pieces and quite a bit smaller. It was rectangular, six inches by ten inches, and located one foot to the right of the painting.

As if in a trance, Tony started mumbling to himself. "Why is that piece of marble so much smaller than the rest?" Out of curiosity, his hand shot forward to touch it. As he did so, a strange sound erupted behind him. "Oh my god, what's that?" he whispered.

Spinning around, he saw nothing. The noise continued. Gripping his flashlight, he swung his arm back and forth. The beam traced out a pattern on the floor. Then he saw it. It was in the direction of the noise. "Oh my lord, the floor is opening up!"

No sooner had the words left his mouth than the noise stopped. There, at the foot of the massive bed, was a four-foot-square hole in the floor.

The eerie silence pressed on him as the gaping hole awaited inspection. "What the hell? Is this a secret hiding place?" mumbled Tony. Walking ever so gingerly, he guided his movements by flashing his light on the floor, so as not to be surprised by something else. As he stood over the hole, his light illuminated a marble-lined chamber below. Slowly, he bent over, squatting on his knees. "What's in here?" he asked himself as he prepared to investigate. He held his breath and put his head into the hole on the floor.

Although the opening was only four-foot-square, the chasm beneath the floor was a cubic square of at least eight by eight feet in length and width and eight feet in height. At first, Tony saw nothing in the inky blackness. Then, cautiously moving his light, he spotted something. It was a box—no, two boxes, one larger and heavier than the other. The bigger one looked like it had to weigh at least twenty pounds, maybe more.

Tony winced as something shot his beam back into his eyes. *What's reflecting my light beam?* He shifted it a little. His heart was pounding. Squinting, he muttered, "Something is reflecting my flashlight—it's like a highly polished mirror."

Then he saw it more clearly. *Wow! They look like gems—they're stars! Yes, rainbow-colored gemstones in the shape of stars. Is that gold? That box must be made of bronze or brass or maybe gold. It looks like there's a little window on the top of it. Why would there be a little window on this thing? What are those little things that look like gold mirrors?*

The dim light was just enough for something strange to catch his eye. *Those are weird symbols! Why would they be on those little wheel things? Is there a combination lock on this box? What's that crazy old man hiding under his floor? What is he doing up here?*

Readjusting his body, Tony slipped. *"Oh no! No! No!"* he screamed as he scrambled to grab the slick marble floor. Throwing his leg out as fast as he could, he managed to catch the side of the opening with his foot and brace himself to keep from falling headfirst into the chasm.

"Oh my god," he gasped. "I damn near fell in this trap!" Catching his breath, he again flashed his light on the object he'd spotted moments earlier.

Cautiously, Tony moved so as not to slip again. He squirmed to adjust his body and tried to make out what was on the ornate metal box. His flashlight was reflected by the gems outlined in gold on its side. His heart took off. He took a deep breath and held it. He studied the top of the box.

"There are nine little wheels that appear to be made of gold, each with weird-looking symbols engraved on them," he muttered. He tried to read the symbols on the gold wheels, but there was not enough light. "They are in a row and resemble a combination-locking mechanism. What the hell is this thing?" Confusion began to dominate his thoughts. "There are also five little windows with a gold shutter behind each one. In the middle is another window with glass over it," he whispered to himself.

His heart pounded in his chest. Finding the box had piqued his interest. Adjusting his body, he lowered himself a bit farther into the opening to get a closer look. His movements caused the beam of light to dance around the blackness. It landed on yet another object of interest. The image of a skull, lying lifeless on the floor between the boxes, flashed before Tony's eyes like a demon looking at him from Hell.

His heart dropped. "Is that? Oh shit! It is! It's a human skull!"

Suddenly, the loud noises started again. The slab of marble started moving, pinching his arm, which was dangling in the hole. As the opening to the chasm began its timed closure, Tony panicked. His sleeve was now caught in the moving mechanism. Yelling for help, he rolled over onto his back and managed to free his arm. He was just barely in time. The door to the vault slammed shut and silence took over.

He looked at his sleeve. Part of it was missing. A small piece of the cloth was pinned under the marble slab that sealed up the vault.

"Oh, damn!" he said in a state of shock. "My god, this is just crazy!"

While Tony lay on his back, trying to gain composure, the beam from his light found another painting—on the wall, opposite the painting of Jeannie. It was a multicolored oil painting of a man wearing a black robe decorated with gems and gold-rope trim. The man was standing over a young girl's body, holding a knife in one hand and her heart in the other. Tony gawked at the figure

"*No!* Is that him?" He squinted. "Is that Crazy LeRoy in the painting?"

His fingers clutched his light, which bobbed around, but he couldn't tear his eyes from the painting. He gasped as his body stiffened, then began to shake. "My god! That man in the robe—it is him! That monster is holding a human heart dripping blood."

As he recovered from the shock, he turned his head quickly, so he saw only a brief glimpse of the large black bird in the painting, blood dripping from its beak. Clutching his flashlight as tightly as he could, he bolted for the doorway, screaming, "This is a house of horror! I've got to get out of here. This guy is crazy!"

Buzzing with excitement to tell his buddy the monkey story, a triumphant Danny headed toward the house. *I can't wait to let Tony know what's happened! Tony will split a gut when I tell him that a monkey just wiped Eddie's face in hog mud—the washbowl of hog heaven!* He reached for the back doorknob with a huge grin on his face. Just then, the door slammed open

Danny felt Tony's body slam into him, the impact knocking him sideways against the doorjamb. They exchanged bewildered looks. "Hey, you almost knocked me down!" Danny shouted.

Tony didn't answer. Danny didn't turn his head. He grabbed Tony by the arm. "What were you screaming about in there? What's going on? Did you see a ghost?"

Tony tensed up. He started shaking and pulled away. His face grew long, and his voice turned serious. "Let's get the *hell out of here!* This is an evil place of Satanic practice!"

Danny hadn't expected that kind of response from Tony. "What? Tony, what are you saying?"

The expression on Tony's face said it all. Something was dreadfully wrong. Danny grabbed Tony's arm again and felt the trembling of his friend's body. "Slow down, Tony!"

But Tony lunged away. His sleeve tore again, leaving Danny standing baffled, a piece of Tony's sleeve in his hand.

"Tony, what's your problem? Come on! What's going on?"

"Danny, you won't believe what's in that house!" Tony said. His voice was quivering. His body was shaking.

"Tony, you're really scared! Why? What's in there?"

"I just want to get the hell out of here! This is a gruesome place! It's a Satanic hellhole. I'm going home. That crazy son of a bitch is evil! Danny, I just don't want to talk about it. It was a bad idea to come up here."

Tony's ramblings got Jeannie's attention. She peered through the door of the woodshed that housed LeRoy's green 1948 Ford pickup. "Why was it a bad idea to come up here?" she asked.

She really didn't want an answer to her question. She had picked up only part of the conversation between Tony and Danny. She had masterminded the adventure, and now she was wondering what the problem was. She didn't want to be blamed for a fiasco, so she changed the subject.

"That's a nice truck! Danny, you'd like it—it's almost new. I don't think Crazy LeRoy has driven it in the seven years he's lived in CoalVille."

Danny cut her off. "Forget about that damn goofy truck. While you've been snooping in that old woodshed, something's happened to Tony."

"*What?* Tony, what happened?" Jeannie looked at him and could tell he wasn't acting normally.

"Sorry, Jeannie, I—er, ah—I know you wanted to look around more, but I just want to go home. You wouldn't believe what's in this house. That crazy old fool has a human skull. LeRoy is a devil. Let's get out of here! This is one creepy place. Ah—er—there's something dreadfully dark and evil going on up here. I just can't talk about it anymore. *Let's go!*" Tony fell silent momentarily and stared at Danny and Jeannie with a spacey look.

Then he blurted, "He's crazy—crazy enough to kill us if he knew we were snooping in his house!"

Jeannie's mood could not have been more serious. Her face was grave as she voiced the thoughts dominating her mind. Facing Danny and Tony, she said, "Nobody in CoalVille knows about this place." She paused, and her face showed lines of concern that reflected the seriousness of her words. "Did you guys hear me?" Not stopping for an answer, she charged on. "If word gets out that this place exists—well, you get the picture. The trail leads back to us!"

Silence fell as they looked at each other. Then Tony asked, "What about Eddie and Terry?"

It was Jeannie who answered. "I don't think they saw anything. It was too dark where we were. If they had seen the palace, they would have said something when Danny and I confronted them." Then she made her point. "We have a problem, guys! This is our secret, and it has to stay a secret or—you get the picture. We'd be in big trouble, maybe even to the point of our lives being in danger!"

Her words hung in the air like the sounds of bells banging away in a church steeple. Danny's heart sank. *I knew it! That old man is hiding something—something a hell of a lot more dreadful than we could possibly imagine!*

CHAPTER 11
Pirate Log Day

It was the fourteenth of March 1958. An unusual hubbub filled the cafeteria of CoalVille High School. It was not the rumbling and grinding of the tattered conveyor belt that carried trays of dirty dishes and uneaten food through a service window to the kitchen; the machine was motionless, silent, and empty. Although there were a few scattered trays on the old steel tables, mostly shoved to one corner, no attention was being given to food or to foreboding thoughts of evil, only pictures. The noise was the chatter of kids marveling over their latest acquisition—the 1958 yearbook.

"Damn, this is neat! Karen did a great job putting the yearbook together," Danny remarked as he sat next to Jeannie and Tony at the lunch table. "This is one of my favorite days. The annual is about us, not all the bullshit class work. What do you guys think?"

All high school students had been issued the annual school yearbook, the Pirate Log, at the start of lunch period. Danny's attention was not on lunch—it was on pictures of Jeannie and her cheerleading partners and of him and his Pirate teammates.

Sitting next to Danny in the cafeteria, Jeannie wrapped her arm around him and squeezed his biceps. "Yeah, it's a cool book this year. Your basketball pictures are great!" she said, watching him flip through the pages.

"Why do we have to go to class on the day they issue the yearbook? I hate going to class on yearbook day, especially the last one of the day—that damn American history class," Danny remarked with a disgusted look.

As the end of the lunch hour approached, Jeannie closed her yearbook and picked up her canvas bag. "We had better head back to class," she said.

"I agree with Danny," Tony commented. "This is Friday afternoon—I'm sick of school."

Jeannie put her annual in her bag and flung it over her shoulder. She reached to touch Danny's hand. "Danny, just hang on for two periods. We can have fun in Miss C's class—we'll make plans for an after-school adventure." She turned and started skip-walking toward the door. "See you guys in two hours," she said as she headed off to her English class.

Danny lifted the pencil he was holding and put it behind his ear, leaving the end of it sticking out of his hair. "Let's go, Tony. Crap, another math class. Do you understand that bullshit algebra stuff—x-y-z equals something? How stupid!"

Tony laughed. "Don't worry, Danny. I'll help you get through Mr. Hall's math class. It'll be okay. Let's go. We're late."

The last class of the day finally arrived. Tony and Danny walked out of their math class and headed down a hall buzzing with conversations about the yearbook. Danny was flipping the pages of his as he walked, not paying attention to Tony.

Tony spotted KateLynn, the girl who had captured his attention and wrapped his heart around her finger. "KateLynn, stop," he called to her.

She stopped and turned, recognizing his voice behind her. "Hi, Tony." As they walked up to her, she teased Danny: "Danny, Danny, look up!"

"Oh hi, KateLynn. Have you seen Jeannie?" said Danny, lifting his head and glancing quickly in her direction.

KateLynn smiled. "I think she's already in American history class. I wish I was in that class with you guys instead of Latin. I hate Latin. Nobody speaks that crap. Oh, I'm late. I've got to run."

Tony grabbed her arm before she got away. "Sign my annual. You have a few minutes. Who cares if you're late? Anyway, if you miss a few minutes, you won't have to listen to a full hour of that Latin crap!"

She took Tony's yearbook from his outstretched hand, and then she grabbed his hand and pulled him next to her. "I'll sign this only if you promise to go out with me."

Tony grinned. "You got it!"

Danny watched. "KateLynn, it would be a pleasure if you signed my book also."

"Sure, Danny. Just a minute and I'll finish my note in Tony's."

Finishing her perfectly crafted, poetic love message to Tony, she looked up. "Hand me your book, Danny—just a quick note." She scrawled hurriedly and handed it back to him. "I've got to run. I'm really late. Say hi to Jeannie."

Miss Carter glared at Danny and Tony as they walked into her room five minutes late.

Danny swished Jeannie's hair with his hand as he walked past her on the way to his seat. Smiling, she rolled her eyes at him and quickly pinched him on his hind pocket before he sat down. Sitting in the seat in front of her, he reached his arm behind to grab her leg, but she was quicker and moved it.

Miss Carter didn't notice the horseplay going on between Danny and Jeannie. Finishing her board writing, she wheeled around. First she looked nonchalantly at the back of the class, then at Danny.

I hate this class. Good Lord, a history class at the end of the school day on a Friday afternoon! Danny thought. He frowned, his facial expression broadcasting his disgust.

Miss Carter noticed his expression. "Class, during the migration west, Wyoming played a major role in history, especially on two fronts that dealt with transportation. Let's look at these two issues. What were they? Danny, can you help us?"

Why in the hell is she bugging me again? Is she pissed at me because I threatened her pet, Eddie? I hate this class—who cares about two fronts? Transportation— good grief!

Danny's mind was on treasure, not transportation. *I know that some time long ago, there just had to have been Spanish explorers who looted Incan treasure. Then pirates would have stolen it from the Spaniards and hid it someplace around here. It has to be around CoalVille, buried in these hills—I just know it.*

Danny stared at the cover of his school yearbook, the Pirate Log, sitting on his desk. It's funny how the human mind can play tricks, especially when you are daydreaming about treasure. At first, Danny's Pirate Log looked just like the CoalVille High school yearbook—after all, that's what it was. But the human mind is complex, and it can create surreal images—figments of the imagination.

Danny's mind was drifting. No longer did his Pirate Log look normal. It seemed his mind was playing tricks on him. He stared at his annual. The

Boar's Tusk was smack in the middle of the front cover, just behind the Pirate. *Why is the Boar's Tusk on my yearbook? I know why our mascot is the pirate, but the Tusk? I know! Pirates buried their treasure in the Scarlet Desert. I'll bet they put it some place where they could find it easily.*

He reached out and touched it. *What the hell is going on? Am I imagining this?*

Had his mind played a trick on him as he was daydreaming? Maybe that was what was happening—figments of imagination had crept into Danny's mind as he daydreamed of finding pirate treasure in the desert. Who knew? *There's a pirate standing at the Boar's Tusk—they buried something there, I know they did! Yeah, they put it near the Boar's Tusk—it's a perfect marker.*

Standing behind her desk, Miss Carter tapped her pencil. She was waiting for Danny's answer to the question she had just asked him. She paused. He looked up but did not answer. She tapped her pencil again and asked sarcastically, "Mr. Roberts, can you enlighten us as to where your mind is and what you are thinking about?"

Danny flinched. He said nothing.

The only motion by Miss Carter was her hands moving from her side to the desktop. "I'm waiting," she snapped as she leaned forward.

Shit, lady, Danny thought. He hesitated, then blurted out, "Yes, Miss Carter. I think there's treasure around here!"

She straightened up. His answer startled her. "Oh? I had no idea, Danny. Just what on earth are you talking about? Are you here—or someplace else? I thought the subject was transportation! Evidently, Danny, you want to study something else during this hour—is that not so?" She smiled at him.

At that comment by Miss Carter, the entire class erupted into laughter. Eddie chuckled to himself. *Go get him, Miss Carter. He deserves it after what he did to me yesterday.* He rolled up a piece of paper around an orange peel and flicked it to the floor. He then pointed to the garbage and grinned at his freckle-faced buddy, Terry. They gleefully watched Miss Carter rake Danny over the coals.

Eddie was sitting in the back of the class, while Danny and Jeannie were in the front. Loving every moment, Eddie took advantage. He wrinkled his nose at Terry and gave Danny the bird while Miss Carter's attention was elsewhere. He was still furious over the hog incident at Crazy LeRoy's house and wanted Terry to take note.

Miss Carter slowly tapped her pencil on her scratched wooden desk, then continued. "Mr. Roberts, the subject is transportation, not treasure. Can you get your mind back on track and tell the class about early transportation in Wyoming?"

Danny looked at her seriously. "Wagons and trains, Miss Carter. If it weren't for wagons, the West would still be a wild frontier, and if it weren't for trains, CoalVille wouldn't be here. Coal from the CoalVille mine powered the locomotives that pulled the trains."

She smiled at him and responded, "Very good, Danny. I see you've read part of your assignment. But how did the wagon trains help Wyoming?"

Danny fidgeted in his seat. *Now what the hell is she up to?*

For a few moments, Miss Carter said nothing. The class waited with anticipation. She then continued her questioning. "Please help us out. What more can you tell us?"

Holy rat shit, lady, what's wrong with you? Danny wondered why he was getting the brunt of her afternoon questioning. *I hate this class.* He turned his head sideways and glanced at the back row of students. *Those bastards, Eddie and Terry. They're giggling under their breath. What have they got going with her now?* His face lit up with a grin. *Well, I'll give them something to laugh about!*

He rubbed his tongue across the edges of his upper teeth. "Farts and outposts," he grinned. "Miss Carter, if the wagons had not come through Wyoming, we wouldn't have the farts and outposts."

Silence engulfed the class. Danny opened his mouth in feigned shock and then slapped the side of his cheek with his hand. All the students heard the loud pop. Not waiting, he corrected himself. "I mean *forts* and outposts."

Miss Carter thought, *You smartass. You're playing with me. All right, two can play. This is my territory!*

"Yes, Danny, we all know what you meant," Miss Carter said, looking at Eddie. "Next time, choose your men wisely. I mean—ah, ah—choose your words wisely."

I've got her! Danny grinned from ear to ear. *Too bad, Miss C!* "Men? Choose what men, Miss Carter?" he shot back as he noted that she was looking at Eddie. "Touché, Miss Carter!"

Although there should have been an outburst of laughter from every student in the class, there was dead silence. The students kept their amusement bottled up. But if silent laughter was golden, Danny had found his treasure—he knew what everyone was thinking. Then his eye caught a quick glance from Miss Carter.

Why'd she look at Eddie and then at me? He's her pet. Is she comparing me to him? Does she want a new conquest? She's not for me!

Jeannie didn't miss a trick. Her mind took off. *One for Danny—zip for Miss Carter.*

From the back of the room came the distinct smell of human gas. Danny giggled to himself. *Has to be a fart and not an outpost—someone cut the cheese!*

Jeannie's face lit up. Watching the dynamic between Miss Carter and Danny reminded her of just how skilled Danny could be when he had to think fast, but she was not concentrating on Danny, Miss Carter, or American history. No—her thoughts were on their next after-school adventure. Their Thursday adventure at LeRoy's house had been a bust, but that wouldn't stop her from planning the next one.

She slid her hand under the desktop, raising it just enough to get her hand inside. She grabbed a small piece of paper as she contemplated her plan. *Here's what we do: quickly get together after class, catch three of Alex's horses, and ride out to White Face Cliff.*

She scribbled out her message and waited. The cue for her to pass her note was Miss Carter turning and writing Monday's assignment on the blackboard. She giggled to herself as she planned out a more adventurous outing—a search for hidden treasure in the desert. She would play on Danny's fascination with tales of Incan treasure, stolen by pirates and buried in the Scarlet Desert.

She knew the horses would be easy to catch. *Boy, are we going to have fun. I can't wait for this darn class to be over so I can race through the desert with Danny and Tony—bareback on Alex's horses.*

Tony caught the twinkle in Jeannie's eyes and knew something was up. He watched her hand pull back Danny's shirt collar and saw the note disappear.

Danny felt the touch on his shirt. *Damn it, Jeannie. You did it again! You do it because you know where your notes end up.* He squirmed and fidgeted in his seat, trying to stop the paper from sliding down his backside. He looked at Jeannie and Tony, who had grins on their faces. He too got a grin on his face as he watched Miss Carter. *All right, you guys. Someone else must be smiling along with you—it must be the gods, because she keeps on writing and writing and writing!*

Danny unbuttoned the lower part of his shirt and reached his hand behind his body to grab the note before Miss Carter turned around.

He read it to himself: *Let's catch ASH's, then off to WFC! We'll have a quick meet after class to figure out when and where! Then off to Ziz we go!*

He chuckled to himself. *Typical Jeannie—she always has to get those plug horses, but what the hay. They sure are fun to ride. Besides, Eddie and Terry can't catch a frog, let alone a horse, so they'll be left in our dust. We're going to have a ball this afternoon. No, not a ball—a blast!* Nodding his head, Danny stretched his hand across the aisle to slap the note into Tony's outstretched hand.

Beaming, Tony mouthed his response under his breath. "Sounds super!"

Eddie and Terry, not missing a trick, decided not to follow up on what was going on between Danny, Jeannie, and Tony. They speculated that the three friends would be stomping up to Crazy LeRoy's nasty house again. But Eddie was thinking of payback. *I need more time to plan how to get back at Danny and do him justice for that nasty trick he pulled on me yesterday. Don't worry—I'll figure something out that's really bad to do to that jerk.*

The bell finally rang, and none too soon. The mad dash for the exit door left Miss Carter, as usual, standing at the blackboard. Only a half-finished assignment was written on it.

Oh, well, I'll catch up on Monday, she thought as she walked to her desk.

CHAPTER 12

The White Face of Ziz Reveals the Path

"Our adventure yesterday at LeRoy's was a bust. Will our adventure today be a boom?" wondered Jeannie to herself as she raced bareback on Skipper through the Scarlet Desert, over nature's multicolored quilt of spring flowers and purple sage. She answered her own question. "I hope so!"

Springtime showers on sage-covered hills filled the air with an aroma that reminded Tony of a potpourri market. *This is what the gods must have every day to freshen up their playgrounds, and today, Mariah—the old wind—is bringing this gift to us.*

As Mariah kicked up, Danny watched Jeannie riding her horse, heading for White Face Cliff. Her long black ponytail streamed in the wind, flowing in rhythm with Skipper's mane as the horse moved in full gallop.

Jeannie had taken a chance on the weather. She had slipped into a pair of tight-fitting shorts, exposing her long legs to the afternoon sunlight. *I love this*, she thought as she kicked Skipper in his sides with her heels. *I'm glad it warmed up so I can finally wear shorts.*

Clutching the reins of CoCo's bridle as he watched Jeannie race through the desert, Danny wondered if anyone from CoalVille had ever noticed them take Alex's horses. *Who cares?* His heart thumped. *Whoa—*

Jeannie's soft, white, bare legs and Skipper in full gallop. How cool is that?

They rounded the hill, bringing White Face Cliff into spectacular view. The scarlet rays of the afternoon sun set the cliff ablaze with breathtaking colors.

Danny's excitement mounted. His heart was skipping beats not only because he was watching Jeannie's body bouncing up and down on Skipper's back but also because of the folk legends. He'd always been curious about them—tales of buried treasure in the hills around CoalVille.

That white sandstone cliff is my favorite stomping ground. Those petroglyphs have to mean something—those carvings of the sun, a star, and three images of people holding hands must tell a story. But what is it? Is it a treasure map?

Jeannie was the first to reach their destination. She reined Skipper in, jumped off him, and tied him to a sage bush next to a large sandstone rock. She cried out excitedly: "Hey, guys, this is Friday, and we don't have to go to school tomorrow—*hallelujah!*"

Danny swung his leg off CoCo, jumping to the ground. "You know it! I just love this place—I wish we could sleep out here tonight, Jeannie. We'd have fun, wouldn't we? But we can't."

He watched her every movement. Her sparkling eyes caught his. "It would be fun, Danny. Maybe we ought to plan a trip alone, without Tony," she beamed. "But alas, actually, we don't have a lot of time to spend—so I guess we had better make the most of it."

As she jogged by him, she quickly stretched her arm out and gave him a quick slap on the back pocket of his Levis. He pivoted on one foot and tried to grab her. She turned her head, gazing at him, and giggled, "Slow on the uptake!" He laughed.

Jeannie continued her jog toward the pond nestled at the base of the cliff. She picked up a rock and skipped it across the surface. The ripples reflected the afternoon rays with the same brilliant burnt orange painted on the cliff directly behind the pond.

As Danny stood motionless, watching the love of his life playing with nature's wonders, an electric current seemed to course through him, charging his body with excitement. As he watched Jeannie playfully enjoying the moment, he visualized what it would be like for him and

Jeannie to discover a treasure. He sighed as he thought about it; he knew everyone thought it was impossible. He visualized a chest filled with gold coins. *That old fart KeeLord found some gold. There's got to be more. Wouldn't that be a kick in the ass if we stumbled onto treasure?*

His eyes lit up as his imagination went wild. *My god, wouldn't it be wonderful if we could find a priceless treasure that would free us from the stifling cycle that grips the residents of CoalVille. Each new generation of boys follow their fathers to the monster—the mine—to play miner's Russian roulette.*

He spoke. "I think a pirate made those markings up there a long time ago. I think he wanted to tell us something."

Tony had been watching Danny, standing only twenty feet from him. He knew his friend so well. *Ever since we met, Danny has been sharing his dreams of treasure with me.* But Tony was a realist, not a dreamer. He scrunched up his face, rolled his eyes, and gaped at Danny. "Yeah, and I think you've lost your marbles, Mr. Roberts." He pointed to the spot on the cliff where the petroglyphs were carved. "The only thing I see is some old Indian markings."

Jeannie overheard his conversation. She looked where he had just pointed with a stern look on her face. She was not pleased with his comment. "Watch what you say, Tony," Jeannie snapped at him. "Those markings on that cliff are *not* 'Indian markings'! You're talking about sacred Kashome writings. There is a difference!"

Taking his eyes off Tony, Danny glanced at Jeannie swiftly, trying to read her body language. "Jeannie, just because you're part of the Kashome Nation doesn't mean that those writings up there were made by one of your Kashome ancestors," he remarked, sheepishly.

She didn't buy his remark. In fact, she found it offensive. "So, smarty pants, you tell me—just what is it? You think you know everything! Just who in god's name do you think you are?" she said sharply.

Danny had stuck his foot in his mouth. He didn't want to make matters worse. His only comeback was *pirates.*

"You don't know, Jeannie. Maybe it was a pirate who put those markings up there," he said, now even more sheepishly.

Her response was far from sheepish. "Yeah, sure. And pigs fly!"

Tony was well aware that he had instigated the back-and-forth. He saw no reason for the bickering to continue. He quickly jumped to his feet from the rock he'd been sitting on and put his hands in the air, forming a T with them.

"Okay, guys, time for a truce." Tony spoke quietly but in an authoritative tone. He had no intention of letting tensions get out of hand. "We came to have a good time, and we only have fifteen minutes left before we need to head for home." He paused. Then he asked a question. "Why is this cliff called White Face Cliff by some and White Cliff of Ziz by the Kashome people? I know this is not a widely known fact, but Jeannie, you referred to it as Ziz in your note yesterday. Do you remember?"

She knew what Tony was up to. *He's just being diplomatic. Well, that's okay.* For a moment she said nothing. Then, following a short silence, Jeannie started to answer him. "Tony, it is—"

For whatever reason, Tony immediately jumped back into the conversation. "Jeannie, I don't want to cut you off, but that question was rhetorical," Tony said before Jeannie could say anything. "I was just trying to provoke thought!"

Listening to Tony and Jeannie, Danny had found a comfy spot to relax. He put his hands behind his head, resting it on the rock. He could tell that Tony had good intentions with his question about Ziz, but it just wasn't getting the job done.

"I think I know what Tony is trying to say," he said with a knowing smile.

Jeannie walked to the rock he was leaning on and resting his back against. His legs were stretched out straight, resting on the ground in front of his rock. She stepped over his body, straddling his legs with hers. Standing over him, she looked down at his smiling face. Reaching over her head, she grabbed the silk scarf she used to decorate her ponytail. As she untied, it her long silky hair draped around her face.

"Yeah, what?" was Jeannie's reply, dangling her scarf in a swishing motion over his face in a teasing manner. "I see you smiling."

He looked up at her standing over him, her bare legs on either side of his. He laughed. He slowly moved his arms and gently placed his hands on her calves. "Well, Tony was just thinking out loud and wondered who Ziz is. As a matter of fact, I would like to know also."

The longing for a girl pulled at Tony's heart as he watched the dynamic between his friends. He had no doubt what was on their minds. *God, I'd love it if KateLynn were here. This is no fun for me. Next time, I'm bringing her.*

From the corner of her eye, Jeannie caught Tony watching them. She dropped her scarf on Danny's face. He slid it a bit to uncover one eye. Jeannie was now smiling at both Danny and Tony. She giggled and said, "I have no idea who Ziz is."

Then, more seriously, she continued, "The Kashome people have called certain places in the Scarlet Desert by certain names for centuries. Who knows why they do it. Usually it's just the Kashome people who recognize the names of a place. They're the only ones that have knowledge of the names. I guess Tony just picked up on something I said. Sorry for the confusion, Tony."

Jeannie wasn't satisfied with what she had just said to the boys. In fact, she was thinking about her own comments. *Yeah, who is Ziz?* She laughed to herself. *I don't think any of us knows what the heck Ziz is, let alone who it is!*

She smiled and winked down at Danny, still straddling him. She turned quickly and also winked at Tony. That was all it took. They knew it was her way of saying, *Okay, guys, all is cool.*

Jeannie stepped away from Danny so he could move from the rock he'd been resting against. At first, he pulled his legs up, bending his knees. Then he leaned forward and wrapped his arms around his folded legs. His head remained still as his eyes searched for something. As he sat on the ground with his back pulled slightly forward from the rock, his eyes focused intently on the cliff. They wandered up and down gray-and-white sandstone formations. The afternoon shadows made the cracks and crevices seem like lines drawn by human hands.

Danny suddenly stood up. Out of the blue, he remarked, "Look, you can see the face of a man on the cliff. Look up there." He pointed his finger to a place on the cliff that reflected a sliver of sunlight.

Tony had been looking at the pond of water at the base of the cliff, but quickly diverted his attention to where Danny was pointing. "I see it."

The boys' conversation captured Jeannie's attention. "Yeah, I see it also. Kinda neat, Danny. You've got a good imagination!"

The sun was less than two hours from setting. Its afternoon rays made the cracks, crevices, and petroglyphs remarkably evident. Tony concentrated on a specific spot—the eyes of the face on the cliff.

"Wow!" he said. "Good observation, Danny. I never noticed that face before. You guys, look at the eyes of the face. They're looking at those three figures of people holding hands and some other markings on the cliff," said Tony.

Less interested, Jeannie spotted a comfortable spot to rest—a large white sandstone rock that had been polished smooth by the elements over the eons. Watching Jeannie lie back on her comfortable rock, Danny moved from his spot. "Your rock is more comfortable than mine," he said, reaching for her hand as he sat next to her.

For a few moments, all three kids enjoyed the unusually warm afternoon. Danny and Jeannie lay back on their rock, holding hands while watching clouds drift overhead in slow motion. A brilliant yellow meadowlark not far from them provided an interlude of song.

Tony was sitting quietly, fifty feet from Danny and Jeannie. He fiddled with a piece of paper while dragging his foot in the sand. Growing a bit impatient, he looked at his watch and then at the cliff again.

Danny came up on one elbow and put his face over Jeannie's. The temptation was almost more than he could stand. He was about to move closer, his lips only inches from Jeannie's, when Tony yelled, "Wow!"

Danny and Jeannie sat up, still holding hands. Danny's eyebrows pulled together as he thought, *Tony, this had better be good. You screwed up my kiss!*

Tony pointed to direct the others' attention once again to the petroglyphs on the cliff in front of them. He watched Danny, wondering if he was looking at the same thing he'd just pointed out. *He does see it. I knew it. There's something peculiar up there.*

Then, suddenly, all three kids saw the same thing at the same time. They cried out in unison, "Look at the words by the three figures!"

Tony stood up from his resting spot and started walking closer to get a better look. "What do they say?" Tony mumbled. His mind was racing.

That's strange. I wonder why I never noticed those words. They're almost hidden by the cracks and crevices in the rocks on the cliff!

Danny did not move. He squinted intently so his eyes could focus, seeing the words clearly. He had no idea what they meant. "It looks like 2 CRÓNICAS 20:16 and EXODO 33:2," Danny shouted.

Jeannie glared at the strange writing. *Why didn't I notice this before? I've been here hundreds of times. Well, maybe I did see it before but just never questioned it.*

She released Danny's hand and clapped hers, startling him. "I've got it, guys—I've got it!" she exclaimed excitedly.

"You've got what?" Danny asked, with a puzzled look. She said nothing, just smiled at him. He noticed her excitement. "What do you have?" he asked again, now grinning and waiting for her response.

"Stand up, and I'll tell you," she said, jumping to her feet while tugging on his hand. He stood up. She put her hands on either side of his face. She turned his head so their eyes locked. "Well, Danny," Jeannie said in a cool, authoritative voice, "it's from the Biblia Reina-Valera."

Danny didn't move. Their eyes remained locked. "What are you talking about? What's a Bubbly Reinaiana Valderas?"

Jeannie dropped her hands from his face. She laughed. "Danny, it's an old book."

Danny's eyebrows lifted. "How do you know that? Are you just winging it, Miss Smarty?"

Still laughing and smiling, she answered, "No! Danny, I'm not winging anything."

Danny's voice was deep and manly. "Like I said, Jeannie, you just lost me and probably Tony also. What are you talking about? Good grief, girl, what's Bubbling Reinaiana Valderas? It doesn't sound like a book to me! Are you sure it's not a wild animal?"

She tugged at his arm. He looked at her.

"No! It's not a wild animal." Jeannie said, batting her eyelashes at him. "It's a seventeenth-century Spanish-language Bible!"

Danny was puzzled. *I don't have the foggiest what she's saying. Hell, I'm lost!* His eyes wandered up and down her body, and he motioned for the two of them to once again sit on the rock. They did.

He said nothing more. His mind was racing, but he wasn't interested in an old Bible. He dropped his hand to her bare thigh, stroking it gently with a feathery touch. *Whoa—she sure is cute explaining some goofy-sounding Reinaiana Valderas book or whatever it is. God, she's gorgeous!*

Jeannie stiffened. Her entire body became rigid. She got a startled look on her face.

Danny's fingers felt her tense. He sensed her uneasiness. "What is it, Jeannie? I hope I haven't upset you."

In a frightened voice, she said, "Look at my other leg. There's a scorpion on it. My god, Danny, help me!"

The scorpion took a few steps. Its pincers gently touched the flesh of her leg as it navigated its way up her thigh, making her skin tingle with each tiny step. At first, its tail was directed out straight, dragging against Jeannie's bare skin. Suddenly it stopped and curled its tail, stinger in strike position. Its right pincer grabbed her flesh, preparing to strike. The deadly poison was only microseconds from entering Jeannie's body.

But Danny's strike was quicker. He grabbed the scorpion and crushed it with his bare hand.

Jeannie's body was shaking uncontrollably. She screamed, "Hold me, Danny! Hold me close!"

His massive arms and hands took her body and pulled it close to his. Their faces met, with no more than six inches between them. She found his hand with hers, squeezing it and staring into his eyes, "My god, Danny, that really scared me," she whimpered. He felt her shaking. Her hot breath fell on his face as she spoke. "You were unbelievable. How did you do that?" She stopped and looked into his eyes. "Hold me tight, Danny," she repeated, puzzled but relieved. Her body relaxed as she asked, "How can a human react faster than a scorpion once its strike is under way?"

Danny had no answer. He said nothing for a few seconds. He held her body next to his until she stopped quivering. "Are you okay, Jeannie? That scared the hell out of me too."

She motioned him to stand. They did. "I don't want to sit on that rock anymore. I'm terrified of those things."

Tony watched the episode. He felt it was time for some humor—something that would get Jeannie's mind off the scorpion. "So you're telling us some kook wrote that stuff up there—some Jesus freak?" Tony asked.

Jeannie took the bait. She settled down.

"No, Tony—no kook and no Jesus freak! I really don't think so. Look at the 'T' and the 'S' on the object the three stick people are holding. It's the same handwriting—same format as the 'T' and the 'S' in the Biblia Reina-Valera reference." She pointed to the petroglyphs. "Danny, do you see the petroglyphs of the sun, a star, and three people holding hands?"

Danny knew the tense moments were over. He knew it was time for fun. He crafted a careful answer to Jeannie's question. "I—well—maybe—yeah—where?"

Jeannie laughed. "Danny, don't give me that 'I-well-maybe' stuff. You know exactly what I'm talking about!" She motioned for him to look where she was pointing. "Look at what the three people are holding—there are the letters 'T' and 'S' on whatever is in their hands. Do you guys see that?" She made the same gesture to Tony.

Danny appeared not to have heard her. For a few minutes, he stood silently. He was in a mood to have fun. He blinked at her, then answered. "Yes, your Holiness-Highness-Princess-Wizardess. Do you think we're blind?"

Jeannie knew what he was doing. She thought, *Two can play this game!* "Danny, if you call me that one more time you'll be sorry," she said, feigning a stern voice.

Danny didn't know if he was pushing her buttons, if her comment was for real, or if she was just playing with him. To be on the safe side, he responded, "You're right! You're always right, Jeannie—good work! And you know what? You're beautiful! And I do think you're a gorgeous princess!"

Oh my gosh! What did he just say? She watched Danny smiling at her. *Yeah, Danny, I'm her holiness-highness and I can't wait to get you alone. I'm gonna have fun with you!* "What are you guys doing tomorrow?" she asked.

Tony was content to enjoy the outdoors and let Danny and Jeannie have fun bantering. He was happy to see Danny was no longer in a state of depression. He knew all too well what Danny had gone through with the unexpected loss of his dad.

"I don't know. What do you have in mind?" replied Danny.

Jeannie took the lead. She had a plan. "I'll go home tonight and translate using the Reina-Valera," she answered.

"There you go again!" Danny said playfully. "What? What on earth are you talking about, Jeannie? What is this Reinaiana Valderas or whatever you said? It's an old book? What do we need an old book for? Sometimes you talk in riddles or in your own little world of language that only you know." He smiled at her.

Jeannie giggled. *You just wait and see, Mr. Danny! Princess Jeannie is going to have lots of fun with Prince Danny!*

Jeannie started walking to Skipper. The afternoon sun had lost its warmth, and she was getting chilly. She stopped for a moment and turned to face Danny. "Danny, it's not a Reinaiana Valderas, or whatever you just said. I already told you that it's called the Reina-Valera, and it's a seventeenth-century Spanish translation of the Bible. You weren't listening. We have a very old copy on the bookshelf in our living room." Laughing, she turned and started walking again toward Skipper.

Danny followed her, knowing it was her way of saying it was time to head back to CoalVille. He still didn't have a clue what she was talking about. "Jeannie, I'm lost. What does a seventeenth-century Spanish-language Bible have to do with White Face Cliff?"

She didn't answer, just kept on walking.

He realized she must have some plan in mind. *I have no idea what she's up to. An old book?* Not wanting to be outdone, he hollered to her, "Who cares about an old book? I don't. Let's get those horses back before Alex gets off work."

I've got him going. That's good, she thought. She untied her horse and led him to a large rock next to Danny's horse.

"We'll come back tomorrow and spend the day," Jeannie said, kicking her leg over Skipper and jumping on his back from the large rock she was standing on. "I'll translate the petroglyph references this evening—maybe we'll get lucky and figure something out. Let's meet at seven at the top of Long Hill in the morning."

She kicked Skipper in the sides and set off for CoalVille at full gallop. Danny and Tony mounted their horses and followed in hot pursuit.

Jeannie turned her head to Danny as he raced up alongside her on CoCo. "Danny, we're going to have some fun tomorrow!" she yelled, so as to be heard over the sound of the galloping horses. *That Danny is such a neat boy! Wow—I wonder where our relationship is going. He cares about me. He didn't let that scorpion bite me.*

Danny hollered back, "Sounds like a plan." He watched Jeannie pull away on Skipper, who was a much faster horse than CoCo or Tony's horse, Black Tail. As she raced ahead of him, his mind seemed to follow her. *Does she know she is pulling on that string she's tied to my heart? I think she does—she knows how and when to pull on it! Who knows what will happen?*

The smell of sage filled Danny's nostrils on the ride back to CoalVille, but it was not sage that was on his mind. *What do 2 CRÓNICAS 20:16 and EXODO 33:2 mean, and who put those words on the cliff of Ziz?* He had always called it White Face Cliff, but for some reason, the name *Ziz* stuck in Danny's mind.

CHAPTER 13
Pirate Legends

"**M**om, do you think that pirates were actually here in CoalVille at one time?" Danny asked, breaking the silence that had prevailed while he and his mother sat quietly at the dinner table.

Darla laughed at his comment. She dropped her fork, startling him. "I just saw a pirate peek through the window. He made me drop my fork!" She had her own way of getting his attention.

Danny chuckled. "Mom, I'm serious. Don't you think that the folklore might have validity? What if the pirates carved a treasure map on the side of a cliff?"

She smiled. Then, she entwined her fingers, locking her hands together. She covered her face with them and slowly slid them down her face, feigning a serious look.

"Son, you know that the school mascot is the pirate. That's the name of the school's yearbook—Pirate Log."

Danny laughed even louder. As long as Danny could remember, his mother had always been able to come up with pantomime skits that made him laugh. He loved it, and she knew it.

"I'm serious, Mom," he said. "I know all that stuff about our school's annual, the Pirate Log, but has anyone ever found anything—you know, like real treasure?"

She put her hands back on her "serious" face. This time, when she removed them, a smile dominated her expression.

"Danny, if they have, they haven't told a soul. Who knows? You do know that when Mr. KeeLord went missing, they discovered three hundred thousand in gold coins inside the walls of his house! He was the old man who lived next to Crazy LeRoy in Upper Camp. When they tore down his rickety, ramshackle house, they found the gold. Some people think he stole it, but all we know is that they were very old Spanish gold coins."

From his chair, Danny could smell his mother's freshly brewed coffee. For a few moments, the quiet of the evening returned as his mind drifted. His mother watched him eating as she sipped, steam rising from her cup. Then Danny looked up. His mind was churning. *Where in the hell did KeeLord find that gold?* There was a hint of frustration displayed on his face.

He blurted, "Yeah, Mom, I know all that—but what if it wasn't stolen money, but money from treasure? Mr. KeeLord spent a lot of time roaming around the hills of CoalVille. What if he found a treasure—the Spanish gold coins? He hung around LeRoy a lot—what if Crazy LeRoy was in cahoots with KeeLord, and they found the treasure?"

Danny tensed up as he mentioned LeRoy and KeeLord's names. Now his mind was swirling with thoughts of mystery. *That crazy old devil. Why does he live in a palace? Nobody has a clue except Jeannie, Tony, and me. Weird! I wonder if LeRoy had anything to do with KeeLord's disappearance—could the skull Tony saw have been his? Why would he have a human skull in his house?*

"Danny—are you okay?" Darla sensed her son's tension.

Danny thought about what to say. He flicked his peas with his fork.

"I'm okay, Mom," said Danny, watching his mom looking at him with an expression of concern. "I think the Spaniards left some of their gold coins in the Incan treasure, and the pirates got the entire loot. That's what I think happened. I think that old man died with the secret of hidden treasure, but I'll bet LeRoy knows something. I think that crazy old man is hiding more than who he is!"

Darla tensed. She gently stretched her hand across the red checked oilcloth that covered the small table. Looking intently at her son, she softly touched his hand. Her mind filled with thoughts of the crazy man. *Oh, Danny, you're lost in thoughts of a hunt for lost treasure. I hope your hunt doesn't get you involved with LeRoy. I don't like him. He just looks creepy!* She couldn't help but recall the many discussions of lost treasure that they had had as a family.

She sweetly patted Danny's hand and said, "Well, Danny, who knows? I've heard of a legend that marauding Spaniards stormed ancient South American Incan towns and villages. They carried off countless amounts of gold, silver, and precious gems. That vast treasure was being transported back to Spain, but then it was seized by pirates. The pirates decided to take the Incan treasure far inland from the southeast coast of what's now the United States to a high desert plateau—to make sure the Spaniards couldn't find it. Who knows? But, Danny, it's just a legend."

As she talked, Danny studied her every move. He could tell she hadn't made the connection. *That's good—she didn't focus on my comments about LeRoy and KeeLord hanging around together. I don't want her worrying about me going up to Crazy LeRoy's house.*

Darla smiled at him. *Johnny used to get such a kick out of Danny's infatuation with lost Incan treasure buried around CoalVille. Ever since he was a small boy, he has dreamed of finding lost treasure. I guess that's because being poor and growing up in a godforsaken coal camp would make anyone dream of riches. When you're poor, you can always be "make-believe rich," and it doesn't cost anything.*

With fondness in her eyes, she looked at Danny. *You silly boy, there's no buried treasure around here, only a wretched coal mine that took the life of my lover—my handsome husband and your father.*

Noticing the tears gathering in her eyes, Danny thought, *Mom is crying—I wonder why? Did I say something that upset her?* "Mom, I think we're going to be okay. Somehow, Mom, we'll get some money, I just know it. Mom, I love you! I'll always be here for you!" he said, smiling at his mother. He knew that her heart was aching.

Her long slender fingers grasped his and squeezed them. "Oh, Danny, that's sweet of you to say. I have my job at the Granite Springs hospital. We'll get by." She brushed tears from her cheek. *I just have to be strong for him. He's such a dreamer and thinks that somehow we'll find a pot of gold. If only that were the case—if somehow Danny and I could find a pot of gold—oh, that's just foolishness. What's wrong with me?*

The petroglyphs carved high on the cliff of White Face—2 CRÓNICAS 20:16 and EXODO 33:22—were now indelibly embedded in Danny's mind. *Hmm. The Bubblia Vergeina Valederaldels or whatever Jeannie was talking about—she said it was Spanish. Yeah, that's it! The pirates knew Spanish because they took the treasure from the Spaniards! I don't think Ziz is a Kashome name. Ziz must be a pirate. The Kashome people must have gotten the name Ziz from the pirates. The face on the cliff certainly looks like a pirate. And those eyes looking at the writing—yes! It has to be a clue to a treasure—a treasure map!*

Where would that old fart KeeLord get three hundred thousand in Spanish gold? He found the clue on White Face Cliff! Somehow, I think LeRoy is mixed up in this mystery. KeeLord must have hidden the gold from LeRoy—maybe that's why KeeLord went missing! Hmm! Maybe Tony found the connection!

The distraught look on his mom's face troubled Danny. He could only guess what she was thinking. *It has to be that she would like to be rich, but we're poor, and I keep talking about treasure. Maybe I should change the subject.* He stood up, walked around the table, tapped his mother on the shoulder, and said, "Stand up, Mom. I've got something for you."

She did. He grabbed her shoulders with his strong hands, then gently turned her so they were facing each other. He put his arms around her and squeezed. "You're the greatest mom on earth. We'll always have each other. Mom, we're going to find the good life! You just wait and see!"

He dropped his hands from her waist and threw them over his eyes. His fingers intertwined. He waited for a moment and then slowly slid them down his face, exposing a radiant smile.

Darla's eyes filled with tears. Lifting her hand, she touched his face, and he took her in his arms again. She trembled, saying, "Danny, I just love you! I couldn't ask for a better son! You're the best!"

CHAPTER 14
Sacred Legends

I *have to get to the bottom of this puzzle,* thought Jeannie.

It wasn't just Danny who was reflecting upon their discovery. Jeannie had also drifted into a fantasy world of legends—but not pirate legends. She had been brought up with Kashome legends. *Who wrote the markings on White Face Cliff? Whoever did it must be part of the Kashome people. I need to figure out the verses we found today and interpret their meaning. My mother knows all of the Kashome legends. She can help figure this stuff out. I know I've heard those goofy legends many times before—I've always thought they were a bunch of hogwash.*

She walked to the front room where her mother was. "Mom, would you tell me again the legends of the Kashome people? I know you've told them to me before, but could you tell them to me again?" she asked. She had a puzzled look on her face that surely meant something.

Jeannie's mother, Soft Wind, could tell that her daughter was ready to listen. *Maybe she has grown up. I remember when I was a little girl and thought the legends were boring.*

Soft Wind was tall, thirty-three years old, and beautiful, with long, shiny black hair and deep-set brown eyes. Sitting on the living-room couch, which was freckled with hand-sewn patches that marked each repair over the past twenty years, she looked at her daughter and said, "Well, Jeannie, the father of our nation was Kashom. And you know that you're part of the legend. Your real name isn't Jeannie—it's Neferzul, which means 'Beautiful Keeper of the Golden Key.'"

Jeannie's face was serious. She listened intently, then asked a question: "I know that, Mom, but why am I called Neferzul?"

Knowing she was interested, Soft Wind realized this was a prime opportunity to pass on the culture of the Kashome people, who had lived in the Scarlet Desert, a place they held sacred, for centuries.

"There are three legends that the Kashome people keep sacred. As a direct descendent of Kashom, I'm the one who holds the written accounts of the legends—just like you will when it's time. Let me go and get the goatskins. I'll read them to you." She turned, her face instantly breaking into a joyous smile. "In fact, this is an occasion, Jeannie. I'll make us some coffee and then get the legends."

Her hand reached into the cupboard next to the stove. She pushed the stacked pots and pans to one side, looking for her favorite coffee pan, and spotted it—speckled white paint on blue porcelain.

Listening to her mother run water in the sink, Jeannie asked, "Mom, can I help you?" There was no answer. Next came the sound of the pan of water being pushed across the stovetop. Jeannie waited.

"No, this is my treat," replied Soft Wind, pulling open the cupboard drawer next to the sink. She reached in and took out a neatly cut piece of white cheesecloth and a prized possession, an old silver spoon. The spoon had once belonged to Kashom's second daughter and had then been passed down for generations until Soft Wind had inherited it from her grandmother.

Soft Wind spooned the right amount of fresh-ground coffee into the cloth, tied it closed with string, and tossed it into the boiling water. It was just a matter of minutes before the aroma of fresh-brewed coffee filtered through the air into the living room. Soon she walked through the living room door with two cups of coffee, balancing them with every step. Jeannie sprang to her feet and took one. "Good job, Mom. They're filled to the brim, and you didn't spill a drop."

"Thanks, Jeannie," Soft Wind said as she set hers on the coffee table.

Jeannie watched her mother go to her secret hiding place—a hole hidden under a throw rug on the living room floor. Soft Wind rolled back the rug, lifted up a loose board, reached into the hole, and brought out a bronze box.

She opened the box and took out two goatskins with writings on them in the native language of Kashom. For a few moments, silence pressed in on them. Holding the two skins in both hands, Soft Wind looked fondly at her lovely daughter. Jeannie became uneasy under her mother's stare. She fidgeted in the stuffed armchair, which she was sitting in crosswise, with her legs hanging over one stuffed arm and her back resting against the other.

Soft Wind was pleased that Jeannie was maturing and could possibly be the Chosen One who would fulfill the mission of her people's legend. She turned her head, noting Jeannie's uneasiness, and found a spot to sit in. Sinking into the old couch, she folded her knees to her side.

"Okay, we have our coffee and our legends," she said as she got comfortable. A smile emerged on Jeannie's face. Encouraged, she went on. "Jeannie, here are the legends. The first is the Legend of Kashom. I'll read it to you, and then we'll talk about it. This is the legend."

The Legend of Kashom and the Golden Key

A long time ago, a man with reddish-blond hair, light-tan skin, and deep-set blue eyes came to the Scarlet Desert from the land of Kopaz. His name was Kashom, and he was a royal prince. His younger sister, Princess Aerapondes, had been murdered by the high priest of the royal court of Kopaz. The murderer's name was Gorom Mochcom. He had drowned her in a river; her body plunged over a giant falls and was lost forever. Kashom was on the river's bank when his sister drifted by. He tried to rescue her, but her body was pulled over the edge of the great falls by the raging current.

King Dalvin blamed his son, Prince Kashom, for the murder of Aerapondes, because the goroms were clever and lied to the royal family. Because of those lies, Kashom left his homeland and abdicated his position as heir to the royal throne. He traveled the Highway of Time, and now he holds he gift of eternal youth. He never dies and has waited for centuries to regain his royal position.

The evil gorom wanted Aerapondes's golden key and Kashom's golden watch. Together, they can unlock the power of the sun—the star at the center of our solar system—by transforming its energy. But the golden key has an even greater purpose. It is required to unlock GAMMAZEL and the energy of the giant star, Kolar, at the center of the universe, which will allow Viracocha to win the war of the gods!

That golden key and golden watch were special gifts from the gods—the supreme god, Viracocha, and his wife, the goddess Neferdor. Viracocha personally gave the golden watch to Prince Kashom. Neferdor personally gave the golden key to Princess Aerapondes. The transformed sun energy can open the Highway of Time and endow travelers with the Pearl of Time—eternal youth.

Neferdor loved and adored Aerapondes and considered her to be her own living doll. She gave Aerapondes a special name, which was Neferzul.

After Gorom Mochcom killed Princess Aerapondes, he conned Kashom into using the golden key and golden watch to venture onto the Highway of Time. They both ended up in the Scarlet Desert at the Boar's Tusk. And as far as the Kashome people know, Mochcom still lives in the Scarlet Desert. He is the emissary of the dark god Zuron, who personally gave Mochcom the black ring that protects him. The energy from the ring is a beam of purple light, and it is the reason why Kashom was unable to kill him.

The gods were furious with the royal family of Kopaz because they failed to protect Aerapondes and the precious gifts used to open the Highway of Time from the goroms. When Kashom came to the Scarlet Desert, Viracocha took the golden watch back from the dethroned prince. Then Kashom had a harrowing battle with Mochcom and managed to regain the golden key from the evil disciple of Zuron. We are not sure how Kashom overpowered Gorom Mochcom to get the golden key, since the evil gorom has a black ring that protects him. Because Kashom was able to get the golden key from Mochcom, we believe that is why Neferdor allowed it to remain with Kashom's family under the condition that it would be passed down from generation to generation to the eldest girl in his bloodline.

In his new home in the desert, Kashom discovered that there were only a few inhabitants there, remaining from a tribe called the Ancients. For some unknown reason, most had died off. One, however, the daughter of the chief, was a teenage girl. Her name was Star-of-Night. Kashom fell in love the moment he laid eyes on her. They married shortly after they met. His wedding gift to her was a lovely golden medallion with a blue, sapphire-colored, star-shaped gemstone at its center. Eventually, all of the Ancients died off, and the only indigenous inhabitant left in the Scarlet Desert was Kashom's beautiful wife. Star-of-Night mourned the loss of her family and friends. But Kashom was compassionate, and together, they started their family. Kashom and Star-of-Night were the genesis of the new race of inhabitants who came to live in the Scarlet Desert—the Kashome nation.

Kashom and Star-of-Night had a beautiful daughter, Moon-of-Day, and a son, Yellow Moon. Their daughter had soft white skin like the petals of a rose, silky black hair, and sapphire-blue eyes. She was entrusted with the golden key. Her beautiful features marked her as the Chosen One, fated to redeem her father's honor and restore him to his rightful place as heir to the royal throne of Kopaz. She was the second keeper of the golden key that was given the sacred name of Neferzul.

Against his father's wishes, Yellow Moon, a young warrior, went hunting for Desert Eagle, the king of all eagles in the Scarlet Desert. He took Moon-of-Day on the hunt with him, but she mysteriously fell into a crevasse and was lost forever.

Kashom and Star-of-Night mourned the loss of their daughter. With Moon-of-Day's death, their other daughter, Skip-with-Wind, became the next keeper of the key. Because she did not have shiny black hair, sapphire-blue eyes, and soft white skin, she was not given the sacred name of Neferzul. Kashom said he could not be restored to his rightful throne until another who looked like his murdered sister, Aerapondes, came forth from his bloodline.

Star-of-Night grew old and died. But because he had traveled the Highway of Time, Kashom never died and stayed eighteen forever. He remains to this day in the desert, his whereabouts unknown to all.

The new Chosen One will have shiny black hair, sapphire-blue eyes, and soft white skin like Aerapondes and Moon-of-Day. She will be called Neferzul and will hold the golden key of Neferdor. Together with her partner, the man who holds the golden watch of Viracocha, they will travel the Highway of Time, redeem Kashom's honor and be thrust center stage onto the battlefield of the gods.

The golden key has been passed down from generation to generation in the LoneTree family.

Skip-with-Wind gave the key to her daughter, Ripple-in-Pond.

Ripple-in-Pond gave the key to her daughter, Golden Cloud.

Golden Cloud gave the key to her daughter, Clear Water.

Clear Water is my mother, and she gave the key to me, and now you have it.

The Kashome people wait for the supreme god Viracocha and his wife, Neferdor, to reveal their emissaries, TRPOV and TRPON.

TRPOV will be designated by Viracocha's gift of the golden watch.

The Neferzul who is in possession of the golden key of Neferdor at the time when TRPOV is gifted the golden watch of Viracocha will become TRPON.

Viracocha told Kashom that, as part of his purgatory, if he is to regain his royal status, he must aid TRPOV and TRPON in the fulfillment of their missions and declare to them who they are and let them know they will be valiant warriors for Viracocha and Neferdor in the battle of deities.

Lifting her cup, Soft Wind sipped the warm coffee. She clutched the cup tightly, cherishing the warmth on her fingers. Her glance at Jeannie told her that her daughter was still listening.

"Mom, I am so confused!" Jeannie said as her mother finished reading.

"Yes," Soft Wind replied.

"Yeah, Mom, this is just mumbo jumbo!" shot back Jeannie. Soft Wind listened as Jeannie continued. "What do you mean, Mom? Kashom will declare who TRPOV and TRPON are? Who or what are TRPOV and TRPON? They will be center stage on the battlefield of the gods and be valiant warriors? What is that all about?"

The old handmade wooden coffee table, with its layers of paint, sat like a monument between mother and daughter. Its shabby appearance reflected its hard years of steadfast service. For as long as Jeannie could remember, it had supported countless coffee cups during discussions with her mother. Some were serious, and some were not.

Setting the goatskin on the table in front of the couch, Soft Wind relaxed. Jeannie sensed this would be a serious discussion.

For several moments, Soft Wind said nothing. She smiled with pleasure, noting the attention Jeannie was paying her. "We know nothing about TRPOV and TRPON, except they are somehow connected to the gods. We can only guess, but we suspect that TRPOV stands for 'The Royal Prince of Viracocha' and TRPON stands for 'The Royal Princess of Neferdor.' We don't know for sure, but hopefully Kashom will reveal that secret to us. That's what our legends tell us."

She bit her lip and then ventured another aspect of the legend of Kashom. "For centuries, the eldest daughter of the bloodline of Kashom has been given the surname of Lone Tree and entrusted with the golden key. Kashom waits for the Chosen One to come forth from his posterity."

But then the discussion took a sad turn as Soft Wind reflected on her first love, with a young man who had been but a brief part of her life. "Jeannie, your father was Billy Harris. He died shortly after you were born." A tear spilled from Soft Wind's eye and rolled down her cheek. "We were so in love!"

She smiled sadly and took a deep breath. "Even though your father traveled to the Land of the Dead when you were young, that is not the reason you do not have the surname of Harris. But for sure, your father knew that you were special."

There was a moment of silence. Looking fondly at Jeannie, Soft Wind continued, "Your surname is Lone Tree. You're now the keeper of the golden key. Only the eldest girls in the direct bloodline of Kashom have the surname of Lone Tree. You're the sixth generation in his direct bloodline. We do not know for sure why our last name is Lone Tree. Kashom wanted it that way. Who knows for sure? Maybe someday we will have that answer."

The slap of Jeannie's hand on the chair startled Soft Wind. Since she had not been looking directly at Jeannie, Soft Wind had not seen her sit up in haste. Readjusting her body, Jeannie had just about fallen off the chair she was sitting on. Quickly grabbing the chair's arm, she diverted her fall.

For some reason, it had never dawned on Jeannie. Now it did. "What are you saying, Mom? Are you telling me that Kashom is my great-great-great-great-grandfather?"

Noting that everything was under control, her mother nodded. "Yes, Jeannie, I am. You're of royal blood. All who are entrusted with the key are of Kashom's lineage. You're my daughter, the sixth keeper of the key. In addition, you are only the third person with the royal blood of the Kopaz family to be called by that special name, which is Neferzul, and that's sacred! Jeannie, it could be that you have a special role to play. You meet all the requirements."

Soft Wind then made a startling statement. "Jeannie, only three planets circle the herculean star at the center of the universe. They are Volob, where Supreme God Viracocha and Supreme Goddess Neferdor dwell; Zolob, where Dark God Zuron dwells; and Kopaz. It is on Kopaz that the royal family of Prince Kashom and Princess Aerapondes lived. The high priests, also called goroms, also live on Kopaz. Unfortunately, the royal family of Kopaz does not know that the high priests are disciples of Zuron. Prince Kashom is the only one of that royal family who knows this secret, and he is here in the Scarlet Desert. He cannot tell his story, or explain that he was tricked by the evil Gorom Mochcom, or let them know that this evil high priest killed his beloved sister, Princess Aerapondes."

Hit with such a strange and foreign reality, Jeannie was taken aback. It might just as well have come from a fantasy novel. Her mind whirled. She gasped, clearly flabbergasted by what her mother had just told her. *Whoa, this is way too much! This is much bigger than I thought or could even imagine!*

Making eye contact with her mother, Jeannie confronted her with these troubling questions. "But what does all of this mean?" *I want to hear about the petroglyphs at White Face Cliff.* "Mom, what do our people know about Kashom?"

Soft Wind beamed as she looked affectionately at Jeannie. She sat her coffee cup down. She had now come to the point she wanted to make, and she selected her words carefully. "Well, nothing is for certain, but over the centuries, our people have spoken of Kashom's former life. I just gave you a brief synopsis, but I can add a little more. They say he came from another land, the world of Kopaz—the planet that revolves around the star Kolar at the center of the universe. That's what he told the ancient ones that he met in the Scarlet Desert when he arrived here. My grandmother, Golden Cloud, said that her grandmother, Skip-With-Wind—Kashom's second daughter—told her that Kashom loved his sister, who had been murdered by the evil Gorom Mochcom. Somehow, Kashom got the golden key back and vowed never again to let it fall into the gorom's hands. He said the gods were furious because they personally gave it to his sister, Aerapondes, and he let it fall into the hands of the Gorom Mochcom. Jeannie, I never doubted my grandmother—the Kashome people have always believed in our legends."

If Jeannie's mind had ever been stunned with amazement, it was at that moment. Suddenly, it was dawning on her that a key once owned by a twelve-year old princess now belonged to her. Her mind whirled with puzzlement. *How did Kashom get the key if someone else killed his sister? Did I hear correctly what Mom said earlier...a gorom...a fight?* Her mental questions kept coming. *Do I have this story correct? Okay, the key came from the goddess Neferdor. The goddess gave it to Princess Aerapondes. Kashom was tricked by the gorom who killed his little sister and took her key. Kashom and the gorom used it to come to the Scarlet Desert. They had a fight and Kashom got it back. Now I have it!*

Slowly, Jeannie lifted her leather pouch. Now, she knew her golden key was much more than a family heirloom. She could not stop her questions as she took the key from its beautiful beaded-leather pouch and held it in her hand. "Mom, how does this key work, and what do you think it is for? Is this the very key that was ripped from the neck of the young princess before she was murdered by the evil gorom?"

Soft Wind leaned forward and gently reached her arm across the coffee table. "Would you hand it to me?"

Jeannie met her mother's outstretched hand with her key. "Here, Mom."

Her mother set it on the wooden table between them, putting her right index finger on it. "There are two rings of symbols on this key. The symbols in the outer ring symbols are made of precious gemstones. The symbols in the inner ring are slits in the gold surrounding the gemstone star at the key's center." Grabbing the edge of the table with her other hand, she leaned forward and spoke quietly. "Jeannie, the Kashome people believe the key you're entrusted with is indeed the very one that was torn from the beautiful princess's neck. That key once belonged to the gods."

For a moment, Soft Wind said nothing else, gazing at her daughter with a serious face. Her finger was still on the key. Then, she spoke softly. "These symbols will unlock something, Jeannie. We do not know how it works. Our legends say it unlocks the power of the star Kolar and will be used by Viracocha to win the deadly war game being played by the gods."

With a serious look, Jeannie asked, "How?"

Soft Wind gave a short answer. "I believe the discovery of that mystery will be the role of the Chosen One."

The mystery was right before her eyes. She shuddered just thinking about the role that she could play. Fear was gripping her inner soul. As she listened to her mother talk about the symbols, Jeannie realized that she did not have a clue about what the symbols were used for or what they meant. What her golden key unlocked was a mystery to Soft Wind, but that mystery had just been handed to Jeannie.

Pounding with every word, Jeannie's heart made its presence known as her questions continued. "Mom, what's a gorom? How did Kashom get the key from that evil person? Why is this key so important?" Jeannie's need for answers that, until this time, she had dismissed as nonsense was now a stark reality that would change her life forever.

There was a moment of silence, and then Soft Wind responded: "Well, Jeannie I don't know for sure. Some of our people, the Kashome elders, believe that a gorom is an evil person—an evil high priest, in fact. And as for how Kashom got the key—well, we don't know all the details. We know they battled. We know the gorom has a ring that protects him. All we know is that somehow Kashom managed to get Aerapondes's key from the gorom, despite the fact the Mochcom has a powerful ring to aid in his defense. The key may be used to unlock something—but whatever it unlocks has never been found—at least not to my knowledge. We know from our legends, as I read to you a few minutes earlier, that it has something to do with unlocking the power of the sun and the star Kolar. Our legends tell us that your key unlocks something called GAMMAZEL. We don't know how it works. The symbols on your key must have something to do with it. Someday we may have that answer."

The only sound was the wind rattling the weathered siding on the old house as Jeannie and her mom sat silently for a few minutes.

"There is something I need to tell you," said Soft Wind delicately. She had noticed that Jeannie did not seem to be grasping what she had just said. She was about to be more specific and give her daughter the warning when Jeannie interrupted her. "Mom, tell me about the young princess who was murdered. Did your grandmother tell you anything about Kashom's younger sister?"

Jeannie's questions piqued her mother's interest. Excitement filled her soul. For generations, the Kashome people had passed down the legends. But for Soft Wind, this exchange was special. She could hardly contain her feelings of exuberance as she thought, *Jeannie is learning about her role. She's the third Neferzul. Maybe our people will soon experience the joy of the Pearl of Youth, eternal youth, and my daughter will be the one who brings us that glorious gift from the gods!*

There was no point in dodging it. The gravity of it was real. Soft Wind could not deny that Jeannie would play a special role in the fulfillment of the legend. What she couldn't know was just how special.

"Jeannie—again, this is just a story my grandmother told me. I don't know if it's true, but there's something very curious about what she said."

Jeannie's eyes flew open. Once again, she interrupted her mother, and it was obvious she wanted to know every detail. "What was curious, Mom?"

Her mother's deep brown eyes gazed at her for a moment. She picked up Jeannie's golden key from the table and clutched it. Speaking reverently, Soft Wind said, "She told me what Kashom's sister looked like."

Pausing briefly, she gazed at her lovely daughter. "Jeannie, she was beautiful, just like you. You must remember that my grandmother told me this story when I was a small girl—you were not yet born. My grandmother said that the young princess had shiny black hair, sapphire-blue eyes, and soft white skin, like the petals of a rose. She looked just like you."

Her mother caught her by surprise with the last statement. "S-she looked just like m-me?" stuttered Jeannie, with a perplexed expression. Her mind whirled with questions. *What is my mother telling me? What is this all about?*

Soft Wind sensed that Jeannie was deep in thought. She stood and walked to the chair in which Jeannie was sitting crosswise. She gently took her by the hand, and in a sweet voice, she said, "Jeannie, you have soft white skin like the petals of a rose, silky black hair, and sapphire-blue eyes. Jeannie—I, well, ah, to put it bluntly, was very surprised when you were born. Our eyes in the LoneTree family have always been dark brown, and our skin color is light tan. And likewise, your father's family had tan skin and dark-brown eyes."

Silence fell. In those special moments, there was a once-in-a-lifetime connection as mother and daughter held hands and locked eyes. It was time to play their role as descendants of the royal family of Kopaz. They contemplated their journey as royal heirs and where it would take them. They had no idea. The one thing they knew was that their pathways would be governed by the Sacred Legends.

Sensing the deep attention of her daughter, Soft Wind had one more revelation to make. "Jeannie, I don't know if I've ever showed this to you, but this leather pouch I keep with the legends has a lock of hair in it. My grandmother told me it was Aerapondes's hair. She said that this was a prized possession of Kashom—he brought it with him to the Scarlet Desert. On Kopaz, the royal family exchanged locks of hair. This was one of their traditions. Our people have kept this lock of hair with the legends for centuries."

She opened the pouch and removed the lock. She held it in ceremonial fashion, drawing it across her cupped hands with arms outstretched. Contracting her fingers around the lock, she squeezed it. Drawing back her arms, she released her fingers and gently took the hair from her left hand with her right. She replaced the lock in its pouch. Returning to her seat on the couch, she put the pouch on the table between them.

Jeannie's eyes followed her mother's every movement. She picked up the leather pouch carefully. "This hair belonged to Aerapondes?" Jeannie was dumbfounded. "It's the same color as mine! She looked like me?" Jeannie was trying to make sense of what her mother was telling her.

Even though Soft Wind had already told Jeannie of her sacred name, Neferzul, she wanted to drive the point home. She made a statement that Jeannie had never expected. "Jeannie, I believe you are the Chosen One!"

Maybe Jeannie had not been paying attention, maybe it was just because she was a teenager, but up until now, Jeannie had not fully grasped the complete meaning of who she was. Maybe her mother knew that, and that was why she was repeating what she had to tell her daughter.

Jeannie gasped as she looked at her mother. "My heavens, Mother, what are you saying? Are you trying to tell me something?" Jeannie was obviously concerned with what her mother had just said. Her mind raced with questions—questions that begged answers—answers that could change her life. *Am I the Chosen One? How can this be? It makes no sense to me. How can I restore a fallen prince to his rightful throne in the faraway land of Kopaz in a time long ago?*

"Mom—are you telling me that I'm the Chosen One? Are you telling me that I'm from his lineage, have the golden key, and have the appearance that makes me the Chosen One? Are those the requirements?" Jeannie struggled for words as she contemplated what her mother was telling her. "And what about the war of the gods? Am I involved in that?"

"Yes, Jeannie, you have all of the requirements. Whether it turns out that you are in fact the Chosen One is still to be determined—only time will tell."

Again, silence engulfed the room. Mother and daughter stayed still, holding hands. Their minds locked together—both contemplating the possible fulfillment of their people's sacred legend, their thoughts running in parallel. *Centuries of waiting may be on the brink of ending with the emergence of the Chosen One.*

"Wow! Mom, did your grandmother tell you the name of the evil gorom?"

"Yes, Jeannie, she did. Remember, it was in the legend—Mochcom. My grandmother told me he was also called Príncipe Alma Negra, which, as you know, is Spanish for Prince Dark Soul."

Soft Wind bit her lip as she spoke of Prince Dark Soul. Her look of concern was evident as she continued, "Evidently, those goroms wanted to get access to something very special that can be unlocked by the golden key—something that would give them eternal youth and, more importantly, win the war for Zuron!"

Fiddling with her golden key, Jeannie tried to make sense of the symbols, the slits, and their geometric design. She was lost. But her mind froze at what her mother had just said. *My god, Príncipe Alma Negra? How creepy!* "Mom, this is way crazy! Win the war for Zuron? The prince called Dark Soul wants my key? What's it all about? How can my key be used to help the evil god Zuron?"

"Jeannie, it's a mystery to all of us. We do not know why the goroms want your key. All we know is that it will help the Kashome people. It is eternal youth that the Kashome people seek, and your key will play a role in that." She smiled at Jeannie. "The Pearl of Youth—the essence of the Kashome legend—is eternal youth. Perhaps someday soon our people will find it!"

"This stuff just doesn't make any sense. If the evil gorom killed Kashom's sister and stole the golden key—the very one I have in my possession—how did Kashom get it? Boy, I'm glad that is ancient history. I'd hate to have a gorom try to kill me to get this key—holy crap!"

Soft Wind was pleased that her daughter was interested in the Kashome legends. By now, the coffee in both cups was cold. A hot refill sounded good. "I'll be right back," she said, getting up from the couch with cups in hand.

Her smile was like a new light in the room as she walked back through the kitchen door balancing the hot drinks. "Here, Jeannie," she said. She waited until Jeannie took her cup and then set her own down.

The afghans folded neatly on the back of the couch looked inviting. She reached for them. Tossing one to Jeannie and covering her folded legs with the other, she prepared to give her next lesson.

"The second legend of the Kashome people is called the Legend of the Boar's Tusk. I'll read it to you."

Snuggled beneath the afghan on the lumps of the old couch cushion, Soft Wind started reading the Legend of the Boar's Tusk from her goatskin. "In a land far away, in a time long ago, a young prince lost his honor. He left his family and lush tropical homeland in disgrace because of lies told by an evil high priest. The young prince, whose name was Kashom, ended up in the Scarlet Desert."

Jeannie interrupted abruptly: "Mom, I'm kind of tired." She smiled at her mother. "This sounds like what you just told me. Can you tell me the rest some other time?"

Soft Wind grinned. "Yes, my dear. We have all the time in the universe!" She looked longingly at Jeannie for a short time and then broke that precious moment of silence. "There is something I must say. It will sound strange, but it's sacred. As Neferzul, you must know this." She stared at Jeannie for a moment and then added, "It is part of the Legend of the Boar's Tusk."

For Soft Wind, it was time to school Jeannie in one of the most important phrases from their legends. "Jeannie, I told you one of our legends, the Legend of Kashom. There's two more that I believe have something to do with your key."

Jeannie was not in the mood for change of subject. She was more interested in the royal princess—the princess who had once owned the golden key that she was holding in her hand. She was intrigued by the mystery. Little did she know that her mother was about to expose another piece of the mystery. But Jeannie had no idea what her mother was talking about. She was ready to go to bed. "Mom, do we have to do it tonight?"

"Yes! I must tell you the essence of the Legend of the Boar's Tusk!" Soft Wind spoke without hesitation and in a most serious voice. "Also, I must tell you the essence of The Legend of Sky Fire and its connection to GAMMAZEL!

Soft Wind gathered her thoughts. "I'll start with the Legend of the Boar's Tusk. You must know this, as it may save your life! As I said, it's sacred. It has something to do with the Pearl of Time. This evening, I'll only take the time to tell you the sacred part! When it happens, as Neferzul, you may be required to act quickly. In the fulfillment of your role, you will not be given time to sort things out. You must not forget this: 'Yellow Moon, an old man, climbed to the top of the Boar's Tusk and looked down at the young man—his father, Kashom—and said in a loud voice, "Father, it is finished—the keys unlock the bottomless pit by the star of the chamber!" Then he thrust himself from the top of the monument and fell to his death at the feet of his father.'"

Jeannie's eyes widened. Her mother was scaring her. Afraid to ask any more questions, she looked at the ceiling. A perplexed expression gathered on her face. Her mind filled with questions she would like to ask her mother, but she lacked the courage.

Soft Wind appraised Jeannie's reaction and said very fervently, "Your key must be a part of a set of keys that unlock the bottomless pit by the star of the chamber. Evidently, that sacred statement in our legends has something to do with unleashing the power of the sun, which will lead to the essence of what our people seek—the Pearl of Time, eternal youth."

Soft Wind had made her point. There was no question in her mind that Jeannie was grappling with one of the most important parts of their legends. She looked on as her daughter stared at the ceiling.

Jeannie tensed a bit. The very thought of dealing with a bottomless pit frightened her. *This is scary! It is way weird! What is this all about? That statement she just read to me—"Father, it is finished—the keys unlock the bottomless pit by the star of the chamber"—does not make any sense. Whoa! I don't want to go anywhere near a bottomless pit!*

She dropped her eyes and gazed at her mother, her thoughts continuing to tumble. *How can a bottomless pit be unlocked by a star? Weird! Do keys unlock the pit by using the star? This is goofy! I'd ask her what it means, but this stuff is scary.*

Even though her mother had lost her, Jeannie nodded, not necessarily understanding, but accepting the fact that her golden key was real. It was not a myth. She had no idea what would come next in her journey as Neferzul, but the clues on White Face Cliff might help. She wanted to change the subject.

"Mom, I know all of this stuff. I'm—what time is it? Mom—well—I just—can we talk about this another time? I just need to think about this stuff."

"In just a minute, you can go to bed, but I am not through!" said Soft Wind. "Jeannie, there is one more very vital thing you must know. As I mentioned, there is another function of your golden key, maybe the most important one! I told you the Legend of Kashom mentions that GAMMAZEL is unlocked by your key. I don't think you realize the significance of this."

Her heart pounding and her eyes wide open, Jeannie blurted out, "Mom, you are scaring me. Do I need to hear all of this stuff?"

Without a moment's hesitation, Soft Wind said, "Yes!"

Growing tenser with each second, Jeannie knew she had no options left. Her mother was not about to let her only daughter be exposed to the gravest of danger without some knowledge of what lay ahead.

"Can I hold your hand?" asked Soft Wind.

Jeannie moved from her chair to be next to her mom on the old couch, and they held hands as Soft Wind continued. "I just told you that your key must be a part of a set of keys that unlock the bottomless pit by the star of the chamber. Evidently, that sacred statement in our legends has something to do with unleashing the power of the sun, which leads to the essence of what our people seek—the Pearl of Time, eternal youth. But there is more!"

It was time to divert the conversation back to the subject of GAMMAZEL.

"More?" asked Jeannie with an expression of bewilderment.

"Yes, it is not only the power of our sun that your golden key unlocks, but also the power of the star at the center of the universe. It is called Kolar," said Soft Wind with a smile, as if to convey to Jeannie how proud she was that her daughter would be one of the gods and goddesses who resided in their pantheon on Volob, the herculean planet that revolved around Kolar.

"Are you sure, Mom?" asked Jeannie, even more puzzled.

Looking as serious as she had ever looked, Soft Wind said, "I said something earlier that I do not believe you grasped. Yes, your key unlocks GAMMAZEL. And you must never reveal this until the answer to the Ancient Riddle of Zuron is revealed, and only then."

Jeannie interrupted. "Mom, this is crazy stuff! What is GAMMAZEL?"

Soft Wind paid no attention. "We do not know what GAMMAZEL is. And this is the warning I must give you, Jeannie: keep this secret safe and do not reveal it to Danny or even the Royal Prince of Viracocha, not until you know the answer to the Ancient Riddle of Zuron."

"Mom, you are really scaring me. Zuron is the dark god, and now I have to know an answer to an ancient riddle?" blurted Jeannie. Then she added, "How will I know that the answer to the riddle is the correct one? And what is this Ancient Riddle of Zuron?"

The afghans had fallen to the floor. The lights of a passing car were dancing once more across the old plastered walls, and the cracks were like figures in the dance.

It was a bit chilly, so Soft Wind grabbed the afghan that had been covering her and tossed it over her and Jeannie's legs. Then she said, "We do not know the Ancient Riddle. Only the gods are privy to that. And when the time comes, you will know the answer is correct, as it has something to do with another of our legends, the Legend of Sky Fire." Soft Wind took a deep breath. "You are familiar with the Legend of Sky Fire, and since it is getting late, I will not bother repeating it."

Jeannie's jaw dropped. Her questions were not finished. Jeannie stared at her mother's dimly lit face as the glow of the moon made its way through the living room window—a window that had welcomed the moon's rays for generations—and shed light on the pair sitting on their threadbare, tattered couch.

With a puzzled look on her face, Jeannie asked, "Mom, why doesn't Supreme God Viracocha know the connection between the riddle's answer and the Legend of Sky Fire? This is way too weird for me!"

"Jeannie, you know that Kashom was tricked by Zuron's disciple, Mochcom. Mochcom is clever. He knows the Ancient Riddle of Zuron. And there are only two beings in the universe that know the answer to the riddle—the dark god, Zuron, and his trusted disciple, Gorom Mochcom."

All was quiet, except that the wind had kicked up and was rattling one of the windowpanes. The moon's light continued to make its way through the window, but the chattering sounds seemed to be an impending warning.

Soft Wind spoke clearly. "Mochcom and Zuron are the only ones who know of the connection between the riddle's answer and fire in the sky! Evidently, Kashom overheard Mochcom say something about the riddle and that the answer was connected to a scent and fire in the sky!"

Jeannie was listening. Her mother continued: "Kashom knew that at some time the Neferzul who would help solve the Ancient Riddle of Zuron would come from his posterity." Now, with conviction, Soft Wind made her point: "Jeannie, I am positive that you are that Neferzul. Kashom wanted to do all he could to help you succeed in your mission, which is essential for Supreme God Viracocha to be triumphant in winning the war! And to help you, the Kashome people have the Legend of Sky Fire. It was Kashom who created this legend. He did it to help solve the Riddle of Zuron."

Soft Wind gave Jeannie a serious look as she made her final point to her only daughter. "Jeannie, you must guard your golden key as if the universe depended on it—because it does! If Zuron's disciple, Mochcom, gets your key, the war of the gods is lost, and Viracocha will no longer be the supreme god of the universe. Zuron will!"

Jeannie wanted the discussion to end. She was frightened but did not want her mother to know. She wanted to change the subject. *This is way too much*, thought Jeannie. *This night of legends has turned into much more that I had ever imagined.*

"Good night, Mom," said Jeannie as she got up and started down the hall leading to her bedroom. Then she stopped, turned, and came back to the living room where her mother was still on the old couch. There was something else on Jeannie's mind.

CHAPTER 15

Zanzee, the Mystical Egyptian Cat

Soft Wind was tired from sitting on their worn-out, uncomfortable couch. "Is there anything else you would like to know, Jeannie?" she asked. She could tell that Jeannie was not interested in the Legend of the Boar's Tusk, but she knew her daughter was curious about something.

The old couch had seen better days. She turned to adjust her body on the sagging cushion, wrapping her afghan around her as she looked at Jeannie. Soft Wind sensed that Jeannie was searching for knowledge.

Jeannie followed her mother's movements in the dim room, shadows dancing on the wall as cars drove past, their headlights shining through the windows. She waited for her mother to get comfortable before posing her next question. "Mom, do you know what language Kashom spoke?" *I need to know about the Spanish.*

Soft Wind had been right. Jeannie had finally transitioned from a young girl to a young adult. Yet there was an element of curiosity. "Jeannie, why do you ask? Of course he spoke our language—the Kashome language, the language he brought from Kopaz. It was the language that the common people speak on planet Kopaz. But you know that Kashom also brought another language with him. He said it was a sacred language that only the royals spoke. The eldest girl in each generation in direct lineage from

Kashom is taught to communicate in this royal language. I know it. You know it. But we hold it sacred and do not use it for common conversation."

Her mother was telling Jeannie something she already knew, so she broke in and said, "Mom, I already know all of this."

Soft Wind paid little attention to what Jeannie had just said. She continued, "Not only do we have a spoken language; we also have a written language. We can speak and write Kashome. And likewise, our sacred language, which Kashom called the 'Royal Language,' we can speak and write. You also know that our legends—the ones I just read to you—are written in our sacred language." She paused for a long thirty seconds, contemplating what to say next. "It's interesting that Kashom called his sacred language the 'Royal Language.' We don't know what that means. Perhaps it was a language that only the royal family spoke in Kopaz. Who knows?"

Jeannie could care less about the royal language. She had been taught the sacred language as a small child and could speak and write it fluently. However, her thoughts were elsewhere. *Royal language? What's up with that? That might just be a fairy tale! We don't know for sure. Yeah, I know it. Mom made sure I could write using those goofy symbols and talk using even goofier sounds, but who cares?* She looked puzzled. "Mom, do you think he could read, speak, and write Spanish?"

Leaning forward as a passing car's lights streamed across her face, illuminating her smile, Soft Wind said, "I'm sure he could, Jeannie. The ancient ones he met in the Scarlet Desert spoke Spanish, so I'm sure he learned to communicate in Spanish. We all speak Spanish because it's our second language. Our first is Kashome, our second is Spanish, our third is English, and our fourth is the one we call our sacred Royal Language."

Listening to the car sounds, now coming from somewhere down the street, Soft Wind paused and looked at Jeannie. *I wonder why she's so curious about what language Kashom spoke?* "Is there anything else, Jeannie?"

"Yeah, Mom, I do have one more question. Why do the Kashome people call White Face Cliff by the special name, 'Cliff of Ziz'?"

The question caught Jeannie's mother off guard. It was now Jeannie who was waiting. There were no distracting car lights or sounds, only the light coming through a lampshade Soft Wind had made. It hung low on a homemade lamp constructed from galvanized pipe. Mr. Jones, their neighbor, had given it to them two years ago on Christmas, and Soft Wind displayed it so as not to offend him. But the long shade served to hide its ugly appearance.

Soft Wind was now trying to craft answers about the cliff in the desert. She had no idea really what answer to give. She had always prided herself on her knowledge of her people's culture, but her daughter had just stumped her. Jeannie continued to wait.

It was now Soft Wind who wore an uneasy look. "Jeannie, that has always puzzled me. I don't have the answer. I just know that our people are the only ones that call White Face Cliff by the special name of Ziz. It's interesting that we keep that name special and don't talk about it. Like I said, Jeannie, I just don't know—it has always been a mystery to me." Soft Wind smiled at Jeannie. "Is there anything else you would like to know?"

"No, Mom. I'm just interested in the history of our people," she answered as she gazed at her mother's eyes, which glowed in the faint light coming from the handmade pipe lamp on the side table next to the couch.

She's looking at me in a funny way. She knows I'm up to something. This business about the Spanish references on White Face Cliff must have something to do with Kashom. What does he have to do with Ziz? I wonder if my Mom knows anything about the petroglyphs with the Spanish references to the Biblia Reina-Valera? Hmm, this is very strange. I want to know how the writings on the cliff are tied to our legends. Oh, well, I can read and write Spanish, so I'll search for the answers myself. I must figure out what the Spanish writings mean—I must not let Mom confuse me with legends of my people.

Jeannie stood up. She walked to the bookshelf at the north wall of the living room and retrieved the Reina-Valera, their Spanish-language Bible. Soft Wind was curious but said nothing. She followed Jeannie's movements from the bookshelf to the small end table with her schoolbooks on it next to the stuffed chair. Jeannie took her seat again. She proceeded to look up the two verses: 2 Crónicas 20:16 and Exodo 33:22.

"Hmm," said Jeannie. She read 2 Crónicas 20:16 to herself: *"Mañana descenderéis contra ellos: he aquí que ellos subirán por la cuesta de Sis, y los hallaréis junto al arroyo, antes del desierto de Jeruel."* She then looked at Exodo 33:22 and again read to herself: *"Y cuando pase mi gloria, yo te pondré en una hendidura de la peña, y te cubriré con mi mano hasta que haya pasado."*

Soft Wind continued watching Jeannie, remaining quiet. Jeannie took her pad of paper from her book bag and wrote on it.

Jeannie translated 2 Crónicas 20:16 as she wrote, "To morrow go ye down against them: behold, they come up by the cliff of Ziz, and you shall find them at the end of the brook, before the wilderness of Jeruel."

For the second Bible verse, Exodo 33:22, Jeannie wrote, "And when my glory passes by, I will put you in a cleft of the rock and cover you with my hand until I have passed."

Hmm, Jeannie wrote something down from our Reina-Valera. I wonder what? thought Soft Wind. Aloud, she asked, "What are you doing, Jeannie?"

"Oh, nothing. I wanted to check something I read about in our ancient civilization class. Just fiddling around."

Okay, Jeannie thought, *now I have them written down. It's getting late, so I'll let Tony and Danny help figure out what this mumbo jumbo means tomorrow. We're going to meet in the morning at the top of Long Hill at seven, so I'm going to call it a day.*

Tinkle, tinkle. Jeannie heard the familiar sound and knew what was coming next. "Meow, meow." It was Jeannie's kitty, Zanzee, who had walked into the room and started the familiar meowing that meant he wanted something. He was sleek. He had shiny black fur. His eyes were sapphire-blue. She looked at him affectionately.

It was not a secret that Zanzee was ancient and had never died. The question was why. Maybe that was the genesis of Jeannie's next question:

"Mom, is Zanzee a gift from the gods?"

Quick to laugh and quick with her answer, Soft Wind was pleased to tell Jeannie more of the cultural history of the Kashome people. "Yes! Kashom told our people that a very long time ago, Queen Nefertiti of Egypt was given Zanzee by the goddess Bastet, daughter of the sun god, Ra—and Ra is the son of the supreme god, Viracocha, the only offspring of his union with the goddess Neferdor."

Soft Wind gazed at the ceiling and thought for a few seconds. She looked at Jeannie. Another car drove by, so Soft Wind waited to speak until the lights from that car were no longer shining through the front window. "The Egyptians spell the sun god's name *Ra*. Some spell it *Re*. Our people spell it *Ra* just like the Egyptians. I believe this is true, as I've already said, because we have the closest connection to the gods through Kashom. Viracocha and Neferdor created the sun and gave control of it to Ra. Because Ra did a good job controlling the sun, Viracocha's favorite wife, Neferdor, gave her son a special gift that could never die. That gift was Zanzee. Bastet wanted human royalty to have access to Zanzee's powers, so she begged the cat from her father, Ra, and gave Zanzee to Queen Nefertiti."

Jeannie's eyes were wide open. Her mother's words prompted a question: "Mom, I've been studying ancient Egyptian culture in school. My school books say nothing about our gods being the parents of the Egyptian gods. You just said that Ra is the son of the supreme god and goddess, Viracocha and Neferdor. Where did that come from? The Egyptians never mention it in their hieroglyphic records—or do they?"

Soft Wind laughed. "Oh, Jeannie, do you not know that the gods have mysteries? They are circumspect and tell humans only what they want them to know, which is very little! Maybe that is why your schoolbooks on ancient Egyptian culture are missing so many god-human interactions!" Her smile grew wider, and she spoke softly. "I'm sure our people, the Kashome People, know more about the gods than any other group of humans on Earth. That is because Kashom was intended to be TRPOV. We believe Kashom was personally in touch with the gods. But when Kashom was tricked by the goroms and his sister was murdered, he fell from grace."

Jumping back into the conversation, Jeannie said, "Mom, I don't care about all this Egyptian god stuff. What about our people? What can you tell me that is really neat about the Kashome people?"

Soft Wind showed her delight in the teachings of her ancestors by explaining the beliefs that the Kashome people had held sacred for centuries in their home of the Scarlet Desert. "The gods play a major part in our culture. Zanzee, your kitty, is connected to the gods. Our worship to honor the gods for giving us the sun is sacred. When you were a little girl, I told many times the story of how the gods named our sun." Jeannie nodded. "Okay, I won't repeat that story, but the god's name for our sun is *Seen Far as a Distant Star*. So you may just have to learn some new things."

Soft Wind had Jeannie's attention.

"Jeannie, my grandmother, Golden Cloud, was very close to her grandmother, Skip-with-Wind. You know that Skip-with-Wind was Kashom's daughter. What my grandmother told me was not speculation. In essence, I have a direct line to the source, Kashom, about our people. I say this so you know it is true!"

Jeannie sat silently in her chair. Taking in every word that fell from her mother's mouth and hearing about the culture of her ancestors lifted her spirit anew.

"Although we do not know all the details, what my grandmother told me was that the gods visited planet Earth only once. It was the god Ra and his daughter, the goddess Bastet, when they visited Egypt. It was a long time ago."

Soft Wind stopped. She wanted to make sure Jeannie was listening. Jeannie was, so Soft Wind continued. "I'll get back to the god Ra in a minute, but first I want to talk about our sun. Jeannie, the sun has hidden powers we have yet to discover. The Kashome people worship the sun—we believe it has the power to open the Highway of Time and give travelers to faraway lands in distant times the gift of eternal youth. That is why the Kashome people give thanks each year to Viracocha during our Festival of the Sun, Intipraimi. Zanzee has a special part in that festival—he accompanies you during the golden key dance."

For a moment, Soft Wind reflected on performing the golden key dance in her youth with Zanzee, who had been her cat even then. *I loved holding Zanzee in my arms with my golden key around my neck, leading the dancers in full festival costume to the ceremonial ring. Zanzee and I would stand side by side in the center of the ring. At a special point, those dancing around Zanzee and me would stop. I would take my golden key from my neck and hold it up to the sun. Zanzee would stand erect and dance around me on only his hind legs. The festival would end with a grand feast honoring Viracocha.*

Jeannie noticed her mother's daydreaming and said, "Is that all, Mom?"

Jeannie's remark startled Soft Wind. She snapped her head around, now looking at Jeannie, and said, "There is a little more you should know. Be patient another minute or so, and I'll finish."

Zanzee's ability to sense emotions told him Soft Wind would like some company. He leaped from the braided oval throw rug to Soft Wind's lap. Her face burst into a smile. "When I was a girl like you, Zanzee was never far away. And now that he's your cat, I'm so fortunate he is still close by!"

Purring loudly into the stillness of the night, Zanzee filled the silent darkness of the room with his familiar, comforting sound of contentment.

Soft Wind's heart rose with Zanzee's sounds of joy, and she continued. "Ra has taken good care of the sun, and we honor his goodwill to all creatures on earth, which are alive only because of the sun."

It was at this point that Soft Wind wanted to make her story come alive. Certainly, Zanzee was real. He would never die. Jeannie had known this about her cat for as long as she had had him, which seemed like forever.

"Jeannie, Zanzee is a central figure in our festival to honor the sun. So where did Zanzee come from? One of the stories my grandmother told me is the story of how Zanzee came to be in our family. Evidently, at one time, Kashom's family visited Egypt. We know that Prince Kashom was part of that royal delegation that visited Egypt on planet Earth. We have Zanzee because Nefertiti was generous and gave him as a gift to the royal family of Kopaz. My grandmother said her grandmother, Kashom's daughter, talked a lot about Kashom's visit to Egypt. The purpose was to give the Egyptians instructions on how to build pyramids. My grandmother told me that Kashom once said there was a great pyramid on the grounds of the royal palace in Kopaz."

Jeannie broke in, "A pyramid on planet Kopaz?"

"Yes, Jeannie, that is what I said. The royal family in the land of Kopaz, or planet Kopaz, built a pyramid long before the Egyptian pyramids were built here on planet Earth."

Again Jeannie interrupted her mother. "Are you sure, Mom?"

"Yes!" replied Soft Wind. "Queen Nefertiti gave Zanzee to Kashom for his generosity in showing the Egyptians how to build pyramids. And as I said a few moments ago, Queen Nefertiti was given Zanzee by Bastet, the daughter of the god Ra."

Soft Wind glanced at Jeannie and noticed she was listening with intent interest. Smiling, she continued speaking proudly about the culture of her people. "We know a little about Zanzee's life in Kopaz. According to my grandmother, Zanzee lived in the palace with the royal family of Kopaz. Zanzee was Kashom's cat and comforted him in times of trouble. Kashom was going to give Zanzee to his sister, but then she was murdered, so later he gave him to his daughter, Moon-of-Day. Since that time, the eldest girl in the Lone Tree Family is the one Zanzee comforts—that has been tradition for centuries. He has special powers. Clearly, he never dies. Zanzee was my cat for twenty-eight years; now he is your cat and comforts you."

A long, drawn-out pause interrupted Soft Wind's recital of the legend of Zanzee. She selected her words carefully, knowing the impact they would have. "Jeannie, there is something I have not told you about Zanzee. Legend states that Zanzee will help the Chosen One navigate the path to restore Kashom's honor."

Caught totally by surprise, Jeannie asked, "How, Mom?"

Now, it was Soft Wind who was at a loss for words. "I don't know. What we know is that Zanzee is a special cat with a special role to play in the events to come."

Jeannie lifted her hand and motioned for Zanzee to come to her. "Thanks, Mom! I'm glad to know all that about Zanzee. I've always known that he's special. I think we're going to go to bed. Good night, Mom."

The cat leaped to her side. She picked him up and walked to her bedroom. Holding him tightly, she snuggled her face in his fur and whispered into his ear, "Oh, Zanzee, you know just when I need your company." She swung him back and forth in her arms and cradled him like a baby. "Zanzee, those gold earrings give you away. Have you never come to me without shaking your head and clinking your earrings? You love to make them go *tinkle, tinkle*—don't you? Well, I can make them go *tinkle, tinkle* by making you be the baby!" She giggled, and he purred.

She walked through her bedroom door, still with Zanzee in her arms, stroking his shiny black fur as she teased him. "Zanzee, my friends all ask me where you came from and who put the earrings in your ears. They want to know why you have two in your right ear and only one in your left ear. And all you can say is meow? Zanzee, you're a good kitty, but I'm still trying to figure out what you're good for. Oh, I'm sorry! Just kidding! I know—I don't want to hurt your feelings. You're my best friend. You keep me company all night long, sleeping right by my side."

Jeannie lifted him to her face and kissed his nose. She giggled and asked him a question. "Do you know what I tell my friends, Zanzee, when they ask me where you came from? Well, I tell them that the Egyptian gods gave you to me to guard my path through life and keep me company. What do you think about that?"

Zanzee gave Jeannie that familiar look that told her he wanted to go to bed. He looked her in the eyes and said, "Meow, meow."

"Okay, I know! Let's go to bed, Zanzee. I'm tired too," said Jeannie, jumping onto her bed.

Zanzee waited for Jeannie to get under the blankets and then jumped on top of the covers, snuggling next to her.

This cat is so neat, Jeannie thought as she drifted off to sleep. *He would never let anything happen to me.*

CHAPTER 16

The 1955 Chevy— What a Wild Ride!

*C*lang, *clang, clang, clang, clang!* rang the alarm. *It must be five thirty,* thought Darla as she reached over and turned off the alarm on her nightstand. *This is now the third week I've been back to work. I guess it's okay. It's tough with only one income—I wish Johnny were still here. Oh, how I want him back!*

She stood up and took the long nightshirt from the back of the chair next to her bed. Looking in the mirror, she recalled having done the same thing so many times with Johnny still in bed, but then her nightshirts had been much shorter, covering only her upper body and exposing her long legs.

She walked to the bathroom and washed her face in cold water. "It's just too hot to have that coal-burning stove fired up in the kitchen during the spring and summer months," she sighed, recalling that cold snowy day in February when, no matter how hot the stove got, it couldn't warm her heart.

Listening to sounds coming from the bathroom—his bedroom door was not completely closed—triggered Danny's recollection of the events of yesterday.

We have a full day—can't wait to find out what Jeannie figured out about the writings on the cliff. I better get up and talk to Mom before she heads off to work, he thought.

"Mom, when will you be home?" Danny hollered from his bedroom.

She was looking in the oval mirror above the sink. Its silver backing was peeling away after many years of use. She was applying her wine-red lipstick when she heard her son call. She reached for her dress, which was hanging on the door hook. "Danny, I'll be out until around five this evening. I have to go to the grocery store. Mr. Jacobs at the Granite Springs Market said he wouldn't worry about our charging groceries. He knows I only get paid once a month, and that's two weeks away."

Her motherly instinct set the tone of her instructions. "Danny, if you take the Chevy out today, make sure you have your driver's permit with you. I've left five dollars on the kitchen table to fill your truck with gas. Sam Maretti will have his gas pumps open for six hours today. Fill it up before you take off, so you won't run out of fuel in the desert. I know that's where you'll be headed. Also, write down your mileage—you only get seventy-five miles a week."

Darla looked at her watch. *Oh no! I'm late. I only have thirty minutes to get to work.* Finishing getting dressed, she dashed out of the bathroom with her makeup in place, grabbed her jacket from the back of a kitchen chair, and headed for the door.

"I'll do that, Mom, and I'll also wash the truck."

Danny heard the door slam. "She didn't hear me," he said to himself. He had wanted to walk his mom to the door and wish her a good day. *I guess I missed saying good-bye. I should have gotten up sooner.*

Danny scurried around his bedroom, getting ready for his outing in the desert with his friends. He grabbed his clothes from the closet and his boxers from his chest of drawers. He headed to the bathroom. His mind filled with excitement. Washing his face, he anticipated the adventure he would have with his newfound love and his best friend.

Today, I'm going to be just like James Dean—blue Levis and a white T-shirt and a red-hot Chevy! My dad sure liked James Dean. He looked a lot like him, too. I guess that's why Dad loved racing around in his truck and always repeated James Dean's quote, "Dream as if you'll live forever; live as if you'll die tomorrow."

He flicked the light switch on his way out the back door. He jumped down the stairs three at a time, thinking of what he would need for their outing. Tossing his lunch sack through the open window of his truck, he headed to the woodshed for the rest of his gear.

As he loaded the stuff he thought they would need at White Face Cliff—shovel, pry bar, pick, bucket, water, and toolbox—he kept thinking about James Dean. Having gathered his things, he was ready to go. He was about to jump in his truck and take off, but paused. "Oh shit. I almost forgot my special treat for Jeannie."

He raced back into his house, opened the fridge door, and grabbed a bag of chocolate-chip cookies that his mother had made the day earlier and a covered dish with a piece of pie in it.

"Okay," said Danny as he bounded down the back porch stairs with cookies and pie in hand, "I think I've got everything." As he jumped into the driver's seat, he started thinking about the details. *Hope Jeannie and Tony bring some Pepsi. That little creek that starts from a crack at the bottom of the cliff has clean water, but I like Pepsi!*

Popping the clutch, spinning the wheels, creating a cloud of dust, he raced to meet his friends. *This truck is a looker. I know heads turn when I go by. I feel like I'm on top of the world in this thing.*

Waiting at their designated location, Jeannie and Tony didn't even have to look up.

"Here comes Danny. Jeannie, those glasspacks purr just like Zanzee," said Tony.

She frowned. "Not so fast, Tony. Zanzee doesn't sound like that bucket of bolts Danny calls 'pure class'!" *Boys and their cars—good grief! Don't they know that life is not all about trucks?*

Danny gunned the engine to get its RPM up to three thousand and let the truck coast to the top of Long Hill, where Jeannie and Tony were standing.

He stared through his windshield as he cruised up to them. His eyes were fixed on Jeannie standing in her tight-fitting cutoffs, their white frayed trim wrapped snugly around her upper thighs. Her white T-shirt, displaying her thin body and small breasts, matched his.

His glasspacks were making their familiar *paderrrr, paderrrr* sound as his truck came to a stop.

"Okay, Danny, we know you have a cool truck." That was how Jeannie greeted him.

He grinned, eyes still fixed on her, watching her every movement. *Cool, Jeannie! You're just too cool!* "You guys ready?" He motioned for his friends to get in. "Jeannie, quit being a critic. You know you love this truck. You just wish you had it."

Danny reached his arm around her, his right hand on her upper thigh, and pulled her close to him, his radio blaring out Johnny Bacon's smash hit, "You're My Angel Divine." The last verse of the song finished:

> *Pretty pretty blue eyes from the gods above*
> *You fell from heaven to bring me your love*
> *You're my beautiful angel divine*
> *You're sixteen and you're all mine*

Jeannie beamed and her heart pounded. *Wow! It's happening. He just put his arm around me. Oh, Danny, I just love you! Yeah, do you know what, Danny? You're sixteen, and you're all mine!*

"Danny, sing to me the last verse of Johnny Bacon's 'You're My Angel Divine,' 'cause you can belt it out ten times better than he can."

Danny smiled, feeling the warmth of her body against his arm. "Oh, Jeannie, do I detect a bit of bias?" But he couldn't wait any longer to quiz Jeannie and changed the topic. "Jeannie, do you have this stuff figured out?"

"Did you guys bring lunch?" Jeannie didn't hesitate with her comeback.

He chuckled. "Sure did—you know the old story about the desert gopher," Danny chuckled with a grin on his face.

"Yes, Danny, that's your favorite story—we know all about the little varmint putting his behind over a sandhill and hunching over to take a you know what. That's not my point, and you know it."

One hand on the wheel, the other on her thigh, he gave her a love slap.

She glanced upward at him. "What's in your lunch bag?" She tenderly pinched his leg. "Did you guys bring a good lunch, or did you just bring a couple of pieces of bread and hope you could sponge part of my lunch?"

He smiled. "It's going to be a great day, Jeannie. I've got something real sweet in my bag for you. I know you have a sweet tooth! But you'll just have to wait!"

The Granite Springs radio station DJ set a joyous mood for the three teenage kids on their way to adventure in the front seat of the 1955 Chevy. "How's everybody doing in radio land? This is Daren Blake, your Saturday morning DJ. Stay tuned—we have lots of rock and roll songs coming your way! We just heard 'You're My Angel Divine,' by Johnny Bacon. Are you ready for the twangy sound of Duane Eddy to get you in the swing of things to rock and roll your day away?"

"You bet, Daren Blake. Give us Duane Eddy!" Danny hooted.

The radio was blaring Duane Eddy's "Rebel Rouser," the wheels were spinning, and dirt was flying—and unfortunately for them, Eddie and Terry were standing on the side of the dirt road. As the three grinning CoalVille teenagers whizzed by the bullies in the red Chevy, they gave them the middle-finger salute. A cloud of dust left the bullies coughing and rubbing dirt from their eyes—the truck would be a sight to remember.

"Did you see the expressions on Eddie's and Terry's faces when we all gave them the finger? What idiots! They think we're headed to Granite Springs to cruise Main. The only cruising they're going to do is in their shoes 'cause they don't have wheels. Too bad, so sad, you jerks!" said Danny with a grin on his face.

The conversation got serious as the three teenage kids headed off on their adventure. Danny was trying to keep his eyes on the road, but his attention was more on Jeannie than the road. Jeannie was watching Danny and fiddling with his leg, letting her fingers dance up and down it. Tony was looking out the window with a serious look, watching the sagebrush whiz by as Danny's truck raced down the highway. He was thinking about petroglyphs and Jeannie's remarks about deciphering them with an old book.

"Well, how about the stuff on the cliff? You said you would figure it out!" blurted out Tony.

Not taking her hand off Danny's leg, Jeannie snapped, "I said I would write out the translations, not figure it out—that's your job, Tony."

That caught Tony, as well as Danny, off guard. "Okay, so you didn't figure it out—but what in the Sam Hill is it?" asked Danny. "You know us boys. Our curiosity is so great that we're energized with anticipation to the point we could—as I always say—fly to the moon and back just thinking about the possibility of treasure."

Winding her bare legs around the shaft of the transmission floor shifter, Jeannie decided to have some fun with the boys. "Okay, here it is." Jeannie saw the anticipatory looks on her two friends' faces. She pulled out a piece of paper from her canvas bag. Tony said nothing as he watched her retrieve her notes, but as soon as she did, he said, "Let me see your papers." Jeannie handed them to him.

He stared at the writing on the paper. The first one read, *"Mañana descenderéis contra ellos: he aquí que ellos subirán por la cuesta de Sis, y los hallaréis junto al arroyo, antes del desierto de Jeruel."* And the second one read, *"Y será que, cuando pasare mi gloria, yo te pondré en una hendidura de la peña, y te cubriré con mi mano hasta que haya pasado."*

Jeannie was not about to let the cat out of the bag. She had one over on the boys—she could speak Spanish, and they couldn't. *They'll just have to wait until I'm ready to fill them in on the clues!* she thought as she giggled. Before long, she was distracted not only by the bright morning sun rising above White Mountain directly in front of them, but also by the thrill of barreling down the highway in her true love's red racer.

Tony wasn't interested in playing games. "Jeannie, you win—just tell us what this gibberish means." Tony showed his frustration with her by the grimace on his face.

She pulled her eyes from the mountain and the brilliant morning sun back to her bag. She reached into it to fetch another piece of paper. "Boys, I think we can get to the bottom of this just by looking at the English version," said Jeannie in a sweet voice. She knew how to play Danny and Tony like a couple of fiddles.

Jeannie was always up for having fun, and that she was going to do. Her father, Billy Harris, was of Greek descent and had left her his parents' Greek Bible. Although she did not speak Greek, Jeannie had done a little copying from that Bible.

"Here's the paper with the translations you boys can understand."

Danny glanced from the road to Jeannie's papers. The first one read, *"αυριον καταβητε επ' αυτους ιδου αναβαινουσιν κατα την αναβασιν ασας και ευρησετε αυτους επ' ακρου ποταμου της ερημου ιεριηλ."* The second read, *"ηνικα δ' αν παρελθη μου η δοξα και θησω σε εις οπην της πετρας και σκεπασω τη χειρι μου επι σε εως αν παρελθω."*

"What's that shit? Damn it, Jeannie," he said with a stern voice. "You're trying our patience. What in the name of Judas Priest are you up to?"

"Danny! What did I say about your cussing? You know I don't like it. Could you try harder not to use those words around me?"

"Whoa! Sorry, Jeannie, I'll work on it." He nodded sheepishly, knowing she had reached her limit with his swear words.

Having grabbed his attention, she giggled and pinched his leg gingerly. "I just thought you guys would like a little Greek Bible study!"

Danny smiled as he thought, *Two can play your game, Jeannie.* He gently pinched her thigh and slid his fingers under the white fray of her cutoffs as he said, "Jeannie, enough is enough! This truck knows the way back home and will certainly exercise that option if you don't stop the games and cut to the chase!"

She smartly moved his hand away from her leg. "Okay, guys, but you have to admit, your buttons are easy to find—and easy to push," Jeannie said with her cute little smile.

He curled his fingers tightly, realizing he had overstepped his bounds. He turned to her and gave her a sad look, but his eyes were sparkling, and it quickly turned into a smile. She smiled back and imitated his sad look. He laughed.

"Here's what you're looking for." She pulled another piece of paper from her canvas bag. "I'm only going to translate the important stuff—that is, unless you guys want all the Bible-churchy, chitty-chat stuff."

Danny did a quick finger dance on Jeannie's lower thigh and then quickly moved his hand. She pointed a finger at him and shook it in his face. Danny winked at her, shook his head, and moved his fingers on the wheel, tapping them in rhythm to Elvis's song "Jailhouse Rock." He laughed again. "Jeannie, not like Elvis. No wooden chair for my dance partner and no Bible lessons—just get to the point, the important stuff!"

At that, she giggled. "So am I your partner? If so, you get the good stuff. Here goes. This is the first one. It's from the second book of Chronicles—in Spanish, 2 Crónicas—chapter twenty, verse sixteen. 'At the cliff of Ziz… you shall find them at the end of the brook, before the wilderness…'"

If Danny wasn't listening closely, Tony sure was. But Danny's attention was on Jeannie's face and voice. "You are doing good stuff! Keep going!"

"And this is the second one, from Exodus, chapter thirty-three, verse twenty-two. 'I will put it in a cleft of the rock…I will cover…with my hand…'"

Even though he had no idea what she was talking about, he knew her well. She took her native cultural beliefs seriously. He would have to fit her beliefs in with his game plan for having fun with the girl who had captured his heart. "So, what does all of this jibber-jabber mean?" Danny asked Jeannie as he looked out over the hood of his pickup and then glanced quickly at her paper.

"Well, guys, I think we have our work cut out for us."

"No kidding!" was Tony's response. He had been listening to Danny and Jeannie carry on, and he wanted answers—not lovers' play.

This spring was especially warm. Springtime in Wyoming could bring unpredictable weather, but no one could object to the beautiful day that was beginning. The sun was just starting to show its face above the distant hills. The brilliant pink silver-lined clouds reflecting the rising sun couldn't have been more spectacular. The 1955 Chevy truck, carrying three teenage kids deciphering clues, was headed on an adventure. It was starting to be obvious to Danny, Jeannie, and Tony that someone was using ancient petroglyphs and a very old Bible to communicate clues about something; the questions were what and why. Yes, the three kids were looking at clues embedded in verses from la Biblia Reina-Valera, but they still had to decipher what they meant.

Danny grabbed his Hollywood girlie steering wheel knob and yanked it. "Hold on, guys," he said as he negotiated the turnoff from the blacktop pavement onto the two-rut dirt road leading to White Face Cliff.

His red truck tilted as he cranked the wheel with his left hand, right arm still around Jeannie, and careened onto the dirt road leading to White Face Cliff. He gunned it. Wheels spun, kicking up a cloud of loose dirt. Suddenly, his truck hit a large hole in the road and shot upward, with all four wheels going airborne. He took his foot off the pedal. The truck smashed into the dirt on all four. He hit the brakes. As the truck slowed, a cloud of dust surrounded it.

Jeannie screamed. *"Don't hit the antelope!"*

Danny yanked the wheel with both hands, cranking it in the opposite direction. His truck careened again, this time sliding sideways toward a head-on collision with a pronghorn antelope. The animal made a sudden leap into the air. His truck scraped the white rump of the pronghorn, spinning it around. It stumbled and lay still in the sagebrush.

Suddenly angry and defensive, Jeannie screamed again. *"You killed it!"* He hadn't expected that.

Danny slammed on the brakes with both feet. He jumped out. Jeannie gave him a blank look. Danny was not looking at her. His heart sank, not knowing what to expect. He swung around looking for the antelope. He spotted a brown and tan leg sticking out of the sagebrush. Jumping over the brush in front of him, he was there in three seconds. Clearly dazed, the animal rolled its head. They exchanged baffled looks. The animal's large round eyes watched Danny's every move. Its eyes widened. It regained its senses and realized it wanted nothing to do with this man.

The pronghorn sprung to its feet, jerking his head around. It leaped over the brush directly in front of it. It wasn't hurt—only frightened and stunned. Its legs moved with lightning speed. It raced away, then stopped about fifty feet from Danny, cocking its head to the side as they exchanged looks for the last time. Danny's front fender had merely ruffled its fur. Running forty miles per hour, it would live to race again another day in the Scarlet Desert.

Danny jumped back into the truck. The moment his door slammed shut, he said, "He's fine." Jeannie's silence oppressed him. White as a ghost, Danny took a deep breath and repeated, "Scared but fine."

Jeannie glared at him. She was furious. Her silence ended. "What were you thinking, Danny? Are you trying to get us killed?"

His look was somber. He was sheepish. "No," he said. His glance from the corner of his eye caught her glare. "Sorry, Jeannie, I was totally in the wrong. It won't happen again."

Jeannie did not let up. "Danny, if I've told you once, I've told you a hundred times—drive no faster than twenty miles per hour on this winding rut trail! We're not in the Indianapolis 500 through the sagebrush to White Face Cliff. So get your lead foot off the pedal!"

Putting his truck in gear, getting their journey underway again, he slapped her bare leg gently. His only words were a repeat of what he'd said a moment ago. "Sorry, Jeannie. It won't happen again."

A long silence ensued. Then he laughed. "At least not for the rest of this day."

Jeannie got the message. He was a boy with a toy; she was a girl with more sense than the boy. She grabbed his arm. With her other she touched his lips with her finger. "Danny, it's okay. Just be careful. We'll have fun today."

The trio's excitement grew as the truck made the final turn to reveal the cliff no more than three hundred yards in front of them. The morning sun brought life to the face on the cliff. They had always known why it was called White Face, but at seven ten that morning, with the breaking sun making the face glow like pure alabaster, the sight took their breath away.

"Wow! Isn't that something?" said Danny.

The run-in with the pronghorn was now far from Jeannie's mind. Her thoughts were centered on the teachings of her mother from the night before—the sacred Kashome legends, the centuries-old legends of a desert people that yet captured the curiosity common to all humans since the dawning of time, the very essence of eternal youth.

She was not listening to Danny's remarks about the cliff; she was thinking, *I've always known why it was named White Face. The white sandstone is spectacular in the morning sun. But now I know the reason why it's also called*

Ziz. It's the clue that was hidden in the petroglyphs. She rehearsed it in her mind. *At the cliff of Ziz…you shall find them at the end of the brook, before the wilderness. Did Kashom add the name of Ziz to the cliff? Is he trying to communicate with us in some strange way? It must be his way of communicating with the Chosen One. Why else would the name of this cliff—the name of Ziz— only be in the Kashome culture?*

But then it dawned on her. Her mind filled with questions. *What is Kashom telling us in the clue? The end of the brook? What is he talking about? Where's the end of the brook? Did he put something there?*

Danny was also puzzled, and the expression on Jeannie's face piqued his curiosity. He parked his truck and said, "What are you thinking, Jeannie?"

She didn't answer but just giggled and pointed.

He got the message. "Okay, let's go," he said, and all three walked together toward a clump of cedar trees growing in an outcropping of rocks.

When they reached the trees, which were only a stone's throw from the clear-water pond nestled at the base of the cliff, Danny took Jeannie's hand. He grabbed her by her waist and boosted her onto a large rock, slapping her rump. He jumped up on it and stood beside her.

She snuggled against him, but her mind was still engulfed in questions surrounding the clue. Focusing her attention on the spring, which was spewing water from a crevice near the bottom of the cliff, she noticed something.

Hmmm, the little stream of water makes its way down the side of the cliff and forms a pool at the base. Her eyes followed the journey of the water. *It collects in the pool, but then continues on its way in a small brook that starts at the other end of the pool. The little brook meanders away toward the adjacent desert sands.* Jeannie looked at the point on the cliff where the water seeped from the crevice and thought, *Hmm! It's the mouth of the face on the cliff where the water comes from—how interesting!*

Danny held onto Jeannie's hand as they stood pressed against each other on the rock. She gazed, saying nothing. He had no idea what she was so deep in thought about. He didn't care.

Tony walked past them on his way to the pond.

Jeannie continued her silence while staring at the cliff. Danny wasn't about to interrupt her meditation. He knew she was still a little peeved about the pronghorn incident.

Her mind raced. *The obscure face on the cliff created by the cracks and crevices must be the face of Ziz. Yes, how interesting! Ziz's mouth is spewing out the water. Someone is telling us this water is a clue to finding something! What is it? Yes, there's much to ponder about legends. Where did they come from? What do they mean?* She thought about what her mother had told her. *Kashom was a royal prince. He lost his honor and his position as heir to the royal throne. His honor and position can only be restored by someone who takes the place of Moon-of-Day. Will it be me? Am I the Chosen One? What does that have to do with this place?*

CHAPTER 17

Uncovering Secrets—First Clue

S he was positive it was him. Her mind scrambled for direction. *Someone is trying to communicate with us by using petroglyphs and one of the oldest books on earth—the Biblia Reina-Valera!* Jeannie had her own ideas, but fate and luck were not her standard fallback. Reality grounded her reasoning, and legends were her guide. *It has to be Kashom!*

She dropped Danny's hand and jumped off the rock they'd been standing on. Moving through the purple sage, she selected her footing so as not to step on a rattlesnake, trip in a gopher hole, or get tangled in a desert cactus. She headed to a different vantage point.

He watched her and wondered, *What's she doing now? Where's she going?*

She reached the edge of the pond. Deep in thought, she stared, her eyes wandering up and down the cliff. Searching for answers, she gazed at the petroglyphs high on the wall in front of her. Michelangelo would have been hard pressed to create a more magnificent masterpiece than the one Jeannie was looking at. The morning sun painted its glory on the white sandstone in brilliant shades of orange, yellow, pink, and scarlet, making the petroglyphs worthy of any cathedral ceiling.

She was not watching her path, and she walked around a red-ant hill and accidentally kicked a rock next to it. Suddenly, she felt a piercing sting on her leg. She saw an angry little ant pinching her flesh with pincer fangs and stabbing a needle-shaped object protruding from its round, red behind into the skin on her leg. A drop of blood oozed from the pincer hole and ran down her thigh, and she screamed, "You little bugger!"

Dancing around the red-ant pile, which looked like a small red pimple on the desert sands, she kicked it again.

She got bitten! Danny chuckled to himself. He yelled, "Jeannie, what are you doing? Have you got problems?"

Jeannie was not about to let a nasty little red ant divert her train of thought. *That darn Danny is laughing at me. I'll show him. I'll figure this petroglyph out, 'cause I know that someone is telling us something big time!* "Danny, you lunatic, what's your problem?" blurted out Jeannie, glaring at him. "Why are you still standing on that rock? We have things to do out here—more important than your laughing and making fun of me. I'm onto something *big!*"

Jeannie wrinkled her nose at him as she flipped her head, her hair catching the early morning rays of the sun with a flash of light as she ran to a rock that protruded into the pond. She hopped onto it and said, "Okay, little red ants. Try swimming to get to me."

Danny's eyes tracked her every movement. He laughed under his breath. *I love it when she gets peeved at me!* He hollered, "Do you want company?"

Slipping her shoes off, she dangled her feet in the water. She looked at him nonchalantly and said, "I do."

His first instinct was to take off and fly to her as fast as he could, but he put his hand over his mouth and lightly bit his lip. *Hmm, I think I'll play hard to get.*

Snickering to himself, Tony watched the dynamic between Jeannie and Danny. But their bantering was not Tony's real concern. No, he could tell by the intent look on Jeannie's face that she was onto something. He continued to watch. *Jeannie is figuring out something much bigger than a little red ant.*

"Earth to Jeannie, Earth to Jeannie, come in," Tony said as he watched Jeannie sitting on the rock, with the water slapping at her legs. He'd picked up the set of notes she'd been studying earlier. *She has a certain look when she's contemplating something important,* Tony thought as he wondered what she was so fascinated with. *This pond of water, that water coming out of the cliff—what does it mean?*

Her voice took on a commanding tone, competing with the sounds of Mother Nature's myriad of chirping birds, as if to wake the morning sun. "Okay, guys, what do you see?" asked Jeannie, not taking her eyes from the cliff.

Danny snickered, but Tony quickened his pace, walking toward the pond; his eyes were fixed on the cliff as he walked. "What do you mean, Jeannie? We see White Face Cliff," Tony said, with a puzzled look on his face.

Jeannie knew she would have to choose her words wisely, as the mystery of the petroglyphs had been hidden for centuries, but she had an idea—she was certain it was tied to the reference in her Reina-Valera.

For a moment, her mind was blank. Then it hit her. "Danny, come over here. Hurry!" she called, jumping to her feet, "You too, Tony."

Danny's game of hard-to-get ended. Hitting the ground running, he jumped from his rock. His stride was full of excitement. *She's got something figured out. I don't know how she does it, but she does!*

The sun had reached a height where its rays turned the water's surface into a giant mirror reflecting the mysterious face on the cliff—the cliff called Ziz by the Kashome people.

Jeannie flicked her fingers through Danny's hair as he came to a halt, standing directly in front of her. From her vantage point on the rock looking down at him, her finger pointed up. He got the message. He put one hand on the edge of the rock she was on and vaulted himself onto it.

He extended his arms; his hands grasped her waist. His thumbs softly slid over the waistband of her shorts. She put her hands over his and smiled, then nudged him gently with a twisting body motion, pushing him slightly to the right.

She pointed to the cliff and said, "I'm talking about the obscure face and what's coming from it." She spoke so softly that the morning breeze nearly drowned out her words.

Standing on the ground next to them, Tony was ecstatically curious, but Danny was content to tease Jeannie in a fun-loving way. His eyebrows dropped and his lip curled, but before he could speak, Tony spoke up, his impatience clear. "What? Now what are you talking about? What do you mean—something coming from it?" asked Tony.

Quick with her response, she looked down at him and said, "My point is the water!"

His hands went straight up. "So? What about the water? What do you mean the water?" Tony blurted.

While Jeannie had turned to talk to Tony, Danny picked up a five-pound rock not far from his feet. He threw it.

Kabloosh! Jeannie jumped. Danny laughed. "Got water?" he said, chuckling.

Jeannie giggled. "You'll think water, Mr. Danny." She smiled at him. "Good rock toss, but it's now time to get serious. And that's an order, Danny."

Danny laughed louder. "Aye, aye, lady general!" But watching her intently as she gazed at the sky, he realized that Jeannie was ignoring him. *Why is she looking at the sky? What's she thinking now?* "Okay, what are we going to do today—stargaze, moongaze, cloudgaze? Let's not spend this entire day gazing!"

Not looking at him, Jeannie pointed to the sun. "Danny, do you know anything about unraveling clues? Have you ever looked to the sun, stars, moon, or sky to guide your thoughts?" Jeannie replied gently. "My people's legends help guide us to interpret signs."

"Jeannie, there you go again—your legends are driving me bats! We need to find the treasure, not chase your goofy legends!" said Danny, wrinkling up his nose and making a weird face. "What on earth does the sun have to do with this mystery?" he said, chuckling.

Looking at him, she laughed to herself as she thought about her people's culture of worshiping the sun. *Danny, soon you'll know how important the sun is and the power it can unleash.*

At this point, Tony had no clue what Jeannie was up to, although he suspected she had reason for her reference to the water. Her reference to the sun, moon, and stars was a mystery to him also. He was waiting for her to reveal her hypothesis.

For centuries, the petroglyphs carved on cliffs in the Scarlet Desert had remained mysteries—at least the ones on White Face Cliff. Tony suspected Jeannie was about to unravel a mystery. He suspected Danny was lost.

Jeannie laughed easily. "Darn it anyway, Danny, you sure look cute with that face you put on. I just love that little smirk and wrinkled-up nose!" She broke into a huge smile. "But I'll say this. It's legends that will take us to where we are going—if there's treasure there, so be it. But the treasure might be something way beyond what you can comprehend, Danny Roberts—so there you go!"

Danny wasn't impressed by Jeannie's patronizing diversion. "Jeannie, here you're trying to figure out your damned legends and getting no-place. We need to find the treasure!"

Jeannie's response was quick and sharp. "Okay, guys, you figure it out. You guys think you're so damn smart! If you're the king wizards that you think you are, well, you go figure it out!" She walked to the edge of the rock hanging over the water. Flipping her head away from Danny, she sat down not more than five feet away, dangling her feet in the water again.

Danny thought, *Tony and I are no match for Jeannie when she gets pissed. If we're going to have any fun today, we need to kiss her boots.* In two steps, he was by her side. He grinned down at her. "Jeannie, you win—what's on your mind?"

While swirling her feet in the pond, Jeannie had arrived at a revelation seemingly conveyed from the depths of that water. She was 99 percent positive she was on the right track. She'd made mistakes in the past, but she counted them as lessons, and they were leading her to maturity. She was waiting for the opportunity to reveal her revelation. She needed her notes from the Biblia Reina-Valera. She also realized that Danny needed coddling. Tony was good.

"Okay," said Jeannie, "let me go back to what I was saying a few minutes ago. I think someone is trying to communicate something. I haven't figured it out yet, but I think we are on the right track."

Danny listened intently but had his own view on the subject of lost treasure. "How do you know that? What makes you sure you're right?"

His remarks and a quick glance in his direction told her he was off track—someplace else. *Danny, how do I get you on board?*

Danny wasn't quite ready to move on. What he wanted to do was just have fun with Jeannie.

Jeannie knew exactly what was going on. She looked at him intently, thinking, *He's just come through the depths of darkness following the loss of his dad. I'm well aware of what he needs. I'll let him play, at least for the time being.* She motioned him to follow her as she jumped from the rock and started walking. He followed. She smiled, clearly cheered.

Tony was left at the pond, preoccupied, standing several hundred feet from them as he fiddled with Jeannie's papers.

Jeannie walked along the edge of the pond, Danny following. All Danny could think about was the beautiful girl he was falling in love with— this young girl wearing skimpy shorts and a tight T-shirt, walking by the pond at the base of White Face Cliff. As she stopped, he reached for her shoulders with his hands. He turned her to face him. He softly whispered in her ear, "You're right! You're always right! But I'll say this!"

She listened. He said nothing. His hands moved to her back, his fingers feeling her flesh beneath her tightly stretched T-shirt as he slid them up and down over her ribs. His thumbs under her arms made her giggle. He dropped his arms, placed his hands firmly with outstretched fingers on the back pockets of her cutoffs, and pulled her body closer to his.

"Whoa," she said as a distressed thought crossed her mind. *Is it me or my body he's interested in—or both?* Up to this point, she hadn't known for sure. She grabbed his hands on her rear pockets and moved them.

He flinched and let her go. Puzzled, he looked directly at her, debating whether to say something else. Tony looked up from his study of her notes. He was anxious to get moving. "Okay, let's continue," said Tony. "Jeannie does have a point. Let's assume that someone is trying to communicate using the Biblia Reina-Valera. Okay, Jeannie, it's your turn. What do you need?"

With tact, Jeannie gave Danny an assignment. She put her hand on his face, brushing his hair out of his eyes, and said, "Danny, would you go to your truck and get my Spanish notes? The translations I read on our drive out this morning?"

"Sure, Jeannie. Where are they?" Danny asked.

"On the seat—the canvas bag," she said, watching him take off in the direction of the small hill that his truck was parked behind. Danny had a spring in his stride as he ran back, carrying Jeannie's notebook.

Taking her notes from his outstretched hand, she said, "Thanks, Danny! We have two clues. I think the order is important. Let's use logic and assume that one comes before the other. Okay, here's what the first one says: 'At the cliff of Ziz, you shall find them at the end of the brook, before the wilderness.'"

She paused and said nothing. She looked at the cliff. Danny and Tony followed her movements. She pointed at the face on the cliff. "The Kashome people refer to this cliff by the name of Ziz. That is something we don't talk about outside of our culture. What I mean is that just among the Kashome people, it is referred to as Ziz."

Still pointing, she remained silent for a long minute. Danny waited. Tony was curious. She selected her words carefully. "I have an idea," she said. "I think Kashom named this cliff Ziz. He wanted only the Kashome people to recognize it by that name."

It was now time. Jeannie was ready to reveal what had come to her as a clue from the water of the pond. "Here's what I think," she said, looking at the face of Ziz on the cliff. "He's communicating with us. He wants his communication to be understood by only the Kashome people. It is puzzling! I believe Kashom is referring to the face on the cliff—a face he calls Ziz. Look at where the water comes from—maybe there's a connection between the face on the cliff and the water that comes from the mouth of the face. Yeah, that's what Kashom wants us to see. There's something about the water coming from the cliff."

Danny didn't buy it. He had his own ideas. "Jeannie, how do you know that? I think it's a map telling us where the pirates buried their gold. Isn't that why we went snooping at LeRoy's house? You're the one who organized that fiasco. You said he might have some of the pirate's gold up there. Do you remember?"

His statements caught her off guard. Her mind reeled. *Damn it, Danny. I did take us on a wild goose treasure hunt at Crazy LeRoy's house. Now what do*

I say? She stared at him for one second and then looked to the sky. The sun had turned the clouds a fiery orange. The incident earlier with his hands on her rear pockets was heavy on her mind. Tensions were on the rise.

Then, just like that, there he was. *Tinkle, tinkle.* Jeannie's head snapped around to look in the direction of the sound. *That has to be—*"Meow, meow!" She spotted Zanzee standing by the brook.

It was not Jeannie alone who deserved the credit for this revelation about the mystery of the petroglyphs on the Cliff of Ziz and how they were tied to the water. She was also being helped by Zanzee, who was the navigator.

"Zanzee, good boy! You're here!" Her discussion with Tony about the name of the sandstone cliff was momentarily forgotten.

Danny's train of thought on pirate treasure came to a screeching halt. Twisting his head around, he looked in the direction of the sounds. He threw his hands in the air. "How did your cat get here?" he asked as he watched Zanzee's black tail darting to and fro above the tops of the sagebrush.

That started a vigorous discussion. "Danny, he's an Egyptian cat. He has special powers."

Danny jumped onto the rock Jeannie was standing next to. *"What?"* Her response made no sense to him. He wondered how she had come up with that statement Looking down at her, he said, "Egyptian cat? Special powers? I don't get it! That's just loony!"

He was continuing to dig himself into the proverbial hole. Little did he know that she was tense not only because of his comments about her cat, but also something he was oblivious about—her concern that it was her body and not her mind and heart that he was interested in.

She flung her hand at him as if throwing something his way. "Danny, you know nothing! Zanzee is an Egyptian cat, and you know it! How else did he get way out here? We're five miles from town. He must have special powers."

Zanzee's movements had surprised Tony so much he'd had little time to react to the banter between Danny and Jeannie. He'd been thinking about how to settle their tensions, but now his focus was elsewhere. He felt a pulse of joy and yelled in a loud voice, "Jeannie, you shall find them at the end of the brook, before the wilderness. It's the brook that Zanzee is walking by—he's showing us where to look! Yeah, it's the brook that someone is telling us to focus on—and Zanzee knows it! You're absolutely correct, Jeannie—there is a connection between the name Ziz and the water coming out of the cliff!"

Danny's attention was finally piqued. "Tony, that's brilliant—you're right!" He jumped off the rock and started whistling his shrill trademark whistle. When Zanzee heard the shrill whistling, he darted for cover in the sagebrush.

Watching Zanzee race for cover in the desert, Jeannie ignored Danny. Then, suddenly, her face lit up with a smile. *My mother told me about Zanzee's special role—he will help the Chosen One navigate the path to restore Kashom's honor. He must be doing that.*

She took off running in the direction of the brook, Danny and Tony following. When she got to her destination, her attention was quickly diverted from her cat to a startling discovery.

She screamed, "*We got it right!*" Her ringing words of amazement hung in the air like the sound of a shotgun blast. "Look, this little brook just disappears into the desert sand!"

"Got what right? You just scared the crap out of me! Now what are you talking about?" Tony asked her with amazement.

She was panting—out of breath from her run. She uttered between breaths of air, "Danny and Tony, it's the Reina-Valera verse you guys got excited about, but it's more than just the connection with the name of the cliff. You recall what that verse said: 'You shall find them at the end of the brook, before the wilderness.' I'm standing at the end of the brook, and this desert beyond the brook must be the wilderness! We know where to look—thanks to Zanzee! Something is hidden in this wilderness. Yeah— the wilderness is the desert!"

Tony beamed. He said, "Jeannie, here are your papers," and he waved them in the air above his head.

Danny was concentrating. *The brook disappears just as Jeannie pointed out. So we're onto something. Water comes out of the crack in the cliff—the mouth of*

Ziz. It runs down the side of the cliff and forms a pond. Okay, then it comes from the outlet of the pond at the base of the cliff and goes in this little brook. It starts a journey into the desert, but only goes so far before it's swallowed up by the desert sands and disappears. Yes, that's it! The desert is the wilderness, and the brook ends at the edge of the desert or the wilderness. Basically, it's very sandy here, and the water in the brook gets absorbed. It only goes so far—that cuts down our search area.

Then, out of nowhere, Danny said, "Maybe there is something mystical about that cat."

Jeannie nearly said something but caught herself. There was a sudden shining in her eyes. *I misjudged him. He's only treated me with respect. How could I think otherwise?* She turned to walk to where he was standing. "What are you thinking, Danny? You look deep in thought!"

"Jeannie, I've got it!" said Danny with the biggest grin on his face. "Thanks to you, we know where the treasure is buried!"

She chuckled to herself. *That's my Danny. I just love him.*

They stood in excitement at the end of the brook that disappeared into the sands of the Scarlet Desert. They had begun to unravel the clues, but they still had no idea where the clues would lead them, or what they would find.

CHAPTER 18

Uncovering Secrets—
Second Clue

Jeannie gave Danny her princess smile, as he called it. She giggled to herself as she watched him dream of treasure. *That silly Danny is still thinking about his buried treasure. Oh well, I guess it can't hurt anything—anyway, neither Tony nor I can change his mind. He'll chase after his treasure until we find it or something else. I think it will be something else, but who knows what.*

She stood at the end of the brook that disappeared into the sands of the desert. She looked to the sky as her eyes sparkled with tears. Her heart was pounding, not only because of the young man standing next to her, but also because of their success at unraveling the first clue. They were standing exactly at the spot to which the clue—*you shall find them at the end of the brook, before the wilderness*—had directed them to go.

She spotted a flat rock next to an extraordinarily large sage bush that was ideally suited for a work area. It was on the bank of the brook at the point where the water vanished, making its final descent from sight as it rushed with a swirling motion into a hole in the sands of the desert—a rather large hole, created over eons.

"God, Jeannie, don't get too close to the hole the water is draining into. Shit, if one of us fell into it, who knows where we'd end up," said Danny with genuine concern.

"Don't worry, Danny. This flat rock is ten feet from the hole," she said, laughing at his concern. A midmorning wind was blowing slightly as she gently grasped Danny's bare, hairy arm and said, in her sweet girlish voice, "Danny, let's lay this paper out on this rock and go over each word very carefully. Sometimes, there's a hidden meaning, and sometimes there isn't—so we just need to sort things out."

She felt terribly excited as she started her discussion. "Okay! I think the first part of the verse from second Crónicas isn't that important. I think the only message in the first part is telling us where to start—that is, 'at the cliff of Ziz.' Yes, water comes from the mouth of Ziz and ends up in the brook. I think the important fact is this: 'you shall find them at the end of the brook, before the wilderness.' That tells me that we need to look at the end of the brook. Danny! You were right! Good work! It couldn't be clearer. If the brook didn't end but just kept meandering on and on like an endless river, well, you get the picture. We would have a real problem—but it ends, so that tells us where to look."

Danny put his finger on his mouth and blew her a kiss, which was his way of telling her thanks.

Jeannie didn't have to say another word. *That Danny, bless his soul, he's a great guy. He always knows how to give a compliment, even when he knows he's a big part of the solution.*

Straightening her paper on the rock so they could all see it, she pointed to the second clue and said, "Onto the next one."

Tony wasn't able to see the paper from where he was standing. He asked, "Jeannie, what does the Exodo one say?"

She made a face by rolling her bottom lip under her upper lip. She wrinkled up her nose and said, "Some goofy stuff like 'I will put it in a cleft of the rock...I will cover...with my hand...' That doesn't make any sense!"

Tony listened to the words with intense excitement and shouted, "Yeah! I got it! Suppose we reinterpret the words, so instead of saying 'I will put it in a cleft of the rock,' it reads, 'I will put it in the crack of the rock.' You see, in ancient times, *cleft* sometimes referred to a crack in a rock—so maybe there's a big rock with a crack that has something hidden in it?" Tony stopped and looked directly at Jeannie and Danny. "So, my friends, we have to find a rock with a big crack in it!"

Tony could see he had the attention of his two friends, so he continued. "Now the good part. 'I will cover…with my hand…' Wow, do you guys get it?"

"Tony, you've lost me on this one, but please go on," Jeannie commented in a cool tone. Her papers fluttered in the wind. One took flight—ready to skim into the brook and disappear into the desert. Danny quickly grabbed it. "Thanks, Danny. It didn't go down the sinkhole. That saved me from running back to your truck to get my Biblia Reina-Valera and retranslate."

Tony knew that he was getting one up on Jeannie. *Boy, for once I get to figure something out.* "Okay, here's what we need to look for—a rock that's in the shape of a hand, someplace at the end of the brook!" Tony said, beaming all over with enthusiasm.

Danny looked totally ecstatic. "Jeannie, I think Tony just figured it out—so let's go!" he said, as he too lit up with excitement.

She didn't buy it. She frowned. He watched her body language and predicted what was coming next. "Not so fast, Danny! Go where and do what? Are we on a wild-rock chase? First, Tony talked about a rock with a crack in it, and then he talked about a rock in the shape of a hand. What story does he want us to believe—the crack or the hand?"

Her comments were as he had expected. He was ready. This time Danny didn't let Jeannie have the upper hand. "Jeannie, you bet that's what we're going to do, so get with the program. We're on a wild-rock chase— so let's go!"

Jeannie realized Danny and Tony were right. *I guess sometimes you swallow your pride and get with the program, as Danny calls it. Darned Tony— why'd he have to figure it out? Oh well, it's okay. I can't do everything.*

Clapping his hands, Danny seized their attention. "So! Where do we start?" Danny was anxious to find the treasure.

Jeannie was a master of taking control. She knew it. She waited for her opportunity, and she realized it was now. She jumped back into the conversation and said, "Look—we still aren't there yet."

She hesitated. It was her way of grabbing attention and maintaining it. The sound of the rippling brook dominated the scene while the two young men waited for Jeannie to say something. She took advantage of the opportunity to be the leader again. "The clue says, 'will cover...with my hand...' Well! We need to analyze this some more—so what does it mean?" There was a long silence this time. Then she continued. "Tony may be onto something—but we don't know exactly what it is. It could be a rock shaped like a hand—or maybe it's a rock with a hand on it."

But her position of leadership lasted only a few seconds. She knew she was grasping at this juncture. She would wait for a more opportune time to take charge.

Sensing that she was fumbling and really didn't have a clear idea what she was talking about—*hand-shaped rock or rock with a hand on it*—Tony began to retort. He was going to charge on with the idea of a rock carved in the shape of a hand, but then stopped. He had a better idea.

"How about this? A rock with a hand petroglyph on it," Tony said as he visualized a hand on a rock. "Yeah! The first part says, 'I will put it in a cleft of the rock.' It's telling us to look for the rock with a hand carved on it. The second part says, 'I will cover...with my hand...' That's telling us the rock with a hand carved on it is covering something up. Yep! We walk by it, see the rock with a hand on it, and voilà—the treasure is under the rock!" Tony looked at his friends to see if they were following his line of reasoning. "Let's suppose that whoever carved the petroglyphs on White Face Cliff also carved something on a rock—like a hand."

"Good idea, Tony. Let's look for a rock—a special rock," said Danny.

The excitement level among all three kids was definitely on the rise. But these teenagers had been excited many times by things in the past. What would keep the excitement would be finding something—the kids knew that false hopes led to wild-goose chases that ended in disappointment. They had been down that false-hope road many times. "If it's nothing more than a wild-rock chase—as Jeannie put it—then, as Danny would say, it's nothing more than embellishment of legends." Tony smiled at them.

Jeannie knew the immediate task was to find a hand. Thoughts filled her mind. *A hand on a rock someplace at the end of the brook—or, as stated by someone unknown telling us what to do and where to go, we look for something at the end of the brook, covered by a rock with the petroglyph of a hand on it.*

Jeannie exerted her leadership skills and set the search in motion. "Here's what we do, guys—one person on one side of the brook and another on the other side. I'll bring up the rear and go back and forth to leave no rock unturned. Let's go!" She never let go of the thought that she had started the day with. *Could it be that someone is trying to communicate with us by using petroglyphs and one of the oldest books on earth—the Biblia Reina-Valera—to point to clues?*

CHAPTER 19
Zanzee Points the Way

J eannie was certain Zanzee would be back. She was a Neferzul, and she was 99 percent positive she was the Chosen One. She never doubted the cat's mystical powers. He'd never let her down in the past. He had already saved her life once from the deadly fangs of a rattlesnake. He was a gift from the gods. They had given him special powers. He would never die and could travel over any distance throughout all time. She had no idea how he would do it, but she was sure he'd use his powers to find the path for her to fulfill her mission to redeem Kashom's honor.

They had been searching for ten minutes, and Jeannie decided it was rest time. From the corner of his eye, Danny spotted her sitting. He waved at her, letting her know all was cool. He and Tony kept searching. Jeannie had trouble relaxing. The haunting question loomed in her mind: *How can I help the royal prince of Kopaz bring the gift of eternal youth to my people—a gift they've waited centuries for?*

She looked to the sky for answers. And then suddenly, glancing down, she spotted two black eyes set in a steely gray face moving cautiously toward her hand. The blue-bellied lizard had been catching the morning rays, stretched out on the rock she was sitting on. The creature moved cautiously to inspect her soft white fingers. It was like a cat full of curiosity. It slowly moved its little feet and inched forward.

Jeannie flicked her fingers. In an instant display of speed, it raced in the opposite direction. Its long gray tail curved to steady it as it disappeared under the rock.

Jeannie laughed to herself. *Zanzee is not motivated by curiosity. His actions are directed by the gods! Will he be the navigator again today? I hope so!*

A loud voice thundered through the air. "Jeannie, why are you sitting? It's treasure-finding time! Come on! Let's go!" hollered Danny.

She jumped to her feet and raced to his side, laughing easily. "All right! Get to work, Mr. Danny!"

He bent over and rolled over a large rock, moved his head, and glanced up at her. He puckered his lips, smirked, and answered, "Look, Jeannie, your interpretations have set us on this venture—what have you found?" Looking at her, he hesitated. Then his eyes opened wide, and he laughed in delight.

Nonchalantly, she answered, "Oh, nothing!" as she skipped away and started jumping back and forth over the brook. He laughed again. They all went back to work looking for the special rock. They searched in silence; only the sounds of the desert creatures filled the air.

After a long five minutes, Jeannie sighed. "Have you guys found anything?" she asked, her voice competing with the song of a meadowlark perched on the scrub cedar tree not far from the end of the brook.

Danny kicked at a large rock. He had a frown on his face. He answered, "Nothing but old rocks that have been here for centuries."

His frown persisted and grew larger with the ensuing silence. She had no idea if it was for real. She was still figuring him out and wondered if it was his way of displaying humor.

Then he asked, in a somewhat discouraged voice, "Jeannie, do you really think some mystery person is trying to communicate with us?"

"*Yep!*" Jeannie said without hesitation as she hopped over the brook. In her mind, it was clear who was leading the search. *He's not a mystery man. He's Kashom.* But for now, she had a challenge—to bring Danny on board. Selecting her words carefully, she continued, "Danny, I don't know. I guess all we can do to find out is do our best. If we don't find anything, well, what have we lost? These things are for sure—someone put those markings on White Face Cliff and the Biblia Reina-Valera references, and they describe this small brook we're following to a T—is that not correct?"

He listened to her as he punted a rock he'd just turned over. It rolled down a small incline onto an anthill. He chuckled to himself. *Little red creatures, you just got a big knock at your door!* He smiled slightly, but his expression soon faded back to a frown.

Jeannie said, in all seriousness, "Danny, put a smile on your face."

Danny had had a good teacher—his mother. He entwined his fingers, locking his hands together, and covered his face with them. Then he slowly slid his locked hands down his face, exposing a smile.

Jeannie laughed. "That's good, Danny, real good! Seriously, Danny, I guess all we can do is hope—hope that we'll find the rock with a hand on it—hope that we're led to something worthwhile. Hope is all we have. Do you know that hope is a good thing? Hope is the difference between having a good life and having a bad life. Danny, if we have hope, I believe the gods will step in and help us!" But the expression on Danny's face reminded her that she didn't have to philosophize to him. *Danny is the one with hope—his hope is really the driving factor behind our quest for adventure.*

Danny seemed at a loss of what to say in return. First he looked at her. Then he fumbled with his hands. He rolled the sleeves of his T-shirt around his biceps a little higher in an effort to relieve the pressure. His massive arm muscles were being strangled by his sleeves.

Sensing his uneasiness, she smiled wistfully, and her love for him grew deeper.

His head turned, and he was looking intently at her now. "Jeannie," he said in a quiet voice, "you're my best friend. I know I kid around and tease you sometimes, but that's because I think so much of you. You've been my strength when life turned bleak for me—and yes, I realize that hope is the force that gives me the strength to forge on." Watching her, he got a lump in his throat. He motioned to her. "Come over here by me. I want to hold your hands. I want to be near you." His voice choked up.

Jeannie was lost for words, but she was not lost for thought. *Oh, my wonderful Danny, you're my pillar of strength. I just hope that we find the lost treasure you're looking for.* Walking up to him, she said, "Danny, here are my hands. I want to hold you. Come close."

She pulled him into her arms and embraced him. As they held each other, time stood still for Jeannie. *Wow! His body is next to mine! My heart is pounding—my body is trembling!*

For a long moment, Danny looked at her, his eyes filled with compassion. "Jeannie, do you ever think about the future, and where our lives might end up?" He held her face in his hands and gently whispered in her ear. "Do you have a little twitch in your heart? I sure do!"

Her eyes locked with his. "Danny, you have no idea! If you think your heart has a little twitch in it—mine is going crazy with twitches! And, yes, I do think about our lives and the future."

Tony picked up the rock he just rolled over. He threw it into the brook, making a loud splash to get their attention. "Okay, you guys. This is not *Gone with the Wind*. This is *Back with the Rock*! Jeannie, you're not Scarlett O'Hara, and Danny, you're not Rhett Butler. We're not Gone-with-the-Winders. We're Rock-Backers, so get with the program!"

Danny and Jeannie laughed hysterically. "Yep, Tony, you sure can make us laugh! Humor is good!" said Danny. He gave Jeannie a love slap on her rear with his large right hand and said, "Yeah, Jeannie, we'll have fun later. Right now, Tony wants us to find the treasure. Let's go!"

This time Jeannie did nothing to provoke him. Her eyes flashed encouragement at him.

With a zip in his stride, Danny started walking toward the brook where Tony was standing. "You're right, Tony. We need to find the lost Incan treasure. When we do, I'll give my mom a giant gemstone."

Jeannie listened to Danny talk about his mom. A tear ran down her cheek. *I know how much he dreams of finding riches: the gold, silver, and precious jewels that he wants to give his mother. He thinks the treasure will make the pain of losing her lover and his father go away. Bless his heart! He does love his mom.*

She thought about their lives in CoalVille. As Jeannie watched Danny, she realized that he represented the entire community of CoalVille in so many ways. Her mind whirled. *Be patient, my love. The gods will help us.* Watching him walk toward Tony, she said, "Danny, hope is a good thing." He stopped and turned to look at her. "We must hang onto the hope we have. I think our lives are changing." Jeannie blew him a kiss.

"Yeah, Jeannie—hope is a good thing!" This time Danny sighed as he spoke. *Is there hope for a better time in a distant future?*

And with that, the hunt for a special rock was under way once more. Jeannie watched her friends turn over rocks. They shook their heads and went to the next one.

Her heart ached. She desperately wanted success. *They turn over a rock and find nothing—they walk to the next one and turn it over. They keep doing it over and over—and each rock is turned over in vain. I know Danny needs his friends more than ever. I must be there for him. He wants desperately to find his lost Incan treasure—the treasure he thinks pirates hid someplace around CoalVille so long ago.*

It was hard for her to watch him. His dreams of finding treasure in the Scarlet Desert were coming up bust. Jeannie was a realist, and her thoughts were more down-to-earth. *Finding treasure is what a lot of people dream of—but those dreams are just fantasy!*

She couldn't let the boys know that she had doubts. She was caught between the hope of fulfilling her mission as Neferzul and being a realist about not finding hidden treasure.

The sun was climbing. Its rays were heating up the desert. Jeannie called to the boys. "Hey, guys," Jeannie yelled out, "found anything yet?"

They answered in unison, "*Nope!*"

Her mind searched for answers. Then it hit her. It was like a ton of bricks fell on her doubting brain. *It's the Biblia Reina-Valera connection. It has to do with the Bible verse—yes, that's our clue.* She pushed away the doubts that clouded her thinking and screamed, "Guys, let's study the verses again—there may be a clue we missed."

She startled Danny. He didn't get it. "Isn't that what we have been doing?" he asked, giving Jeannie a puzzled look.

Jeannie held her ground. "*No!*" she said emphatically. "We've been walking along either side of the brook near the end of its journey, rolling over rocks and looking at them." She pulled her note from her back pocket and said, "This is what the verse says. 'You shall find them at the end of the brook.' Well, the 'you' is 'we,' and we haven't been searching at the end of the brook. Now, let's look at something else in this verse—it says, 'you shall find them.' It doesn't say you *may* find them, or you *might* find them, or you *could* find them. Do you get my point? *Shall* is a very strong word. Basically, it says if we search at the end of the brook we'll find them, *so let's get finding!*"

It was quickly agreed that her suggestions would head them in the right direction. The tempo was on the rise. Jeannie was revising the search operation. She had always been the leader of the pack. Now she took charge again and blurted out commands to her friends. "Danny, get the pry bar from your truck. Tony, you make a grid around the end of the brook—make it twenty feet by twenty feet, using one-foot squares for the grid size. We'll try one poke per square."

"Aye, aye, lady general!" Danny said. "Your command is our wish, Your Highness!" His eyes sparkled as he chuckled with delight. Running in the direction of his truck, he thought about his love's words: "The gods will step in and help us out." *Yeah, Jeannie, maybe the gods will smile on us today! I hope they do! Let's hope the gods help us find the treasure!*

Reaching over the side of the truck bed, he grabbed his iron pry bar, which was lying next to the shovel and bucket. As he carried it back to the end of the brook, he watched his friends draw horizontal and vertical lines on the ground. They used tree branches as tools. Their grid was taking shape, centered around the sinkhole where the brook vanished into the desert sands. He thought, *Wow, there are going to be a lot of pokes in the ground.*

That thought must have been traveling the airwaves, as Tony's next remark was in sync with what Danny was thinking. "Jeannie, do you know what an area of twenty square feet divided into one-foot squares means? We have to poke the ground four hundred times!"

Danny's keen eye noticed a movement. He walked to Jeannie's side. She was busy making lines in the dirt, so she didn't notice. But what he saw was out of place five miles from CoalVille in the middle of the desert.

"Hey! There's your cat—back again—down by that bush. What do you make of that?" Danny yelled unexpectedly. "He's over there, digging for something! What do you think he's doing there? What's he digging for? Hey, he helped us once. Maybe he knows something!"

"I knew it!" Jeannie screamed. "I am the Chosen One!"

Danny's jaw dropped. He took his eyes off Zanzee. "What the hell did you just say?"

Oh my god, what did I just say? thought Jeannie. She scrambled for words. "Oh, I meant to say that I'm your chosen one! You chose me!"

He didn't buy her comeback. He knew he'd heard what he'd heard. "Jeannie, who's the Chosen One?"

With no words to give, she ignored him. She said nothing for a long thirty seconds. He waited patiently. Then, changing the subject, she continued, her voice filled with exuberance. "He's telling us where to look—he did it once, and now he's doing it again."

He thought, *Oh well, I guess it's not important. We've got bigger fish to fry.*

Jeannie reached a new level of excitement. Her mind raced. *Oh my god! Zanzee does have a special role—he's navigating the way for Kashom to redeem his honor. I am the Chosen One. What do I have to do?*

"Yeah, you guys!" Tony jumped into the excitement. "He's standing by a sagebrush that is a lot bigger than all the rest, and he's digging, telling us it's underground!"

Danny remembered the large bush. It was at the spot where the brook vanished into the desert sands. "It's the marker!" yelled Danny.

Their excitement was building. Tony knew this was the big test. Either they would find something, or they would pack their bags and head back to CoalVille. Tony's heart pounded. He looked at the flat rock next to the bank where the brook disappeared. "We were here earlier. If you didn't know what you were looking for, this rock and bush would not seem out of place. But that is not the case," Tony said.

"Tony, take the pry bar and poke all around that bush—everywhere— all around it, in it, the whole area surrounding it," Jeannie shouted with excitement.

Tony lifted the pry bar high above his head with his entire might and drove it into the ground as hard as he could. The pry bar came to an abrupt stop with a loud THUD.

"Ouch," Tony squealed. "Damn it! That hurt!"

The sound of the impact and Tony shaking his hands energized Danny and Jeannie. They raced to where he was standing. Danny's face lit up like a neon sign—specifically, a Coors Beer sign saying, "It's party time!"

The excitement could not be stopped. "What did you hit?" shouted Danny.

"Damned if I know!" yelled Tony.

Danny didn't wait for an explanation. He grabbed the pry bar and started poking it into the ground at the base of the large sagebrush. "Jeannie, run back to the truck and get my shovel," Danny shouted with overwhelming joy.

This time it was Jeannie who was filled with ecstasy as she raced through the desert in her body-tight white T-shirt and skimpy cutoffs. She was back in a flash. "Here ya go, Danny," she squealed as she handed him his shovel.

It didn't take long for Danny to uncover the top of the object. "This thing is only one foot below the top of the ground," Danny shouted, throwing dirt from the hole as fast as he could. Sand started falling from around the edges back into the hole. He realized the shovel wasn't working. "Jeannie, you and Tony use your hands."

They hung their arms and heads into the hole as they lay on their bellies, scraping away the sand. Jeannie's white T-shirt was turning brown. She didn't care.

They removed dirt from the top of the rock and piled it in mounds away from the edge of the hole. Danny used his shovel to systematically scrape it back from where they were digging.

Then, suddenly, the noonday silence in the Scarlet Desert was broken with shouts of joy that hung in the air like the persistent sound of a bell in a church steeple on a Sunday morning.

"We've found it! Look at that! Eureka!" Tony yelled. He brushed sand from the impression in the rock, his fingers tracing the indentations of a handprint.

"Yep, it's a hand," Tony shouted. "We've found it!"

If excitement had been treasure, three teenagers on a warm spring day in the desert had just struck it rich.

Danny turned to Jeannie, reached out, and found her hand. He gently pushed her hair from her eyes and grinned. Tears ran down her cheek. His hands brushed dirt from her shirt.

He couldn't stop smiling. "I told you the pirates were here! I'm so happy, guys. We found it—we found it—just look at it! Ain't that the most beautiful thing you've ever seen. I just know that Pirate Pete was here. Some old pirate put his hand on this rock and made an imprint of it. He did! I just know he did!" Danny was beaming from ear to ear.

"We did find it." Jeannie touched Danny's face with her hand. Watching Danny bask in his glory, she chuckled under her breath. *You silly boy. No, Danny, not pirates. I think it has to do with the Legend of Kashom—you don't even know who he is, but maybe we'll all find out. Tony is on the right track, but Tony, it's more than a petroglyph. It's a marker. Yes, Danny and Tony, what we have just found is the mark of a new journey that will change our lives forever.*

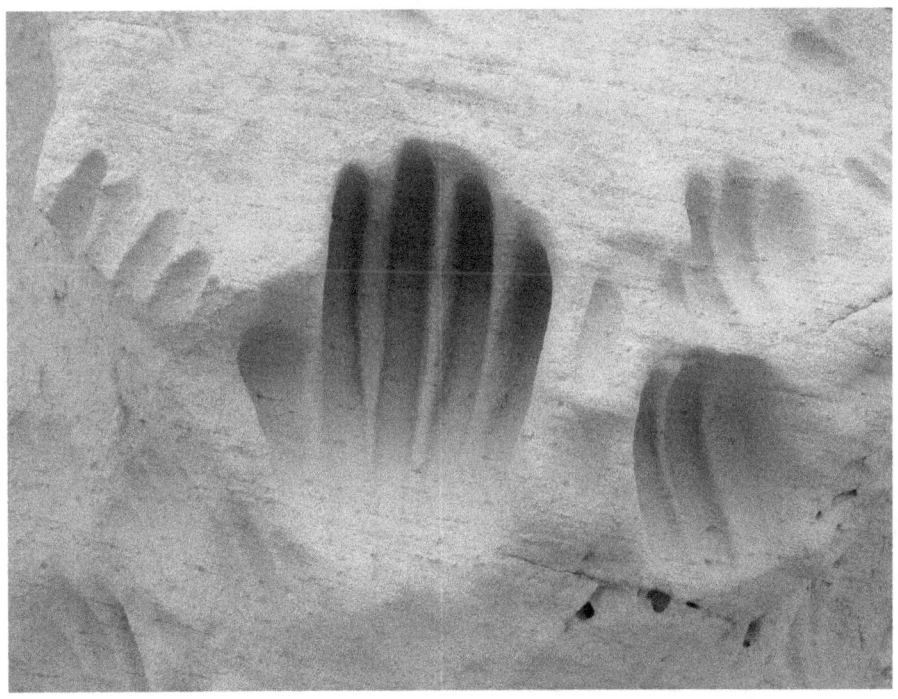

Danny gently grabbed Jeannie's arm and pulled her to him. Her feet went airborne as he lifted her body and swung her around. He carefully slowed his swinging motion and set her feet on the ground. "Jeannie, you were right on. Look at this thing—just look at it! It's a rock with a handprint on it! We've found the clue! We're on our way! Yes! Jeannie, hope is a good thing!"

, Danny's dream of finding treasure intensified with visions of pirate loot. *The rock with a hand on it is covering up the Incan treasure—I just know it is. There's a treasure just waiting for us!*

CHAPTER 20

Supernatural

Aconstant gurgling sound erupted from the hole that marked the spot. The sparkling brook's water received its final rays of sunlight at the sinkhole where its journey ended. A swirling current caused by the desert sands gobbling it up was its last farewell before it disappeared into an unknown darkness beneath the ground.

"Oh my god, Danny! Be careful! Don't get near the sinkhole. Dig on this side. I don't want you falling into an abyss!" screamed Jeannie.

The ground beneath Danny's feet was hard and barren. He felt safe.

"Don't worry," he said, jumping over the hole he'd started to dig next to the large sage bush. "We'll get this done without anyone getting hurt."

Danny surveyed the possibilities and determined the best spot for Jeannie and Tony to help him. "I need some help. You guys stay on this side of the rock, and you'll be fine," he said, pointing to where he wanted them.

Age-old dirt had held the rock firmly in its resting place for who knows how long. Danny used his shovel to dig around the sides of it, while Jeannie and Tony removed the dirt that Danny scraped free. Systematically, they piled it several feet from the hole Danny was digging. Ten minutes passed, and finally the large rock with the hand petroglyph on it was ready to be moved out of its hole.

A plan was needed. Danny looked at the situation and thought to himself, *No, not quite yet—that's one heavy rock. I'll need to dig a trench as a pathway, so we can roll it out of the hole.*

Digging a ten-foot trench in the shape of a ramp leading from the hole, Danny, in a matter of seconds, had his face covered with sweat and dirt. This time he piled the dirt between the hole he was digging and the sinkhole the brook vanished into.

"Okay, let's roll this rock out!" hooted Danny. "Got this trench good and wide. Let's move it!" He looked at Jeannie with his ear-to-ear grin and said, "I told you the pirates were here!"

"Danny, why do you have to be so dramatic?" Jeannie said in her sweet little way.

Wiping sweaty dirt from his brow, he replied, "Jeannie, we have treasure to find, and we're looking at its hiding place, so let's quit worrying about drama!"

The rock was much bigger and heavier than even Danny imagined. He motioned for Tony to help him. Together, they got behind the rock and tried to budge it.

He stepped back away. *Hmm,* he thought. *Now what?* His hand came to his face with his thumb under his chin and index finger over his lips. Tapping his finger, he glanced up at her. "No luck. Come on, Jeannie—get in here with us and start pushing."

Jeannie accepted his request with glee, but even together, all three kids were unable to budge the rock. Danny had an idea. "Tony, grab that log over there," he said, pointing to where he was looking.

Tony kicked the log with his foot to roll it over. He was deathly afraid of snakes and wanted to make sure one was not hiding under it. There was none.

"Here, Danny," Tony said as he handed him the log and jumped back into the hole.

"All right, we'll use this as our lever," Danny said, pushing the end of it several feet under the rock. "Okay, good to go."

He grabbed the end of the log sticking out from under the rock and put his weight on it. The rock budged. He managed to move it one foot. He didn't know what to do next. He pondered. He spotted a smaller rock not far from the large sage bush.

"Tony, get that smaller rock over there. We need it. This damn thing is heavy—it's putting a lot of pressure on this log. Hurry!"

Quickly, Tony jumped out of the hole and raced to get what Danny had asked for. It was the size of a basketball and very heavy. He locked his hands together with interlaced fingers to form a sling in which to carry it. He carefully got back into the hole and placed it behind the large rock, stabilizing it so Danny could release the pry lever.

The plan was now in motion. They used the pry lever to move the rock a small distance, put the smaller rock behind it to keep it from rolling back into the hole, and repeated the process.

It took fifteen minutes of pushing, cussing, and grunting to finally get the rock rolled to the top of the ramp. Danny held onto the end of the log sticking out from under the rock, stabilizing it while he waited for Tony to move the smaller one into place.

The gurgling sound captured Danny's attention. Waiting for Tony to do his job, he turned and gazed at the sinkhole only a few feet away. He stared at the brook vanishing into its abyss.

"Man alive, this thing is heavy!" Jeannie commented as she took her hands off the rock.

Danny turned his head from the direction of the brook to look at Jeannie. At that moment, the log flipped out of his hand. The rock started rolling back into the hole.

Tony was kneeling directly in its path. He had his hands on the smaller rock. He jerked them away so as not to get them crushed when the two rocks smashed together. Scrambling, he tried to get out of the way of the rolling rock. He fell on his back, lying in the trench directly in the path of the oncoming rock. Both his eyes flew wide open, and his first vision was white puffy clouds drifting in the blue sky above. He froze. Rigid as a statue, he braced himself to be steamrolled by the rock looming just up the trench.

He screamed in panic, "Help me! My god, help me!"

Momentarily, the large rock stopped its movement as it crashed into the smaller one. Its motion was not arrested for long. The smaller rock was pushed into the soft desert sand by the weight of the larger one.

Thoughts of horror raced through Tony's mind. *This thing is going to roll over me and crush me to death. I'm going to die!*

Lying prone on his back, his arms extended in reflex motion, Tony frantically reached his hands and searched for something to grab. They dug into the loose dirt. His fingers squeezed around the desert sands, which sifted through them like the sands in an hourglass. With only seconds away from sure death, he screamed, "Oh my god—get it off me! Get it off me! It's going to crush me!"

Her face contorted with horror, Jeannie screamed in terror as she watched helplessly.

Tony's face wrenched as he braced for death from the crushing rock.

Danny panicked. For a few seconds, he stood motionless. He gawked at the small rock disappearing under the large one as it started its downward journey in the trench again. His mind filled with thoughts of doom. *That rock is going to kill Tony!* Then, quickly, he jumped around the rock and straddled Tony with his legs. He placed his hands on the rock and gave it a giant shove.

"Hold on, Tony!" screamed Danny. "I'll get this thing off you!" He stared down at his friend's face lying on the ground between his legs. Their eyes locked. Every muscle in Danny's body bulged as he did battle with the rock. He never took his eyes off Tony.

Jeannie was in sheer panic. Every inch of her body shivered out of control as she watched the episode unfold in front of her. Her shrill screams of horror filled the air as she watched her two best friends stare death in its face. Her mind filled with horrific images of their bodies crushed under the rock. *My god, Danny! We need the gods' help! Help us!*

With all his might, Danny gave the rock a shove. Miraculously, it stopped its downward motion. Slowly, inch by inch, he was able to roll it back up the trench.

With one last shove, it was out of the hole and stabilized. "Holy shit! That is one heavy rock!" he managed to say between gulps of air.

Jeannie's heart soared. She could not believe her eyes. She stood gaping at him. He had looked like Atlas holding the Earth in his hands— but instead of the world, he had held up a rock of death with a hand carved on it "Danny, that rock moved for you," she squealed. "Where did you get that strength?"

His white T-shirt was soaking wet with sweat. His body was shaking. He used his forearm to wipe away the sweat that was running down his brow into his eyes.

He looked at her and managed to smile as he said, "Jeannie, it just happened. Maybe the gods stepped in to save Tony's life. I don't know—it just happened." Danny took a deep breath. Turning his head, he looked at his best friend lying prone in the trench behind him. "Tony, are you okay?" Then, in jest with the biggest smile on his face: "Tony, what the hell are you lying down for? Are you taking a nap? We've got treasure to find! No nap time now!"

Tony's face tried to smile, but it couldn't. His body released the tension that had overtaken it. He started shaking. "Sorry, Danny. I'm cold. I think I'm okay! My leg hurts—it's not—I—I don't think its broken, but I think it is bruised very badly!" He was struggling for words and shaking as he looked up at his best friend. "Danny, you saved my life. There are not enough ways on the earth to say thank you. As long as I'm alive, I'll never forget this day." He stopped speaking and just stared at Danny. Then he said, "Let me get my breath. I'll lie here for a few more minutes. My energy is sapped."

For a few moments, there was silence. Mother Nature's creatures, scurrying around their homes in the desert, made the only sounds the three teenage kids heard as they remained motionless, thinking about their escape from the hand of death that had just passed them by—thanks to Danny.

Danny's efforts to shake off the tension delivered by the hand of fate remained on Tony's mind. His jovial method wasn't working.

Jeannie had something else on her mind. First she looked at Tony in the hole, then at Danny. A puzzled expression crept over her face. She broke the silence. "Danny, you were unbelievable! Are you supernatural?" Her eyes never left his. Her facial expression left no doubt that she was serious. She questioned him again. "Are you?"

Dropping his forearm, wet with dirt and sweat, he said, "Jeannie, as I said, sometimes things happen I can't explain. Anyway, let's move on."

That was not good enough. She asked, "What was that green light under your shirt?"

This caught him by surprise. He wrinkled his brow as he answered with a question, "What green light, Jeannie? What are you talking about?" Her stare did not go away. Her look meant business. He answered once more, "Oh, that! It's just my emerald ring on a chain around my neck. The sun must have shone on it."

Danny pulled the neck of his T-shirt down and showed his ring for a brief second.

Jeannie remained puzzled. She had a strange look on her face as she thought, *That was weird! Oh, it probably was the sun—the chain it is on must have flipped partway out of his shirt when he jumped behind the rock and started pushing.*

Danny redirected his attention to his friend in the hole, still on his back and queasy. "Tony, you okay? You're sure?"

Looking up at his lifesaving friend, he said, "Yeah, Danny, I'm okay, thanks to you! I owe you my life! How can I ever repay you for what you did? You're one hell of a guy! None better!"

Danny detected the mood change. He jumped at the chance to add humor and move on. Smiling, he hooted, "So what the hell is my best friend doing in a hole? We've got treasure to find. Get the hell out of there! You owe me nothing. I'll cherish your friendship until the day I die!"

He reached and grabbed Tony's outstretched hand. For a few precious moments, they said nothing. He just grinned as he helped Tony stand and held him until he was steady on his feet again. He put his arm around his best buddy and gave him a bear hug.

The somber mood had lifted. Conversation between all three returned to normal.

"Tony, you're my best friend," Danny said, laughing, still with his arms around him, "and I'd save your life again. But do you know what?" He paused and dropped his arms from Tony, then turned and looked at Jeannie. He reached out and gently touched her face with his sweaty, dirty hand.

She didn't care how dirty he was. He was her hero. Then he caught her by surprise. "I'd go to the ends of the earth and back for my love standing next to me!" At that statement, their eyes locked. Then he laughed and said, "Besides, we have bigger fish to fry right now than talking about rolling a rock off my best buddy! Look at that rock—just look at it!"

Jeannie tingled all over with joy, her mind exploding with thoughts she'd never experienced. *Oh, my gosh! He called me his love! It's not just my body he's interested in—it's me. He's falling in love! And so am I!*

Jeannie's eyes filled with tears as she stared at the boy who had just set her heart on fire. She moved close to him and touched his face. Her spirit raced to a height where it had never been. It was at that moment she knew—yes, he was special. He was a boy—a boy with boyish dreams of finding lost treasure—but he was much more. He would risk his life for his friends. He'd do anything for her.

The smile she flashed at Danny was like the noonday sun warming the earth. Knowing it wasn't just her body he was interested in set her heart in motion. It pounded like a drum in her chest. *Oh, my gosh! We've found the mark to start our journey—the journey of Kashom's legend—and I have found my love.*

CHAPTER 21

Treasure or Hoax?

❧

A slight breeze fluttered the blades of grass between Jeannie's feet, tickling them with gentle strokes. Without warning, daylight dimmed as a cotton-white cloud drifted quietly overhead and hid the face of the sun. With the sudden decrease in the sun's brightness, Jeannie turned and looked to the sky as a tear rolled down her cheek. She knew her journey had begun. She had no idea where it would take her. *We have started our journey to an unknown future. I know our lives will change; I know we'll have a better tomorrow—a tomorrow that could fill our lives with happiness. We are solving the clues—we found the rock with a hand on it. What will we find under the rock?*

The fondness in her heart for the young man standing next to her was gripping her entire body with emotions that rippled across her skin, causing it to tingle. She glanced at Danny from the corner of her eye. His deep-set green eyes were showcased by strong cheekbones, wet with sweat and dirt that glistened in the sun. She reached for his hand as her mind churned with thought. *He just saved Tony's life—what a super guy! He has a gift that sets him apart—his strength! Have the gods graced him with something special?*

Time was marching on, the sun making its daily journey. The desert sky was alive with the silent motion of a golden eagle gliding effortlessly as it circled its unsuspecting prey on the ground. Jeannie's glance at the eagle reminded her that they were exhausted from moving the heavy rock and needed nourishment as well. To her, it was evident from their expressions that Danny and Tony were getting to the end of their energy levels.

"You guys, good job—let's take a rest and have lunch. If I do one more thing without food, you can just bury my dead body in that rock hole," said Jeannie.

For a few moments, Danny and Jeannie stood next to the large rock with a hand carved on it. Their eyes locked, and their hands met. His fingers entwined with hers and he pulled her next to him.

She stood on her tiptoes and gently put her cheek on his. She sweetly whispered into his ear, "Danny, you just saved Tony's life. You're special— you know that! You mean the world to me!"

It was now Danny who had sparkling wet eyes from emotion. His hands found her face. They held her as he whispered into her ear, "Jeannie, I feel the same about you—I'd follow you to the ends of the earth!"

A momentary flash of joy coursed through her body. She looked to the sky, where the sun was nearing its zenith.

Danny was not looking at her now. He glanced at Tony, sitting not far from them. He was still tense from the rock incident. Realizing Jeannie had had a good suggestion, he said, "You're right—we need a break. I'm exhausted, and Tony has to be hurting."

At twelve fifteen, the sun reached its apex. A temperature five degrees warmer than the morning made it a perfect sixty degrees.

Jeannie spotted the perfect dining spot. It was clear in her mind— lunch hour in the shadow of a lone scrub cedar tree near the water's edge at the base of the cliff. The view from a Fifth Avenue New York restaurant could not have been better. The mirror surface of the pond was alive with images of white clouds floating through the deep blue sky. A light afternoon breeze sent ripples dancing across the surface, making the reflections of clouds quiver and pulsate in rhythm with the sudden flurry of air.

Jeannie could always count on Mother Nature. She had never let her down, and now she had her desert table ready for guests. She'd been working on this rock table for centuries, honing and polishing it with rain, wind, and sand. It was perfect for three desert treasure hunters to have lunch on.

Jeannie picked a bouquet of bright red desert flowers and set them in the middle of the flat rock. She used a handful of prairie grass for a whisk broom to sweep loose sand from their lunch table.

She grabbed Danny's hand, pulling him gently, and pointed to where she wanted him to sit. It was a perfect spot—a little shade from the cedar tree and a little sun.

"Okay, guys, time for lunch," she said.

Sitting next to him, she recalled a comment Danny had made earlier during their joyride in his red racer. She was curious what was so sweet in his lunch bag. She slid over closer to him and touched his face.

"So, Danny, what's in your bag—meat loaf or peach pie?" Jeannie asked in her sweet, girlish voice. "I know you have something good in there."

With a slight smile, not looking directly at her, he replied, "Actually, Jeannie, which would you like? I've got three things: ham sandwiches, chocolate-chip cookies, and peach pie!"

"Just a bite of your pie and a couple of cookies! You know my sweet tooth," sighed Jeannie.

A quick glance at Tony told Danny that he was being left out of the conversation, so he asked, "What would you like, Tony?"

Tony lay back quietly on the rock under the shade of the cedar tree. He said nothing. He seemed to think of Mother Nature's table was more of a bed.

A quiver of concern jangled Danny's body. "Are you okay?"

This time, Danny got Tony's attention. Tony rolled to his side and looked at him. "Oh, I'm okay. My mom made me a kielbasa sandwich— my favorite." Not being hungry, Tony rolled onto his back again. He was preoccupied with something flying overhead. It was unusual for a vulture to circle humans. Tony's curiosity was piqued by the black bird's unusual flight pattern.

Jeannie suspected his preoccupation was with a golden eagle gliding through the sky. It was a perfect opportunity. She was experiencing the miracle of young love, bringing two hearts together in the Scarlet Desert. Their quest for treasure had started their adventure, but love was now the guiding light by which they would forge their path into an unknown future.

Danny heard her giggling. She had picked up a branch from the cedar tree and was teasing him by flicking his hair with it. "Don't you guys just love this time of year?"

Danny reached out and grabbed the branch she was holding. He wound his fingers around it and gave it a little tug. She didn't let go. He whistled his shrill trademark whistle. She dropped it. He said, "Gotcha!" She laughed.

She grabbed his lunch sack and put it behind her. He grinned and put his hand on the rock and pretended it was a mouse. He let his fingers walk across the rock and onto her legs. Laughing, he said, "Got lunch?"

She giggled and pulled her arm around, holding it in front of him. "Yep!"

The fifteen minutes of lunchtime—mostly Jeannie having fun with Danny and Tony staring at a black bird—were soon gone.

Jeannie's thoughts drifted from Danny to something more serious, and she mused, *The sun is giving warmth and life to everything in this paradise called "home on the range." I wonder where Kashom is? He had to be the one who carved the hand in the rock—is the sun still gracing him with warmth? I hope so!*

Suddenly, Danny snapped his fingers forcefully to get everyone's attention. He couldn't wait to get back to the task of finding what was hidden beneath the rock. His mind was filled with thoughts of treasure— thoughts he'd had ever since he was a little boy. But now the thoughts were not just dreams. *This is not a time to wait, but a time to find the mysteries of treasure.* His rising levels of curiosity and excitement led him to say loudly, "I'm not waiting for you guys. I'm going to get the treasure. Just remember, you're dealing with *the* Danny Roberts, and when I'm rich, you poor folk will be licking my boots, and that's a fact." He laughed as he looked at Jeannie and Tony, who were engaged in small talk.

He jumped to his feet and raced off as fast as he could—which reminded Jeannie just what a great athlete he was. *Where does he get that speed? Where does he get his strength? His speed with the scorpion was incredible, and how was he able to roll that rock off Tony?*

Danny put his hand into the impression on the rock. As he waited for his friends to join him, he thought about the handprint. *The person who made this hand impression must have been about my size. I wonder how old he was? His hands were the same size as mine.*

Since his friends were still not moving as fast as he wanted them to, Danny blurted, "Come on, guys. Get over here! We have digging to do and treasure to find."

Jeannie waited patiently until Tony had finished his lunch and said, "I guess we had better hustle. Danny is impatient."

Tony laughed in delight, gobbling down the last of his sandwich. "Yeah, I'm done. Let's go. He's chomping at the bit!"

It was just a matter of minutes until the digging started again. Danny was at the helm with his shovel in hand, digging like a backhoe powered by a John Deere engine. Once more, the intensity of their excitement was on the rise.

Then it happened. A loud *clank* sound filled the air like the peal of a church bell as Danny's shovel came to an abrupt stop. The trios' emotions were flying higher than rockets; their spirits had been launched to the surface of the moon.

"We did it!" screamed Tony, his eyes wide open. He grabbed Jeannie's arm. He was shaking, no longer from the cold sweat that had swept over him an hour earlier but from uncorked, effervescent joy. He felt like he was on top of the world. Jeannie squeezed his hand with cries of delight.

Tony's breathing began to grow labored as he watched every move Danny made, realizing that a life-changing event was unfolding before his eyes.

"That *clank* sure is different from the *thud* noise caused by the rock!" Tony shouted. "That's a metal sound!"

His hands shaking, fingers grappling to hold his shovel, Danny couldn't look up. His fingers slipped on the handle. He dug faster with high-powered intensity, trying to expose the secrets of the treasure box. Dirt flew wildly with each scoop as he struggled to maintain control.

If the friends' excitement had been high when they had discovered the rock with the hand impression on it, the thought of a metal treasure box raised their excitement level to the height of the sun, which was showering its warm rays on the treasure hunters. Without hesitation, Tony jumped into the hole and helped Danny.

Jeannie watched the boys as they scraped away loose dirt from the buried object. Her eyes said it all. They twinkled like stars on a dark night. It was if she were in a dream world and witnessing a fantasy adventure unfolding before her very eyes. She could keep silent no longer. "It's a box—a metal box!" she screamed with shrill excitement. Her screams pierced the crisp springtime air at White Face Cliff, competing with other screams—howling screams from a black vulture flying overhead.

Little did they know that not far from where they were playing, having fun with their discovery, Mochcom, hiding behind his disguise of mental retardation, was stalking them. He was seeking the same treasure, but his hunt was not for riches. His eye was on controlling the power the treasure could release.

Jeannie's fantasy adventure came to a screeching halt. The howling screams of the vulture overhead drew her eyes upward and sent a chill down her spine. *Eerie! That's a creepy bird!* she thought.

Danny caught her looking at the sky. He knew it was something she did all the time, but this was unusual. They had just discovered something that could change their lives, and she was sky-gazing. "Come on, Jeannie. Quit staring at the bird. We've got treasure to get, and I want it!"

Tony's keen eyes saw the bird circling above again. He cringed. Watching Jeannie and Danny sent an uneasiness through his body. His sixth sense told him Jeannie was worried, and surely nothing short of imminent death would distract her attention from their treasure.

Jeannie gave Danny a brief, blank look. She lifted her head to look at the sky once more. The bird was gone. She looked away from where it had been flying and jumped into the hole with Danny.

His dirty, sweaty arm wrapped around her waist. Dirt was everywhere, but she didn't care. They were standing hip deep in a hole eight feet in diameter and four feet deep.

"I think we've removed most of the dirt around it," whispered Danny.

She squeezed his hand. "Danny, why are you whispering?" Jeannie asked.

He grinned. "Oh, Jeannie, I don't know." He looked at her. "It's your sweet little voice we need to hear—not mine!"

He studied the box, carefully examining every inch of it. His hands and fingers were all over it. "It has a little handle on one end, but it would be better if two of us lifted it out," Danny said as he placed his hands under one end. He nodded his head as he said, "Help me, Jeannie. Let's lift it out of here."

Jeannie and Danny grabbed opposite ends of the box and raised it to a point where they could set it on the sand near the large sagebrush. As they lifted the box from the hole, a tear came to Jeannie's eye.

Her mind was full of so many thoughts. *Boy, this thing seems heavy—or maybe I've lost my strength because of the excitement.* She didn't want to show weakness by dropping the corner she was holding or letting her friends see the tear in her eye. *Danny has finally found his treasure.*

Tony moved to the edge of the hole and helped them set the box on the dirt. His heart thumped loudly.

Danny put his hand on her cheek. "Jeannie, are you crying?" he asked, noticing the tear run down her cheek. He wiped her face with his fingers, leaving a streak of dirt. He laughed and said, "Oops! Now your face is dirty."

Her dirty face didn't matter to her. She mumbled to herself, "I've found the first piece of the mystery that the Chosen One will need."

Danny, his hand still on her face, strained to make out her words.

She sensed his awareness of her muffled utterance, so she moved closer and caressed his cheek gently. Wet with tears, her dark blue eyes smiled in their own special way. "No, Danny—I—well—I—I'm just as excited as you are. Our lives will change after today, I'm sure," she said in a low, sweet voice.

"Let me help you guys get out of the hole," Tony said, extending his hand.

He reached for Jeannie's hand and steadied her as Danny grabbed her waist and boosted her out. Next, he extended his hand to Danny. Instantly, Danny vaulted out of the hole, using Tony's hand to steady his jump.

Danny walked to Jeannie, picked up the box, and pressed against her. As they held the box to their sides, both of them were fiddling with it. After thirty seconds of fiddling, Danny pointed to the flat rock where they had had lunch. It was not only a perfect lunch table, still bearing Jeannie's centerpiece of bright red flowers, but also a perfect workbench. He said, "Let's set it there. It's a great spot to open it."

Huddled around the treasure box, they had one thing on their mind—the box's contents. Jeannie reached into Danny's back pocket and grabbed the white cloth that was sticking out of it. She stepped between Danny and Tony and pointed to the lid.

"How do we open this thing?" Jeannie asked as she wiped the dirt from it with Danny's handkerchief. Her cleaning exposed four T-shaped clasps—one at each corner of the box. *That was a dumb question—just snap back the clasps.*

Saying nothing, Danny watched her clean the lid. Then his hand searched for his Swiss Army knife. He found it in his right front pocket. He pulled it from his pocket and opened the screwdriver blade. "This will flip the T-clasps back—then, I think, we can lift off the top."

He pried the clasps back slowly and carefully lifted the lid from the box.

At last, there it was—an open treasure box displaying its contents to the bright desert sun. But the question was, what was it?

Danny's heart dropped. Jeannie's hand fell to her side. None of them had expected what they were seeing.

"What the hell is this? Where's the treasure? Is this a bow and arrow? A metal bow and arrow? Somebody is playing a joke on us!" Clearly, Danny's excitement had dropped to total disappointment, as evidenced by his facial expressions.

Both the bow and arrow were ten inches long and made of solid brass. At one end, the arrow had a sharp pointed head; on the other end were two feather-shaped vanes.

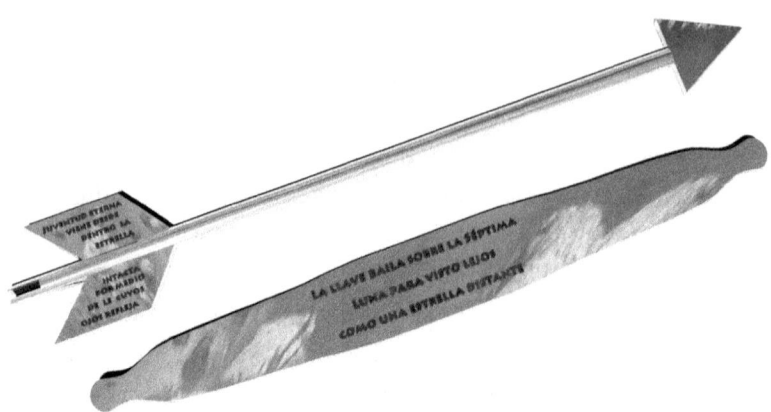

Jeannie grabbed Danny's arm and felt his tense body. Staring at him intensely, she could sense his disappointment. But then, she noticed something that made her squeeze his arm more tightly.

"W-what's that? It—it looks like gold! Is it?" She pointed to an object just partly visible, which was positioned under the bow in a cradle of its own.

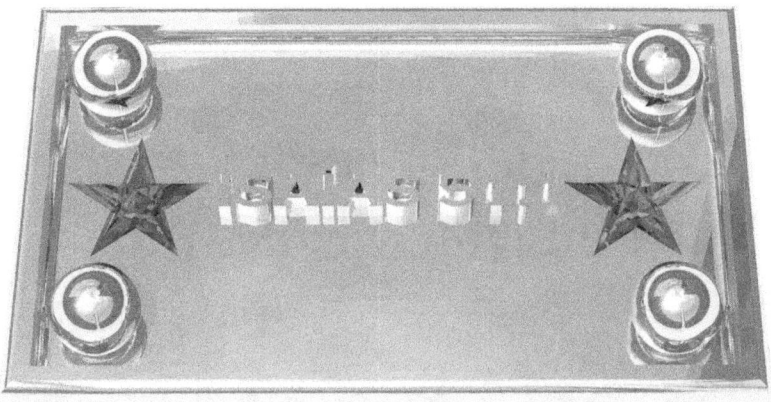

Danny stared, awestruck. He reached to grab it. "It's solid gold—it's pure gold—look at the gems—look! L-look at those four silver balls! It has jewels on it—look at these green stars! I'll bet they're emeralds! We—we are—we're rich! We've found it! We've found a treasure!"

CHAPTER 22
The Black Disciple

"A penny for your thoughts," Jeannie whispered in Danny's ear, her hot breath on his neck. Again, she took the silk scarf from her hair and teasingly touched his face with it, as if tickling him with a feather. His facial skin twitched spontaneously in response.

He pretended to ignore her. Her scarf was catching on his five o'clock shadow—his body was developing, and so was his beard.

"Prickly face, my love," she said, as she gently ran her hand across his stubble. She was watching him intently and knew exactly what he was thinking. He kept fiddling with their discovery, and she kept fiddling with him.

Danny looked at the gold slab carefully. His fingers stroked the emerald-green stars inlaid at each end, then moved along the outer edge. It was rounded, with no sharp corners. He caressed the yellow, silky gold and rubbed over the letters engraved at its center.

"I love your ponytail, Jeannie," said Danny. "It sways with a wiggle when you walk. But I also love when your silky hair is draped around your soft, white face." She giggled, and then he said, "Do you think this stuff has been here since the pirates took it from the Spaniards?" He glanced at her, still pretending to ignore her fiddling.

She knew how to get his attention. She'd just gotten a new hobby—having fun with Danny as she taught him the real meaning of the treasure hunt they were on. But she understood that would be a challenge. She was schooled in the culture of her people, which was centuries old. Her challenge was to get him on board with the Legend of Kashom and enjoy the ride with her first and only love.

"Danny! No, I don't think so. In fact, I don't think pirates put it here."

This time he looked at her, smiling, and thought, *Two can play this game.* "Well, you know that Spaniards stole the treasure from the Incan empire hundreds of years ago, and the pirates stole it from the Spanish conquerors!" he responded, keeping the game going.

At this point, she didn't know if he was serious or not, but there was no doubt in her mind. She was serious and knew it was not pirates. "I know all that, Danny—but pirates didn't put this stuff here!" Jeannie said, trying to make her point.

Tony had been listening to the playful bantering between Danny and Jeannie. He was back to his old self again, the rock accident a thing of the past. "And your point is, Miss Lone Tree?" Tony asked, as he listened to his friends engage in their pirate-or-no-pirate discussion.

Now it was time for Jeannie to make her point. There was no hesitation. "My point, Mr. Lopez, is that Peg Leg Peter the Pirate would never carry a brass bow and arrow and a little piece of gold thousands of miles to this godforsaken desert," Jeannie asserted.

"She's got a point—why in the name of Mother Mary would they?" Tony nodded his head in agreement.

Danny felt he had just gotten zinged by his two friends. Jeannie was clever, and he didn't have a comeback. He jumped into the conversation. "Wait, wait, wait," he said, wanting to be heard. "So why all the Spanish—on White Face Cliff, on the bow, on the arrow, on the gold plaque? Come on! The Spaniards had to have had something to do with all this stuff! By the way, who gets it? How are we going to divide this up?"

That statement sent a totally unexpected ripple through Jeannie's feelings. Suddenly she was faced with a new challenge. "We don't!" she snapped. A whole new dynamic had just emerged, and she quickly realized some rules had to be laid down. She stood quickly and used dramatic acting to make her point. She laughed and bowed slightly as if addressing royalty, then waved as if she were a stately politician. "Guys, here are the laws. What we find, nobody knows—or ever will know! Where we go, nobody knows—or ever will know! What we find stays with us! We do not talk to anybody about what we find—I mean anybody! Our secrets are our secrets and nobody else's! Nobody has dibs—*nobody has dibs*!"

The game wasn't working. Danny chimed in again. "Wait, you guys. What about my mom? Tony's mom? Tony damn near died an hour ago. What if he did? I don't know if I like these laws."

Suddenly, Jeannie knew she had a problem on her hands. It had to be settled fast. Her hand went up, one rigid finger in the air. "Guys, we do nothing with the treasure now. We'll figure it out later. Period!"

Danny had no comeback except to be a wise guy. "Well, I guess she made that perfectly *clear*—we're the braves, and she's the chief! She has *power*—we have none, nope, none at all!" Danny poked Tony's side to get his reaction.

Danny's attempt at humor fell on deaf ears. Tony was far from being a fool. He was street-smart and had realized Jeannie knew exactly what she was talking about. In quick retort to Danny's smart remarks, Tony stated his support for Jeannie. "Danny, she's right—fall in line," he snapped.

That caught Danny off guard. He said nothing. He frowned, his eyebrows pulling up in a way that expressed his disagreement.

Tony straightened now. His finger moved to the treasure box and tapped it while his mouth pulled down into a stubborn line. "If word gets out that we found a treasure at White Face Cliff, everybody and his cousin will be out here digging up the desert. We would be the losers! And who knows? We could find ourselves in real danger! Maybe even dead!" he snapped, even louder.

For a long moment, Tony looked at Danny. Jeannie remained silent. Tony drove his point home. "Danny, do you want to get us all killed? Do you want Jeannie in an early grave? Are you just thinking about your own welfare and not ours?"

Silence hit them like three tons of bricks.

After Tony's slam dunk, Jeannie's next move had to be to show a bit of diplomacy and soothe Danny's hurt feelings. These were stormy waters she had to navigate, but she was up for the challenge. For a long moment, she looked at Danny. Then she took charge. "Well, let me be blunt. I think there is more to this treasure than the few objects we just found. I don't know what more there is, but my hunch is that this stuff is just the tip of the iceberg!"

He was reading her body language. He wondered what she meant. *More? Just the tip of the iceberg?* He felt it might be time for some humor. "Your Royal Highness—my sweet princess—what thinkest thou to make such a bold statement? Knowest thou something we know not?" He chuckled.

Fortunately for Jeannie, Danny had just ended the contention and opened the door to peaceful harmony. Not slow on the uptake, Jeannie fired back her response. "Prince Danny, have you read the inscriptions on the bow, the arrow, and the plaque?"

Now he was stuck. He tried. But all he could do was stick his foot in his mouth. "No, Your Royal Highness, I have not." Danny laughed as he realized he'd just been zinged by Jeannie. He poked Tony in his side again.

"Well, my dear prince, you have much to learn!" Jeannie said with conviction.

Tony laughed to himself. *Well, do I keep score? If so, one for Jeannie and zip for Danny!*

Ka-boom! The crack of distant thunder brought all three kids back to the present—the serious present. The towering pillars of rock at the Boar's Tusk defined the northern horizon. Now black clouds hid them, and lightning was making a pathway for the approaching storm.

Jeannie cringed, knowing that the unpredictable path of the storm might lead right to the White Face Cliff. Her glance at Tony and then at the distant storm clued him in on her conclusion—make hay while the sun shines, for the storm is coming.

"All right, Your Royal Highnesses—what do we do next?" Tony asked soberly, as he listened to Jeannie and Danny cutting up.

"Let's see." Danny looked at his watch, resting in the palm of his hand. "It's one thirty. We only have a few hours left—let's spread this stuff out on the lunch-table rock and start figuring out what the inscriptions say."

It wasn't long until the aftermath of the storm reached them. A distant rain shower brought the fresh smell of sage to a large surrounding area. The storm headed west, leaving them in bright sunlight.

Jeannie savored the moment. *I love the smell of sage after a rainstorm—I wonder if we'll be blessed or cursed with rain this afternoon.* She got up from the spot she'd been sitting on and walked a few feet to the box, with its contents lying next to Danny. She picked up the gold plate and took a closer look at what was on it.

"Yes! Yes, you guys! There's more—much more! Our journey has just begun!" Jeannie's heart was pounding as she stared at the piece of gold in her hand.

The sun glistened on the gold and revealed the words "ISAÍAS 51:1."

"Hold this, Danny." Jeannie gave him the gold and took off running, taking off at a high-speed sprint to Danny's truck.

He watched her and yelled, "Where are you going?"

Not turning back, she yelled, "To the truck to get something! Be right back!"

He had parked his truck around a small hill from where they had been sitting, so as she raced around the hill, he lost sight of her.

She stopped just short of the door. She was out of breath. She heard something that sounded like a flapping noise behind her. She flinched but guessed it was just the wind. It wasn't. She heard it again. Her heart pounded. She had no idea what was behind her. She reached for the handle, flinging open the passenger door. She was about to jump into the truck when something heavy hit her in the back. She fell to the ground.

The tremendous force that slammed into her back felt to Jeannie like a ton of bricks had crashed into her. With no warning, she had no way to break the fall, so her face dug into the dirt, the collision delivering a smashing blow to her nose. Blood trickled out of her nostrils and seeped into the sand. She could only gasp with horror. Nothing had prepared her for this. She was face down in the dirt. Something was on her. She raised her head and screamed. Then she felt the weight lift from her back. She knew it had moved. Her mind raced in terror. *My god, what's going on? What is it?*

She turned her head in the sand and saw a large set of talons out of the corner of her eye. She screamed. The creature jumped back. She flipped over. Staring her in the face, not more than two feet from her, was a giant black vulture. It let out a howling scream and hit her with its outstretched wing.

She screamed again. The bird was relentless, not affected one iota by her screams. She grabbed a handful of dirt and pebbles, flinging them into the bird's face. Blinking wildly, it screamed and howled even louder.

Jeannie's screams sent a paralyzing shock through Danny's body, like a bolt of lightning had just hit him. Danny heard her second scream and the horrific howls from the vulture. His mind exploded with visions of Jeannie fighting for her life. He bolted to his feet and raced through the desert, hurtling over brush, hills, and rocks as if they were nonexistent.

He had no idea what was happening, but his unbelievable speed quickly propelled him around the hill, bringing him into full view of the episode taking place at his truck. The black bird of death was reaching for her jugular with its talons. Black Vulture was schooled in the art of death, and for him, Jeannie helpless on the ground was an easy kill.

The vision of the vulture ripping Jeannie's throat from her neck intensified Danny's motivation to tax his muscles to their ultimate strength. His incredible strength and speed propelled him to the rear of the truck within seconds.

Black Vulture's awareness alerted him to the intruder, and he flinched. That was his mistake. With lightning speed, Danny scooped up the rock at his feet and flung it at the bird.

Only the reflexes of Black Vulture, honed over centuries, kept the rock from its mark.

"Shit! I don't miss. What am I dealing with?" screamed Danny.

The force and speed of that throw were beyond human ability, thought Black Vulture. He had no intent of tangling with this unexpected force. He swiveled on his talons, hopped five large steps, and took off, raking at the air to get his flight in motion.

Danny turned his head from watching the departing vulture to Jeannie lying on the ground. He picked her up. Holding her in his arms like a small baby, he gently pulled her closer to his body and asked, "Are you okay?" She was crying. He kissed her cheek. "It's okay, Jeannie. He's gone. I have you now. He won't hurt you ever again."

He gently helped her stand. Her eyes were filled with tears. He wiped her cheek. Her entire body broke into a cold sweat, and she shook in uncontrolled jerks. Danny wrapped his arms around her and held her even closer as her body trembled next to his.

She stood on her tiptoes and put her face on his. Then she whispered, in a shaky voice, "Thank you, Danny. I don't know what it would have done to me if you weren't here. Thank you, my love. Thank you! Thank you!" Snuggling against him as close as physically possible, she started to regain her composure. He could feel her relax against him, and he felt relieved. "Can you walk?" he asked softly.

"Yes, my love," she whimpered. She dropped from her tiptoes and took a step back. Her hand came up, and she touched his lips. "You saved my life. Danny, I just love you."

Danny took her hand. "I'll carry your stuff. Let's go back to the pond where Tony is waiting," he said with a catch in his voice. He didn't want her to know; he was almost certain that she hadn't made the connection. He had, however. He was not dumb. His mind drifted to the incident that had occurred a few weeks back, and he cringed. *That bird was at my dad's funeral. I don't think Jeannie noticed it. I was curious then, but now I know there's something weird going on. I wondered why that bird was so close to the people at my dad's funeral. What the hell is up with a giant bird hanging around humans?*

Jeannie felt his body go rigid. She was not dumb either. She was aware that something was troubling him. "Danny, what's wrong?"

He stopped, turned, and embraced her, holding her next to him. "I'm just upset. That bird got me rattled. I'll be okay."

CHAPTER 23

The Further We Dig

Little did the three friends know that the deadly hand of fate hung over them.

As he watched Danny and Jeannie round the hill on their way back, Tony searched his mind for answers. He could find none. Events had him stumped. Within the past two hours, close encounters with fate had upended his and Jeannie's lives. In both cases, the young man now walking toward him had pried loose the fingers of death from its victim.

Tony was convinced. He had thought his close brush with death had been a random act of nature. Jeannie's had not been. The distressed look on her face had revealed an emerging threat. Tilting his head, he followed the vulture's sudden and swift flight through the deep blue sky. Its screaming howls sent a chill up his spine.

Suspecting someone was behind Jeannie's brush with death, he scrambled for answers, searching through the caverns of his mind. Someplace in the recent past, he had noticed the presence of that vulture, but he could not recall where. The question was this: Who was behind this vulture's actions, and when would it strike again?

Danny and Jeannie walked up to Tony. Tony thought questions were unnecessary because he already had the answers, but he asked anyway. "What happened? Are you guys okay?"

Danny's words came out slowly, and his face was distressed. "A large black vulture attacked Jeannie. I got there in time. It flew off."

Nodding his head, Tony said, "Yes, Danny, I saw him take flight." They exchanged a worried look.

Then, Danny slapped Tony's back cheerfully, a signal that they should shift the mood. Tony noticed how Danny's tone changed and how he took charge of moving forward and leaving terror behind.

"She's okay. Let's forget about the whole vulture thing and move on. We came to have fun today—let's not let a bird destroy it," said Danny, pointing at the gold plaque on the rock next to him.

Tony took the hint. He turned to Jeannie and asked, "What did you get?"

She also wanted to put her scrape with death behind her. "My Reina-Valera," she answered quietly. "We have another reference to look at."

Danny felt the knot in this stomach loosen just a bit. The gloomy mood caused by that terrible bird—the black disciple of Prince Dark Soul, although none of the three yet knew that truth—waned. The lure of hidden treasure once more dominated their thoughts.

Danny couldn't deny the success they had had with the petroglyphs they'd discovered on White Face Cliff. He thought, *Yes! There's no compensation required for success. Those Biblia Reina-Valera verses on the cliff just behind me were not a hoax or a wild-goose chase—they were pay dirt!*

"What is it, Jeannie? Where do we go next?" he asked. His eyes locked with hers. He knew Jeannie had identified another clue—another Reina-Valera verse. Their hearts started pounding.

Jeannie felt back to her old self. A smile crossed her face. Her eyes lit up. She decided to bring back the joyous mood back with a little drama. "Okay, I'm ready! We're on a treasure hunt! And guys, we're going to hit pay dirt—I can feel it in my bones!"

She looked up the Spanish verse and read it aloud. "*Los que seguís justicia, los que buscáis á Jehová: mirad á la piedra de donde fuisteis cortados, y á la caverna de la fosa de donde fuisteis arrancados.*"

She winked at Danny and Tony, who were standing together with their mouths open. "Oh that's right! Neither of you can speak Spanish! So, let's see, what does this say? What do we have here? What's this all about? Oh yeah, you guys are waiting! Do you want to know what it says?"

Danny was pleased to see her having fun again, but he was also impatient. "Hurry up, Jeannie! You're fooling around," he said. "Just get to the point and tell us what it says."

"Brace yourselves, guys! You'll like what you hear! This is a good one! Tony, you did a great job figuring out there was a hand petroglyph on the rock—this one is even easier. And Danny, let me say this to you: you will find your Pearl of Time, I'm sure."

She laughed with delight. Her look was now a bit teasing as she stretched out her response. "Yes, Tony and Danny, I do know what it says. Hang on, here it comes!" Jeannie then translated the verse for them. "Look unto the rock whence you are hewn, and to the hole of the pit whence you are dug."

That verse was music to Danny's ears. He responded instantly. Jumping to his feet, he started a high-speed sprint to the end of the brook. Then, momentarily, he stopped and turned. "Tony, grab the shovel," he shouted to his friend, who was still a hundred feet away. "We need to dig deeper!"

Jeannie's mind shifted into high gear as she watched Danny and Tony following the clue. This verse was not that difficult. After all, interpreting the phrase "Look unto the rock with the hand on it and dig deeper in the hole you have already dug" would not be difficult, for even a slow learner. And for darned sure, Danny and Tony were not slow learners. In the poverty-stricken environment of CoalVille, when adversity arose, you rose above it by lengthening your stride. You avoided whining and excelled. Danny and Tony knew how to excel when the need arose.

Danny was the first to jump back into the hole. Why not? He was after his treasure. First they had found the rock with the hand on it in the hole. Next they had found a bronze box buried under the rock. Now they were being instructed to dig deeper.

"Dig faster!" yelled out Tony. Their success at unraveling the Biblia Reina-Valera verses on White Face Cliff had elevated his excitement. "Danny, dig faster! You know what? There is—yes, there is treasure down there!" yelled Tony.

The tempo increased. Danny's strenuous effort was visible. Desert dirt mixed with sweat snaked down his face. Tony took the cue. "Danny, let me take over. You've dug down about two feet—it's my turn."

Danny willingly jumped out of the way as Tony took over. He sat on the side of the hole and turned to Jeannie. She moved behind him and put her hands on his shoulders. He looked up as she commented, "Danny, as I said to you before—hope is a good thing!"

The greater part of Danny's hope had left him with the death of his father. The only hope he had left was to get out of CoalVille. The mystery of what might be buried captured his imagination. It might be a means of escape.

Sensing his anxiety, she motioned him to stand and reached for him. "Danny, give me your hands." Standing close together, they looked into each other's eyes. They didn't have to say a thing—their eyes said it all. Jeannie's eyes, deeper blue than the sky above, were smiling and filled with tears of joy. Danny could feel her mood had lifted and she was relaxed. He was elated. "Jeannie—did anyone ever tell you have beautiful eyes? Did anyone ever tell you that you are beautiful?"

Her mouth pulled up in a joyous line. She smiled brightly at her hero, feeling a deeper love for him. "Yes, Danny! You! And nobody else better! You'll kick their butts if they do!"

He chuckled. His heart flipped. "Yep! Jeannie, if someone else even looks at you, I will kick his butt! And, yes, hope is a good thing—I'll not forget that," Danny said as he gently pulled her into his arms.

Jeannie's head slowly tilted upward, and she lifted her eyes as well. Her hands gently wrapped his face as she pulled it to meet hers. She slid her lips across his cheek, then moved her mouth to his ear and gently nibbled it. "Danny," she whispered, "we have to have hope." She paused, giving Tony a quick glance. He was preoccupied digging in the hole. She slid her fingers through Danny's hair and whispered more softly, "That's what the Kashome people believe—there's hope in all good things. Without hope, life becomes meaningless."

Danny wondered where she was going with her discussion. Then it happened. The sound was loud and clear. Tony's shovel hit something that made a loud *clank*.

Jeannie screamed, "Right now we're on the verge of a huge discovery! A huge big hope!"

Danny's eyes flashed. His mouth flew open. His lungs filled with a huge gulp of air. "Jeannie, I don't care if you just shouted in my ear," yelled Danny. "That sound tells me we just struck pay dirt!" She felt his body tingling as he squeezed her hand more tightly. "That's it—that's it—the old metal-to-metal sound—that's music to my ears!" he shouted.

Danny's heart was pounding. His mind was going wild with visions of treasure. Suddenly he was engulfed by the thought of holding lost Incan treasure in his hands. *What if this is a metal treasure chest filled with diamonds, gold, silver, and royal crowns—what if we really found a lost treasure—could it be? My god, is this our ticket out of this hellhole?*

Tony worked even harder to clear away the dirt from the metal object. *Clank, clank.* The repeated sound came from the hole each time Tony hit the metal object with his shovel.

Despite Jeannie using every muscle in her body to keep herself calm, it was impossible. She was not in control of her emotions. Her body was trembling, but not because of fear. It was a state of excitement that gripped her like nothing else in her life ever had.

"Be careful! Don't break it! Tony—don't screw it up!" Jeannie shouted. "We don't want to damage whatever this is."

He stopped digging and looked up at her. "You're right, Jeannie," Tony responded, trying to calm his almost uncontrollable joy.

"Did you bring a small spade?" Jeannie asked, glancing at Danny.

"Yes, and a coal bucket. I'll run back to the truck and get them."

He took off running full speed. He stopped and turned around and said, "If that damned vulture comes back, I'll kill it! Just take a few minutes to catch your breath. I'll be right back."

He continued his high-speed sprint.

It was a perfect time to relax and escape the heightened emotions that had dominated the past moments since the new discovery. Tony and Jeannie took a few minutes to rest while Danny ran to get his bucket and tools.

"What do you think this is?" Tony asked.

She was quick with her response. "Well, I could say something about lost Incan treasure, but I won't! Tony, I know Danny would like it to be some lost Incan treasure. I have another idea. I believe it has to do with the legend of Kashom—the man who never dies—the man the Kashome Nation is named after. I guess I'm superstitious."

She studied Tony's face as she spoke, trying to detect any reaction from him as she talked about her people. His wide-open, deep-brown eyes and slight smile told her he was listening.

"How's that, Jeannie? What do you mean?" Tony asked, clearly interested. "You know my ancestors are Latino, and we have very close family ties and cultural beliefs also."

Jeannie was convinced. Tony was sincere and wanted to know about the legends of her people. "I don't know, Tony. I just have a weird feeling. My people believe in legends. It's hard for me to talk about them with someone who isn't Kashome—but there's a legend that has been handed down for generations. I'll tell you part of it." She paused to get a feel for Tony's body language. *I think he understands where I'm coming from.* Putting her fingers over her lips, she spoke softly through them. "Kashom was a royal prince. He lost his honor and position as heir to the royal throne of Kopaz because he was careless and allowed Mochcom, the disciple of Zuron, to murder Aerapondes, his little sister, and take her golden key. Kashom was tricked by Mochcom. and both ended up in the Scarlet Desert. Kashom was able to get the key back from Mochcom. However, his honor and throne can only be restored by someone who takes the place of Aerapondes. Kashom thought that would be his daughter, Moon-of-Day. She was killed because her older brother, Yellow Moon, was careless and lied. The person who takes the place of Moon-of-Day will hold the key to traveling the Highway of Time and to redeeming Kashom's honor."

Tony responded with respect for her cultural beliefs. "I didn't know that, Jeannie—thank you for telling me. I know your people keep things like that very sacred. It's special to me that you've shared sacred secrets."

"Yes, they do, Tony. There's something else you should know," Jeannie continued. Tony's intent look told her he was sincerely interested in what she was about to tell him.

"What's that, Jeannie?" he asked with a serious look.

"Kashom is my great-great-great-great-grandfather," Jeannie answered in a hushed voice. "My mother feels it is very likely I will play a special role in the fulfillment of this legend. Even though Kashom thought it would be his daughter who would restore his honor, I believe it will be me." Jeannie was about to show Tony her golden key, but hesitated.

Tony was totally caught off guard. His eyes and facial expression exploded with curiosity. "You're kidding me! You! Why?"

"No, I'm not kidding. Maybe you'll understand now why I feel we're onto something big."

Danny raced up, huffing and puffing from exertion. He had not stopped from the time he'd left for his truck until he got back to where Jeannie and Tony were. Between gulps of air, he said, "Here's the stuff—spade and bucket." He put them on the ground next to the hole. "I'll take my turn, Tony." Glancing at his friends, he calculated quickly. His awareness was keen. He asked, "You and Jeannie really look serious about something. What have you guys been talking about?"

Jeannie's response was also carefully calculated, as she knew Danny was not interested in legends, but she still delivered it with tact. "Oh, Danny—we were telling tales out of school. Do you want us to repeat them?" Jeannie laughed as she waved her hands in the air.

Danny leaped into the hole. His head never moved to look at her. His attention was on discovering the secret he was standing on. "Heavens, no! I want to get the treasure!" He took the lead as the hunt for hidden treasure and secrets returned to full swing. Tony had discovered where it was, but it was still covered with dirt. It wasn't buried deep. Danny's shovel found it within minutes of digging.

Jeannie and Tony beamed as they witnessed Danny scrape dirt from the top of another bronze box.

Jeannie picked up the coal bucket and pressed it into Danny's outstretched hand. "Danny, just start filling the bucket up—we want to get to the treasure." She laughed and pantomimed filling the bucket with dirt. "Just keep going with the bucket brigade, Danny—you're doing just fine!"

She let out her breath in a deep expression of encouragement. The young man of her dreams was standing in a hole looking at his dreams—a bronze treasure box. It hadn't been even a month ago that she had stood at the back of a chapel, wanting desperately to hold this young man full of heartache and pain in her arms. Her heart soared as she stood watching both their dreams become realities.

It was clear to her. The gods had a hand in directing the journey they were on. She had no doubt that soon her love would also know that. She was 100 percent positive that his dreams of pirate treasure would fade away. Soon he would bask in the glory of everlasting young love over a journey through time that had no ending. But for now, she was content to let him bask in the glory of chasing after hidden pirate treasure.

His head turned to her. "Yeah, you hope it's a treasure, don't you?" Danny smiled at his friends.

"Well, Danny, what do you hope?" Tony asked teasingly, clearly indicating by his strange little smile that he knew what his friend's answer was.

For the next ten minutes, the bucket line emptied dirt out of the hole.

"Careful now, Danny—don't hit the box with the spade," Jeannie said as she directed the digging operation.

Bucket by bucket, the sides of the box were uncovered.

"I think this box is bigger than the last one!" shouted Danny, as his dirt-covered hand went up to give Tony a high five.

"I think you're right, Danny, but it also looks like you're dirty, sweaty, and tired. Do you want me to take over?" asked Tony. His friend's face was marked with brown dirt lines running down his brow.

"No, Tony! I'm fine—we only have a few more buckets to go."

After five more minutes of hard work, the box was fully exposed. Danny handed Tony the last bucket of dirt. "I think we can lift it out now. This one has handles—one on each side—that will make it easier to get it out of this hole." He handed his spade to Tony. "Okay, let's get it!" blurted out Danny.

Tony and Danny slowly lifted the box out of the hole. Danny's hands gripped it as if it were a bird with wings, and if he let it go, it would fly away.

"If ever I could fly to the moon, it's now," he said with excitement.

The boys lifted the box out of the hole. Jeannie pointed to the spot where she wanted it. They carried it a few feet to a cedar tree. Her mind was racing. *I hope for Danny's sake that whatever is in the box is exciting. What I suspect is that Kashom has put something in this box that has to do with our legends. I know Danny may be disappointed, but he may soon realize that the treasure we will find is far more valuable than he could ever imagine.*

Tony's head cocked. He asked with a puzzled expression, "Jeannie, don't you want to carry it back to the pond? We have that large flat rock where the other box is."

There was no pause. "Nope!" she said. "Let's see what's in it first. We'll carry it over there in a few minutes. What's that hole on top of the box?"

Tony brushed sand off the box with his handkerchief and blew loose dirt out of the curved slit he'd uncovered. "Danny, don't you think that looks like the same shape as the brass bow in the box we just found?" Tony asked.

Before Tony could say another word, Jeannie chimed in. "Yep, I think so!" She noticed something else. "Hey look! There's another hole on the top of it, just below the slit for the bow. That looks just like a keyhole." Jeannie continued to explore the exterior of the box. "It's also made of bronze."

"You're right, Jeannie—it's a keyhole, but we don't have a key!" Danny looked a bit frustrated.

"Hold on to your zippers, folks," Tony said with his I-know-something smile. "I think the arrow tip fits into that keyhole."

"Darn! Tony, you're my man! You figured it out." Danny let out a shrill whistle while clapping his hands. He pointed to Tony and then to the direction of the pond. Jeannie followed his sign language but ignored his musical whistling. She mimicked Danny's pointing with a cheerful giggle.

"It's over there by the pond, on the flat rock," she said. "Tony, run quick like a bunny and get the box with the bow and arrow, while we let Danny do his war-chant whistle thing."

Danny's head snapped around. He frowned, eyebrows pulling up in a way that looked sad rather than angry. "I'm not one of your Kashome braves! That's it, Lone Tree—you'll never see me do that again. So, Princess

Jeannie, no more whistling from me."

She just fixed him! Tony smiled as he ran to the flat rock. His mind raced as he raced. *I wonder what might be in the new box we just uncovered—it could be something really neat!* Tony picked up the bronze box containing the brass bow and arrow. Suddenly an eerie sensation gripped Tony's body; he had the strangest feeling someone was watching him. A black vulture's howling screams overhead shifted his thoughts of treasure to fear of being watched. *Oh my god, there he is. He's back.* The cold chill of raw nerves sent waves of goosebumps rippling along Tony's extremities.

Mochcom was standing about a mile from White Face Cliff, his watchful eyes tracked the movements of the three kids not far from their parked red pickup. His arm waved in the wind, his coat sleeve flapping about it. He motioned for Vulture to return. *Vulture is doing a good job*, he mused. *I asked him to guide me to where they were. I've been curious about these kids for the last few days.*

Steely gray eyes peered from beneath the brim of his floppy hat. Long, perfectly manicured fingernails raked through his goatee. Nervous fingers flicked and pulled at the hair of his beard. His eyes squinted tighter with each pull. *What are they doing?* His inability to get a closer look because of the vast distance between them annoyed him.

"Are they searching? I didn't think it was here. It's at the Boar's Tusk. It has to be. What are they doing down there?" rasped Mochcom.

Dirt flew in a small cloud through the sagebrush as Black Vulture landed. His ten-foot wingspan broke his final descent, and he collapsed his wings around his body with his final hop after landing. His head turned to Mochcom, and he blinked. Lifting his head, he roared a howling scream through his curved beak.

"Good work, servant," Mochcom growled. He motioned to Vulture to stay behind him. His long fingernails dug into his shovel handle, leaving a distinct indentation matching the hundreds already in the wood, impressed there by decades of his nervous habit. He pulled it close to him, using it as a makeshift crutch as he started his trek through the sagebrush and sand.

"Yes, Vulture, we'll keep a closer watch on them. I wonder what Neferzul is doing with those boys. She was with them when I first spotted her. I wonder if she has the golden key. I hope she does. We'll keep watching her. Oh yes, this could be my chance to get the golden key again. I knew if I waited patiently, another opportunity would come to gain supreme control over eternal youth."

He stopped, turned to Vulture, and pointed to the sky with one arm; he waved the other at the bird. The black bird of death raked his wings and took to flight. Mochcom resumed his trek. "I'm on my way. Soon I'll fulfill my mission from Zuron and sit at his table!"

His long black coat flew open in the stiff wind. It fluttered around his bony legs with each gimpy step.

Tony's uneasiness was accelerating. Puzzled, he reached again into his mind. It was blank. He could not remember where he'd first seen that huge vulture. Emotions stirred within him. Control of them was now paramount. He didn't want to scare Jeannie by telling her that the vulture was back.

Walking up to Danny and Jeannie, still unable to master his fear, Tony handed her the box to her with quivering hands. "Here you go, Jeannie."

"What's the problem, Tony?" Jeannie was concerned.

He had no good answer. "Oh, I guess I was just thinking about the danger we all would be in if someone found out what we've discovered here."

Jeannie sensed Tony was feeling afraid of something more specific. He was not only shaking, but his voice choked up when he responded to her question. She was a woman, and her instinct was to comfort him.

"Don't worry about that, Tony, we're okay. Nobody knows what we're up to! Look—the only ones that know what we are up to are the gophers, desert rats, snakes, lizards. You get the picture. We're fine."

Danny listened to Jeannie comforting Tony as he watched the silhouette of a man walk over a hill on the distant horizon. *There's LeRoy Nabal—what's he doing? That old bastard is up to something.* He flinched away from the hostile image of the crazy man stalking them and instead looked at Jeannie.

"Danny, what are you concerned about? You have a strange look on your face. What's up?" Jeannie's sixth sense told her Danny was thinking about something out of the ordinary.

Suddenly, something caught Danny's eye, and he turned quickly. He cringed, still staring at the horizon. *Hmm! Not only was that crazy old man watching us, but that vulture is following LeRoy. It just flew over the horizon after him. Holy shit! I was right.*

Now her sense of awareness was keen. Something was going on that smacked of danger. "Danny," she screamed, "why aren't you answering me?" He didn't answer. "What's up with you?" screamed Jeannie, more loudly.

Her startling outburst signaled him to quickly move the discussion in another direction. He did. "Nothing, Jeannie! Everything is cool," he said, turning his head to look at her. "We're fine. I'm just excited about finding the lost Incan treasure. You know me. All's cool!"

Jeannie didn't see the vulture or LeRoy. Her instinct told her Danny and Tony were concerned about something, but she had no idea what it was, and they weren't telling. For now, her only choice was to move on.

The bronze box now became her focus. As the Chosen One, her interest was in the century-old secrets in front of her—and she wanted the secrets out of the box. "Tony, Danny's right—it will be okay, we'll be fine. We're on the verge of something big—I don't know how big, but our lives are going to change, change forever!" She looked at Tony, grabbed his arm, and gave it a reassuring squeeze. "We'll keep our find a secret. We're a team—don't ever forget that."

The treasure box once more took center stage. It beckoned the finders to open it, and they proceeded with pleasure.

Jeannie carefully opened the smaller box and removed the brass bow and arrow from their respective cradles. She inserted the bow in the slit on top of the larger, second bronze box.

"It fits! It fits! See what I told you? I was right!" yelled Danny.

Jeannie inserted the arrow tip into the keyhole on the top plate of the box—again, a perfect fit. Then, she gently twisted the arrow, and all three heard the *click click.*

For a moment, Jeannie did nothing. There were no more sounds coming from the box. She asked, "Do you think the lid is free now?"

Danny cocked his head toward Jeannie. A faint smile started to develop. "Yep. I'm gonna give it a try," said Danny, as he put his hands on the lid. There could be no denying that he was anxiously waiting to view the contents of his treasure box. His fingers grabbed one end and slowly raised it a tiny bit. It lifted freely. "Yeah, oh yeah, the lid is free to open. Here goes." Danny pulled the lid from the box.

"Yeah, you did it!" shrilled Jeannie, as her eyes flew open wider than they had ever been.

Three teenage kids who had known nothing but poverty—not even the luxury of a new pair of shoes—had just found their treasure in the Scarlet Desert. Their hope for a brighter future was right before their eyes.

"Oh my god of mercy! Look at that! It's—it's a treasure! We found it—god, we found it! I can't believe we did it! Wow!" shouted Danny.

Danny's heart bounded. His hands reached to touch the treasure. They shook with excitement. He was at a loss for words. His eyes filled with tears. For the first time in his life, he was looking at something of unbelievable value—something that would change their lives forever.

CHAPTER 24

Treasure

Danny's fingers stroked the gold tablets, and his eyes sparkled like the gems as he thought about the tablets they had just discovered. Their journey had started. On this warm spring afternoon in March of 1958, three poor teenagers searching for adventure in the Scarlet Desert had found it. Where would it take them? To the depths of darkness, or to a prize of great value—eternal youth? They had no idea. For now, they were content to bask in the glory of what they had just found.

Danny wondered if their treasure could be a way out of poverty for him and his love. Jeannie wondered if this was the key to an endless journey through time. Tony was content to search for answers surrounding the mystery of the treasure. All were looking at their treasure with different agendas, but the reality they had not yet grasped was darker. Could it lead them to danger, even death?

"This looks like a three-ring binder, except its pages are pure gold! Yes! Solid gold! And the notebook is this beautiful red-colored metal box!" Jeannie squealed with joy. She very carefully lifted the set of gold tablets— pages of pure gold bound together by three white-gold rings—from their resting place, a golden cradle in the bronze box. She set them on the flat rock.

Her fingers moved across the silky gold cradle. She let them slip into the indentation. "Wow! The cradle for this thing is made of gold! Can you believe this? I had no idea what we would find. Yeah, but what is it, and what is it for?"

Danny's fingers followed Jeannie's, but his reached for the gemstones inlaid on the gold. Awestruck, Danny started stroking his treasure. Never in a million lifetimes had he imagined his boyhood dreams would actually come true. He touched an item of gold worth a fortune. He burst out with a shout of joy, "My lord! Look at those beautiful gemstones cut in the shape of strange letters. This thing has to be worth a fortune."

Jeannie put her fingers on his as they stroked the gold together. "They're beautiful—look how shiny and bright they are. You can see the blue sky and clouds reflecting in them as if they were mirrors!"

She lifted her finger and pointed to a lone cloud in the sky. His eyes looked at hers and then at her finger. She dropped it and pointed to the cloud's image drifting across the mirror surface of the gold tablet. "See!" she giggled freely. She flipped the tablets one by one on their white-gold binding rings.

Tony stood looking over Jeannie's shoulder as he studied their content and made similar comments. "These things are unbelievable! They're beautiful! There are even more illustrations! What's this all about? Look at the gemstone symbols. They're inlaid in the gold. Wow! Unbelievable."

Tony was fascinated by the symbols etched on the golden tablets. They surely had a story to tell that was centuries old. He understood the nondestructive character of gold, protecting the message it bore from the elements of nature. "Guys, whoever wrote all this stuff was well educated. Gold is the only element that won't deteriorate. The creator wanted this to survive centuries."

Tony tapped his finger quietly on the gemstone symbols. His head bobbed in rhythm to his finger. He pointed to one. With a puzzled expression, he lifted his finger to his lips and remarked, "These symbols etched into the gold look familiar. I know I've seen them someplace." Nobody was listening. But Tony was overwhelmed. He pointed to the gold and asked loudly, "Have you guys ever seen symbols like the ones etched into these gold tablets?"

The thought of ancient writing on golden tablets sent Tony's mind in search of something he had read about. "Hey guys, this is cool. I read about the Persian king Darius, the first who, thousands of years ago used golden tablets to record what he wanted others to know. He knew gold lasts forever! He used cuneiform script on golden tablets!" Danny and Jeannie listened with blank looks. Tony waited for them to comment. Neither said a word, so Tony added, "What do you guys think?"

In perfect form, Danny said to his best buddy, "Tony, you just took off on a tangent that has nothing to do with treasure right before our eyes. What the hell are you talking about—cunny-form script?" He rolled his eyes and wrinkled his nose while shaking his head. "Tony—who cares about the symbols? It's the gold we care about! Who gives a rat's ass about a bunch of goofy-looking symbols? Holy Mother of Saint Andrew, just look at that gold! How much do you think it weighs? That damn thing must weigh at least twenty pounds—it's worth a fortune!" He stroked it with one hand while holding Jeannie's with his other. He tracked the change of expression on Tony's face as he made his comments.

Jeannie turned from Tony and gave Danny a somber stare. Danny stiffened, pointed to the gold, and then blurted out, "If this isn't pirate treasure, I don't know w-w-what it—yeah, just look at that stuff!"

Aware that Jeannie was listening, Danny gave her a sideways glance. She merely clasped her hands. Her eyes didn't blink. Knowing she was watching his every move, he stuck his fingers between two of the gold tablets. In a quick move, he flipped the top one over the rings. It flopped on the opposite side, making a soft thump. She didn't say a word.

"Look at all the pirate writings on those gold tablets. You know it! Some one-eyed, wooden-legged pirate wrote all that stuff. Flip the page, Jeannie. I want to see the next one," Danny yelled excitedly.

She didn't move and didn't help flip another page.

Her body language wasn't filtering through to him. Danny's mind couldn't stop. Dollar signs were everywhere he looked. He thought, *My god—I'm looking at a fortune, a fortune that will get Jeannie and me out of CoalVille!* His thoughts exploded into words. "Wow! We're rich! We'll finally get out of that damn coal camp when we sell this! We're on our way!"

Jeannie sensed his driving motivation—poverty. But that wasn't good enough, and she was ready. "Danny, I'm sorry to break your bubble—but no pirate wrote this stuff. You just need to get your marbles rolling in the right direction and realize that this is something much bigger than pirate gibberish, and what's more, this is *not for sale!*"

His face dropped with a surprised look, not necessarily angry, but with a hint of sadness. She unclasped her hands and dropped them to her side. His eyes followed them. He reached to touch her hand. His fingers intertwined with hers. Her arm was limp and heavy. His look did not deter her. Now speaking sternly, Jeannie made her position clear. "This is a sacred Kashome treasure. It is part of our culture. There is no way this treasure is for sale."

A little smirk appeared on Danny's face, but he said nothing. His stare continued. He dropped her hand.

Looking squarely into her eyes, Danny said, "Jeannie, you don't know what you're talking about. How do you know it's part of your culture? Where did you get that from? We're poor, and this is our ticket out of a godforsaken coal camp! What do you mean—not for sale? This is how we get out of this hellhole—who wants to live in a coal camp forever? Who wants to be poor forever? I sure don't! This is our ticket to a bright future. You know it as well as I do!"

He blinked. He thought he'd made his point. He hadn't. Jeannie was ready with her next response. "Danny, you have no idea what's involved here. It's a priceless treasure that is worth more than money. You don't know what these tablets are about—much is in Spanish, and I can tell you it has nothing to do with pirates. These tablets will guide us to a treasure beyond your wildest imagination. By selling now, all chance of discovering that priceless treasure would be gone. We won't lose anything by holding onto them."

Danny had no idea what she was talking about. At that point, he didn't care, and whatever she said, he didn't buy it. His facial muscles tensed as their eyes remained locked.

Tony sensed an escalating argument in the making. He studied his best buddy's body language as Danny glared at Jeannie. "Hmm, I don't know, Jeannie. When was the last time you had any money?" Danny looked at Tony and then at Jeannie. Danny's eyelid twitched as he said, "Right! Never! My god, Jeannie, think about it! We're poor! This is our ticket out of *hell*!"

At this point, Jeannie snapped at him, "I told you, Danny, that we will make the decision only after all chance of discovering the priceless treasure is gone. If we sell it now, we kiss the big treasure good-bye!"

Now her comment registered. Her statement caught him by surprise. "What do you mean, big treasure?" he questioned.

The only answer she had was feeble, but she gave it a shot. "What did we find after we found the box with the bow and arrow?"

Tony saw her losing ground, and he had to support Jeannie. His best friend had just saved his life, but Tony was not stupid, and he realized that Danny was letting emotions rule his reason. Tony moved closer to Danny. "I agree with what Jeannie just said. We don't lose anything by waiting." Tony hesitated and put a finger on his twitching lips. "I think we have something big—but we don't know just how big it really is."

Looking at Jeannie, he said, "I think you are correct in your assessment! This could be the start of a long journey." Then, jerking his head in Danny's direction, he added, "And Danny, let me say this to you. You have no idea how to sell this gold."

A slight breeze picked up Jeannie's papers and tossed them off the rock. They skimmed over the sand and blew against the stalk of a large sagebrush. They fluttered in the wind like the giant wings of a dying butterfly.

As Jeannie walked over to fetch her notes, Tony continued to reason with Danny. "If we tried to sell it before we know what we were doing, well, you get the picture. Somebody would end up with the gold! We'd have nothing!"

Danny crossed his arms and squinted his eyes even more.

Tony glared at Danny as he shouted, "I've already told you, we would most likely end up dead! You know damn well what I'm talking about! Jeannie has the right idea. Listen to her! We hold onto this! We hide it, so nobody knows we have it! You got it?" For a long moment, he looked at Danny. Jeannie remained silent a few feet away, clutching her paper with tense fingers and overtaken by a sad heart. Danny shook his head stubbornly.

Then, Tony erupted. He was desperate to drive his point home. Pointing his finger at Danny, he said, "Danny, do you want to get us all killed? Do you want Jeannie in an early grave? Are you just thinking about your own selfish welfare and not ours?"

Silence hit them like three tons of donkey snot, smothering all sounds but for the fluttering papers in Jeannie's hand.

Danny was by no means ignorant. He was street-smart—he knew doing something foolish with the treasure would put them all in danger. He was in a bind. He had never had Jeannie's support for selling, and Tony had just dropkicked his plans off the nearest cliff. All he had left were questions.

Danny walked to stand behind Jeannie. Grasping her shoulders, he turned her to face him and said in a calm voice, "Okay, Jeannie. You've made your point, you and Tony. Just how long do we hang onto them?"

Tony had provided a slam dunk once again. It was up to Jeannie to navigate rough waters and soothe Danny's ruffled feelings.

She took a deep breath and let out a sigh as she answered him in an unusually sweet voice. "Danny, this is the deal. We hold onto them for a time—how much time I don't know, but long enough to exhaust all avenues for finding other clues that could lead us to the ultimate treasure."

He said nothing. For what seemed like an eternity, she looked at him. Then she took charge. Her hand searched for his and found a forlorn set of fingers. She quickly grabbed them and squeezed tightly. Now she would make the important point. With a gulp of air, she felt a twinge of anxiety. "I said this earlier, but I'll repeat it because I don't think you were listening. I'll be blunt. I'm positive there's more to this treasure than the few objects we just found. If you were listening before, you must not have understood what I said. I don't know what more there is—my hunch is, and I'll repeat my words, this stuff is just the tip of the iceberg!"

This time he was listening. He was reading her body language. He wondered what she meant. *More? Maybe it is just the tip of the iceberg?*

Danny's breathing was heavy. Then it hit him. A long line lifted his face into a bursting smile. *She's right. My god, she's right.*

Curiosity shot through her body. Her little smirk turned to a joyous smile.

Standing in front of her, Danny took her shoulders in his hands and looked into her eyes. With a shaking voice he said, "No more harsh words will ever escape from this mouth of mine. My love, 'I will fight with you no more forever!'"

Before he could utter another word, her hand came to his lips. Tears streamed from her eyes like pouring rain. She sweetly said, "Danny, you are my Chief Joseph! And like that great leader who had the wisdom to fight no more forever, you have found your treasure—true happiness, knowing the beast of contention can no longer live within you."

Danny's emotions were nearly overcoming him. It was time for some humor. His hand softly wiped away the tears rolling down her cheeks. "Okay, your Royal Highness," said Danny as he chuckled. "You mentioned the iceberg. What's under the tip of the iceberg? Maybe the *Titanic!*"

He had somehow wrapped himself around her without coming in actual contact. Her heart took off like a rocket, but she had her way of bantering with him. She stepped back a foot or two, put on her sweet little smile, bowed, and gestured in a royal fashion as she asked, "Prince Danny, you goofed around in Spanish class! Right? Do you know what the inscriptions on the bow, the arrow, and the plaque are all about?"

He couldn't stop his laughter. He threw his hand in the air. She stepped to him, lifted her hand, swatted his briskly, and intertwined her fingers to lock with his. His hand locked with Jeannie's, Danny said, "Well, my dear, I just started a journey down humor road! But guess what? I ran off the damned road, and now I'm stuck."

It was *déjà vu* all over again. Bursting into laughter, she said, "Nothing to say at all, my handsome prince?"

"Nope!" Danny said and laughed as he realized he'd just been zinged by Jeannie.

He poked Tony's side and winked.

"Well, my dear prince, you are a slow learner. All we have to do is look at your report cards! But you are learning, so I'll give you a little credit!"

Jeannie said with a cheerful giggle.

Tony laughed to himself as he thought, *Well, as the score keeper I'd say it is at least two for Jeannie and zip for Danny!*

Tony walked to Jeannie's side. Danny still had his hand wrapped in hers. Tony focused on both of them and said, "You're right, Danny—you too, Jeannie. Uh, what's next?"

Jeannie reached and grabbed Tony with her other hand. She put her arm around him for support. He sensed her gratitude. Tony touched Jeannie's face.

Danny stiffened so abruptly that Jeannie flinched. His reaction to her support of Tony caught her off guard. Her only conclusion was that he had had a twinge of jealousy. That made her happy. But now she had a problem—mending feelings.

Quickly turning to face Danny, she reached for his hand. She moved closer to him. Her hand slid down his stomach, letting her fingers dance around. Before he could say a word, she was on her toes with her lips in his ears.

"Danny, my love, trust me," she whispered sweetly. "Soon we'll all experience a joy and pleasure from this treasure that all the money in the world could not buy. We're on a journey to a magical place that few have ventured. Trust me, my love."

She kissed his cheek and gave him a love tap on his rear pants pockets with both hands.

Danny could not resist. He stepped back, nodded, did a little bow, and whirled his hand, mimicking her mock royal gesture. She laughed easily. He swatted his hands on her rear pockets and said, "Whatever you want, Jeannie. I trust you, my love."

With the bonfire of contention that had erupted over selling the treasure now extinguished, she was content to let the boys play with the treasure while she drifted into deep thought.

She rehearsed the Legend of Kashom. A thousand questions came in a rush to Jeannie's mind. *Did Kashom bury these gold tablets out here in the Scarlet Desert? Why? What is in these tablets? Did he write them? Is this a roadmap for the Chosen One to redeem his honor? I'm certain I'm the Chosen*

One! What happens next?

While Jeannie was daydreaming—or at least that's what Danny thought she was doing—he was exploring their new treasure. His outburst broke the short silence. Her meditations came to a screeching halt.

"Holy smokes! I think there's another compartment in the bottom of this box." His finger tapped the gold cradle. "I think this thing comes out." He had their attention. With no hesitation, Danny pinched his fingers on a flange of gold sticking up. He started lifting the heavy gold cradle. He had it six inches above the box when his fingers started losing their grip.

Jeannie's hand flew with lightning speed, saving the heavy piece of gold from dropping out of Danny's fingers. She said, "Careful, careful, Mr. Muscle Man! Can't drop it!"

He chuckled freely as they lifted the cradle for the tablets out of the bronze box—exposing another compartment.

"Oh my god of mercy! There's a bunch more gold in the bottom of the box. Look at that thing! What is it? Let's get it out of there!" hollered Danny.

The three crowded about the object—all excitedly speaking at once. Their lives were changing faster than they could ever realize. Going from rags to riches was not commonplace in CoalVille. Danny set the item on a flat rock.

"This is weird!" shrilled Jeannie. "This thing is made out of solid gold. It looks like a miniature sundial of some sort with a pointed hat on it. Wow! It also rests in its own gold cradle."

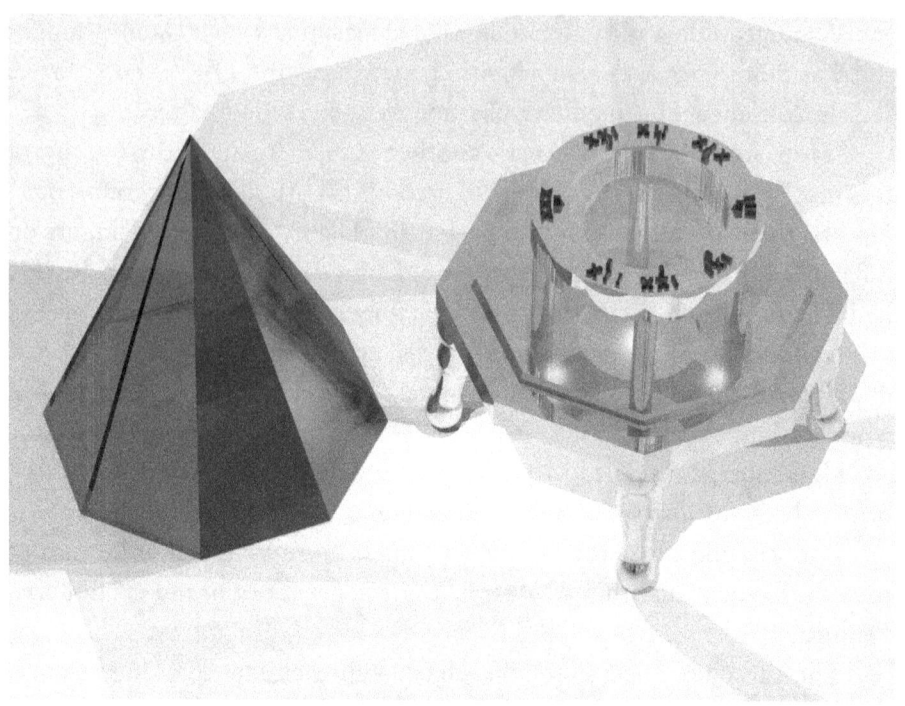

Tony clapped his hands and nodded his head as he jumped into the excitement. "This is too much!" he shouted. "The design of this is strange—what's this slit for?" He pointed at the object Jeannie called a hat. "You're right, Jeannie. It looks like a pointed hat. Let's call it the dunce hat—sure looks like one!"

Danny was following Tony's finger as he pointed to the strange-looking device. "Yeah, Jeannie, this thing is solid gold. It's a treasure for sure," Danny shouted, parroting Tony's gesture as he pointed toward the sundial.

"But what's it for? What does it do?" questioned Jeannie. Jeannie's mind was racing all over the place. *We have much to figure out. What's this all about? It has to be connected to our legends—but how?*

Their excitement left them in a giddy labyrinth of speculation and bewilderment.

"Hey guys! My lord, this thing is beautiful! It's a work of art!" yelled

Tony. "Just as you said, Jeannie, this looks like a sundial. But look, there's a little arrow by each set of roman numerals. What is this thing? What's it for?"

A strange smirk crept across Danny's face. He poked Tony in the side, but Jeannie didn't notice. Then her glance caught them exchanging funny little facial expressions. Now Danny turned to face her. He was staring at her, remembering the words that had jumped out at her to cause the bonfire of contention that had only just been extinguished.

Danny's face went serious as he said in a strong voice, "This thing weighs fifteen or twenty pounds—that's a lot of gold. My god, that would make us all rich!"

His comment was calculated to get a response from Jeannie. He waited for comeback. Nothing happened. Then it did. She pointed a finger and shook it at him. She giggled, knowing it was his way of having fun with her.

She was onto him, and he knew it. Danny had flubbed his chance to push her buttons. He put a frown on his face. She laughed. He entwined his fingers together and put them over his frowning face. Slowly, he moved them down, exposing his smiling face. She laughed more generously.

"The beat goes on," yelled Tony. His keen eye spotted something else. He grabbed Danny's sleeve and tugged it. Danny dropped his attention from Jeannie. He chuckled freely as he looked to where Tony was pointing. "Yeah, Danny, there's even more! Look! There's another gold plaque," said Tony, tapping his finger on a slot in the interior of the box. "It has some more Reina-Valera verses."

Jeannie seized the opportunity. "Danny," Jeannie asked, "can you understand why this is not for sale? The trail is just beginning!"

"Yes, I see your point," he sheepishly responded.

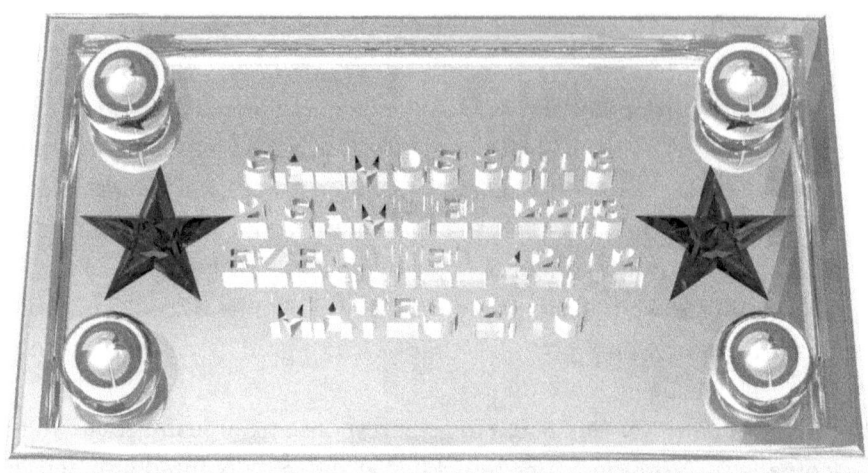

But LeRoy and Vulture were not sheepish. They continued their vigilance, spying on three kids from afar. Although they could not make out the details of Danny, Jeannie, and Tony's activities, they suspected a find was in the making. LeRoy turned to Vulture and rasped, "What do you think, my servant? Do we make our move now, or do we wait?"

Vulture hopped in front of LeRoy. His head bobbed as he squawked his answer, *"Aak! Aak!"*

"Very well then. We'll wait until we know for sure. I've waited for centuries to get my hands on what Neferzul has. So waiting a little longer to be positive is but a second in time compared to the centuries I've already waited."

CHAPTER 25

Bow and Arrow Lead the Way

T hey were looking at a set of keys they had no idea were keys. At this point, they had no idea what purpose the brass bow and arrow served, other than opening the second box. They did not suspect the bow and arrow were keys with other purposes as well. They did not suspect the riddles inscribed on them would provide clues that would work in combination with other keys as yet unfound.

Tony was a master at solving riddles. He prided himself on his reasoning and sound judgment being able to tackle any riddle he came across. He would be the first to wonder why he couldn't eventually solve any riddle that came his way. Certainly, he knew he had not yet found one that could stump him, given enough time to decipher it. Unfortunately or fortunately, whatever the case might be, a set of riddles had landed in his lap.

Jeannie was exhausted from the adventurous activities and intense excitement that had consumed the past several hours. She suspected her two friends were in the same state. "Do you guys want to take a break? I know I sure do. All of this excitement has got my heart rate so high that if I don't take a rest, I'm sure it will beat its way out of my chest." Jeannie sighed as she looked at Danny and Tony. *I think Danny and Tony need a few minutes to think about our find.*

Danny's body language and facial expression echoed her desire to take a break. Likewise, Tony was also ready for a take-it-easy kickback.

"Jeannie, we're in the same state you are. What's your suggestion?" asked Danny.

"Let's go over by the pool and sit under that shade tree," she said.

Taking a break—time to reflect—had always been a favorite moment for Jeannie. She pondered the quest they had started. *Could it be that we're about to embark upon a journey like the sands in the hourglass that measure time as they fall through the narrow passage? Are we destined to take a journey on the Highway of Time—the highway that is mentioned in the Legend of Kashom— the highway that has no beginning or end?* Shadows lengthened as the sun descended toward the western horizon. *How different this afternoon is from this morning,* Jeannie thought as she stared at the skyline over White Mountain. It stretched for miles, just a few clouds in the sky above it. They were streaked with burnt orange from the afternoon sun.

Jeannie mumbled, "Wow! That looks like a mountain of white ice cream topped with orange caramel."

Tony jumped. His deep-set brown eyes flew open. Shadows streaked across his cheekbones, making them jut out. "Jeannie, what are you talking about? Ice cream with orange caramel? We have mysteries to figure out. Let's save the ice cream until this evening," said Tony. Then he laughed freely.

Jeannie thought for a long moment. She was lying comfortably on the rock next to Danny and was not interested in bantering with Tony. Still, to be polite, she said, "Oh, I was just thinking."

She rolled over and lifted herself up on one elbow. Her head was now directly over Danny's face. She looked down at his napping eyes. She spotted a clump of prairie grass at the edge of the rock. Carefully, she reached out and grabbed it. With a feathery touch, she slid it across his nose. His eyes still closed, he swatted at it, like he was trying to kill a pesky fly. Jeannie waited a long moment. She touched his nose again with the furry end of the grass.

Danny's head came up, and he forced his eyes to open. He reached around her before she could move and pulled her body on top of his. She exhaled hot breath down his neck.

Tony carefully sneaked to the end of the rock. Jeannie and Danny didn't see him. He filled his tin cup with cold water and tossed it at them before quickly dropping to the ground at the foot of the rock.

"Good Lord," Danny shouted, gasping from the onslaught of cold water splashing on him. "What the hell is wrong with you, Lopez?"

Tony said nothing. He lay still beneath the edge of the rock, out of view, but Danny could hear him chuckling. He bolted to his feet, jumped off the edge of the rock, and raced to the bottom. There Tony was, lying on the ground, arm outstretched, cup in hand.

Danny pretended like he was going to take the offering of the cup. Instead he grabbed Tony and threw him over his shoulder like a sack of potatoes. He walked to the edge of the pond and threw the other boy. *Kabloosh* came the sound as Tony hit the water. Everyone chuckled.

Tony crawled out of the water soaking wet. He didn't look at his best buddy. He walked to where Jeannie was standing and said, "Well! We have a lot to think about."

She gaped at him as if he were a rat that had just jumped ship and then climbed back aboard, dripping wet. Then she smiled politely and motioned for Tony to continue.

"Here are my thoughts. I think that first, we need to figure out just exactly what we have!" Then he stopped abruptly. He looked at Danny. His hand motioned him to come to where they were standing. He turned to Jeannie. She gave him a long, searching look.

Getting serious was the furthest thing from Danny's mind. Jeannie was quite puzzled, and she had no idea where Tony was headed. Her glance at the lengthening shadows suggested they did need to move on. They had yet to figure out the Spanish inscriptions on the bow, arrow, and gold plaque. Still, she give Tony a little more rope to see if he was ready to hang himself. She nodded to Danny and pointed to the treasure. He rolled his lower lip and nodded back.

Tony suspected that all were on board. "Okay!" said Tony. "Let's get started." He grabbed Jeannie's note pad. "Danny and Jeannie, we're onto something big. Earlier, Jeannie brought up some guidelines. We verbally agreed, but then a big disagreement ensued when we discovered more treasure. We just need to stick together. I have a suggestion—we need a written agreement. I think we ought to be bound in secrecy by a pact we sign."

Danny bobbed his head in agreement. "Sounds good to me. I can live with that," Danny said. "How about you, Jeannie?"

"Fine with me! We're a team," she answered politely. This was something she'd had on her mind, so she'd let Tony charge on.

Tony was anxious to let Jeannie and Danny know his plan. "Okay, here's the pact that I propose: First, we call our group the 'Pirates in the Desert.' Second, we don't tell anyone—not even our parents. Third, we don't do anything with what we have found without the mutual consent of all the Pirates in the Desert. Fourth, if one of us leaves our group, we're still bound by secrecy, and whoever leaves cannot do anything with our treasure without the mutual consent of the remaining Pirates in the Desert. What do you guys think?" Tony looked to his friends for agreement.

Danny was gazing at the pond. He was swaying in rhythm to the sound of a meadowlark singing not far off, on the top branch of a scrub cedar. Jeannie's eyes roved to him. She reached and snatched his sleeve and gave it a huge tug.

Danny stopped for a moment, gazed at her, and smiled to himself. He thought, *This shit is boring. Boring!* He reached around her and pulled her next to him. His head lowered to her ear, and he whispered, "Boring!"

"Tony, I think that's great!" said Jeannie. She gave Danny another yank. "How about you, Danny?"

"Oh, that's great," Danny said with a snicker.

Jeannie retrieved her note pad from Tony and took a pencil from her canvas bag. "Tony, tell me again exactly what you just said, and I'll write it out so we can all sign it." He did. She wrote it out, and they all signed it.

"Okay, great! We're in agreement, so there we go. That's taken care of. Now, back to you, Jeannie," remarked Tony. "You said a few minutes ago that you were thinking. You get my attention when you're deep in thought. What were you thinking?"

She tapped her pencil on her paper. Tony didn't wait for more. He jumped to his feet and headed to the spot where they had assembled their findings—not more than ten feet from where they had lunch. He grabbed the brass bow and arrow and gold plaque.

Quickly, before Tony got back, Jeannie pressed next to Danny. "Danny, you and I are going to have some real fun in an hour or so. So, my love, if you want to have fun with me, you have to pay attention and let Tony do his thing for an hour." She stood silent, looking at him. He thought about that and then slowly nodded. His eyebrows rose, and his mouth pulled up into a smile. "Good," she said.

Tony walked back, treasures in hand. He showed them to Jeannie and said, "We need to get into the Spanish translations—there's a boatload of translating to do. Did you see all of the Spanish words on the inside curve of the brass bow, the brass vanes of the arrow, and gold plaque?"

"Yep! I did!" said Jeannie. With Danny on board, or so she thought, they were good to go. Jeannie's assessment was quick and exact. She was a master of getting things headed in the right direction. She grabbed the brass bow. "I suggest we start with this. We'll get to the arrow next. We know they were used as a set of keys to unlock the second box we found, but I think they have a bigger role—additional messages that we need to translate." Jeannie was being her serious self. Resting the bow in the palm of her hand, she pointed at it and then the inscription. Surveying it rapidly, she said, "Here's the message on the bow in Spanish. It says, '*La llave baila sobre la séptima luna para visto lejos como una estrella distante.*'"

Danny finally woke up. His face was on fire with an expression of delight, listening to Jeannie's flawless Spanish—only one of her three native languages. But Danny was unaware that Jeannie spoke a fourth—a sacred language. "Good job, Jeannie," Danny said. "Now give us the scoop in English."

"Okay, here we go. 'The key dances on the seventh moon for seen far as a distant star.'"

Jeannie tilted her head up to see Danny's face. He gazed down with a look of interest. "Did you listen carefully and write it down, Danny?" Jeannie asked as she looked at him.

"Yes, I did!" he said, screwing his mouth to one side. He read from the paper in his hand. "The key dances on the seventh moon for seen far as a distant star...don't you think the grammar is a bit weird? It seems it would make more sense if it said, 'The key dances on the seventh moon for that seen afar as a distant star?'"

She laughed as she said, "And...Mr. Grammar Man?...Ah, you did get an *A* in Miss. West's English Class—but this is a riddle!"

Danny had a comeback. Not wanting to be outdone, he hesitated a few moments, thinking of a response. "Well—here's the answer to your 'And?' question, Miss Princess Jeannie." Danny twisted up his face with a disgusted look and said exactly what was on his mind. "That's the biggest pile of written mumbo-jumbo crap I have ever laid my eyes on."

Jeannie and Tony burst into laughter. Danny's disgusted expression reminded them of a frozen iceman who had just seen the light of day.

Suddenly, still laughing, Jeannie screamed exuberantly, "I think I got it! I think I got it!"

There was no doubt in her mind; she had captured their attention, so she continued. "Doesn't one of the planets have seven moons?" she asked rhetorically. "What are the names of the moons? So there you go. Easy! Isn't that right?"

Danny was lost, but Tony didn't buy it. He was the master at riddle solving, so this was his opportunity to take the lead from Jeannie. "Jeannie, that was certainly a brilliant bunch of BS!" blurted out Tony. "The ones closest to Jupiter? The ones closest to the Earth? The names of the moons! Which moons? Good grief! Do you even know how many moons are circling Jupiter?"

Now, very methodically, he stood and assumed the role of the professor. "Here are my thoughts on the interpretation of the writing on the bow," he said in a stately manner. Drawing out his voice like a politician delivering a speech, he continued. "To figure out the riddle, which is what I think it is, we need to apply logic, and this is how you do that. We answer these questions: What key dances? Where does it dance? How does it dance? For what or whom does it dance?" Smiling broadly, he finished his pantomime. He stepped back and bowed.

Danny laughed freely. He waved his hand in a rolling motion to get the show on the road. With a nod of his head, he said, "Tony, you got us laughing—yep, you're the professor. Let's get on with finding the answer.

I want the treasure. Okay? Let's go!" His comments created a jovial mood. "Keep going, Mr. Professor Man—you've got the floor!"

Tony grabbed Jeannie's pad of paper and pencil. His eyes rolled comically as he wrote down some notes. Finally, he dropped the pad of paper at his side. "All right, I'll continue. You see, Jeannie, an answer to a riddle isn't just a guess." Locking his eyes with hers, he paused, ready to drive his point home. She bit her lip, fighting the temptation to throw a thousand questions at him.

He bowed again, strutted a few steps in a circle, and continued, "To figure out the meaning takes thought, and this can be done by asking questions that start with these words: how, what, where, when, who, and for whom or for what. This line of reasoning will get us thinking in the right direction—at least, that's what I believe."

Jeannie was struggling. Tony was charging ahead, leaving her behind on her own turf. She was agitated by her loss of control in a territory she considered hers and hers alone. Sheepishly, she said, "You're probably right, Tony. Let's see if your logical way leads to the same conclusion—that is, the seventh moon is one of the moons of Jupiter. Which one is the seventh moon? That's a good question, isn't it?"

Watching the dynamic between Jeannie and Tony unfold, Danny had picked up on what Jeannie was up to. She was getting ready to pounce, like a cat ready to spring on a mouse. However, she had a problem—no mouse was coming along, so she had nothing to pounce on. He had no idea where Tony was headed. Assuming a referee role, Danny decided to wade in. "Jeannie, sorry to cut your line of reasoning off, but I think Tony is on the right track. Let him continue," said Danny.

Tony winked at his buddy. He'd realized what had just happened and was pleased that Danny gave him his support. "Okay, guys—if we're going to figure this out—we need to work together," said Tony, smiling at Danny in thanks for his moral support. "Here's what we're trying to decipher. First it says, 'the key dances.' Next it says, 'on the seventh moon.' And last it says, 'for seen far as a distant star.'"

For once, Danny was listening. He hung on every word Tony said. Then suddenly, he decided to interject his two cents. "Tony," he cut in. His hand shot up.

Tony noticed immediately and abruptly stopped. "Yes, Danny, what do you have?"

Danny dropped his hand slowly, his palm down. He pivoted and stepped back two feet. Now, he carefully selected his words. "Okay," Danny said, "you proposed that questions to answer the riddle should start with the words how, what, where, when, who, and for whom or what. Well, let's look at the answer to the 'for what' part."

"What do you mean, Danny?" Tony looked at his friend with a puzzled expression.

It was an odd twist of fate. Suddenly, Danny found himself at the helm of riddle-solving. Delight raced through him. He was in their ballpark and hitting a home run. He chuckled so quietly only he could hear it. "Well, it says the key is dancing for something. That something is 'seen far as a distant star.' So that means the key is dancing for something that is viewed or seen as a distant star. Could that something be a moon of Jupiter, like Jeannie just suggested? No! Moons are not stars! Neither is Jupiter! But our sun is! Guys, we need to find a star." Then Danny paused and looked at the sky. "We know that stars move around in the heavens as the seasons change. Maybe we need to consider the 'when' question also."

Jeannie was politely quiet. She let Danny have center stage. She was listening carefully to every word he was saying but giving no indication to him of what she was up to. The cat was ready to pounce on the mouse. She waited for the right moment to spring. The moment came, and suddenly she jumped into the conversation—cutting him off in the middle of his sentence.

Smiling, she stepped onto the stage of riddle solving. "If you were far away from our sun and looked at it—what would it be? What would you see? Wouldn't you see a star? Yes! Our sun would appear as a star if you viewed it from a great distance. From the gods' vantage point, our sun appears as a star. You see, guys, 'seen afar as a distant star' is our sun because, as I said, the gods view our sun from a very far distance!"

Danny spun around and gaped at her with amazement. Listening intently, he realized she was like the proverbial cat pouncing on the mouse.

He wanted to rush on but had nothing to add and no place to go. She had just stolen his thunder. He had gotten the logic down about the star, but she had nailed which one it was. "Well, I'll be damned! Our sun!" he blurted. "Good job, Jeannie!" Both thumbs popped up as he looked at her.

Tony didn't give an inch. He tried to protect his turf. "What gods are you talking about?"

Jeannie snapped without hesitation, "I'm talking about the gods and customs of my culture." Then her eyes flew open and the words just tumbled out. "My god! I've got it! Guys! Oh yes! I've got it! I've got the answer! Holy crap! It's Intipraimi!" she screamed. "Tony, sorry to cut you off! I just figured out what is going on! It's not only what is dancing, but also *when* it's dancing! You guys are the best. Yes, I was jumping all over the place and guessing—Tony reined me in—Danny used logic—you guys are *super*! Okay, let me continue." The smile on Jeannie's face was as big and bright as the sun in the western Wyoming sky.

Now she was at the point she wanted to be. Danny was caught off guard—just like Tony. She was center stage, and she loved it.

"Got what, Jeannie?" asked Danny with a puzzled look on his face, startled by Jeannie's sudden outburst. "You guessed last time, and we know that was a flop."

She had no need to hesitate at this point. Clapping her hands, she screamed, "Danny, I do have it! Yes—the answer to the riddle is Intipraimi!"

"*What?*" Danny was dumbfounded. "What the hell is an Intipi-Rayme?" Jeannie burst out laughing at his look of bewilderment. "Jeannie—what on earth are you talking about? You are not making a bit of sense."

She laughed again. She hadn't had this much fun in a coon's age. "Hold on, Danny—it's not 'intipi-rayme'! You'll know what Intipraimi is in just a minute." Jeannie now spoke in a calm, low voice. "I know I jumped the gun the first time about the moons of Jupiter and all that crap, but this time I really have it. Guys—the answer to the riddle involves something used in the ceremonies we inherited from Kashom."

Now she had their attention. If she had caught them off guard seconds ago, she really had them going now. Danny and Tony wondered what conversation they were involved in and what planet it was taking place on.

"*What?*" both boys said in unison. "Jeannie, what are you talking about?" They could not believe what they were hearing.

"Listen, guys, just listen!" yelled Jeannie.

"Okay, Jeannie, you've got the floor. Go ahead," Danny shot back. Then suddenly, he jumped to his feet. "Wait!"

That totally caught her by surprise. "What now, Danny?" she snapped.

He stood looking at the sky for a long minute. She waited, wanting to get his attention. He turned to her and asked, "Something you inherited from Kashom?" That brought another question to mind. "Jeannie, how can you inherit something from someone you're not related to? You're not making a bit of sense!" He looked puzzled. "Hell, Jeannie, do we even know if this guy is for real?"

Her face broke into a smile. Danny had no idea what she was up to. He continued his stare, longing for more questions to ask, but none came to mind.

At that moment, she stepped in front of him and touched his lips. "My love, you're learning, but I see it will take a lot more time." She giggled, turned, and strutted ten feet to the flat rock. She picked up her canvas bag and took something out. She clutched it tightly with both hands and walked to his side.

"I guess you forgot. Kashom is my great-great-great-great-grandfather," said Jeannie.

"What?" asked Danny. "When? You never told me that!"

"Oh yeah, it was Tony I told. *Sorry!*" said Jeannie.

Danny said nothing, just watched her. He looked like a deer standing in the headlights of an oncoming car. Her smile grew larger. Her eyes twinkled more brightly. Jeannie took something from a beautiful beaded-leather pouch—a golden medallion locked in a bezel on a gold chain. She took it out of its bezel and laid it on the flat rock next to her.

"Okay, this is the golden key! Gorom Mochcom, the disciple of Zuron, ripped this golden key from Prince Kashom's little sister's neck and then killed Princess Aerapondes."

Jeannie had the boys' undivided attention. They stared at it.

It was solid gold, three inches in diameter and half an inch thick.

Strange letters from an unknown alphabet had been cut from colored gemstones and inlaid in a band of white gold around its perimeter. Slits were cut through it in the shape of what appeared to be pairs of mirror-image symbols. In its middle was a brilliant blue gemstone cut in the shape of a star. The star was set so that light could pass through it.

"Remember, Tony? Earlier I told you the legend of Kashom. My mother says that because of my lineage, my distinctive appearance, and my golden key, I will play a special role in the fulfillment of this legend—and this is the key." Jeannie stopped and pointed. "It was given by the goddess Neferdor to Aerapondes personally!"

"My god! Wow!" said Danny. "Holy mackerel! That's the most beautiful thing I have ever seen! I—I—except for you, Jeannie."

His humor died quickly. Danny wasn't dumb. He walked to where she was and picked it up. His eyes never moved from it, and with a questioning look, he asked, "Jeannie, did you say that your golden key at one time belonged to Neferdor?"

"Yep!" Jeannie said. "Now you know what guides me!"

She giggled freely, thinking about the statement he had made moments earlier. *He not only thinks it is beautiful, but is starting to understand there are things in the universe that are way beyond pirate treasure.*

"Can I see it, Danny?" she asked, having a revelation to make. He handed it to her.

She stopped to catch her breath in her state of excitement. It took only a moment, and then, she was ready. "Let me explain. A few minutes ago, I said that the gods view our sun from a very far distance."

She looked at Tony and added, "It was when Tony asked, 'What gods are you talking about?'" Tony smiled, knowing he had offended her and was now showing gratitude for her cultural beliefs.

She turned her focus to Danny and continued," My mother told me that when Viracocha gave our sun to Ra to take care of, there was a celebration for that grand occasion on Volob. The gods and goddesses walked out of their pantheon and Viracocha pointed to the black sky and said, 'Seen far is a distant star!' Those standing next to him agreed and Neferdor ventured a name for our sun. She stepped forward and proclaimed, 'Yes, my husband, we shall call our son's star, *Seen Far as a Distant Star!*'"

Jeannie knew she had it figured. She was excited. "Okay, this key dances." She put her finger on it. "The key dances on the seventh moon. Now here's the important part. It's not a physical moon my key dances on—like our moon that circles the Earth. The riddle is talking about a month of the year when my key is involved in a dance. And yes, as Danny said, it could be a 'when,' and that is correct. Good work, Danny, great observation! And my good friend Tony, thank you for getting us on the right path with your logic! Okay, enough accolades. Let me continue."

She inhaled a large gulp of air. Her hand went to her mouth, fingers stretched over it. She slowly closed her fingers and looked at Danny. He was listening. She batted her eyelashes at him. He pointed to his mouth. He then made a motion of taking something out of it and pointed to his foot.

Tony and Jeannie both broke into laughter. She walked to Danny, reached into his back pocket, and took out his handkerchief. She waved it in the air.

Tony and Danny said together, "Jeannie, you're not the one who needs to surrender."

Her face went serious. This was her territory and hers alone. She spoke reverently, "The festival of the seventh moon is a celebration when my people give thanks to the creator, Supreme God Viracocha, for giving us the sun. My people are grateful because we know that the sun is the source of all life on earth. The seventh moon is called Intipraimi—the name of the seventh month of the year. I told Danny a few weeks ago about this festival that is coming up in June—but remember, our year, the Kashome year, starts in December. It's customary for the one who has a special name—I can't reveal the name—the one who's entrusted to be the keeper of the golden key of Neferdor to dance at the Festival of the Sun while wearing the key, and I am that person. So there you have it! My golden key dances on Intipraimi—the seventh moon—for the sun! Guys, the answer to the riddle—'the key dances on the seventh moon for *Seen far as a Distant Star*, our sun—is Intipraimi."

A strange little smile erupted on her face as she looked to the sun in the western sky. She had just won the high-stakes game of riddle solving. Tony had lost—professor act and all—but he knew it was for good reason. In a million years, he would never have figured it out. He also suspected the Spanish on the vanes of the brass arrow was a riddle. He had no doubt that this was Jeannie's territory, and he would leave well enough alone.

He walked to Jeannie, smiled, threw his hand in the air, and said, "Good job, Jeannie. Give me five!"

Danny's humor rushed back, and he spoke from his gut. "Well, I'll be damned. Now what do we do?" *Not only did we discover the most beautiful unbelievable find, but the most beautiful girl in the world—Jeannie—is essential to its fate!*

His heart raced, knowing that she had scored a big one. Soon her brilliance and cultural upbringing would become paramount in their quest—even to the point of dueling with the stalking hand of death.

CHAPTER 26

The Golden Key

Jeannie felt her heart flutter as a new revelation struck her. The breath escaped her lungs when the inspiration clicked in her mind. Her eyes roved from Tony to Danny. It was not only the priceless treasure that was jangling her emotions, but her hormones were also raging.

A game plan suddenly entered her mind. She needed to get Tony off chasing answers to riddles and exploring the mysteries of symbols while she and Danny took a hike to explore each other.

Her mind raced. Tony had just lost the battle of the riddles, but he certainly could win the war of symbols. *Yes, that's it. My golden key is the key to putting my plan in motion. As he's having fun fiddling with my medallion, I'll be someplace out of sight having fun fiddling with Danny.*

It was not only Jeannie's mind that was hard at work but also Mother Nature. It was that time of year. The unpredictable spring storms swept through the desert like the random chance of a roulette wheel. Black clouds were moving from the distant hills north of the Boar's Tusk on the Scarlet Desert to the western hills near the White Mountain. Jeannie blinked as a flash of lightning bolted from a dark cloud, striking the towering Tusk. *I'd better hurry and get my plan in motion if I want any fun time with Danny. If the storm moves our way, all bets are off.*

The desert surrounding White Face Cliff was full of life. All of the creatures were enjoying the rays of sun. Jeannie wondered how long that state of bliss would last.

Danny followed the movement of Jeannie's head—first to the storm, then back to her key.

She caught him watching her. A thousand words wanted to tumble out of her mouth, but he spoke first. "Can I hold your medallion?" Danny asked.

As she handed it to him, she looked at his face, not saying a word. Her eyes moistened, and her mind drifted to pleasure. *His long yellow hair is beautiful with the sun shimmering on it. I can hardly see his ears or his eyes because his hair is so long—it's as bright and shiny as the golden tablets sitting on the rock beside him.*

Fondling the medallion, Danny gave her many curious looks. His fingers slowly worked their way around the array of slits and pressed on the brilliant blue star. As he held it to the sun, light burst through the blue-colored gemstone like fire in a dragon's eye.

"Wow, this thing is heavy—how much does it weigh?" he said as he squinted, his eyes outlined by a star-shaped pillar of blue light streaming through the precious gemstone.

"Only you would ask that question," she said, smiling and giggling at the same time. "You have a passion for treasure, but I must warn you: this medallion is my treasure."

His strong fingers touched her bare leg, sliding around her thigh, as he said, "Oh, Jeannie, I would never have it any other way. I have my own treasure—my dad's golden watch and chain."

His fingers tightened as he made his comment about the watch. Because she had been staring at his face for another reason—young love—she detected an obvious, yet subtle, reaction: his suddenly changing facial expression and body language. At first she said nothing.

Danny's mind had gone to a place concerned not with the golden key, but rather with the golden watch. Tension gripped his body as he stumbled over the craziness of it. His thoughts rambled on. *The same symbols that are on Jeannie's key are on the inside of my watch. This is all just weird. My watch never stops. It never needs to be wound.*

His fingers tightened on her leg. The image of the gold note that had shown up next to his parents on their honeymoon night immediately flashed through his mind. *Reveal the secret to no one until they reveal the source.* Aware of his supernatural strength, yet not knowing its source, he heeded the warning in the note. *I can't tell Jeannie. I don't understand. My parents never understood.* He shuddered with a disturbing thought. *God, I hope I'm not a weird monster like a vampire or werewolf.*

His entire body went rigid. The sudden tightening of his fingers caused a concerned question to rush from Jeannie. "What's up, Danny?" she asked.

He retracted his hand from her leg. He quickly diverted the subject back to her golden key. "How heavy is it?"

Puzzled, but unsure, she looked into his face curiously and then felt sadness overtake her. *He must have been thinking about his dad*, she thought. Her voice now tender, she tried to understand the deep emotions that he must have locked inside him. Yet she felt a slight uneasiness as to why his reaction to the thought of his dad's watch was so different from his other reactions to his dad's death.

His face broke into a smile that lit his eyes so fully that they sparkled like the star of her golden key, and as she saw that change, she tossed the watch incident out of her mind.

"Danny, it's heavy," Jeannie said, "so now you know. I don't wear it all the time. I have a little leather pouch that I keep it in. I only wear it on special occasions." She continued to stare at him, and she knew exactly what he was thinking. "So, Danny—have you figured out how much it's worth?"

"You read my mind," he said, grinning from ear to ear.

She giggled in playful reaction and reached to stroke his golden hair as she said, "You don't know how much it's worth!" she replied. "You have no idea what this blue star in the middle is made of, do you?"

"You got me there, Jeannie. What is it?" he said in an inquisitive voice.

"Danny, I know you so well. And you are interested in the value of treasure—let me say this: my key is priceless!" She took it back from him gently and replaced it in the beaded pouch.

Tony was not interested in lover's talk—at least not Danny and Jeannie's lover's talk. He would have been interested if KateLynn were there, but she wasn't.

"We're wasting time, guys," said Tony. "I've got an idea." He was impatient and wanted to know what the riddle on the arrow was all about. He'd picked it up moments earlier, and now he was ready to give her an assignment. "Okay, Jeannie—here ya go. It's your turn, Miss Translator, so do your thing."

Her way of interjecting the drama of a New York Broadway play seemed appropriate in the setting of the Scarlet Desert. Walking onto center stage, the middle of the flat rock, props in hand, first she glanced at the words as her hand floated the paper across her eyes. Then, with a drop of her arm, she looked to the audience of two, threw her head back in Victorian style, and made her recital. *"Juventud eterna viene desde dentro la estrella intacta por medio de le cuyos ojos refleja."*

With a bow and a curtsey, she stepped off the rock she had been standing on.

Danny clapped loudly and gave a whistle or two. "Jeannie, if I didn't know better, I would swear you were Spanish—not Kashome," he said as he listened to her beautiful voice. "I wish I could speak a foreign language. Will you teach me one?" he asked her.

"Which one, Danny?" She teased him with glee. "Kashome, Spanish, or English?"

As she finished her sentence, a thought drifted into her mind. *There is another language I know, the Royal Language of Kopaz, which only the royals know. Hmm, I can't tell him of it.*

Tony's sharp look was followed by words of action. "Guys, we don't have time to fiddle around. Time's a-wastin'. Let's get that inscription translated!"

Jeannie glanced at Tony, clearly hopeful he might soften at Danny's small piece of humor, but to no avail. With a cheerful smirk, she elected to add to Danny's humor. Stepping back on her stage, she stood at the center of the rock for her next scene.

"Are you boys ready for this?" she said with the biggest smile on her face.

His impatient expression did not go unnoticed. Tony's refusal to get into the make-believe world of drama and complete lack of humor were a bit annoying, but Jeannie had other plans for him, so she let him continue to fuss.

"Darn it, Jeannie. Get with the program and just blurt it out!" Tony said, clearly showing his frustration.

Jeannie's quick little bow and royal whirl of her hand sent a frown to Tony's face and produced a giggle from Jeannie.

"Okay, here we go," she said. "This is the secret you boys have been waiting for. 'Eternal youth comes from within the intact star by means of he whose eyes it reflects.'"

"What? That's gobbledygook!" Danny said, twisting up his nose to make a funny face. Danny threw Jeannie a covert glance, plainly fearing an outburst of laughter, but for all the notice she took of him, he might not have been there.

Tony's agitation was clearly visible. His face was a sure giveaway of the locked-up words just waiting to venture out. "All right, guys, we need to figure out what it's all about. Let's get serious! Look, Danny—I don't know who buried treasure out here in the middle of the desert, or why. The simple fact is that they did. We found it—it's ours. And we have to figure out what it all means."

The thought of getting serious about a brass arrow at this point had shot out of Jeannie's mind an hour ago. She had no idea what the answer was and had no intention of diving into another riddle solving chase. At the moment, wrapping her concentration around it to decipher a riddle was not her plan. Wrapping her hands around Danny was.

Tony's words fit right into her plan. The boys were right where she wanted them. Her plan was set to start. Now she had to ensure her words and action met with success. Carefully, Jeannie's mind raced as she thought of her next steps. *I've got to get Tony busy so Danny and I can sneak off. How?*

"The message on this arrow"—Jeannie pointed the tip of it right at Danny—"was put there for a purpose, and Tony's right—it's our job to figure it out."

It worked. "So, Jeannie," Tony butted into the conversation. "What does it mean?"

"Tony, if I knew what it meant, I'd tell you! It may be the answer to finding more treasure. At this point, I don't have the foggiest idea what it means."

Now her game plan flew into motion as she shifted to high gear. "Let's look at all of this stuff," Jeannie said, pointing the arrow at the objects from both of the bronze boxes sitting next to Tony and Danny. "Yes, just as Tony said, someone put it out here. We found it! It's ours! Now we need to figure out what it's all about. I think we need to look at the gold tablets, the gold slab, and the sundial. All of these things have messages. I believe they are somehow connected to my golden key."

She reached into her pocket to get her beaded-leather pouch. "There's a connection to the treasure with my key we need to find," she said, taking it out and holding it in her hand so the boys could see it.

What she said about the connection to the treasure with her golden medallion was something that had actually been puzzling her, but her motive now was far from that puzzle.

Holding back a smile, her mind raced. *Getting Tony off studying this stuff is an ideal assignment for him so Danny and I can scoot away and be alone together.*

Dark clouds moving from the Boar's Tusk in the direction of White Face Cliff meant time was of the essence if she were to have much time with her love.

Tony took the bait. "Jeannie, can I see your gold medallion?" he asked.

Her heart jumped. The very thought of having Danny alone was swelling her heart almost beyond her control. Hiding the shaking of her own body, she quickly pressed her medallion into Tony's hand. "Sure, Tony—here it is. What are you looking for?"

Tony's eyes raced around the outer track of gemstone symbols as his fingers circled the slits on the inner track.

"This is interesting," Tony said. "There are twenty-two gemstone alphabet letters around the outer ring that are inlaid in white gold. They're meticulously cut from colored gemstones." *Hmm—that's a work of art!* "And look at the eleven weird symbols formed by slits that cut through the inner ring of the medallion."

With careful attention, he gently placed her medallion on the rock. His hand reached to his face and gently started tapping his cheek. He glanced at Jeannie, his look a question that had gotten stuck in his mouth. Then he stared at her golden key. "Jeannie, can I have your pad of paper? I want to try something." A smile crossed his face.

Trying Danny's trick of being dumb like the smart fox was her plan, and fortunately, Tony remained serious and preoccupied with symbols.

As Danny watched Jeannie closely, a strange little smile erupted on his face, revealing he had detected a fox at work. At this point, she wasn't holding back any smile. She thought, *It's working!*

"What do you have in mind, Tony?" Jeannie asked as she handed him her tablet and a pencil.

Her eyes moved covertly to Danny with a little flash. To keep Tony out of their sign-language conversation, she pulled her arm tightly to her body, and her hand gave a thumbs up to him. Deciphering what foxy Jeannie was up to, Danny was almost unable to hold back a chuckle, but he managed, and he indicated the vote was unanimous by responding with his two thumbs up.

A cat's curiosity couldn't have been greater than Tony's. His mind was lost in the fascination of unscrambling a mystery, leaving Danny and Jeannie with pounding hearts. "There's something really interesting about how the symbols are organized on your medallion. I think I can figure something out—I think. Maybe—well, I might be able to make a connection between the twenty-two alphabet letters that are cut from precious gemstones on the outer ring and the eleven inner-ring symbols that are made by slits."

Tony reached over and picked up the tin cup that he had been using to drink the water from his Boy Scout canteen. "I need this cup because I'm going to use it to trace circles. And this will take a few minutes," he added, as he started writing and sketching something on the paper.

Stepping next to Danny, her slender body pressing against his tightly, Jeannie watched Tony intently.

Turning his head slowly and sliding his arm around her waist, he asked, "What's he up to?"

"Beats me!" she answered as she thought, *Ah ha, I knew Danny would not be interested in a bunch of symbol crap. Neither am I.*

His fingers moved up her side a bit, and he gently gave a tickle. She giggled very softly under her breath. He spoke loudly: "Jeannie—I don't want to sit here and watch Tony do a bunch of technical gobbledygook crap that I really don't give a rat's butt about." For a short moment, he paused. "Do you want to sit here and watch him fiddle with this circle and that circle and this symbol and that symbol?"

Her eyes lifted with a broad smile, followed by a quick answer. "No! What do you have in mind?"

At that moment, the fantasy cat of the cat-and-mouse game that Danny and Jeannie had been playing jumped out of the bag. Tony laughed at Danny because he understood too well the longing behind his best buddy's need to be alone with his newfound love.

Turning to Jeannie, Danny said, "Let's go over by the pond while Tony does his thing. We can talk and have fun! When Tony gets all of his technical stuff figured out, he can give us the bottom line. This is just too boring for me."

Then, turning to Tony, who was already hard at work on a symbol chase, he said, "Tony, tell us when you get finished. Jeannie and I are going over by the pond."

"No hanky-panky, Danny! I'll give you guys a holler when I'm finished."

"Tony, take as long as you want. We're in no hurry," Jeannie said as she grabbed Danny's hand and started tugging on him. She squeezed his hand and tugged a little harder. "Come on, Danny…we don't have much time."

As Danny stared into her beautiful face, a thousand questions wanted to leap out, but his heart said, *No talking.* They walked with their minds locked on the same track—that first special moment of young love.

They left Tony by himself at the end of the brook where it vanished into its sinkhole. They took off and headed to the rock projecting into the pond, which was out of sight of where Tony was working.

Even though her heart was thumping as she held her lover's hand, the distant lightning was a catalyst that got Jeannie's mind churning—she could not get the events of the day out of her mind. *Our day started with a joyride in a red 1955 Chevy pickup. Our hope was to find adventure—boy, did we ever! Tony has us on the path to figuring out something unique about my golden key! And Danny and I are on a new journey of love. Where will it lead?*

CHAPTER 27

First Love, First Kiss

Finally, Jeannie had Danny alone—all to herself. They were falling in love. As they strolled through desert sands together, new blades of grass brushed across her toes with each step. She wrapped her fingers around his arm, and glancing up at him from the corner of her eyes, she looked fondly at his face. It was the most special day of her short teenage years. She was recording every minute detail and every movement of his face in a secret corner of her mind. Jeannie had rehearsed her every move for these special moments a thousand times over. But deep in her heart, she knew that spontaneous moments of first young love could never be rehearsed.

Tony was busy solving riddles several hundred yards away—out of sight on the other side of a small hill. Danny wasn't interested in all the technical stuff. He didn't care about the riddles, the symbols on Jeannie's medallion, or finding a connection that might reveal what all of it meant. At this moment, he was only interested in the girl who was holding onto his arm. He was content to spend some time alone with her and let Tony chase after the answers to the mysterious symbols.

Even for Jeannie, at this moment, answers to riddles were secondary. Her budding love with Danny was primary. It was just waiting on this warm spring day to burst into the blossom of romance. She felt as if she were the new petals of a rose, feeling the warmth of the sun for the first time. She was content to let nature take its course and discover the true function of the human heart—to bind two young people together in the strings of love.

She dropped her hand and found his. Danny clutched hers, and he swung their arms back and forth as they strolled to the pond at the base of White Face Cliff. Jeannie spotted the perfect spot—the large flat rock she had been on earlier, which protruded into the ten-foot-deep water surrounding its three sides.

He was her star athlete. She was his head cheerleader. They both were daydreaming of a getaway to the town of LaRayme if the CoalVille Pirates went to the state tournament. "Danny, are you getting excited 'bout the upcoming Grizzlies-Pirates game? I sure am! I can't wait for next Friday. It will be a blast!"

He smiled down and looked in her eyes. "Can you imagine being the state champions?" Slightly squeezing her hand, Danny said with excitement, "If we beat the Grizzlies, that will be just too cool!"

She lifted her free hand to touch his hair, which was blowing in the breeze. "Well, we're going to beat them. Danny, you're a phenomenal ballplayer, and you will make it happen. I'm counting the days! We're going to have a party in LaRayme! State tournament, here we come! The school will take the cheerleaders to accompany you guys. I'm so excited that I can hardly stand it!"

"You're the best cheerleader I've ever seen. I watch you when I race up and down the basketball court. You're so cute in your little maroon-and-white miniskirt. You have great legs. Wow! You turn me on! Yeah, Jeannie, you're one super girl, and we will have fun in LaRayme. Yeah! We'll have some time together—just you and me!" He smiled at her.

She tugged at the sleeve wrapped tightly around his biceps. "Hey, we're here. Let's jump up on this rock next to the pond. We can skip rocks across the water." Jeannie reached down and picked up a couple of small flat rocks. Still holding onto his sleeve, she gently pulled on it and pointed where she wanted him to go.

Standing next to Danny on the flat sandstone rock, Jeannie was the first to fling her skipping rock. She squealed in an excited girlish voice, "I got mine to go four skips! Can you beat that, Danny?"

His lower lip rolled down. "I don't know, Jeannie—you're a pretty good rock skipper." Then Danny pitched his.

She laughed. "Ah ha, yours only skipped three times." They faced each other, Danny with his back to the water, and she put her right hand on his left side, feeling his ribs under his white T-shirt. "Let's dangle our feet in the water. Come on. I've already kicked my sandals off."

He chuckled. "Jeannie, you've got skimpy cutoffs on. I have long pants."

Saying nothing, she put her left hand on his right side. Then, with a strange little twinkle growing in her eyes, her right hand fumbled for a place to grab his T-shirt. She gave it a tug, pulled it out, and slid both hands under it. Her fingers outstretched on his sides, looking at him affectionately, she said, "You could take them off! I wouldn't mind!"

Totally caught off guard, he fumbled for a response. "What?"

A smile creeping over her face, like the expression of the Cheshire Cat, she moved her hands and wiggled her fingers, touching his skin ever so lightly as she moved down to the waistband of his Levis. Her fingers gently slid over his rock-hard abs to his fly, and she unbuttoned the top button.

At that moment, Danny was frozen stiff as a board. One thought engulfed his mind. *Holy mother of St. Andrew, Jeannie!*

She looked into his eyes, her fingers barely touching his skin, gently dancing on his hard abs. Then, with a feathery touch, she slowly started gliding them up to his chest. Their eyes remained locked as she reached her arms further under his T-shirt. Her fingers now spread open on his ripped muscles, and she pushed him with all her might.

He flipped backward into the water, and there was a huge *kabloosh*. His face, with wide-open eyes and gaping mouth, said it all as he disappeared. Waiting for him to surface, Jeannie watched the water churning, bubbles rising from the depths. Then she saw him. Watching him flip his head to shake the water from his long shaggy hair as he broke the surface, she laughed and said, "Got water?" Laughing hysterically, she blurted out, "See, it's your fault. I told you to take your pants off. Now they're soaking wet!"

He said nothing, but his face lit up, his mouth drawing into a huge smile. With two strokes of his powerful arms through the water, he was at the rock's edge. His massive hands grabbed it. His strength propelled him out of the water with one leap. He grabbed Jeannie, wrapped his arms around her, and flung the two of them into the pond. The *kabloosh* echoed through the air one more time.

Holding Jeannie tightly with his left arm, he used his right to stroke through the water to get them to the surface. In a matter of seconds, he was at the rock's edge. He grabbed her by her tiny waist and effortlessly hoisted her onto the rock.

Looking at him in the water, Jeannie burst into laughter. "Good job, Danny. Golly, you're strong." Sitting on the rock, her legs dangling in the water, one on each side of his head, she flicked his ear with her big toe. He joined in her laughter. He grabbed her legs and snuggled them against his face. Smiling, he said, "Move back a bit so I can hop onto the rock."

She stood up and looked down at him. His hands grabbed the edge of the rock in preparation to leap out of the water. He glanced up and was caught by surprise. Looking up at her standing on the rock, her legs in an open stance, he blurted, "My god, Jeannie, your soaking wet T-shirt stretched around your beautiful body reveals every detail. My god! Not to mention those skimpy cutoffs!" Danny was caught in an unexpected situation, and Jeannie's upper thighs put him at a loss for words. Jeannie did not move. Danny's eyes remained fixed. Seconds ticked by. He fumbled his words as he tried to maintain his composure. "Jeannie, I can see everything—ah, er—you—you only have skimpy shorts on—" He stopped. "Oh my god! Ahh—you have nothing on under your shorts!" With his mouth wide open and eyes as big as full moons, his fingers tightened on the rock. with only the upper part of his body out of the water.

She cocked her head to the side a bit and smiled down at him willingly. She motioned for him to get out of the water. He used his strength to propel himself to the rock's surface. She sat next to him, scooting as close as physically possible.

Sitting next to Jeannie, Danny wrapped his arm around her waist and pulled her even closer. Still staring at her body, he paused for a while, and then he said, "Do you know what you're doing? I don't think I can control myself."

She giggled, putting her hands on his chest, tickling him with her long slender fingers as she felt his chest muscles. "What do you mean, my love? It seems you also have a soaking wet T-shirt stretched around your handsome body, not to mention the top of your boxers sticking out of your open fly. What are you doing?"

Danny laughed. His eyes followed the curvature of her bare legs still dangling off the rock as she swished them in the water. He reached and put his fingers on them. "Your beautiful skin has been kissed by the sun. Your legs are turning a golden tan. God, you're beautiful!" he said with a catch in his voice.

She turned to him with a serious look on her face. He was puzzled as he thought, *I hope I haven't upset her.* She gently pushed him backward and pointed to the rock. They lay on their backs side by side and looked up at the sky. Then she lifted her hand and pointed at a lone cloud on the distant horizon.

He rolled onto his side with his face only inches from hers. She remained on her back, looking up. He said nothing but looked on fondly at her as his hand reached to touch her wet cheek. She asked, in a quiet voice, "Danny, what are you planning to do with your life?"

Caught by surprise he responded, "What do you mean, Jeannie?" His hand gently wiped away a drop of water making its way from her hair down her cheek.

Now she turned her head slightly to look at him. "You know, Danny— do you want to go to college? What do you want to do for a job? What do you want to be? A doctor? A lawyer? What?"

Again, he said nothing for a long thirty seconds, his eyes telling her he was deep in thought. Then he lifted his right hand and placed it on her stomach, gently sliding his fingers over her wet T-shirt.

The wind was still. The pond was like a mirror, reflecting the face of the cliff. It had settled into its typically unruffled state following the thrashing waves created by Danny and Jeannie minutes earlier.

The human silence pressed on, interrupted only by the song of a meadowlark not far away. As the two poverty-stricken teenagers contemplated their future, Danny's eyes looked into hers. He slowly came up on one elbow, lifted his head, and supported it with his left hand. He moved it slightly so his eyes could follow every contour of her body. They stopped momentarily at his right hand on her stomach and then continued down her legs. He looked past them and gazed at the still water and reflected on her question.

He moved his face over hers and looked down as he said with a wistful smile, "Well, you know my mom works at the hospital. I would really like to be a doctor, but we're poor! I don't even think I will get to college—let alone medical school!"

Silence engulfed the pond. All was still—including Mother Nature's creatures. For a brief moment, he gazed into her eyes and thought of the significance of her question. His hair dripped water onto her face. His hand came off her stomach to brush it off, but she sweetly took it from her face and put it back on her stomach.

Now, his face wore a serious look. "Why do you ask?" He sighed. "I hope I can get out of CoalVille. I'd hate to spend my life in a coal camp!"

Her head never moved from the rock. She looked up at him; their eyes were locked, his face directly over hers as she said painfully, "Oh Danny, you have so much potential. I'm sure you'll be a success in life." She paused briefly and then touched her hand to his lips. "Do you plan to get married and have kids?"

He stroked his fingers through her glistening wet hair and answered, "Sure, Jeannie. I'd love to get married and have kids. How 'bout you?"

Her hand lifted, and Jeannie moved his hair back from his eyes. The moment had finally arrived. "Danny—have you ever kissed a girl?"

Danny's hesitation could not have been briefer. "No! But that is changing right now!" he whispered.

He slowly dropped his head to hers. He put his hands on either side of her face—his long massive fingers entwined in her silky black hair. He pressed his lips to hers, their mouths open wide, and he kissed her.

Time stood still. Jeannie's heart pounded. All she could think about was the good-looking boy who was kissing her. *He's the neatest guy! He's fun to be around. He's strong, tall, a phenomenal athlete, and the best-looking boy I have ever seen!*

After what seemed like an eternity, they both took a huge breath of air. "Wow, Danny, my heart is pounding!"

She wrapped her arms around him and pulled him off his elbow down onto her. His heart was pounding away in his chest, and his breathing was short and jerky as he said, "Mine too, Jeannie!"

Supporting himself so that his chest barely made contact with her pointed breasts under her wet T-shirt, Danny touched her face softly and looked into her eyes. "You have the softest white skin. Your eyes are such a deep blue. Tell me, Jeannie, where did you get your beautiful features? You don't look like your mother. I've never seen your father."

Now her heart was pounding as she thought, *I'm the third Neferzul. I wish I could tell him more, but I can't.*

With a longing look of sadness, she pulled him as tightly to her as possible and whispered, "Oh, Danny—where will our lives take us? We could be happy together. I know we're just teenagers and have one more year of high school, but time goes by fast. We'll have a lot of fun this next year."

Now their bodies were pressed together, and her deep blue eyes filled with tears of joy as she thought of the future that could be.

He rose back to his elbow. She touched his lips and smiled up at him. "Danny—you're the first boy who has ever kissed me. You're the first boy that I have ever kissed," she whispered in a sweet voice.

Danny had never felt the feelings that he was now experiencing. For the first time, true love entangled his body and mind with multiple novel sensations. He attempted to quiet his tingling and quavering muscles, but he couldn't. Her sensitive awareness told her his state as she softly placed her hand on his face and brushed away a tear that managed to spill from his eye.

His head directly over hers, his eyes glistened as he smiled. He gently placed his hand on her face. "Same with me, Jeannie! I've never kissed anyone before. You got my heart pounding!"

As she held the love of her life in her arms, she reflected on their situation—how being raised in a coal camp had defined them. She spoke softly in a wistful voice. "Danny, we are young, just teenagers, but I think we are much older for our age than most other sixteen-year-olds. I think our feelings for one another are more mature than other kids our age. A coal camp is a tough environment. It forces you to take on responsibilities much earlier in life." Pausing briefly, she looked at him longingly and then added, "Do you agree, Danny?"

As their conversation grew more serious by the moment, Danny moved so that they were both sitting. His body tightened as he answered, "Yes! Jeannie, we're not normal kids. As you said, we're much older for our age than most sixteen-year-olds—I know we'll both turn seventeen on the twenty-fourth of March, but we've had to deal with problems that most people never have. When an entire community is poor, it puts added responsibilities on everyone."

He stopped talking. They both sat with their legs stretched out on the rock. He stared at the cliff in front of them and then looked at her again. "Both you and I have been working during our summer months for the past six years. We've been doing adult jobs—twelve-hour days, seven days a week. I work on Mr. Farland's ranch, and you run Mr. Evert's gas station. We never see each other during the summer months. It's always nice when school starts. I'm just glad we are still able to go to school. Some of our friends have had to drop out and go to work full time. They have to help support their families." He sighed.

She turned and held his rigid body tightly in her arms as she put her thoughts into words. Her head moved to his face, and she whispered, "How many times have you gone hungry? How many times has your heart ached because your parents were embarrassed that they didn't even have enough money to buy food? Yeah, we have experienced a lot of life in our short sixteen years."

Danny had deeply savored the playful swim in the pond and the glorious sensations of the love play that followed. He did not want them to slip away. "Let's change the subject. Let's talk about you and me and what our future together might hold for us," said Danny. He wanted to talk about something more uplifting.

Jeannie also wanted to hang onto the moment of first love. "What kind of future do you think we could have? What color eyes do you think our kids will have?" Jeannie tugged on his arm to have him closer to her.

Quick with his answer, he smiled and said jokingly, "Actually, Jeannie, I've thought about that. The boys will have emerald-green eyes, and the girls will have sapphire-blue eyes. What do you think?"

Jeannie giggled freely. "That's neat, I agree—little green-eyed Danny boys and little blue-eyed Jeannie girls."

He chuckled lightly in response.

"Really, what do you think the future holds for us?" Jeannie asked in a serious tone. She reached out, gently wrapped his face in her hands, and looked into his eyes.

His face saddened slightly. "I don't know. Things are changing very fast." He held her close. His next statement caused her pain. "Jeannie, the treasure would allow us to leave CoalVille. We would be rich. We would have the perfect life. We would have our little green-eyed boys and blue-eyed girls. They would go to private school. We'd have a neat car to drive. We would live in our grand mansion with a white picket fence!"

She stumbled for words with pain in her heart, knowing her culture and sacred mission were far above the love of the young man who had just captured her heart. "Oh, Danny, I've thought about that. I do love you, and I know we are poor. God, have I thought of that."

She gently brushed his cheek with her hand as she searched for words. "I could not live with myself if I sold the treasure. I've already told you, it is a sacred part of our culture. Not only could I not live with myself, but if I sold the treasure and took the money, my people would disown me! They would forever banish me from having any association with the Kashome nation. I would never see my family again. I would be an outcast!"

His expression shifted. "I see. Well, let's not dwell on that. Who knows—maybe things will work out for us. We don't know what the future will bring. All we can do, as you always say, is have hope!"

Danny looked at the sun making its afternoon descent to its sleeping place. They stood and took each other's hands. He said, "We should get back to see what Tony has figured out. He's probably wondering what's going on."

Jeannie rose to her tiptoes and pulled him next to her. Their T-shirts, still wet from their frolic in the pond, were all that separated them as she pressed her small breasts tightly against his chest.

He felt her warm breath on his face as she brushed his hair from his ear and whispered to him, "Danny, hold me close one more time before we go back. I just want to be near you. I want your body next to mine!"

Danny and Jeannie stood motionless, locked in each other's arms by the pond at the base of White Face Cliff. For what seemed an eternity to Danny, their lips were locked. For that short time, he felt like he was kissing the most beautiful angel with the softest skin who had fallen from heaven into his arms.

"Danny," Jeannie whispered in his ear as she held him tightly in her arms, "I'll never forget this moment. These few minutes we've had by the pond I will cherish for a lifetime. My heart will have a little message etched on it." She touched her lips to his. She gently slid her tongue across his. She pulled her head back slightly. "Do you know what that message will say, my love?"

"I could guess—the first boy you kissed was Danny Roberts by the pond."

"Yes, Danny, that is exactly what it will say! I'll have that little message on my heart until the day I die."

"Your heart won't be the only one with a little message etched on it; mine will echo yours—the first girl I kissed was Jeannie LoneTree by the pond."

They both said nothing, staying locked in each other's arms for a few more moments. Time seemed to stand still for them, but the shadows were lengthening, and they knew it was time to go.

"I guess we had better go. I don't want to, but it's getting late, and Tony is waiting," said Danny in a stumbling voice.

They took a few steps toward where Tony was waiting.

Jeannie stopped walking. She took Danny's hands and pulled him next to her. He gently lifted her with his strong arms so their faces were next to each other's. She wrapped her legs around his waist and held his body tightly against hers for a few more moments. She stroked his yellow hair with her hands and held his face as she kissed him. Her mind filled with one thought. *I wish time would stand still. I could hold him in my arms forever!*

"Danny, I'm falling in love with you!" she whispered softly in his ear.

"Jeannie, do you know what?"

"What?" she answered.

His voice now choked up as he tried to speak without stumbling over his words. They rushed out in a low, serious tone, yet somehow fraught with anxiety. "I'm falling in love with you! God, I just love you! Maybe we'll have our dreams! Our little green-eyed boys and blue-eyed girls living in a grand mansion with a white picket fence!" he said with a lump gathering in his throat.

She looked at him, a tear rolling down her face. She said with a twinge in her voice, "Oh, Danny! Maybe the gods will step in and give us the dreams we're searching for."

With a longing look of love in his eyes, he said, "I hope so!"

CHAPTER 28

Rosetta Stone

As with the discovery of the Rosetta Stone unveiling the hidden secrets of Egyptian hieroglyphs—symbols that were a mystery for centuries for lack of a translator—Tony made a startling discovery. Jeannie's golden key—her gift from the gods—was their own Rosetta Stone.

Tony looked up. A mountain of excitement growing in him as he grasped Jeannie's key, he waited expectantly for them. His eyes followed each movement of their nonchalant meandering. They slowly made their way toward him through the patchwork of sparsely planted sagebrush, randomly seeded by nature's hand. As they walked and talked, their hands engaged in playful teenage love gestures.

Their eyes were not on Tony but carefully tracing each other's smiles as they made the final steps of their journey of first love from the pond. Tony was first to speak in his effort to redirect attention to his discovery. "You guys have been having fun! Can't fool me! I see your wet T-shirts. What games were you playing?"

Danny avoided Tony's eyes. "What did you figure out, Tony?" He even looked in the opposite direction—ignoring Tony's remark. *He's supposed to be figuring things out—not watching what Jeannie and I are up to.*

Tony took the hint. "I've got three things figured out. Do you want me to explain what they are?"

Following his playful encounter with Jeannie, Danny's mind was far from deep subject matters; instead it was concentrating on Jeannie's body.

"Tony, I don't want to listen to some long, drawn-out bunch of technical stuff that I don't understand. I don't think Jeannie does either. Can you keep it simple? We know you've been working very hard to get this stuff figured out. Jeannie and I are just grateful you have the analytical brain to make sense of these mysteries, but can you just give us the short version!"

Tony picked up Jeannie's key. He held it so the sun was shining through the slits and the blue gemstone at its center. He tilted it so the shaft of star-shaped blue light landed on Danny's face.

"Yeah, I can make it simple. If you guys don't understand everything—well, don't worry about it. We're cool!" He twisted her key and said, "This thing uses the sun and is a translator. I'll get to that in a few minutes." He paused. He had their attention. "Okay, here's the first thing. The eleven symbols in the inner ring of Jeannie's medallion—her golden key—are made by slits. They are very unique. They are mirror images of each other. I'll call them mirror-image symbols. What that means is no matter how you look at her medallion, the symbols don't change."

He placed a piece of paper on the flat rock and held it so the wind didn't blow it away. It didn't take him long. In less than a minute, his sketch was finished.

"Look at my drawing and you'll see what I mean. You can see that the mirror-image symbols are identical, no matter which side of the medallion you're looking at. That is very important, because the sundial, or what I shall call the sundial key, has something to do with Jeannie's medallion."

Front Side of
Jeannie's Medallion

Back Side of
Jeannie's Medallion

"Tony, you drew the same picture twice! Do you know what you're doing? Because I don't!" Danny blurted.

Tony knew without question that he had captured Danny's attention. He could tell by the intent look on his face. Jeannie's attention was never questionable.

"That's exactly my point, best buddy! Both sides are identical. Look at this side," Tony said as he held Jeannie's golden key in the air so Danny could see it. "Okay," Tony continued, "let me flip it so you can see the other side...do you see a difference?" Tony didn't wait for an answer. "There is no difference," he said.

Then, Tony slightly moved the sundial key on the rock he was now sitting on. He picked up Jeannie's golden key from the pad of paper he'd placed it on and carefully put it into the dial.

"Okay, you guys—here's the second thing I've discovered. Check this out! Jeannie's medallion fits into the sundial! To keep it simple, sometimes I'll also refer to the sundial key as just the dial."

Danny's eyes shot open. His mouth gaped. "My god, Tony! You are some kind of a wizard! That's just way cool!" Danny hooted. "Now what?"

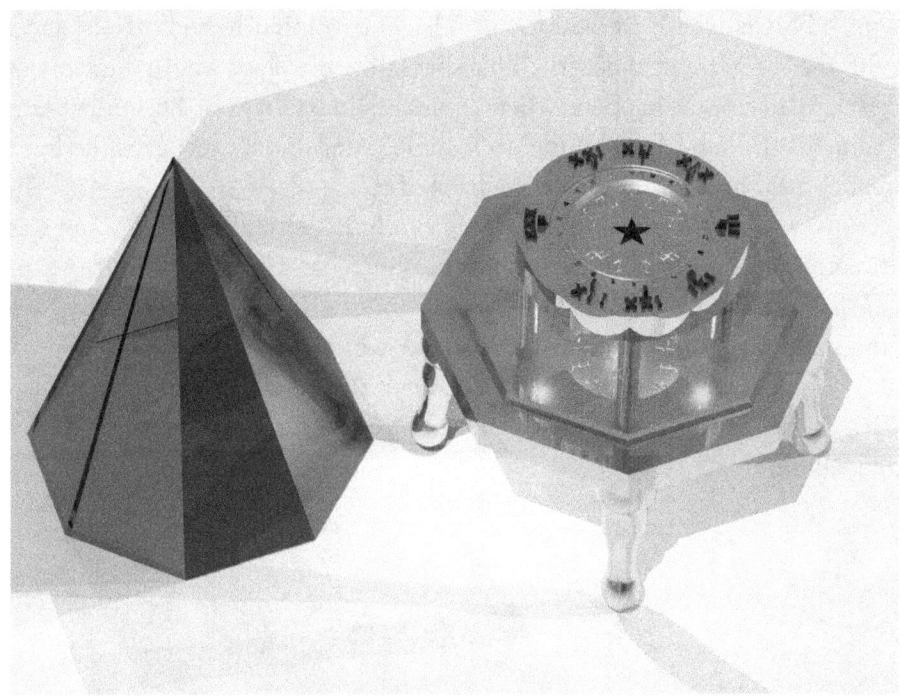

Tony motioned for Danny and Jeannie to sit next to the dial. "As I said, Danny—the mirror-image symbols on Jeannie's medallion are unique. Look at the sun shining on it. Now, look at the images on the gold table just under her medallion. Do you see the mirror-image symbols on the gold table?"

He paused. "The sun shines through the slits and projects images of the mirror-image symbols onto the gold table underneath her medallion."

Danny's face lit up. "Yeah, Tony, I see 'em!" he hooted.

Danny had been holding Jeannie's hand, but no longer. In her excitement, she unintentionally pulled it from him as she clapped. "Hell, Tony! You have discovered something special."

The sun turned the clouds a fiery orange above them. Tony's hand came to his mouth, and he nodded his head. "Hang on, Jeannie and Danny—the best is yet to come!" Tony beamed. He reached for the dunce hat and carefully picked it up. He pointed to the transparent, glass-like panels and said, "This is where we will look." Then he pointed to the metal panels with the slit in them and said, "This slit is the only place where the sun can enter. Watch what happens when I put the dunce hat on the sundial key. It shields the sun from shining on Jeannie's medallion, except for the light that comes through the slit in the back of it."

Tony put it on the sundial key. He carefully twisted it until the sun was directly shining on the back part of the dunce hat with the slit in it.

Jeannie's finger immediately shot to the window panel. She was jumping up and down and tapping on the window.

"Look at that! Just look at that! Can you believe it?" Jeannie squealed. "It's there. The image made by the light is on the gold table under my medallion."

Danny shook his head. "Not in a million years would I have ever dreamed of such a thing!" Danny said with amazement. His eyes were focused on the fascinating device.

The sun shining through the slit on the back of the dunce hat formed a thin sliver of light that streaked across Jeannie's medallion. The line of light crossed the slit for the mirror-image symbol **Ŧ**, thereby projecting its image onto the gold table of the sundial key.

Tony was beaming. "Yes—your golden key and sundial key work together. They must have a purpose. Our task is to figure it out, but I firmly believe your key is a translator. Hang on for a few more minutes and I'll explain."

He inhaled a huge gulp of air and let it out slowly. "Whew! Let me catch my breath." Now he breathed more slowly. "Okay—this would not work if the slits on the inner ring of the medallion were not mirror-image symbols. Somebody knew what they were doing when they dreamed this up!"

"The third thing I discovered is the association between the eleven mirror-image symbols on the inner ring with the twenty-two gemstone alphabet letters on the outer ring. The alphabet letters are in pairs and are color-coded by the gemstones they're made of."

Jeannie was puzzled by his comment. "What are you talking about? An association?" asked Jeannie. She turned to Danny and grabbed his hand again, realizing she had let it go. "Do you have a clue of what he's up to?" Jeannie asked Danny. "He just lost me!"

His weird expression said it all. He didn't even have to speak, but he did. "No! I'm as lost as you are! I don't have a clue what he's doing or talking about. I don't really care either—let's just let him figure it out. If it works—hell, that's all we care about!" Danny gave Jeannie a wink.

Tony threw both hands in the air and said, "Guys—it doesn't matter if you don't understand all the details. Let me take care of them. Here's what's going on. Look at Jeannie's medallion." He set it in front of them.

"This is the association. For each mirror-image symbol there is a pair of color-coded gemstone alphabet letters on the outer ring. I've drawn it out on this piece of paper so it will be easier to see what I am talking about." He set the paper on the rock next to Jeannie's golden key.

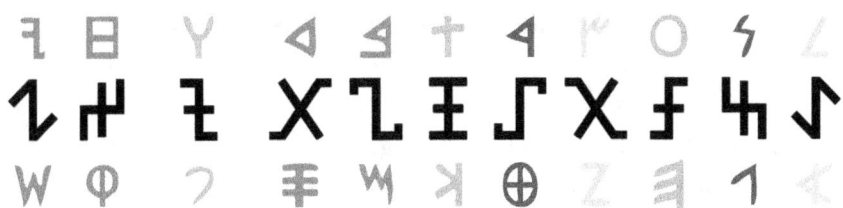

Shaking his head as if awestruck, Danny looked at Jeannie and pulled his eyebrows down with a strange look of curiosity. He shot a glance at Jeannie to detect her reaction. She looked blank, so he asked, "Well, that's real dandy, Tony, but what's it for?"

Tony was now in his domain. He knew it and took full advantage of teaching his friends the hidden mystery that he had discovered. He put his college instructor act in full gear. He was Professor Tony Einstein.

"Danny, have you ever heard of the Rosetta Stone?" asked Tony.

Danny heard Jeannie giggling behind him. He reached his hand behind to give her a little pinch, but couldn't locate the spot her chuckles were coming from. He turned quickly and swatted her on her rear shorts pocket and swung back to face Tony.

Tony had a smirk on his face. He was waiting for Danny's reaction. It was instant. "What the hell are you talking about—Rosita Stone? Have you gone south on us, Tony? I know you are Latino, but what the shit does Rosita have to do with this?"

Tony burst into laughter. He was now in full command. "Danny and Jeannie, the Rosetta Stone was an unbelievable discovery that allowed the modern world to translate the mysteries of ancient Egyptian hieroglyphs. I was using that as an example to demonstrate how symbols can be translated."

Danny's facial expression of bewilderment lingered. He was still lost. "I don't have the foggiest what you're talking about. Are you speaking English or bullshit?"

Tony knew when to ignore his best buddy and when not to. He ascertained that this was one of the former times, so he ignored Danny.

"Danny and Jeannie, I believe the dial with Jeannie's medallion is a translator. The gemstone alphabet letters on the outer ring are translated into mirror-image symbols. The medallion is rotated in the dial so that one of the twenty-two gemstone alphabet letters on the outer ring is next to an arrowhead point. The sun comes through the slit and projects the image of the mirror-image symbol on the gold table."

Danny couldn't stop the questions. "Well, what's that supposed to do?"

he asked Tony. Shaking his head, he pointed to his buddy and said, "Tony, you have the damnedest way of making things horribly confusing. Don't take my comments in a bad way, but I'm lost! I sure hope the hell you know what you're up to."

God, I love this, thought Tony. He resurrected his make-believe professor act and raced on with his "golden Rosetta Stone lecture."

"Danny, I'm glad you asked. Just be patient for a few more minutes—you'll understand soon." Tony tilted his head first to Danny and then to Jeannie.

The excitement on Tony's face could have generated enough electricity to light up all of Princeton University, especially Einstein's office. Jeannie and Danny detected a surprise was coming. Tony's eyes were twinkling and his smile was a sure giveaway.

"Jeannie, your medallion is a key—just as you said—but did you know it's a key to unravel the answer to the riddle on the brass bow and arrow? You figured out the answer to the riddle on the brass bow—Intipraimi." The pace of his breathing increased with each word that fell out of his mouth. "Somehow, I believe, your medallion, working with the sundial key, is used to translate the answers to the riddles into strings of mirror-image symbols. The only thing I can imagine is that these strings of symbols are used to unlock something. Our job is to find out what!"

Tony suddenly looked at the sinking sun, which was fast approaching the western horizon over White Mountain.

"Oh, by the way Danny, what time is it?" Tony asked. "We need to head back to CoalVille. We should hide all of this stuff in the coal shed behind your house. We need to put the rock with a hand on it back into the hole and cover it so that no one will ever suspect what we've been up to."

This was Tony's domain, and he knew it. He was the master of technical wizardry—as Danny referred to it whenever Tony started discussing abstruse theories. He was at the helm of his ship of wizardry, guiding it along a new course with no idea where it would lead. Tony certainly was aware of the significance of his find—the association of the sundial key, Jeannie's golden key, and the sun all working together to unravel a mystery.

With a strange little smile growing on his face, Danny slapped Tony on his back and said, "Let's continue to let Tony solve more of his Rosie Stone mysteries tomorrow. I suggest we meet at my house at eight thirty in the morning—my mom will have already left for work."

CHAPTER 29

Unraveling Mysteries— Jeannie Teases

Tony's old, scuffed-up, round-toed shoe kicked at a broken bottle in the dirt just off the edge of the street. He missed and instead dragged his foot along the ground, creating a cloud of dust. It flew up around his rolled-up pant cuffs, circling the tops of his shoes. He kicked again, but this time with success. The broken bottle took flight, and a cloud of dust from his faded blue Levis flew into the air with the swing of his foot.

As he walked alongside Main Street in CoalVille early Saturday morning, his eyes followed the ragged sawtooth asphalt down the edge of the road. Years of traffic with no maintenance had left Main Street filled with potholes and jagged road edges that no longer even resembled a straight edge.

He heard a rattling sound off to his side. Then his eyes spotted it—a tin can rolling in the middle of the road, being pushed along by the slight breeze that had picked up. He raced after it and gave it a big kick. It flew through the air like a miniature rocket and headed for the weed patch just down the dirt incline off the road. It landed on the other side of the hedge in front of the Calhouns' house. Tony chuckled.

As he walked toward Danny's house, he felt stumped. Kicking away at garbage alongside the road helped Tony search every corner of his mind, but it wasn't there. His challenge was to find some knowledge to determine exactly how Jeannie's key worked as a Rosetta Stone.

A funny little giggle came from behind him. He hadn't noticed Jeannie. He spun around and started walking backward so he could talk to her. She waved and started skipping to catch him.

"Old lady Calhoun will wonder how that tin can got in her weed patch," Jeannie said teasingly.

Tony rolled his eyes and said, "Hell, she probably already knows it was me. I'll bet she was peering through her curtains."

Jeannie was now by his side, and the two walked on together toward Danny's house. "Well, Tony, did you get anything figured out last night?"

He turned his head. "Jeannie, it's a mystery. We need to find more than knowledge. Shit, we need a miracle to help us out. I suspect your gold key is a translator, but have no idea of the role it plays or how to use it. There has to be a big piece of the puzzle missing."

She bobbed her head and merely said, "Hmm!"

Little did they know that the knowledge they desired would unleash a source of power—a source of power that had been sought for centuries—a source of power that opened travel on the Highway of Time and endowed travelers with the gift of eternal youth. Some had even committed murder to obtain this power.

Jeannie gazed at Tony as he talked about the puzzle. She had no problem letting him take his task seriously. Diving into the history of the Rosetta Stone was the furthest thing from her mind. Jeannie was grateful for his unraveling the meaning of her medallion's symbols and how it worked with the sundial key. She had confidence he'd crack the next mystery.

Her little smile persisted. Jeannie had a plan for Tony—just let him charge on. That would leave her alone to carry out her plan—exploring Danny's body and planning for their future.

They walked through the back door of Danny's house. He was anxiously awaiting them, and he greeted them immediately. "Hi, Jeannie and Tony! Come on in—Mom has already taken off for work, so we have my house for the entire day. Would you guys like breakfast?"

"No, Danny. I'm fine for now—maybe we can get a rain check for lunch," Jeannie commented. "Tony may want something."

Tony hesitated, trying to make up his mind. "Oh, I'm fine. Wait. On second thought, do you have a Pepsi and some peanuts?" he asked.

"Sure, Tony," said Danny. already headed to the old fridge with its top coil rattling away.

Her head cocked, and her hand came up. "Danny, grab me one also— Tony had a good suggestion."

Yanking the door open, he slid the milk bottle aside to reach the pop. "Gotcha covered, Jeannie," he said, grabbing three cold Pepsis.

She watched Danny shuffling through his mother's junk drawer looking for a church key. He spotted it under the pliers and claw hammer and said, "Found it!"

He popped the lids off the Pepsi bottles and put a bag of Planters Peanuts in each one. The salty peanuts dropped into the Pepsi, causing it to fizz. They floated and gathered in the neck of the bottles.

Pulling a chair back from the table, Tony said, "I just love drinking Pepsi from a bottle through salty peanuts!" He took it from Danny's hand and set it on the spot in front of him.

Her face broke into a huge smile. "I hope we will make progress today. Tony did a great job yesterday—boy, did he figure out a lot of mysteries," said Jeannie winking at Danny.

Tony turned slightly to his right, looking at Jeannie. "Yeah, while I was slaving away, you guys were playing in the pond and lip smacking. I need to have a little fun too. I should have invited KateLynn over today," he said.

Tony's comment was something Jeannie had been anticipating. Without hesitation, she made her remarks, and they were clear and authoritative. "Tony, I know you and KateLynn are getting involved, but she can't know about our secrets." Carefully watching Tony's expression, she offered him the consolation prize. "Maybe after the big basketball game next Friday, we can double date. We'll have fun. I'll talk to KateLynn during cheerleader practice this week, and then you can ask her if she wants to go with you, Danny, and me to Terry Z's Burgers in Granite Springs. We'll cruise Main and have lots of fun. Who knows, we could even end up on Lover's Lane!"

He smiled. She stepped to his side and slapped at his arm in a teasing manner as she thought, *He's good. That's great.* Then she quickly changed the subject. "Right now, I can't wait to get started. I see Danny has all the stuff out on his kitchen table—great! Hey! Pepsi, peanuts, and treasure—what more do we need to get started? This will be a fun day!" said Jeannie.

The old table vibrated back and forth on its unsteady legs as Tony slammed his hand down next to his Pepsi. He had their attention. "Let's start with Jeannie's golden key—her medallion," he said.

Jeannie glanced at Tony, but he was determined to remain sitting. "What do we know about it so far?"

There was a long pause, and Tony looked past Danny at her. She nodded and said nothing, wondering what his game plan was. "We know that there is an association between the twenty-two gemstone alphabet letters and the eleven mirror-image symbols—and that association is that a pair of letters is associated with each mirror-image symbol. We know that it works with the dial as a translator to derive a string of symbols from a string of the gemstone alphabet letters," said Tony.

Danny was not listening to Tony. He was standing next to Jeannie, holding her medallion. With a downward look at Tony, sitting a few feet from him, he asked, "What do you think, Tony? Do you think these symbols look just like Phoenician or Greek letters?"

"Yeah, Danny, I do," said Tony. "I think you found a clue."

Jeannie's mind was scheming as she watched the boys intently and followed their conversation about the symbols on her medallion. She knew Danny wasn't about to get sucked into a wild-symbol chase, but Tony might.

"Hey, I remember something about another class—our language class. Mrs. Black said that the ancient Phoenician alphabet evolved into the Greek alphabet and then into the Latin, or English alphabet, that we use today," said Jeannie.

"Here's the plan," said Danny. "Jeannie, I'll get my Ancient Civilizations book. Tony can dig through it and see if the twenty-two gemstone letters are from the Phoenician alphabet. If they are, we're in business."

It wasn't that Tony wasn't up for that, but it was a matter of him *wanting* to do it. Danny searched for a reaction. He got none from Tony, only a blink. Danny nodded his head as he spoke slowly. "We know that the letters of our English alphabet associate with the Phoenician alphabet."

Jeannie's eyes looked as if someone had thrown sparkling glitter into them. Danny had just set up her game plan, but he needed her help. "Good suggestion, Danny—we'll give the book to Tony and let him figure out all this stuff."

Tony's eyebrows lowered, not necessarily frowning, but with a hint of curiosity. "Why me? What stuff are you talking about?"

She pointed her finger at him and shook it ever so slightly. "Tony, we don't have to answer that. You know darn well what stuff needs to be figured out. We don't have a clue. You're the one who knows what to do."

Now he did frown. But then he figured out what was going on and asked a rhetorical question. "Why? What are you guys up to?" His frown transformed to a smile as he put his hand to his face with a thumb in the air.

She winked, knowing he was good. "Danny and I have other plans. You just keep busy, Tony!"

Danny got his Ancient Civilizations book from his bedroom. He handed it to Tony and slapped him on the back.

"Tony, I know you can do it. Why don't you look for the association between our alphabet and the Phoenician alphabet? Jeannie and I are going to go sit on the couch. Have fun!" He turned to Jeannie. "Come on, Jeannie. Let's go to the other room. We don't want to bother Tony as he works!"

He grabbed at her hand, maybe thinking he was going to take charge. She stepped back, and he missed. Before he realized what was going on, she had his arm and was pulling him to the door leading into the living room.

Danny laughed and followed, knowing she wanted to be the leader.

As she walked into the living room, Jeannie's attention was grabbed by the brilliance of the sun's morning light rays reflecting from a glass doorknob. The partly open door of his mother's bedroom beckoned silently as the powerful hand of love pulled at her to enter and enjoy the pleasures of young love.

Cautiously moving toward the door, directing a teasing look at Danny's face, she tugged at his arm, inviting him to follow her there. Stepping slowly as the old floorboards creaked, she peered through the crack of the door. Danny was still at arm's length; his view was blocked.

There, in the middle of the bed, she spotted Zanzee. His head motion was unquestionably clear. Her eyes focused on his startling warning. This was not his first message of stark consequences. Once in the past when she hadn't heeded a warning, a rattler's strike of death had been diverted from its mark only by the intervention of her sleek black cat. Zanzee had already saved her once from a deadly snake. She wasn't about to ignore his warning again.

Momentarily, she hesitated. Zanzee, sitting in the middle of the covering quilt, shook his head again and vanished. Her maturity was developing. Entering into the most intimate act of love for a few moments of pleasure could jeopardize her sacred role as Neferzul. She walked past the door, pulling on Danny, her arm locked with his. Frustrated and disappointed, she pointed to the couch on the adjacent wall, knowing that willpower had triumphed over hormones.

A black, round pipe curved its way out of the potbelly cast-iron stove and into the brick chimney on the wall next to the couch. Warmth radiated from the coal-burning stove, which Danny's mother had started earlier. The couch was a perfect warm lover's nest, and Jeannie intended to use it as such. As she made her way to it across the living room, the oval, hand-braided wool rug silenced the creaking of the wood flooring. Her movements and the sound of the floor brought back old memories that reminded Danny of his parents' love play when his mom would dance on the floor, making the boards creak and snap. She called it *floor music*. A small tear rolled from his eye.

Reaching the couch first, Jeannie turned to Danny. Grabbing him, her hands on his chest, her fingers under his arms, she turned him around and said, "Kabloosh on the couch, Danny," as she gently pushed him. He flopped backward onto it and laughed.

She jumped onto it next to him. Facing him, she swung her right leg over his lap and sat with her legs folded under her, her knees on either side of his body. His back was to the couch. She playfully put her hands on his shoulders, looking into his face, and bounced joyfully.

She stopped her bouncing and asked, "Danny, I asked you yesterday what you wanted to do with your life. You said you wanted to be a doctor. I thought about that. You were concerned that you wouldn't even have an opportunity to go to college, let alone med school." Jeannie reached for the hand that he was trying to put on his lap. Her mood changed from playful to serious. "I've been thinking and would love nothing better than to have you be a doctor. Danny, I'd help you reach that goal. I would do anything to make sure you succeed."

A very slight smile graced his face as he answered, "That's sweet of you, Jeannie. College is a year and a half away. We have a lot of time to plan. What are you thinking?"

"Well, Danny, if things worked out for us, I would work and postpone a family to get you through college—even med school."

Serious discussion was not on his agenda at the moment. "We're young, Jeannie. We're only sixteen—almost seventeen, but let's wait a year or so. We have time. Right now, let's just enjoy the time we have with each other."

Pulling her face next to his, he rubbed his nose on hers. He gently took her into his arms and held her close to him. He whispered to her, "You're gorgeous! I'd love to spend my life with you." Dropping his hands from her waist, he moved them up her body until they rested on either side of her face. Her long black hair draped around his hands and hid his fingers as he gently pulled her close to him. Their lips met, and he kissed her.

She slid her hands up his body, her long fingers softly moving under the shaggy blond hair hanging over his ears as their lips locked in a passionate kiss. Their eyes were closed, their tongues swirling around each other.

Danny's face showed lines of extravagant joy—a joy he'd never experienced before. Jeannie softly slid her hands down his face and put them on his chest. She pushed slightly, moving her body from his. "Wow! Danny, your chest is as hard as a rock! Can I see?" Her face now had a strange little smile. She didn't wait for an answer. Unbuttoning his shirt, she pulled it back. Her eyes locked on his chest and stomach muscles, as hard as a rock. She put the palms of her hands over those ripped, bulging muscles and softly pressed on his chest. She slid her hands over his chest muscles; her fingers danced around as she giggled. "Oh, my! I had no idea what was under your basketball jersey! I watched you race up and down the basketball court and could only imagine what your body looked like. Danny, wow! Do you know what?"

His eyes tracking every movement of hers, he asked with a big gulp of air, "What?" He didn't know what to say. He had no idea where she was going next.

He listened intently as she leaned her head next to him and snuggled her face against his. She spoke softly in his ear. "Only I can see your body. The other girls can only dream! They can only see the most handsome Pirate that ever lived race up and down the basketball court with his jersey *on!*"

Her hands were slowly moving down his body. She moved her head slightly so she could see. Her eyes drifted to the belt line of his Levi's. With his shirt unbuttoned, exposing his chest and stomach, his pants waistband caught her eye.

She smiled down at him. Letting her fingers move with a feathery touch, she glided them across his stomach with only the tips touching his skin. His heart was pounding. He sensed she could feel his heart beating in his chest. Slowly, she moved her hand to the top button of his Levi's. Their heads did not move. She slid her fingers under the waistband and unbuttoned it.

Their eyes remained locked. Neither blinked. He felt the next button snap open.

"What's this?" She didn't wait for his answer.

My god, Jeannie. His heart was now thumping so hard that his chest moved with each beat. Danny tensed. *This is wild!*

She moved her hand and grabbed hold of the waistband of his boxers, sticking out of his pants. She tugged on them slightly.

His steady control was gone. His hand holding her was shaking. Danny's heart rate was on the increase. His temperature was rising. Something within him was building. His emotional level was climbing higher than the Empire State Building. In his entire life, he'd never experienced the joy now racing around his body. He felt as if he'd erupt like Old Faithful at any moment.

As Jeannie sensed his uncontrollable physical sensations, a strange little smile crept onto her face. She bent closer to him and softly whispered into his ear, "Danny, cute white boxers with red polka dots."

He had no idea what to say. He tried to steady his hand, but to no avail.

She tugged on the waistband of his boxers—pulling them out several more inches—and sat back slightly. Looking down, she put her hand on his stomach, fingers outstretched. As she slowly closed her fingers, her fingernails gently raked over his skin. Tapping her fingers as she moved her hand, she let them walk across his stomach. Danny got a thousand goosebumps.

"Wow! Your abs are hard as a rock! I had no idea! Do you lift weights and work out?"

His breathing intense and heart pounding, he stuttered, "I—I do! N-now—do I ga-get a peek?" He moved his hands toward her breasts.

She pulled back slightly, grabbing his hand before he could touch her.

"No! Jeannie is having fun with Danny!" Her tongue moved across the lips of her open mouth. Her eyes sparkled like the dew on the petal of a rose. She giggled. "Oh, Danny, someday! Not now! Not here! Tony is in the other room."

He frowned. "Well, that's not fair!" said Danny as he wrinkled up his nose.

"Someday, maybe someday soon!" She hesitated. With a yearning in her voice she said, "Hold me, Danny. Just hold me close. I love you and want to be next to you! I want you for an eternity." *I think it will happen!* she thought.

CHAPTER 30
Intipraimi—A Combination Code

Jeannie leaned against the doorjamb, undecided whether to get a drink of water first or see what Tony was up to. She strolled through the doorway and looked over her shoulder at the table. Tony threw a quick glance at her as his large fingers flipped her golden key over and over in his hands. His stare showed intense thought, so Jeannie made no comment and walked on across the kitchen.

Tony hadn't solved the riddle whose answer was Intipraimi, but he'd discovered the function of Jeannie's golden key. He now searched for the code of symbols that came from the riddle's answer.

Standing next to the old porcelain sink that had once been white but had deepened to yellow over time, Jeannie reached and opened the faucet to let the cold water run. A little stream leaked from a faulty gasket. It snaked down the sides and made its way to the drain. After years of leaking, brown stains of rust marked the many pathways to the drain.

Another glance at Tony told her he was thinking about some deep subject. "How are things going?" she asked.

He said nothing but turned to the paper on which he'd been writing.

Then she reached and opened the cupboard to the right of the sink. No glasses were in it—only plates and saucers. She let the door go, and the breeze coming in from the partly open sink window slammed it shut with a bang. She jumped.

A snicker came from behind her. She turned quickly and saw Danny pointing to the door left of the sink. She giggled, turned, and reached to open it. An array of canning jars and mismatched glasses lined the shelves. By now, the water coming from the vintage cast-iron faucet was nice and cold. She filled a pint jar.

Tony lifted his head and looked at Danny making funny little finger motions to Jeannie.

Danny detected a smirk growing on Tony's face, but before he could say anything, Tony's arm flew straight out like an arrow and pointed at him. Danny's eyebrows lowered, a puzzled look on his face.

"Better button up, buddy," said Tony, his arm pointing to his fly.

Danny never took his eyes off Tony. His hands fumbled for the buttons on his blue jeans. Getting them fastened, he said, "What's up?"

Tony blinked and answered, "Nothing is up with me. What's up with you?"

Jeannie snickered between gulps of water. Her lips tried to make sure the water didn't spill around the jar's threads.

Pointing to Tony, Danny made a *zip-it* motion with his fingers across his lips. A few more snickers erupted, but not from Danny. Then Tony turned again to look at his work on the table.

"Okay, guys, I got it finished," he remarked with a chuckle. "Come on— Danny has his britches buttoned up, and Jeannie has her drink. Horseplay time is over! It's time to get busy and search for answers!"

Setting her empty glass jar in the sink, Jeannie walked to Danny and put her hands on his face, pulling it next to hers. She put her lips to his ear and whispered, "Damn! Why didn't he just keep fiddling around with my medallion or whatever? I think he's jealous."

Danny reached around her and put both hands in her rear pockets and whispered back, "Oh hell, I'm with you." He pushed back a bit and paused. Lifting his hand to her face, he flicked her nose with his little finger gingerly. "I guess we had better see what he's up to. We'll have time in the future to have all the fun we want."

"What did you find, Tony? It had better be good! You interrupted!" Jeannie said as she stepped next to him looking over his shoulder.

"Interrupted?" asked Tony. "I don't think so. You wandered off to get a drink. I said and did nothing!"

Jeannie frowned.

Tony took the hint. He never looked up and decided to go along with Jeannie's fussing. "I'm serious," he said. "You guys didn't give me much choice." He hesitated intentionally. "You guys were off having fun fooling around. You had me slaving away on bullshit."

His comment startled Jeannie. *Oh no. We offended him*, she thought.

Tony's insides were ready to explode with laughter. He knew he was a master not only of serious technical stuff, but also of humor. A loud chuckle erupted from his bowed head. "No, Jeannie, just kidding. Gotcha!"

She reached out and pinched his shoulder. "You devil, Tony. You got me. Yes, you did!" She laughed.

He put his serious look back on as he watched Danny from the corner of his eye, standing motionless less than five feet away. "Looks like the *girl* got the best of the *boy*, best buddy!" Danny ignored him—not even another *zip-it* comment—so Tony motioned him to join them. "Come on, Danny, you'll like what I've found," said Tony, now with a lot of enthusiasm.

Tony jumped up. "Hold on a minute. I need a drink." Before he went to the sink, he moved two chairs next to his and pointed to Danny and Jeannie. "This one's for you, Danny, and I'll have Jeannie on my right side."

Setting his glass on the table and taking his seat between them, he turned to a page on the book. "Actually, it wasn't that difficult. There's a picture that illustrates the relationship between the Phoenician and English letters. I rearranged them in the same order as they are on your medallion. Actually, I have two rows of them—each row has eleven Phoenician letters, so each row represents half of your medallion."

Tony clapped his hands and put them palms down on the table next to a piece of paper he'd been working on. "Here's my assignment!" he said.

(I,J)	H	(F,U,V,W,Y)	D	B	T	R		O	N	L
⇂	⊟	Y	◁	◀	†	◀		O	ϟ	╱

S	Q	P	X	M	K		Z	E	(C,G)	A
W	Φ	⊃	⯛	⋈	⋊	⊕	Z	⫤	⇑	⋉

"Good work, Tony," said both Danny and Jeannie. "Now what?"

Jeannie's head rolled to Danny, and then she pointed to the symbols in the book. "Uh-oh—you missed some, Tony," said Jeannie, pointing to the

 and ⊕ letters.

Tony grinned. "Nope! Jeannie, there are no English letters for those two Phoenician letters, so we are good."

Tony was thinking. His face turned serious, and a muscle in his cheek twitched slightly as he continued. "Well, the only thing we have that has English letters in what we've discovered is the answer to the riddle on the bow—Intipraimi. I guess we could translate it into Phoenician letters using the table I just put together. I'll give it a try."

Tony spent five minutes translating the English letters to Phoenician while Danny and Jeannie looked on. "Okay, here it is—I used the colored ones." He pointed to the paper he'd been working on.

⇂ ϟ † ⇂ ⊃ ◁ ⋉ ⇂ ⋈ ⫤ ⇂

Jeannie's mind wasn't convinced that what he was up to was working. She looked at Danny and rolled her upper lip over her lower. "Well, Tony, you just came up with ten Phoenician letters—what do we do with them?"

His face was drawn into a smile, and his white teeth sparkled like his eyes as he answered her. "We use your golden Rosetta Stone." He quickly turned to Danny on his left and nodded his head. "It's Danny's golden Rosita Stone."

Danny laughed and pointed to Jeannie's golden key on the table. "Tony, I'm on board. Get this ship moving, and get the golden Rosetta Stone rolling."

Danny paused, a quick inspiration popping into his head. He nodded and said with excitement, "Translate them into a string of ten mirror-image symbols using the dial and Jeannie's golden Rosetta Stone medallion." Danny waited for Tony to speak, but he didn't. He turned to look in his direction. Tony had a blank stare and continued his silence. Not waiting any longer, Danny hooted, "Tony, you showed us yesterday how it all works— the dial and Jeannie's key, working together with the sun as a translator. Come on, Tony. Let's get translating with Danny's golden Rosita Stone—I mean Jeannie's golden Rosetta Stone!"

He looked around Tony at Jeannie, who was cheerfully giggling.

Tony shook his head.

Danny's face went blank. "What the hell is wrong with you, Tony?" Danny snapped.

Jeannie's giggling stopped. Tony's heart raced a bit, knowing he had just moved into his territory and his alone.

"Danny, it's a good idea to use Jeannie's key, I mean Jeannie's Rosetta Stone, but you're jumping the gun," Tony said politely, cutting Danny off. "We don't know what arrow point on the key's sundial to use; there are eight different ones. The only rotating part of this system is Jeannie's key. The hood or dunce hat locks in only one position. Nothing else moves."

Danny's face dropped. "What the hell are you talking about now? Eight arrow points?" he asked.

Exploding with laughter, Tony clapped his hands and said, "Yes! Eight arrow points! Look, here they are." He pointed to eight sets of roman numerals with a small black metal arrow point by each set. "Danny, do you see these? Pay attention!" he said as he moved his finger to the first set, making his point indelibly clear. "My finger is pointing to the XXX! Do you see it?"

Danny's finger went to his right eye. He stared at Tony and said, "Shit, Tony, I'm not blind!"

Tony didn't stop. He moved his finger clockwise around the dial to the next set. "My finger is now pointing to the XXI! Do you see it?"

He didn't wait for Danny to answer with another smart remark. He charged on, moving his finger to the next set. "My finger is now pointing to the XII! Do you see it?"

This time Danny cut him off. "All right, you made your point. I see there are eight sets. Now what?"

Tony laughed again. "Thanks, best buddy, for no smartass remarks! You're learning!"

Jeannie got a kick out of the two big boys—one on either side of her—bantering with each other. Danny and Tony were about the same physical size. They were the biggest boys in high school—both extremely muscular; Danny, at six foot three, was only one inch taller than Tony.

She thought, *Wow, they're both handsome and big studs, but they act like two large lions just having fun teasing each other.* Jeannie giggled, watching the dynamic play out. "Okay, Tony, I'm with Danny. Now what?"

Tony loved it. This was his sacred domain, and nobody ventured to take it away from him.

"Okay. Here's the answer to your 'What?' question. We've already discovered that Jeannie's medallion is a Rosetta Stone that translates Phoenician letters to a code of symbols. We just discovered ten Phoenician letters for the answer to the riddle on the bow—Intipraimi. We'll need to align each Phoenician letter with the correct arrow pint on the dial. Otherwise, we'll get a different set of symbols. Crap, there are eight possibilities!"

Tony's heart was pounding. He needed air. He gulped in a big breath and let it out slowly. Then he took one more breath and continued. "We are just shooting blanks if we jump into using Jeannie's medallion and the sundial key without first doing a little homework."

He stopped and looked first at Jeannie's face and then at Danny's to see if they understood what he was saying; they did. "That tells me we need to know which arrow point we use to align each of the Phoenician letters to."

Danny nodded gravely, then pushed back his chair and stood and walked behind Jeannie.

Jeannie looked up at him over her shoulder and shook her head. She could follow the discussion, but she didn't have a clue about how to proceed.

"Well, crap. Now what?" Danny said, bobbing his head with Jeannie's.

Tony's hand rose into the air, finger waving. He smiled at them and said, "Hang on. I've got an idea. Okay, here's what I suggest—we know the only thing we've discovered that has to do with English letters is the answer to the riddle on the brass bow."

For a long moment, Tony paused. "My question is this. Did we see everything on the bow that we were supposed to? The bow is where the riddle came from, so let's look again to see if we missed anything!"

Jeannie stared at him for one second before she understood. "Good idea, Tony," Jeannie said, "I'll get the bow. You just keep thinking, 'cause you always come up with good ideas." Jeannie got up from her chair, flicked Danny's hair, and dashed across the room to get the bow before he could react. "Here it is, Tony," she said as she handed it to him.

The sun was now streaking through the kitchen window. The old coal stove that had heated so many of Johnny's breakfasts before he'd left for a day's work in the mine was cold. The five-gallon bucket next to it was filled with shiny black chunks of coal just waiting for when the fire would be stoked up and ready for fuel.

The warmth of the kitchen was coming from the sun. The rays of light were dancing though the window and reflecting off the brass bow in Tony's hand.

"Get a load of this!" Tony said. "We just hit pay dirt!"

"What? What did you find? You've got a smile on your face—show us what you've found!" Danny yelled. His hand came up from his lap and reached to take the bow from Tony. Rays of sunlight splashed across his arm, making the hair on it look like tiny threads of gold.

Tony handed it to Danny and pointed to the spot off which the sun was reflecting. "Look! This is what we're looking for! Whoever is guiding us is looking out for us because he or she or whoever it is, is giving us solid clues!" Tony beamed. "Look, right here on the top edge of the bow there is an engraving we missed! Damn—this is real subtle. There are three X's engraved into the bow—wow! I think we're on our way again!"

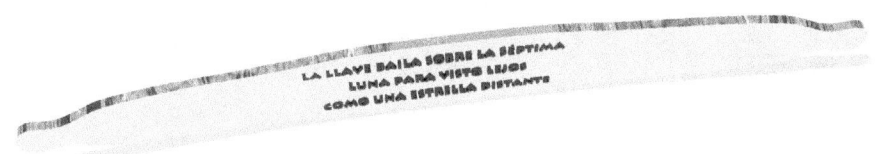

Jeannie's heart shifted into high gear, but she was not quite sure where things were headed. "Super, Tony!" she cheered. "What now?"

Tony's heart was already in high gear, and he had no doubt where he was headed. "Jeannie and Danny, get the dial set up in the best place on the kitchen table—the place where the morning sun coming through the window is the brightest." Bursting with excitement, he shouted, "We're going to do a golden Rosetta Stone translation! Guys, I smell pay dirt."

This time, both Danny and Jeannie raced to the wooden box that Danny was using to hide the treasure in. He'd sat it next to his bedroom door at the other end of the kitchen. Jeannie carried the dunce hat, and Danny the sundial key.

Danny helped Jeannie set her load down and put his next to it. He then rearranged the kitchen furniture and slid the table to a spot where the most sunlight was coming through the window. He moved all of his mother's geraniums off the windowsill so as not to have anything in the way of the sun.

"We're ready, Tony! Let's go! We've got answers to find—we've got stuff to solve—let's go!" Danny shouted.

They were struggling to find a clue—a clue that would give them an idea what they had. And they had just found one. Jeannie clapped her hands and rubbed her sweaty palms together. "What's next, Tony? Seems like you know what you're doing—so what's next?" she asked.

He pointed to her golden key. "We translate the Phoenician letters to mirror-image symbols. We just found this string of Phoenician letters." Once more, putting his right index finger on the paper where he'd written the string of letters, Tony nodded.

Tony's arm was shaking with excitement as he picked up Jeannie's golden key. He took a breath and asked, "Okay, then—is it agreed that we use the arrow point by the XXX to do the translation?"

Danny waved his hand in a forward motion. "Yep! Tony, you're the man. Get busy translating!" shouted Danny.

Tony placed Jeannie's gold medallion into the depression on the sundial key. He aligned the string of Phoenician symbols he'd just found with the XXX arrow point one by one. He adjusted their position so the sun shining through the window was directly on the shield with the slit in it. He thought, *The sun is perfect—it's a beautiful bright day.*

Tony carefully rotated Jeannie's medallion so the arrowhead point was next to the first Phoenician letter. "Okay, Jeannie's medallion is positioned so that the arrow point on the dial is aligned to this," he pointed to the

Phoenician letter, "on her medallion."

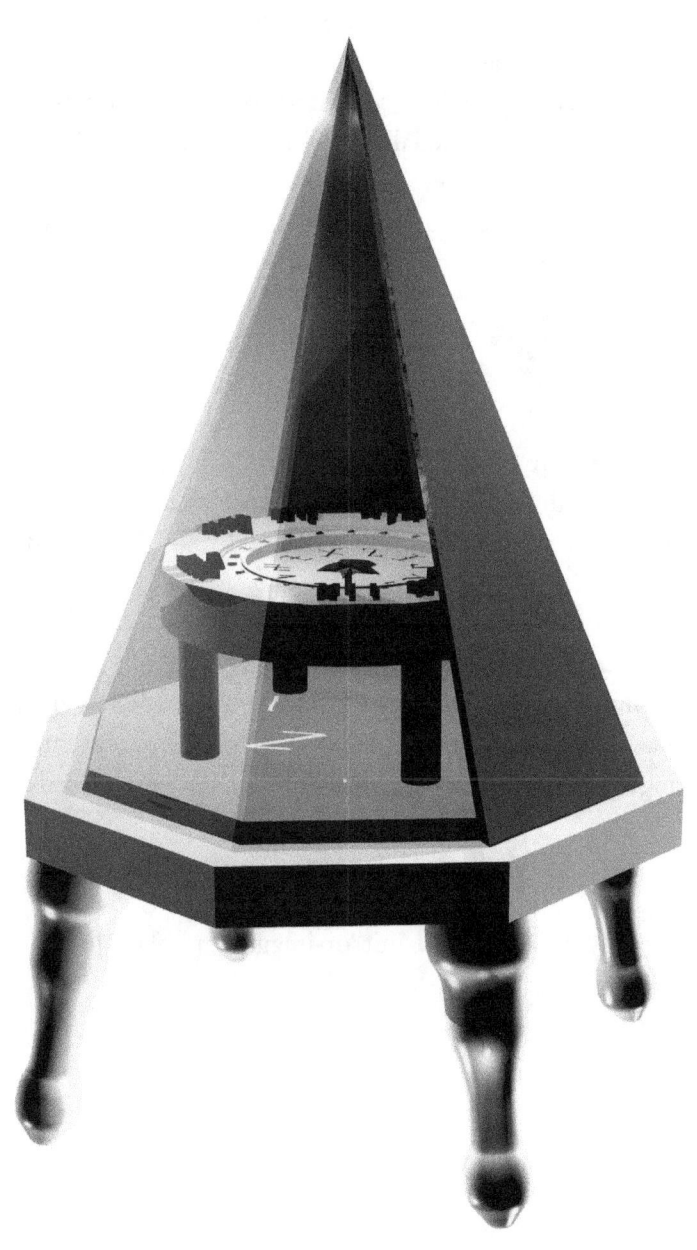

With the sun shining on the metal panels of the dunce hat, Jeannie's golden key was shielded from the direct sunlight, except for a little stream of light coming through the slit. They crowded around the window panel, looking to see what was happening.

"Look—the sliver of sunlight coming through the slit makes a perfect thin line of light across my medallion. This is just too cool," said Jeannie, her excitement growing with every word.

"We did it! We did it! Look at that crazy looking symbol!" Danny pointed to the mirror-image symbol on the gold table under her medallion. "Let's do the next one," Danny said breathlessly. His mind raced on. *I can see we're headed for more treasure!*

Tony took the dunce hat off. "Okay, here's the next one—I rotated Jeannie's medallion so the arrow point aligned to—" he placed his right index finger on the Phoenician letter on Jeannie's medallion.

He replaced the dunce hat. They all peered in amazement as the sun shone through the slit in the back of the dunce hat and caused a sliver of light to cross only the mirror-image symbol on Jeannie's golden key.

"There it is! We did it again! Look!" And there it was. The

mirror-image symbol glowing brightly on the golden table."

Jeannie was now drawn into the excitement that Danny and Tony had no intention of hiding. "Keep going, guys—you're doing a great job."

It was amazing! There could be no denying that the sun and Jeannie's golden key were tied to something. The question was whether Jeannie's key was tied or connected to something even more spectacular. Could it be that Danny, Jeannie, and Tony had found the first connection to Jeannie's golden key? And could there be more? Who knew?

Tony continued the process. "Who's writing these down?" he asked.

"Gotcha covered," Jeannie replied.

For the next five minutes, Danny and Jeannie watched Tony carefully rotate the medallion in the depression on the dial. One by one, he translated the string of Phoenician letters that corresponded to the answer of the first riddle—Intipraimi—into the code of mirror-image symbols.

"Okay, guys, here's the code of symbols." Jeannie had been carefully writing down each mirror-image symbol as Tony worked the sundial key with Jeannie's key and derived them one at a time.

$$\text{ꔰ ꝑ Ɇ ꔰ ꝑ ꝭ ʃ ʃ ꔰ ꝭ ꔰ}$$

"Good work, Tony!" squealed Jeannie with excitement in her voice.

The three teenagers looking for hope had found something. They had some symbols, but that was all, just symbols. Was it a code for something? What followed? Did they have a clue?

"Well," Danny said.

"Well, what?" was Jeannie's response.

"Well, my point is," Danny said, "what do we do with these symbols?"

"We've got another mystery to solve," Tony chimed in. "We can use Jeannie's medallion, working with the sundial key, to translate the answers to the riddles into strings of mirror-image symbols. The only thing I can imagine is that these strings of symbols are used to unlock something. Our job is to find out what they unlock!"

CHAPTER 31

The Disciple of Darkness

Mochcom's long, filthy coat swayed to and fro as he limped through the sagebrush, struggling with each step on his way to the Boar's Tusk once again. Hiding behind the disguise of a mentally retarded person, he had wandered through the desert for centuries, searching for a priceless treasure, a gift from the gods that would give him control of eternal youth.

Gorom Mochcom's deception of Kashom had been short-lived after their arrival in the Scarlet Desert. Prince Kashom had uncovered Mochcom's true character when he discovered his sister's golden key in the possession of the head high priest of the royal court of Kopaz. The battle that ensued had left Mochcom with broken legs and Kashom seriously wounded.

When Kashom and Mochcom left Kopaz, they had used the gifts of the gods to travel the Highway of Time and arrive in the Scarlet Desert. After their battle, Kashom escaped with almost all the gifts of the gods. The only portion that Mochcom managed to keep was the top half of the Sun Energy Transformer. That difficulty resulted in his inability to return to Kopaz, as all of the gifts were required to venture on the Highway of Time.

He mumbled as he walked along. "That dammed Kashom—he cut off my ear. he broke my legs! He broke my legs! Now I struggle—I limp in pain! My walk through life is painful because of the deeds of Prince

Kashom—someday I will have revenge on his family. They will feel the pain I feel. *Vengeance will be mine!*"

His eyes focused on the Boar's Tusk as he stopped momentarily and leaned on his shovel. He held the handle tightly as he rested his foot on the blade, which was partway in the ground.

"Kashom's son, Yellow Moon, spent his life out here hacking away at this piece of rock. The Tusk is different. He did change it—it looks much different from when Kashom and I arrived here hundreds of years ago."

He took his foot from the shovel blade and kicked at a small rock.

"Where did Kashom hide the gifts from Viracocha—the five worox stones and the emerald star? Where are they? I've been to the Boar's Tusk many times over the past several centuries, searching for the gifts. I've dug through the brush—I've dug in the hill the Tusk sits on! Where are they? Are they even at the Boar's Tusk?"

He took his long black coat off and threw it on the ground. A black beetle, disturbed by the sleeve slapping the sand, scurried under it for cover. Mochcom's beady eyes glanced at the movement on the ground. Raising his foot in anger, he stomped on the sleeve through spurts of laughter. His head rolled slowly as his eyes moved from gazing at his filthy coat in the sand to the Boar's Tusk.

"Where are the five worox stones and the emerald star? Did Kashom and Yellow Moon hide them at the Boar's Tusk? Maybe they didn't. But why? Why else was Kashom's son out here all those years? Why? Why? He had to have had a reason!"

Maybe he set up a diversion, Mochcom mused. *Kashom is clever—maybe he wanted to trick me into believing he hid them at the Boar's Tusk because his son spent his entire life out here hacking away at this rock! Maybe he hid the five worox stones and the emerald star someplace else in the desert. Hmm, are they at White Face Cliff? I'll find the gifts! I'll find them!*

He lifted his arms to the sky with a prayer of reverence for his master, pleading for help to find the priceless treasure brought from Kopaz centuries ago.

"Mighty Zuron, Great God of the Underworld, I'm your loyal servant! Praise be to thee! May your dominance as the supreme god be brought about by my humble efforts to control the gifts. I'm the one who carries out your vengeance. Help me find the gifts!"

Mochcom's fingers slid down his mustache. It glistened in the afternoon sun like a gray rod of steel.

He thought of the passing of time as he gazed at the sky. *When I left Kopaz, I was thirty-eight years old—I'm now over two hundred years old. My mustache and beard never change color. It's good to experience the gift—the gift of eternal youth—thanks to Kashom. He fell for the con. I got him once—I'll get him again.*

"I'm your prince—Prince Dark Soul. I carry out your will. Help me! Help me!" he roared with anger. "I need the five worox stones and the emerald star. Great and Eminent Zuron, you helped me get some of the gifts from Viracocha—you helped me get the top half of the Sun Energy Transformer. I've been a good servant. I've taken care of my half!" His steely blue eyes flashed with anger. "Help me get the other half of the Transformer—the five worox stones and the emerald star!"

The howling screams of Black Vulture circling the Boar's Tusk sent a feeling of tranquility through his body.

"Yes, Vulture, you killed Moon-of-Day, Kashom's firstborn daughter—the second Neferzul. You killed her as I watched! You frightened her with your howls and screams. She backed up to a crevice in the rock she stood on. You flew into her with your outstretched talons and knocked her into it! Her death was necessary—just like Kashom's sister—Aerapondes, the first Neferzul."

Mochcom's sparkling eyes followed his servant flying through the air like a fighter jet positioning itself for the kill. Black Vulture dived on a mother pronghorn with her baby racing by its side. At first the attack appeared random and without purpose. Chaos ensued. The mother squealed. The baby panicked. Then, the crafty plan of Black Vulture emerged. His prey—the baby pronghorn—strayed from its mother's side in the confusion. The killing dive left the squealing cries of the dying animal piercing the air surrounding the Boar's Tusk. The tranquil sounds of Mother Nature resumed as the eerie screams of the baby were silenced by Vulture finishing its kill, talons severing its victim's jugular.

"Well done, faithful servant!" said Lord Mochcom, praising his disciple for its valiant effort. "But that is only preparation for our most important kill—that of the third Neferzul."

Those kids were at the White Face Cliff the other day. Mochcom's eyes twitched. He pulled at the ends of his mustache, and he smiled as he mused. *Could it be? Yes! They are searching. Thank you, Vulture!*

His emotions climbing higher than Ben Franklin's kite in search of electricity, Mochcom's dark soul was soaring on the hope of an emerging discovery. His spirit raced on like an electric current, fueled by a strike of lightning, through a kite string in a storm.

"Those kids, yes! Those kids, they know something!" LeRoy grinned. He listened to the howling screams of Black Vulture. "Yes, oh God of Darkness—Zuron, thank you! I'll watch the kids—they'll lead me to my prize! Thank you! Black Vulture is my guiding light. He will lead me to where she hides them. I feel she knows about the gifts—the five worox stones and the emerald star. She is the Neferzul I've waited for!

Watching Vulture eat his prey, Mochcom wondered, "Where would she hide them? Her boyfriend is big and strong. I'll bet he's guarding the gifts. I need to do something to gain the trust of her boyfriend Hmm? He loves his mother. Yes!...That's it! Where? Ah! His house!"

CHAPTER 32

The Garage

It was not normal for Danny's mother to leave her purse at home. He wondered aloud, "Why is my mother's purse next to the treasure box? She needs it."

His hand moved from Jeannie's lap. Zanzee flinched as Danny lifted his arm. Danny stood up and said nothing but just started walking toward the back door.

"Wait, Danny!" Jeannie yelled.

He stopped but did not turn to face her.

Jolted by his concern, Jeannie answered the question that was still hanging in the air. "Danny, I'm sure she just forgot it. She was probably in a hurry and needed to get to work."

Turning before he reached to open the back door, Danny faced Jeannie. With a look of anxiety, he mumbled, "She has never forgotten it before."

Jeannie watched him tense up. He moved from the door and started walking across the room to where his mother's purse was on the floor. His mind filled with stumbling thoughts. *Maybe she took her wallet out and left her purse here. I don't know. She has never done that before. Her driver's license is in it, and Mom won't drive without it.*

Standing over the purse, he reached and picked it up. His heart fluttered as he opened it and saw her wallet.

Danny dropped his mom's purse. He ran to the back door and flung it open. With two bounding strides, he was at the bottom of the porch stairs.

Jeannie panicked. She jumped to her feet and raced to the open door. As she flew down the stairs, taking two steps with each stride, she watched Danny race to the garage. He headed for the side door.

Tony was also alarmed and had jumped to his feet. He was only a few steps behind Jeannie.

"Danny, wait!" screamed Jeannie, knowing that something seemed unnatural but not wanting to raise the level of tension any higher than it had climbed. "I'm sure there is an explanation," she shouted.

Danny stopped momentarily, hesitating, looking first at the garage and then at Jeannie. She ran to catch him.

Her concern flew over his head. He focused on the side door of the garage. Then Jeannie was at his side and grabbing his arm. "Danny, don't get carried away," she said in an effort to get him to slow down.

But that was not what Danny had in mind. He wanted the door open now. His strong body lunged forward as he grabbed the door handle, causing Jeannie to lose her grip on his arm. It was not the casual opening of a garage door. He flung it open with one swift yank, and it slammed against the outside wall of the garage.

His eyes sprang open like two blazing suns as he stared at the '53 Buick Special parked silently not more than ten feet from him. A grungy, filthy, black coat with long tails was draped over the hood of the car. Dangling from one of the pockets was the end of a bloodstained piece of rope. Danny's mind was racing. *What is going on? Where's Mom?*

Jeannie was shaking. Quickly she was at his side, grabbing onto his arm again, trying to comprehend the sight before them.

A breeze kicked up and rustled a piece of paper that was skittering on the concrete floor just inside the door. It was fluttering in a circular motion as the wind blew past Danny's feet; it looked like a whirlwind. It came to rest a few feet in front of him.

The sun broke through the crack in a lone cloud and formed a pillar of light that landed on the piece of paper, making it appear as a brilliant white object against the backdrop of the dirty floor.

Danny's eyes at that moment focused on nothing but the paper. The windowless garage was dark.

He reached and picked it up. Jeannie watched nervously as he flipped it over.

"Oh my God!" he yelled as he stared at a bloody handprint on a page torn from a Bible.

Jeannie had no words. Danny broke into a cold sweat. He bolted toward the Buick, desperately wanting to fling open the passenger door. A shovel was stretched out on the floor, waiting silently to snare the first panicked intruder. He didn't see it. He tripped over it and hit his head on the concrete floor. A sharp pain dazed his senses. Lying on the ground, he saw the bloody blade at the end of the wooden handle. It was still wet. His body succumbed to shock.

At that moment, the sun burst from behind the lone cloud, all of its rays streaming through the car window. Jeannie's hands flew to her mouth. "Danny, get out of here! You can't look at her!" Jeannie shrilled through her fingers, which were curled over her lips. She never looked at him lying prone on the filthy floor only a few feet from her. Her eyes could not move from the auburn-red hair draped over the steering wheel.

Jeannie didn't have to tell him. Danny's heart sank into a hole of desperation as he looked up at her. Jeannie's shaking body and the expression of horror on her face told him the worst.

He rose to his feet. There could be no hiding the scene of death in the front seat of his mother's car. The angel of death had visited the Roberts family again—this time the murderer's hand had made Danny an orphan.

CHAPTER 33

Farewell

Although there was music from the old pipe organ, Danny felt sur-rounded by silence. His mind was empty. With Tony standing on his left side and Jeannie on his right, he was lost in the expanse of drifting time. He could not concentrate on anything. There could be no words to take away his pain, and the echoing sounds from the organ eventually died away between the walls of the old community church. The rays of sun streaming through the stained glass window, with the multicolored figures of the Baby Jesus in Mary's arms could not shed warmth on Danny's mournful soul.

Unlike the preceding funeral for Johnny Roberts, who had been buried alive at the bottom of a coal mine, this funeral was not because the hand of fate had intervened in the coal-mine casino of those playing the insidious game of miner's Russian roulette. No, this tragic death had happened at the hand of a monster, masquerading as a crazy man. He had entered the stage of life wielding a sword of ancient evil and committing the heinous act of murder.

All that Jeannie could do was wrap her arm through Danny's and peek upward from the corner of her eyes into his face, which was staring into nowhere. Her heart, along with Danny's, was shattered into a million numb pieces.

Tony searched for answers about the monstrosity of it all, but he found none. His place was to stand by his best buddy and give whatever was asked for, no matter what. But for now, there was nothing asked, so he stood silently like a sentinel, ready to ward off any demon, ghastly or real, that would seek to threaten his best friend with more tragedy.

Playing the funeral songs for the Roberts family again—for the second time in four weeks—the pipe organ filled the Granite Springs Community Church with the sounds of spiritual praise. Just as at the funeral for Johnny Roberts, Mrs. Hastings nodded her head with each note as her slender fingers pushed on the yellowed keys, filling the chapel with the sound of "Amazing Grace." But now her words reflected on the loved one, Darla, who had been left behind four weeks ago but who was now at her lover's side:

> *Now I am lifted to the skies*
> *On clouds in gentle breeze*
> *To find my lover and the prize*
> *And sail no bloody seas.*
> *Amazing grace! How sweet the sound*
> *That saved a wretch like me.*
> *I once was lost but now am found*
> *Not blind. Johnny, I see!*

Silence fell on the congregation as the concluding note of the song faded into the stark reality that Darla was gone. The onlookers staring at the open casket for the final time could only hope that her soul was saved, that she was no longer lost, that she now had the eyes of an angel that would never be blind again.

As the last resonating pipe fell silent, Pastor Duncan rose from his massive, throne-like wooden chair directly behind the pulpit. He lifted his hands, and the sleeves of his black robe slid down his forearms, exposing his bare flesh as he waved to the waiting crowd of churchgoers, who were yearning for his consoling remarks. Moving with struggling steps, he hobbled forward as his hands came out and reached for each side of the pulpit. He leaned forward and rolled his head back and forth, making eye contact with the line of people sitting in the front pew.

He bellowed out the final words of his funeral sermon for Darla Roberts. "The winds of time blow through the vast expanse of endless space, picking up souls like a storm picks up grains of sand, forging the landscape of a fleeting life not unlike the ever-changing dunes of the desert. Would it not be wonderful if, by some gift from our supreme god, the ravages of time could cease? Our mountains of hope would stand for an eternity rather than be blown away like tiny mounds of dirt. How beautiful will be the day when a life's journey is endless, stretching through time and space."

Pausing for a short moment, Pastor Duncan looked at Danny and then continued. "As we watch our loved ones pass through the veil of death, we long for this glorious gift. But the unknown darkness of the grave blinds us, and that is the pain we carry until we take the final steps of our life's journey."

Danny stood lifeless, not trying to comprehend a word of the preacher's discourse—or even hearing it.

Reverend Duncan motioned for the congregation to rise. "Let us pray," he said.

Throughout the prayer, he stared at Jeannie holding onto Danny's arm. Feeling Duncan's glare like the eyes of a hawk focusing on its prey, she became uneasy, even though she knew that Danny had made amends with Pastor Duncan. Over the past several weeks, Pastor Duncan had visited the Roberts house on several occasions. On the first visit, he had given Darla five hundred dollars. On his second visit, he'd given Danny twenty-five dollars. Maybe it was money that had broken the ice. Who knew?

Not giving Pastor Duncan the pleasure of eye contact, Jeannie took advantage of the moment. She looked at Danny's mother for the last time, resting peacefully in the silk-lined coffin. Her wound was at the back of her head, so her beauty was yet radiating from her face. Sweetly, Jeannie asked, "Danny, can I take a lock of your mom's hair? It's a Kashome tradition. We believe that a lock of hair from a loved one who has gone to the Land of the Dead will, at some future time, point the way back to a family member saving it."

He said nothing but nodded his head and motioned for her to proceed.

Aware of the watchful eyes of the congregation, Pastor Duncan quickly turned his head from Jeannie and smiled to Mrs. Hastings. He signaled for her to start the final song, "There is a Green Hill Far Away."

With music providing the perfect backdrop, Jeannie released Danny's hand and walked to the casket. For a moment, Jeannie just looked. *She's beautiful. Her auburn hair looks like strands of gold with the sunlight shimmering on it. At only thirty-three years old, Darla is gone way before her time.* Gently, Jeannie snipped a lock of Darla's hair and returned to Danny's side.

She took Danny's arm and felt his body go rigid as he watched Pastor Duncan step off the stage, walk to the casket, and close the lid, locking it shut. The reverend then motioned for the pallbearers to take their places. They lifted the ornate mahogany coffin and started the procession to the graveyard.

Having made amends, Pastor Duncan moved to Danny's side and held out a sealed envelope. "Danny, our church has taken up a collection. Here is five hundred dollars. I know it isn't much, but the good folks of our community wanted to do something for you."

Clutching the envelope, Danny said, "Thanks, Pastor Duncan. You've been here for me on both occasions. Thanks again for the money you gave Mom and me last week and your kind words of support.

Jeannie's unwillingness to move let Danny know they were not joining the procession to the graveside service. She had no intention of allowing him to watch his mother descend into the dark hole, knowing he would get lost thinking of the endless journey his mother's soul was about to embark on, traveling to an unknown destination.

As the congregation stepped forward with final condolences, they briefly passed by Danny with a handshake and parting words of sympathy. Then, one by one, they made their way to the chapel doorway. Leaving the church, they joined the procession of cars that wound its way through the streets of Granite Springs, headed for the graveside ceremony.

Within ten minutes, the last three standing in the chapel were Danny, Jeannie, and Tony.

There could be no more bitter, more wrenching sadness than that now tearing at the very fabric of Jeannie's soul. The young man standing next to her—the young man who had stolen her heart—was now grappling with his own heart, not knowing if it would ever be whole again.

She never expected his question. "Was there a purpose?"

The gravity of the question reached to the core of his anguish, but her steadfast vision looked way beyond the surrounding tragedy. She asked, "Our adventure?"

He gave his short answer. "Yes."

As Jeannie stepped to Danny's side and put her arm around him, Tony watched. She reached out with her other hand and touched Danny's face. She looked into his eyes and spoke softly. "Less than three weeks ago, the loose strings of attraction dangled in front of us, two young people searching for hope. But now, the bonds of love that have tied our hearts together will never be broken."

Silence filled the chapel as Jeannie paused. With a gentle smile, she softly grasped his hands and said, "Danny, our love story will ring through the ages. And in some distant time, when young people are faced with the harsh reality of tragedy and despair, if they wonder if there's hope for them, someone will ask, 'Have you heard the story of Danny and Jeannie and the pot of gold they found?'"

There was a sparkle in his eyes as she continued. "Oh, my wonderful Danny. If, by chance, we touch the lives of young people in a time yet to come—if, in their struggles, they discover from our story that the triumph of the human spirit is possible, then yes, my love! Our adventure had purpose!"

With a voice of power, she ventured on. "The winds of change are blowing, and although a tidal wave on the sea of life has threatened to crush us, we have found the treasure of true love."

He listened, and so it was. And in the voice of an angel, she said, "In a year and a half, when we are out of high school, we'll be on our way to having our little green-eyed Danny boys and blue-eyed Jeannie girls. They will fill our cups with more joy and treasure than we could ever dream of. And when they ask us, 'Mommy and Daddy, how did you guys come to be our parents?' we'll answer, 'A pot of gold brought us together,' and then we'll show it to them!"

It was the first time in a long while that he had smiled. But then his next question hung in the air. "Do you think we'll ever escape the clutches of CoalVille?"

Contemplating Danny's youthful innocence, so terribly crushed by a murdering monster, Jeannie searched for words of comfort for the teenage orphan whose pain, she knew, was more than he could bear. Sifting through the bitter sadness that engulfed her soul, she could only fall back on centuries of cultural beliefs that had lifted the spirits of her people. Tears pouring from her eyes, she said in the sweetest of voices, "Oh, Danny, maybe the gods will step in and give us our hopes and dreams of that magical life in a land far away from the miseries of this coal camp."

Yet, at that moment, as her words fell from her lips, a discouraging thought crept into her mind. *Will my golden key ever unlock GAMMAZEL?*

Not knowing her innermost secret, and with the searching gaze of sadness, Danny said, "I hope so."

Watch for the next adventure in the Kopaz series

—SECRETS OF THE SUN—

Beware, for evil lurks in the Scarlet Desert!

Dale Groutage

Dale Groutage was born and raised in Reliance, Wyoming, a poverty-stricken coal camp in the state's southwestern desert. His childhood reading inspired him to pursue a better life, leading to BS, MS, and PhD degrees from the University of Wyoming.

Groutage served as a senior scientist for the US Navy, developing missile guidance and submarine silencing technology. He was inducted into the University of Wyoming Engineering Hall of Fame for his service to his country and honored as one of the top ten engineers in federal government by the National Society of Professional Engineers.

Now retired, Groutage is married with three kids. The former adjunct professor for the University of California and the University of Washington lives in Neenah, Wisconsin, pursuing his passion of writing Epic Fantasy and Science Fiction Novels.